What Goes Ar

A Novel Written and Copyrighted By:
Leslie Rogers

PRINTED IN THE U.S.A.

This book is dedicated to my mother, Cynthia Wood.
Thank you for the love and guidance.

Acknowledgments

First and foremost, I'd like to thank my Lord and Savior Jesus Christ from whom all blessings flow. I give You praise, glory, and honor in my life. The blessings you've bestowed upon me can never be re-paid, but I want You to know I am honored and grateful. The gift of writing is one of the gifts you've graced me with, and I pray with this gift I can express myself to the fullest. Like all the gifts you've blessed me with, I won't take it for granted. I thank you and I love you. To God be the glory.

To Cynthia Wood, my greatest gift from God. Thank you for being the ultimate definition of unconditional love. You were the epitome of what a mother should be. I couldn't and wouldn't ask for God to bless me with a better mother. Your love and support meant the world to me. Words are not enough to express what I feel for you, still. Rest in Peace and know I will always love you! Thank you. Thank you. Thank you. I love you so much. To Henry Wood, my stepfather. May you continue to rest in peace. Thank you for loving my mother and enhancing her happiness.

To the children God blessed me with, without having to endure labor pains, my niece, LaNeshia Rogers. Your intelligence and talents amaze me. I know your choices in life will be wise ones. I'm proud of you and I love you. And your offspring – WOW! Lailah and Anthony Sanders and Ray J, TiTi loves you! My youngest niece, KaWanna Gilyard – I'm blown away with your focus!

To my girls, what can I say? You often hear women can't be friends. Well, we defy the myth. For me to have so many female friends is a true blessing. The support all of you have shown is phenomenal. I appreciate each and every one of you. As I list your names (they're in no particular order) know you all had a hand in me reaching this goal. Arlene and Tim Major, your words always inspire me. Arlene forty-six years and counting. Can't you see us in another forty-six years, still friends and still loving each other? Carol Williams, Kim Wooden, and Zondra Jones – my kindergarten crew. Thanks for showing me real friendship then and now! Sheila Gunn, my rock, my girl, my bestie. You have been there for me NO MATTER WHAT! Words will never describe what you mean to me. Becky Jones, one of the fiercest hairstylists on this side of the Mississippi. What I love about you is you're the same Becky from the sixth grade. The success hasn't gone to your head, and that's why God continues to bless you. Angela May, although we don't talk much you are always there when I need you, and that's friendship. Thank you so much for everything, especially the prayers. Meechy Bradshaw, my ATL connection. You're my girl for life! Thank you for your editing expertise; I couldn't have done it without you. Ann Wallace-Bailey, although we don't talk much (just lots of texting), our friendship is constant. Thank you for everything. Wanda Pelloquin – you are that RIDAH for sure. So thankful our paths crossed. Neicy

2

Crawford, I appreciate you although our bond has changed, we can't negate what we had. Tracey Stephens, thank you for being you, and for always making me laugh and for being the same Tracey no matter what. Misha Marshall, the little sister I never had. You always have my back and your faith in me humbles me. Thank you. Diane Gibson – started from 6th grade and we still here! Thankful for you – always! Tracie Stewart, in the short time you've shown what an awesome woman and friend you are. I'm so thankful we met! To all of you, thank you for loving me and showing me the true meaning of friendship. All of you make me a better me. Much love!

Thanks to all of you for enhancing my life. If I missed you, please don't charge it to my heart but my head.

Always,

Leslie Rogers

PS I have to shout out the city of St. Louis. Special shout out goes to my U. City family - U all know what you mean to me. Thank you for your unwavering support!

PROLOGUE

One of the main objectives in my life is to be drama free. That's all a sistah wants. To live DRAMA FREE. DRAMA LESS. I love Mary J. for making No more Drama! I try and live by it but something or someone always throws some BS in the game which messes up my ultimate objective.

I often ask myself why I can't escape drama. My mother. She's lived a drama free life. My aunts. Both of my grandmothers. They've all lived drama free lives. Me? I can't get any peace. My nickname may as well be the "Queen of Drama" considering all the drama I've encountered. Babymamadrama. The other woman drama. Corporate America drama. Friendship drama. Just every kind of drama. If there's some drama to be had, I've had it, I'm your girl.

Drama seems to follow me like a stalker follows his prey. Closely. I think I've finally figured out why. It's simple. Choices. The choices we make in our lives will ultimately affect us. Be it positive or negative.

I always treat people the way I'd like to be treated. And that's with respect. Aretha Franklin knew what she was talking' about. R-E-S-P-E-C-T! Nothing more. Nothing less. Of course, I expect the same in return, but that rule doesn't apply to everyone. Am I really asking for too much? Are my expectations set too high?

Well....If I'm asking for too much or my standards are set too high, that's life. That's me. That's how I choose to live my life. My parents instilled that in me. I can remember it as if it was the first time my childhood ears heard it. Both of my parents constantly told my sister and I, 'Girls, always treat people in the manner you'd prefer to be treated. Keep in mind this doesn't apply to everyone because you will always come across ignorant people, but that doesn't mean you should act in the same manner. Never look down on people and always hold your head high. Always be proud of who you are and where you came from.' I can't tell you how much we heard that growing up. My parents shared a lot of meaningful things with us; those things stayed with me and helped mold me into the woman I am today.

I am a firm believer in doing unto others, as you would have them do unto you. I believe in all the other sayings as well. I know you all know the popular ones. You reap what you sow. An eye for an eye. What goes around....comes around. I don't ever want anything biting me in the ass because I treated someone like shit. Now, normally I'm the one that's treated like shit, but I'm an optimistic fool. I continue to treat people in the manner I prefer. Disrespect. Lies. Betrayal. I ain't havin' it!

These things can trigger the boomerang effect. You know what I'm talking about. The bite ya' in the ass kinda shit I just talked about. You mistreat someone who's really diggin' you, and then three to five years later when you

4

meet someone, you're really diggin` the boomerang effect kicks in like Jackie Chan. The one you're feeling,' making wedding plans in your head with. They go and do the unthinkable. They dog you. It was inevitable. Some may disagree and argue the point, but when reality sets in, again, it's inevitable. When you do bad things, bad things happen to you. I always find myself saying or thinking, "What Goes Around....I can't believe some of the shit people do. Anyway, when you do good things, eventually good things happen to you. This is my philosophy on life, and here's my story. Well, one of them anyway.

Nia

My mama says I'm too independent, my girls say I'm too picky, and others (who really don't matter) say I read too many romance novels; and therefore, live in a fantasy world waiting on my prince. Well, fuck em' all because no matter what they say, Nia, (that's me) deserves a BMW – black man working (white men need not apply) that is God fearing, ambitious, intelligent, hardworking, childless and knows how to whip it on me Babyface style. I guess that's why I, like so many of the women I know, are single. Black men can be needy, and it's understandable to a certain degree, but DAMN! Can women get a break? What our ancestors went through affected African American women as well, but it's almost as if black men feel like they're in a battle alone. Well, I'm speaking for women everywhere when I say, like Michael Jackson sang, 'You are not Alone'. Black men need to recognize, black women deal with a lot also, and this is our struggle together. Instead of us fighting each other, we need to embrace each other and weather the storms together. Us fighting one another is a losing battle. We know things aren't going to be perfect, but unconditional love is what men and women want and need. I hear so many women complaining our men just don't support us, and they're constantly feeding into the negative bullshit. Most of us just want a black man's love and support. The negativity. We can do without. The struggle is real for us all!

Me? I'm one who appreciates the choice of chocolate we have. You know, white chocolate, chocolate caramel, milk chocolate and the very delicious and the oh so scrumptious dark chocolate, but can I have my choice of chocolate without the it's-the-white-man's-fault-keep-a-brotha-down-although-a-brotha-doesn't-want-anything-out-of-life DRAMA? Please!

Now, I am not one of those women who won't look a man's way if he's not corporate, or college educated. If a brotha is hardworking, and more importantly ambitious, I can deal with a man who isn't corporate or lacks a degree. I'd just love to straddle one of those FedEx men, and just................Ooops! Here I am getting off the subject. Anyway, I'm single because although I don't feel my standards are high, I will not, I repeat I will not put up with any bullshit from any human being with a penis and two testicles. I've dealt with enough bullshit in my thirty-nine years to last two life

5

sentences. Men do what they do, how they do, and when they do because they can. And, oh yeah, let's not forget the other part of this equation. Some women are desperate and allow it. They don't want to be alone, so they settle. They'll share her man. And their man. And your man. In some cases, his man. As long as they have a man. It doesn't matter whose man. If they can get some dick or whatever it is they're looking for. Nope! Not I! I am not the one, the two or the three. Now don't get it wrong or confused. I'm about to be single. But it's by choice. That's right, my choice. My being single doesn't place me in the lonely category. A lot of people tend to think alone and lonely are synonymous. Well.... wrong again.

My girls and I reminisce about our twenties, and we all realize we could've been married but we also realize we'd now be divorced. In some cases, in jail with a case. There's one thing we all agree on and that's, til' death do us part. So, we figure being single and childless at thirty-four is better than being thirty-four, a divorced woman with children we must take care of ourselves. Hell, my ex just proposed after I caught his fine, big dick ass cheating. For a minute I thought he was one of the characters in Eric Jerome Dickey's novel 'Cheaters'. Men who aren't serious always propose when they know they're about to lose a good thing. I don't know why brothas wait until the well runs dry. Or should I say until the coochie runs dry? If they're unhappy, they should be strong enough, which would make them man enough to tell women what's really going on. If men would do this, it would really cut down on the drama. I think I know what it is. Some men just enjoy drama. If they didn't, would they do the bullshit they do? Hell No! I think not! I'll tell you about Ben's tired-big-juicy-dick ass in a minute.

Back to what I was saying, my girls and I drift in and out of the single world, but we're okay with that. Now don't take that as if we're a group of sistahs who don't want men. We love black men! Next to black women, they are one of God's most beautiful creations. They know they have us outnumbered, and that's problem numero uno!

We're strictly dickly! Which makes us heterosexual. Society tries to label single women as lesbians, or old maids. Well, we're neither. If you have children without a husband society accepts it like it's normal, but if you choose the old-fashioned way, the way God intended, something must be wrong with you. It's like they think sistahs without children don't have any because we can't have any, not because we've chosen not to, without a husband. I am constantly questioned about why I don't have children. My answer is always I don't have a husband. Some then have the audacity to ask why I don't have a husband, like there's a line of tuxedo-wearing-broom-carrying men at my door ready to utter, "I do." Times have changed and it's all about choices – some choose to wait for a family, and some don't. Don't criticize me for my choices and I won't criticize you for yours.

With that said, we all want the 'fairy tale'. The husband, 2.5 kids, and a dog, but we will not settle just because our clocks are T-I-C-K-T-O-C-K-I-N-G. As loud as church bells I might add. It's like the nursery rhyme, you know the

6

one......Hickory Dickory Dock.....Time raced against our clock.....The clock struck twelve.....We're still single as hell.......Hickory Dickory Dock.......

As you can imagine we spend lots of time together. As a matter of fact, the year we all turned thirty, we made a pact with each other to not settle, but to marry for Love! Love! Love!

Fortunately, we don't have to marry for money as some women do. I wouldn't label them as gold diggers, because society doesn't label non-African American women going after professional African American ball players as such, but I will say like those women, they're seeking the wrong thing. We've been blessed to have our own businesses. We're not rich, but we're living comfortably. All our parents believed in us being entrepreneurs, and that's something they placed in our heads and hearts at a young age.

Nia and Friends

Alexis Knight is the proud owner of Knight Mortuary. She is a Mortician/Funeral Director, and she loves it. Dealing with dead people is eerie as hell to me, but she really enjoys it, and it's quite lucrative for her. She's jet black and beautiful. People always think we're sisters because of our complexion. She's five feet seven inches tall, and her body is hooked up. A curvaceous black woman's body. She has a flat stomach, small waist, a big round ass, nice legs and 36C perky breasts. She wears her naturally curly hair in a shoulder-length bob. Men go crazy when they see her. Once we were at Lennox Mall in Atlanta, and the way men were acting, I thought she was Janet Jackson or someone famous. They kept coming up to her as if they'd never seen an ass before. She has a problem dating because a lot of the time they're only interested in her body. It's sad because she has the total package. The three B's. Brains, Beauty, and Booty. She's a prime catch, but she doesn't do bullshit.

She attended Beaumont High School in the city of St. Louis, and we met right after high school. She's been an exemplary friend for the last twenty-one years. She has always been there for me. She was my rock after my father's death, and you know she had my back after all my failed relationships. I'm really blessed to have her as a friend.

Kenya Martin and I have been friends since eighth grade, but honestly, it hasn't always been the best friendship. She's a people pleaser, and because she's this way, she has fucked over our friendship on more than one occasion. Now, because I have a forgiving soul, I have forgiven her, but I do have three strikes and you're out policy. She must consider my feelings at some time, but if she doesn't the friendship is over. I told her if she allows one more person, place, or thing to cause problems in our friendship, that's it. Friendship is very important to me. I sincerely believe in treating my friends in the manner I prefer to be treated. The shit she's done, I would've never done, but I guess it's irrelevant at this point. Don't get me wrong; she's a sweet person, sometimes too sweet. I think because we've fallen out before, she's now trying

7

to be the 'perfect' friend', but we know that's impossible. She avoids confrontations like the plague, even if the situation calls for one. I explained to her it's normal for friends and couples, and just people in general to disagree on things, but when a situation arises, deal with it and move on. Well, she doesn't deal with it. She avoids it, which only makes the situation worse. She seems to think if we argue I'm going to end the friendship, but I kindly informed her the only way I'd stop being her friend is if she did the friendship fuck dance again.

She's done some foul shit, but nothing to warrant ending the friendship, not yet anyway. So, Kenya's been on friendship probation quite a bit, but I'm trying to hang in there with her. I try to keep in mind she did have a terrible childhood, and a lot of the shit she does, she's not even aware of. I understand what her mother did to her, but it doesn't justify her doing the friendship fuck dance with me. I guess that's why I keep giving her chances, but I'm sticking to my friendship rule. Three strikes, and she's oooooooout!

Anyway, Kenya has beautiful café au lait skin, thick hips, legs and thighs. She has brown hair with auburn streaks she wears in a short style. She reminds me of the comedian Adele Givens but without full lips.

Her mother tried to ruin her by being verbally and mentally abusive, but with God's grace, she prevailed. Anyone hearing 'You're ugly', 'You're fat', and 'You ain't shit, and 'will never be shit', will eventually believe it. Kenya was strong enough to seek emotional counseling, as well as spiritual counseling, so now she's still recovering. I think Ms. Martin dislikes Kenya because Kenya's father, Mr. Lawrence Billups, wouldn't marry her. At the time Kenya was conceived, Mr. Billups was strictly hittin' it. His intention was to never marry her. She was pissed and inflicted his rejection of her onto Kenya. She was so spiteful she wouldn't give Kenya her father's last name. Ms. Martin held fast to you-may-be-her-daddy-but-you-ain't-my-husband-so-her-last-name-won't-be-the-same-as-yours. She also never had more children to ease the brunt of hatred; Kenya got it all. She thrived despite it.

It didn't matter to either of them. Their last names were different, but the father-daughter bond was there. Ms. Martin resented the fact he could love Kenya with such depth, but not love her at all. With all the love her father gave her, the wounds were still there, and they were deep. Her father's love couldn't and didn't heal them. Fortunately, she didn't succumb to Mrs. Martin's crazy ass. Kenya needs more healing, but she's headed in the right direction. She owns Kenya's Kwik Klean (Triple K to us). She has a staff of twenty, and they clean office buildings, as well as private residences. It has been very successful. I guess all the cleaning she did at her mama's house paid off.

Alicia Fox is a childhood friend as well as my business partner. We own Event Solutions, which is an event planning business. We offer catering services, but we specialize in decorating. Our business is successful after two years of struggle, but those two years made us stronger. I think we're successful because of the services we offer our clients. We do all the legwork preparing a successful party requires, with lots of detail. We prepare the food, find the location site, create, and mail invitations, obtain the desired decorations, and decorate the venue.

We've found most people hate planning and preparing for parties, they only want to attend the event and enjoy themselves. For this reason, our business has really succeeded. We're even handling corporate events now.

Alicia's the one that's very secretive about her personal life, even with me, her girl. She's also one of those women who will simply forget she has friends when she has a man in her life. At one time it bothered me because I don't dis my girls if there's a man in my life, but I realized that's her MO. I feel somewhat neglected, but I've learned if I love her, and I do, I must accept her as she is. She's really a sweet person, but for some reason, she doesn't really do the girlfriend thing. Most women either have a lot of girlfriends, or don't deal with women at all. Alicia's the latter. She has our close-knit group, but that's it.

Alicia's the only one in the group who hasn't picked up any weight since high school. She eats too. She's not one of those salad eaters, this girl gets her eat on, fried foods and all, but no weight gain. I can look at a picture of fried chicken, and BAM! weight gain. I guess all of us can't be itty-bitty.

I also have a girl in Atlanta, her name's Colett. She and I met about ten years ago. Our boyfriends happened to be best friends and that's how we met. Ten minutes after meeting one another, we clicked, and we've been close ever since. People are amazed we're so close, but we trust and love each other, so it works for us. Anyway, Colett has a bachelor's and master's degree in education. She's the Director of a learning center in Atlanta. The center specializes in mathematics and science, two subjects African Americans don't excel in. The goal of the center is to assist those children so they can learn more about the subjects and ultimately, excel. She really loves her job and those children. She loves math and science, and she's determined to show the world African American children can and will excel in subjects normally dominated by Caucasian and Asian children.

She's the youngest of all my friends, at a young twenty-nine. She hasn't entered the DECADE OF DOOM yet, and she constantly reminds me of this fact all the time. She's statuesque like a model at five feet ten inches tall, and very voluptuous. Her skin is the color of butterscotch candy, and she has jet-black short hair she wears very stylish. Her eyes are so black that you can almost look into her soul. She has model cheekbones, a button nose, and a set of full lips. She has the best pair of legs I've ever seen on a woman, other than mine.

Apart from Collet and Alexis, we all attended University City High School together. U. City is what we call it, and it's a suburb of St. Louis, but still close enough to the city of St. Louis to keep us grounded. Although we were grounded, in our opinion at least, we were known as snobs. Nothing could be further from the truth, but everyone judged based on material things, and back then the preppie look was in. You know, Polo knit shirts, Izod shirts, Levi's and of course topsiders. The handbags to carry were Gucci and Louis Vuitton. I had one of each. We all did. We had quickly outgrown the Etienne

9

phase and had moved onto the more expensive designers. I'm assuming because of how we dressed is why we were labeled snobs.

All my girls are beautiful in their own way, and I'm not saying that because they're my girls. All of them have something to bring to the relationship table, but the men we attract are too shallow to recognize that. Men claim they want an independent woman, but I think what they really want is a dependent woman with no ambition. A lot of men fear independent women. My mother once told me, although she and my father raised me to be independent, all men must feel needed. In other words, you may not need him, but you should act like you do so he continues to feel like a man. Once guys realize our ambition will not hinder us as a race, but strengthen us, they should fall in line with us.

Finally, there's me, Nia Elizabeth Witherspoon. I am the oldest child of Ralph and Diane Witherspoon. My parents chose the name Nia, it's African and means purpose in Swahili. It isn't one of those: my-mama-must've-been-on-crack-or-ghetto-as-hell-when-she-named-me-names. My parents chose this name, and from day one, they drilled purpose and success into my brain. In their opinion, my purpose in life is to succeed. I was told I come from great people. To do anything less than succeeding would be disgraceful to my ancestors. So, I made straight A's throughout school, as well as college and grad school. I'm determined to excel in everything I do. I know my parents are proud, which makes me proud. It's sad my love life isn't always successful. That is a different story, altogether. I'm five foot seven inches tall. I've got the no-ass-at-all-syndrome, happily donated by my white grandfather (I'm sure), a small waist, beautiful well-toned legs, and large breasts (36D's). Yes, I am built like a typical white woman, but my dark skin confirms my heritage. I have green eyes and naturally curly hair which I keep shoulder length. Ponytail access is important to me because of how busy I am. I have my daddy's eyebrows, thick and bushy (I keep them waxed), my mama's high cheekbones and full sexy lips. Beauty is in the eye of the beholder, and to my parents I'm gorgeous. I've been told I resemble Kenya Moore, but without the ass. I don't know if I agree, Kenya's gorgeous.

I am thirty-nine years old and childless, and if one more person asks me why I am without a child, I will scream! No babies without a husband. That's my motto! I belong to an elite group. The Few! The Proud! The Babydaddyless! I've also noticed there are more men without children than I thought. Now, don't get it twisted, bruhs got dependents, but there are a few in their thirties who decided they aren't having any children until they marry. Waiting seems to be the 'in' thing. For my girls and I, it's something our parents instilled in us and therefore having children out of wedlock was not our goal.

I'm one of those sistahs who can be very professional when I should be, but I can also be a ratchet when I need or want to be. I think most black women have the ability of being versatile. It's a must to be successful as well as professional while keeping it real on the home front.

10

I have a younger sister named Nandi. She's married with children. She's a Pediatrician in Huntsville, Alabama. Kevin, her husband, is from there. Nandi's thirty-four and her twins, Keenan and Kai are two. Those are Titi's babies. I love my sister, her husband as well as my niece and nephew. I will admit I was a little jealous when she was blessed with a husband and children first. Nandi doesn't know my feelings. I kept them to myself and dealt with my issues on my own. God does everything in His time. It's evident God felt Nandi was ready for marriage and children when He blessed her and I'm sincerely happy for her. We're only six hours apart driving, and we try to visit every six to eight weeks.

My girls and I are a tight bunch, just trying to make it. As time permits, we hang out together and travel together. Thus far, we've been able to take two trips each year. It's easier to get away now because our businesses are established. We have truly been blessed.

I reminisce about corporate America, and I know I'm blessed. Getting booted out of corporate America was a hidden blessing; my health is better and overall, I'm happier. Getting fired was God's way of pushing me into doing something for myself. In the end, I hated working for them, and the corporate bullshit that accompanied it. It has been a struggle, but it has made me stronger.

Prior to Alicia and I starting Event Solutions, we'd discussed starting a business but with both of us working full-time jobs, it was difficult. So, after I was dismissed, Alicia and I decided to take a risk and become entreprenegroes. I thank God for the opportunity to do something satisfying.

I also thank God for Diane Lawson, my mama. She's been so supportive of me, as well as our business. Unfortunately, Eddie Lawson wasn't happy about the support his wife, my mother, gave me, but oh well. I love my stepfather, but I sometimes think he oversteps his boundaries. She is my mother. I know it sounds bratty, but when my father was alive, I didn't have to compete for my mother's affection. We functioned as a family and the love we shared was equal.

Eddie Lawson is a trip and being a part of his family is different. He's very jealous of the relationship my mother and I have. He has two sons, but for some reason, he's not close to them and he doesn't seem to care about their aloofness at all. I've only met them once, and our parents have been together for three years. He tries to make my mother feel bad because she and I are close, and he and his sons aren't, but whose fault is that? Not Diane's or Nia's. Well, enough about step daddy dearest. Let me get back to my girls. Our love is so deep for each other. They've been very supportive of me, and everything I do. Let me explain a particular situation so you can understand the depth of our friendship. Now I can tell you about the big dick ex of mine.

His name is Benjamin Jones, and he is one fine black man! Black men are beautiful, but this one would be in the top one hundred nationwide. That's impressive because there are some fine black men in the U S of A! He is made from the caramel chocolate I described, and he is white-boy hairy. He has hair on his face, legs, chest, and arms. I don't know what it is about hairy men, but I've loved hairy men since Teddy Pendegrass. Although he's hairy he cannot grow any hair on his head, and I do love a bald brotha. He has beautiful dark brown eyes, and his eyelashes are thick and long (like something else on his body). If women had his eyelashes, Maybelline would go out of business. His eyebrows are naturally arched, and he has high cheekbones and full supple lips like Allen Payne. He wears an earring in each ear, either a diamond stud or small gold or silver hoops. He's five feet eleven inches tall, 195 lbs., and he never works out. He has the best looking six- pack I've ever seen considering he doesn't have a fitness regime. All of him is scrumptious. I mean muscular and sexy as hell. He was all that and a bag of chips! Or so I thought. He reconfirmed the fact that; 'just because it looks good, doesn't mean it's good for you.'

We dated for two years, and after one year together he moved in with me. Now, I realize it was a huge mistake. The nigga should've stayed in his matchbox apartment. I own a tri-level townhouse in University City bordering Clayton. Once Event Solutions became stable, I was able to purchase it. It has three bedrooms, three and a half bathrooms, a family room, formal dining room, living room, a finished basement, and a huge gourmet kitchen with state-of-the-art stainless-steel appliances. My favorite room in the house is the family room. It sits off the kitchen. The kitchen and family room are separated by a see-through onyx marble fireplace. The room is very comfortable. It has a built-in entertainment center that holds a sixty-five-inch Plasma television, and a Bose surround sound system. The carpet I chose is onyx, which is complimented by a red leather sectional. There is a large bay window and for window treatments, I have black sheer panels. I draped a red sheer scarf around a brushed silver tone corkscrew rod. The effect enthralls all who see it. The room is very modern. My friends and family are drawn to this room, and this is where I entertain.

Back to Ben, I let his tired ass move in with me, I guess the D-I-C-K caught me at a weak moment. You know how it is. You've chosen celibacy for several reasons. You're tired of the bullshit, you've slept with enough men already, there's no one special in your life and although sex is good, you know fornication is a sin. Right as you're settling into your celibate lifestyle, you meet a man posing as Mr. Right. He's special in the beginning. Gentle. Giving (with his time, his money, and the dick). Considerate. Thoughtful. Affectionate. Everything you think you want. He even wants to spend every spare moment with you. He leaves sweet messages on your voicemail. Then he does, what most women want. He takes you home to meet his mama. AND, the dick. He throws the dick like he's doing the Cha Cha Slide.....Slide to the left....Slide to the right...Cha Cha now ya'll......

In the back of your mind, you remember the promise you made to yourself after the last clown? You promised yourself you wouldn't fall fast. Well guess what? You fail. You do anyway. Now, don't get me wrong, Ben's not a bad person, but a Hoe is a Hoe is a Hoe, soooo!

12

His true colors were bound to come out. Don't they always? Those faking can't fake forever. Unless of course, it's one of these sistahs faking an orgasm for one of these tired ass men who thinks he's swingin' like Tarzan. And he's NOT.

Hell, I even made sacrifices for him. For a very long time, I've wanted an Akita, but because Ben's inhumane ass didn't like dogs, I chose to not get a second dog. He had to deal with Sheba, she was there first. I now understand why he didn't like dogs. He's a dog and doesn't like himself. Another sacrifice for him. Nothing for me.

I'm not one to toot my own horn, but through hard work, and God's grace, I've been successful. Ben on the other hand lacks ambition. He's worked for UPS for the last four years, but he doesn't desire more. I don't have a problem with what he's chosen as a career. I certainly don't want to see him selling crack to our people, like so many people do. When we began dating, he wanted his own landscaping company, but when I brought the topic up later, he acted as if I was speaking Swahili to him, so I left it alone. It's a shame because he has a great business mind, and he knows a lot about landscaping.

Another thing I did not like about him is his lack of friends. He's a NWF. A nigga without friends. Niggas without friends have issues. Now what man doesn't have friends? Hell, most of the guys I know have friends they've been friends with since childhood. This man doesn't have one man in his life he can depend on. His father isn't in his life, and the few associates he has in his life are pathetic. He doesn't have a successful friendship, yet he critiques mine. Now, what's wrong with that picture? We began dating in late 2016 after being introduced by a mutual friend. We were like Will and Jada in the beginning, but we ended up like Halle and Eric in the end. We got along so well and spent so much time together we agreed living together made sense. He leased an apartment, so it made sense for him to end his lease, since I own. Big mistake! The man I loved turned into the bum on the couch. Now I know what Tamia was talking about. He was a stranger in my house. An intruder. He began doing things prior to us living together which were not in his character, like not picking up after himself. Not assisting with the cleaning of the house. Inviting his uncle over to help him junk up the family room. Last time I checked I didn't have any children. Nia was not going to pick up after some grown ass man! The dick ain't that good. Hell, no dick is. He was also hanging out, which was fine, but him coming home at four, five and six in the morning was not! The behavior was totally disrespectful. With him staying out, I got curious.

Call it a woman's intuition. Now, if he was seeing someone else, he was entitled to do what he wanted. We are not married. Thank God. But I'll be damned if he was going to play me for the fool. He was entitled to see someone else, but I was also entitled. Entitled to catch his sorry ass! Entitled to have a companion! I had a strong feeling, so I acted upon it. I called my girl, my partner in crime. It was time to go into my Inspector Bad Chick mode.

13

Alexis

Alexis looked at the caller id before answering, "What's up, Nia?"

"Damn you and caller ID!"

"Whatever girl, that's technology for you. What's up?"

"Girl, this muthafucka must think I'm a fool! I think he's trippin`. No, as a matter of fact, I know he's trippin! I am so sick of his-no-ambition-hanging-out-til-the-wee-hours-in-the-morning-can't-pick-up-behind-his-own-triflin-ass!"

"You know I'm not going to tell you to leave him, but I will tell you, as I've told you many times before, you don't deserve to go through this! So, what are you going to do?"

"I...I mean we...."

"We, what do you mean we? When did you become French?"

"C'mon girl, I need you."

"Nia, are you serious? It's Saturday, and I was about to take a hot bubble bath with Joshua and have a glass of Pinot Noir. Afterwards, I planned on watching 'Best Man' with my Hollywood man."

"And who would that be?"

"Girl don't play. Only the finest brotha on the planet."

Laughing I asked, "Who, Eric Benet? I don't know if you know this, but he's married."

"Ha-Ha, I don't want Eric although he is fine even without the locks, but don't get it twisted, you know my Hollywood man is fine ass-chocolate-drop-eat-em'-up-like-milk-duds Morris Chestnut."

"Whateva. Wait a minute. Who the hell is Joshua? You got a new man you didn't tell me about?"

"Your ass is silly. Joshua Redman is a jazz musician, and his album is ready to play for me."

"Girl, I thought you had a new man. Anyway, I need you. I don't want to ruin your plans, but I wouldn't ask if it wasn't necessary. I know what we're about to do is ghetto as well as juvenile. This is the type of shit we did in our twenties, but I just really need to see it with my own eyes. If you really don't want to go, I'll go alone."

"I wouldn't think of letting you go by yourself. I'll go, but is it really going to make a difference?"

"Believe it or not, I'm finally tired. This mess has gone on long enough. My tolerance meter is overflowing."

"Cause when a woman's fed up."

"Exactly and I'm definitely fed up."

"All righty, how do you want to do this?"

"Call your daddy and see if he'll let us use the Pacer."

"The Pacer! That old piece of shit! What, does Ben drive slow like an eighty-year-old lady sightseeing on a Sunday? That's the only way we'll keep up in the Pacer."

"Girl, don't worry about that, I'll make it keep up."

"Why can't we drive one of our vehicles? I'll feel like Cole on '*Martin*' driving the Pacer."

"Jackass knows our vehicles, and I forgot Cole had a Pacer. Talk about funny."

"Yeah, it was. All right, let me call my daddy on the three-way, hold on..."

Nia

While I was on hold, I asked the Lord to get me through this, and bring everything in the dark, to light.

Lexy came back on the line, "Okay, I'm back. Daddy said we could use the Pacer. He got a good laugh out of it because he knows what we're up to. He told us to be careful."

"Lexy, I really appreciate this."

"It's fine girl, you would do the same for me, as a matter of a fact, remember Kevin?"

"Girl, don't go there! We'll talk about Kevin's wanna-be-a-playa-for-life ass later. I'm going to leave in about ten minutes, I should be there in twenty minutes."

"All right, I'll be ready."

Alexis has a condominium in the Central West End, which is about ten minutes from where I stay. It's a very trendy area that reminds me of the Georgetown area in D.C. The streets are lined with cobblestones and on both sides of the main street, which is Euclid, you'll find art galleries, restaurants, coffee shops, and boutiques with eclectic clothing. It's a great place to hang out, live and people watch.

As I was leaving, guess who walked through the door? Mr. Playa-Playa, himself. He must've just come from the barbershop because his beard was groomed, and his bald head was shining. I guess he went to get so fresh and so clean clean for whatever her name is.

"Where are you going?"

"Well, hello to you too."

"I'm sorry, how you doing Boo?"

"Fine. Lexy and I are going to Landry's for seafood, and then we may go out."

"Oh...okay, I'm going to probably go out too."

"Whateva," I countered with much attitude.

Frowning, he asked, "What's up with the attitude?"

"Nothing." I guess it was not wise to let him know I was pissed, he may want to talk about it, but I'm done talking about it. "Enjoy yourself."
I grabbed my jacket, my Coach bag, and headed for the garage. He was right behind me.
"Can a brotha get a kiss?"
"Sure Boo."
I'll play along with his crazy ass, but he doesn't know he's about to get cold busted but there it is. This time I can hear it. My heart breaking. A slow ache in my heart. A woman's intuition is good, but with it comes a nervous stomach and a broken heart. Why do I always pick these clowns? Then there's two angels perched on my shoulders. The bad angel is saying:
"Niggas ain't shit, they're only good for fucking, and half of them can't get that right! Fuck em' all, buy a vibrator. Then you're guaranteed to get yours."
The good angel was screaming:
"Girl, there are some good black men out here. Just hold on. He's coming. The special one, the one who will treat you like the queen you are. The one God has chosen for you."
I was torn between these two voices. I had to know what was going on. I was tired of speculating. When it came down to it, I was ready to rumble.
I reached Alexis' condo in record time. We then made it to her parent's home in five minutes. They own a beautiful home on Lindell Blvd. This boulevard houses homes of grandeur. Her father owns a successful construction company. I once asked why he kept the Pacer, because he also owns a Maserati, and a Range Rover. He said when he began his company, he could only afford the Pacer and he keeps it as a reminder. It keeps him grounded. I have the utmost respect for him and he's like a father to me. Alexis is so blessed to have both her parents. They've been married for forty-two years. I parked my 4Runner in the back, and Lexy and I jumped in the Pacer. We drove to the Mobil gas station on the corner of Delmar and Kingshighway. Then I called Ben from a pay phone to make sure he was still home. He was. We drove to my townhouse and sat in a spot where we could view the comings and goings of the townhouse, without being noticed, of course. Approximately twenty-five minutes later, he pulled out in his Tahoe. We discreetly followed him until we arrived in the Central West End, on Union and Waterman, which is where his uncle lived. Why am I doing this juvenile shit at my age? Following his funky ass. I guess my eyes must witness his deception. We sat and waited, and he came out about twenty minutes later. We began following him again and this time we ended up in South St. Louis. No one in his family lived in this area, but I was curious to see who lived on this side of town. Who was he going to visit? Well, he wasn't going to disappoint me. I'd get my answer soon enough. We were flying down Vandeventer trying to keep up. We sped by the White Castle on the corner of Chouteau and Vandeventer so fast it was a blur. I knew we passed it because the aroma lingered in the air and my stomach grumbled. He was obviously in a

16

hurry. He turned onto Hunt, which was off Vandeventer. It was one block long and all the houses and duplexes were dilapidated. I had never been on this street, and I wondered what he was doing here. He pulled up in front of one of the dilapidated duplexes and blew his horn. Shortly thereafter, a woman appeared from the side of this raggedy ass, run down duplex, and she hopped in his Tahoe. The Tahoe I helped pick out. The Tahoe I helped pay the sales taxes on. Yes! That damn Tahoe! Again, I wasn't going to be disappointed. I asked God to shed light on the situation and He did. I received the signal and took heed.

When she hopped in his vehicle, they kissed. Not a peck but a Boo-I-miss-you-kind-of-kiss. It was the kind of kiss he and I should have been sharing, not him and someone else.

I got out of the Pacer, walked to the driver's side, and tapped on Ben's window. It scared the shit out of him, but he reluctantly let the window down. His eyes were as big as saucers. I had his ass. He was busted.

"Your shit will be in the garage, and the locks will be changed, as well as the code for the garage door opener. You can get your motorcycle on Tuesday at four and if you're not there, I'll have it dropped off. Since you want to mess around, move in with your friend in this raggedy ass house, in this raggedy ass neighborhood. From this moment on the Sugar Shack is closed." I headed back to the Pacer, got in, and we pulled off.

Busted Ben

Damn, I can't believe I just got caught with big-booty-ghetto-ass Shaquita. Nia straight caught me trippin`. I gotta convince her to take me back. I can't lose her. First, I must get rid of Shaquita because she hasn't moved. It's evident my game is slippin'.

"Girl, get out the truck."

"What! Nigga you trippin. I thought you didn't like her stuck up, educated ass? Fuck her."

"I never told you I didn't care about my lady; you were just something on the side."

"Whateva nigga, enough about your precious Nia, you said we was goin' to eat, I'm hungry so let's go."

I repeated my request, "I said, get your ghetto ass out of my truck."

"Aw, so I'm ghetto now, but this ghetto pussy kept your ass comin' around."

"The pussy was good, but that's all you got. My baby has goals and dreams and shit like that. Your ass is thirty-five and you work at a beauty supply store, what kind of future is that?"

"So, you'd rather be with the no ass having woman of yours who has so many goals she can't fuck you right, than with my ghetto-fuck-you-and suck-you-right-ass?"

"Damn right! And, for the record, she does me right in the bedroom. I chose to get some extra ass. I'm what you'd call a greedy brotha. She wouldn't let me fuck her in the ass, but you did.

"Aw, so it's all about the booty fuck?"

"Without a doubt. Nia's ass had a 'No Entrance' sign, but yours. Yours said, come one, come all, welcome. Sometimes a brotha wants a little ass, so a brotha's gotta do what a brotha's gotta do!"

"Ain't that a bitch! Well, if your girl loved you, she would've given you the ass."

"Say what you want, but my girl has class and anal sex ain't her thang. Love or no love, it ain't her thang. Women like you give up the ass, literally, to niggas constantly, without love. Giving up ass to you is like giving a hand job, no big deal. An everyday occurrence."

"Oh, so you just know me, don't you?"

"As a matter of fact, I do. I mean look at you, your hair's three different colors, you're a weaveaholic, you got three baby daddies, and you got a gold tooth. You don't want anything out of life, and you sleep with a nigga four hours after meeting him."

"You weren't complaining when you got the ass."

Giving her an incredulous look, I responded with, "Of course I wasn't, I wanted the ass, but did you honestly think you and I were going to have a relationship?"

"Well, yes."

"Not!"

"Why?"

"Why? We could never have a future together! Why do you think I've never taken your kids out with us?"

"I figured you didn't want to be bothered."

"Exactly. Why would you want to be with a man who doesn't want to be bothered with your children? Shit, I don't want to be with a sistah who doesn't spend time with her children. The kids spend more time with their grandmother than you. Their fathers don't come around, and I don't want them calling me daddy."

"Oh, so I'm good enough to fuck, but not have a future with."

"That's it sweetheart you don't have a future. Period. You're what they call a less sistah."

"And what the fuck is a less sistah."

"Ambition-less, future-less, life-less, class-less, sophistication-less, sense-less! Those are your qualities."

"You know what Ben."

"What Quita?"

"Fuck you!"

"No, fuck you!" Snapping my fingers, I said, "Oh snap! I already did."

"Don't call me anymore!"

"And the same goes for you."

18

"Remember this, what goes around, comes around."

"What, is that a threat?"

"Not a threat, just a fact."

"Well, whateva. Just do me a favor."

"What?"

She began to lick her lips and gave me the I-want-you-deep-inside-of-me-look. "You want another taste of this?"

"NOT! I want you to forget my cell phone number. The pussy was splendid, but now we've got to end it."

"You low-life-hairy-booty-bastard!"

"The hairy booty you licked, now get yo trifling ass out of my truck."

Twirling her fingers through her ghetto ass weave she had the nerve to ask, "We ain't going to eat?"

"Damn! What part of NO don't you understand? The N or the O?"

"What am I supposed to do about eating?"

"Last time I checked, I wasn't your man, your mama or your daddy and therefore I don't give a damn about how, when, where or what you eat. It's not my problem. See ya' when I see ya'." I threw up the deuces sign.

"I'm going to call Miss Thang and tell her about yo trifling ass."

"No, you're not, you don't know where we live, and our number is not listed. I gotta go."

"Nigga you trippin'. How you gone play me?"

"Play you! If anyone got played, it was Nia."

"Your precious Nia, if she was all that you wouldn't be with me."

"My being with you has nothing to do with Nia. I ain't never been faithful to one woman. I picked you because I knew you wouldn't have a problem with me having a full-time woman."

"Why is that?"

"I don't know you'll have to ask yourself that question. I'm out. Peace."

"But...."

At this point I tuned her out. She got loud and began shouting obscenities, so I politely leaned over her, opened the passenger door, and shoved her ass out of it. She hit the side of the truck with her hand. I closed the door and sped off. Looking in my rear-view mirror, I could see her crazy ass yelling with her hands on those voluptuous hips. I was going to miss that ass, but good riddance. I had to come up with a plan to get my woman back. Unfortunately, I couldn't go home, I wasn't welcome there. I decided to drive around and think. I wish I had a friend I could talk to. I guess I'll call my Uncle Jimmy. At this point, he is my only option.

Nia

We were weaving through traffic and the silence hung in the air like humidity. I couldn't believe what I'd just witnessed. The pain was present, but the fact that I was fed up with his trifling ass dulled the pain. I'd prayed for

19

God's guidance, and He'd shown me the truth. In this case, the truth set me free. I didn't want a pity party. I wanted to celebrate my freedom as well as my womanhood.

Alexis ended the silence. "Are you all right?"

"Surprisingly yes! I prayed for God to show the truth, and He did!"

"Are you sure you're all right?"

"Honestly, I'm in a daze right now, but I'll be okay. I need to have the locks changed, and I want it done tonight. I am so tired of choosing the wrong men."

"I know girl, we all keep going through the worst men in America. They need to do a show on that."

"I'm just sick and tired of all the ups and downs accompanying a relationship."

"I feel ya, but keep this in mind, with all the toads we've kissed, we're bound to come across an African prince eventually."

"Let's hope so girl.....cause I'm tired as hell."

"Do you want to go home, or over to my place?"

"We can go to my place because I want the locks changed, as well as the code on the alarm changed ASAP, I ain't waiting around til' tomorrow."

"Do you think he'll come back?"

"Hell yeah, I got comeback coochie!" Lexy and I began to laugh at my comment. "Seriously, I'm sure he will, but I am too through. If I don't get these locks changed tonight, my explosion will be bigger than any nuclear war occurring."

"If you ain't silly, I don't know who is. All right, we'll go to your house. We can pull up the directory on the Internet for various locksmiths, and ADT. Do you think Ben will try to clown? If so, I can call David. You know he's a cop now."

"I don't think he'll act up but call him just to alert him. Let him know we may need him later."

Alexis

I picked up my cellular phone to call my cousin David. "Hey, David."

"What up cousin? How's Uncle Levi?"

"He's fine. I'm with Nia now and-

"Tell Nia I said what's up. I haven't seen her fine ass in a while."

"I'll give her your message, but right now we have a situation."

"What kind of situation?"

"Nia saw Ben with another woman, and she thinks he may try and clown."

"No that nigga didn't go out like a sucka! Nia's good people, he tripped."

"Yeah he did."

20

"It's his loss."

"I agree with you there. You should've seen the hood rat he was with, and the raggedy ass house she came out of. She had a blonde, pink, and green weave and a big ol' nasty ghetto booty."

"I guess it's true, some niggas go after big asses no matter what the rest of the package looks like. I can't believe he chose to trade in a Lexus for a Kia."

"Oh well, another brotha bites the dust. He'll regret it if he doesn't already."

"Take it from another brotha, he'll certainly regret it. I'll keep my cell phone on. If you need me, I'll be there in less than fifteen minutes."

"Thanks cousin, I really appreciate it. By the way, how's Trina?"

"Trina? Cuz, she left me alone, talking about me being relationship phobic."

"Damn, she pegged your ass right," Laughing.

"Yeah whatever. You women know you stick together. What happened to blood being thicker than water?"

"Blood may be thicker, but the truth shall set you free! I have nothing more to say."

Laughing he said, "Yeah all right."

Nia

After Lexy hung up with David, we rode in silence. I was thinking about the trip tomorrow. Lexy was probably afraid if she said something I'd break down. I was surprised at how well I was handling the situation, but prayer is powerful, and I'd handed it over to God. I'd let go and let God.

Right then, Ashanti's song 'Foolish' came on the radio and I attempted to sing along with her, but Lexy had something else in mind. She changed the station.

"Nia, I don't think you should listen to this song, it may upset you."

"Lexy, thanks for the concern, but I'm not going to allow Ben to control my emotions."

"But-

"But nothing. Do you remember J.D.?"

With apprehension Lexy said, "Yes."

"Well don't act like you forgot. I must deal with this situation head-on, which means not changing the station every time a love song comes on."

"Okay, I'm with you because I remember when I broke up with J.D., I had to endure Toni Braxton's breathe again ass singing 'Unbreak My Heart' and 'There's No Me Without You', but I got through it, so I guess you can endure Ashanti." She changed the station back.

I continued to sing along with my favorite Ashanti verse, "See, when I get the strength to leave you, always tell me that you need me, and I'm weak cause I believe you and I'm mad because I love you so I stop and think that

21

may be you could learn to appreciate me then it all remains the same, that you ain't never gonna change." I turned the volume down. "You know Lexy, that verse is so true. We always stay because of our feelings, and I'm not saying men don't feel or love, but our shit is so much deeper than theirs."

"Yeah, that's the way it seems, but I know my parent's feelings are mutual. My father would be no good if my mother even thought about leaving him."

"I know, but what your parents have is different. The same goes for my parents, their love was so special."

"That's true but to truly believe in love, I mean really believe in it, we must believe someday we'll be blessed with the same kind of love our parents share. Or in your case what your parents shared."

"I hear ya Lex, but I don't think it will happen, not for me anyway."

"You just think so because of what just happened, but you will get through this."

"I know I will, but I'm tired of black men and their bullshit."

"So, you're going date white boys now?"

"Hell to the naw! I'm not looking for anything serious, and I think I'm going to take a break and be celibate."

"Well, that's not a bad thing, but you're not through dating, you just need some time."

"I love you Lexy but whateva!" Lexy began to laugh, and for a moment I wished I could push her out of her father's Pacer.

After arriving at Alexis' parents' home, we dropped off the Pacer. I thanked Mr. Knight, and before we could get in my truck, Mr. Knight asked if he could talk to me. Of course, I said yes, he's like a father to me. He led me into his office and closed the door. I sat in the chair in front of his desk, and he sat in the chair behind the desk. There was complete silence for one minute. He leaned forward and began to speak.

"Nia I'm not going to ask what you and Alexis did tonight and honestly, I don't care, but there are some things I want to say to you. As you know, Ralph and I were good friends and I view you as a daughter. I know whatever you and Alexis went to do involves a man, probably the fella you were living with. When I found out he was living with you I-"

"Mr. Kni-"

"Young lady don't interrupt me. I'll tell you when you can speak." I sat there and continued to listen. I had no other choice. I'd been taught to always respect my elders. He continued, "As I was saying when I found out he was living with you I had a problem with it, but I didn't say anything because you young people can't be told anything. If Ralph were alive, he'd have something to say, and I think it would be what I'm about to tell you. Real men don't move in with women, real men move you in with them or they find a place for both of you. Your father was a great provider and that's what real men do; they provide for those they love. Gladys and I lived together before we got married, but I moved her out of her parent's home into our first apartment. I didn't move

22

her into my parent's home or wait for her to enroll at Harris Stowe and move in with her. I found us an apartment and I paid the rent. The only thing she was responsible for was buying the groceries and cooking. It was a struggle, but we struggled together. My point is this; I knew he wouldn't be right because he shouldn't have moved in with you. You young ladies sell yourselves short. I know times have changed but good men want to take care of their women, not the other way around. These lazy young men don't have to work or be responsible because you all take care of them. Well baby girl, that's not love. You deserve more, but you won't get it until you know in your heart you deserve more. You, Alexis, Kenya, and Alicia deserve good men who want to care of you. It's obvious you all are taking care of yourselves financially, but I know there's more to life, but you won't get it if you continue to sell yourselves short. You deserve a good man, the kind of man your father was. What that means Nia is only dating young men who are gainfully employed and have a lot of ambition. That means not dating a young man with three to four children, even if he does take care of them because you'd be cheating yourself of so much. Hell, he's had three or four, so he's a pro. You want someone who isn't a pro. He's surely not an amateur. The same things I want for Alexis, I want for you. God will only bless you with the best when you start asking for the best in prayer and believing you're worthy. I pray to God you girls deem yourselves worthy. Again, I will never tell you what to do, but I wanted to share my feelings with you."

By this time, tears were streaming down my cheeks. This man, who loved me like he loved his own daughter, had talked to me in such a loving manner, and it touched my heart. It got me thinking about everything, especially my father and his expectations. Mr. Knight was right, and his talk couldn't have come at a better time. We stood up at the same time, and Mr. Knight opened his arms to me, I willingly went into the safety and warmth of his embrace. He held me until my eyes were dry and I was ready to talk.

"Mr. Knight thank y-"

"Nia, you don't have to thank me. Ralph was like a brother to me although we'd only known each other for the length of you and Alexis' friendship. I feel it's my responsibility to watch out for you. That's what fathers do. I know I'll never replace Ralph but be assured I'll always be here for you."

"Thank you, Mr. Knight. Your talk has helped me and made me stronger. I'm going to go home now, but I'll call you and Mrs. Knight tomorrow." I wiped the tears from my cheeks, kissed his cheek, and went to find Lexy. I found her in the kitchen, resting on the island eating grapes. "Lexy, I'm ready."

"Oh, okay." She yelled bye to her parents, and we left.

We got to my place, and fortunately, Ben was not there.

Lexy grabbed some boxes from the basement and headed upstairs to begin packing his belongings. I logged onto Google to pull up the directory. I retrieved the number for a twenty-four-hour locksmith, as well as ADT. Both companies said they could have someone at my home within forty-five minutes. I was in the mood for some music. I began to shuffle all my music through the built-in Bose speakers. As the music began to fill the townhouse, I joined Alexis in my bedroom. She's one helluva friend. Always there. From beginning to end. Through thick and thin.

When I entered the bedroom, she had already packed most of his things in boxes. All his bathroom items were boxed. I went into the walk-in-closet and began placing his clothes in boxes also. I had an old garment bag and placed his suits in it. Lexy was emptying out his drawer, and in doing so she came across a box of condoms.

"Nia, what do you want me to do with these?"

"You can box those up also, I'm sure he'll need them."

"He's lucky you ain't tearing his shit up, because if it were me, I'd do an Angela Bassett on his ass."

Laughing I replied, "Not the Waiting to Exhale scene."

"Yes, the one and only."

"Well, he's not worth it, so I'm not going there."

"Well, I'm really proud of the way you're handling this."

"I've been through so much and all of my heartaches have been my life lessons."

"You obviously learned from them."

"Yes, I have. Thank God."

"So, were you able to get in touch with ADT, and a locksmith?"

"Yeah, I talked to both. They both said they could send someone over within forty-five minutes. That was twenty minutes ago. They should be here soon. Lexy, I really appreciate this, and you know I love you."

"Girl, you don't have to thank me, we're sisters. I'd do anything for you. I wouldn't let you go through this shit by yourself. I will admit I'm surprised you're doing as well as you are. I know how much you love him."

"I do love him, but I've learned to love Nia even more. It took some time for me to get to the point where I loved myself completely, but I just remembered what my daddy always told me."

"And what's that?"

"To always love myself, because when all fails, other than God, you only have yourself."

"That's some great advice."

"It is and my Daddy is probably rolling over in his grave. I had a good example, so I don't know where I went wrong. My daddy wasn't perfect, but he always respected my mama."

"Yeah, he's probably rolling over in his grave, but he knows you'll handle the situation."

"I guess. Hey, do you remember Will?"

"Of course."

"As you know Will turned to won't."

"Your ass is silly."

"Well, I gave my all to Will, and he fucked me over, and I allowed it. I thought if I loved him enough, he'd stop what he was doing. Well, you and I both know that didn't work. I now realize I was never the problem; he just didn't love himself enough. I vowed after my relationship with him I would not allow a man to treat me as he pleased unless it was in a queenly manner. I must love God and Nia. First, and foremost. Earlier tonight I asked God to shed some light, and I said if He did, I would leave the situation alone. Well, He shed the light, and the picture is clear. Crystal clear. Your girl is done with Ben Jones.

Ben

"Yo?"

"What's up Unc? Whatcha doin?"

"I ain't doing shit, just watching 'The Kings of Comedy' and Janice is in the kitchen picking collard greens."

"Tell Aunt Janice I said hi. Where are you watching Kings of Comedy?"

"It's on cable. What's up, nephew?"

"I got a problem."

"I ain't got no money boy."

"I don't need any money, Unc."

"Well then what's wrong?"

"Unc, if you slow down, I can explain."

"I'm your uncle and I love you, but don't talk to me like I'm one of your boys."

"Yes, sir, but remember, I don't have no boys."

"Aw yeah, that's right. Your ass needs some friends, and maybe you'd have some if you weren't so full of yourself. Now, what do you want?"

"Nia caught me with Quita."

"What? Hold on while I pause Bernie Mac's crazy ass. That Cedric funny too, he has made St. Louis proud."

"Yes, sir he has, but can we get back to my problem."

"Yeah. So, your ass got caught? How did that happen?"

"Unc, I don't know. Nia left to go out with Alexis and about forty-five minutes later I left. I came by your place first, and then I went to pick up Quita because I promised her, we'd go to Red Lobster and then head to the motel. When I got there, I blew, she came out, kissed me, and the next thing I knew Nia was tapping on my truck window."

"I know ain't no pussy like new pussy or more pussy, but I told you, you was no good at cheating. Now you done messed up."

"I know, but I need your advice. What should I do?"

"You should pack your shit and get outta her house and leave her alone."

25

"I'm sure her and her girls are having a pack Ben's-shit-party, but I don't want to leave her alone. I love her."

"Is that right? You know, love's a funny thing, cause to me if you loved her, you wouldn't have cheated on her. When you decided to step out, you had to know there might be consequences and repercussions."

"I never thought I'd get caught."

"Who does?"

"I guess nobody."

"Well, you was bound to get caught. You all have been together for two years, and you've been trippin' for two years. She never did have all of you. You always held back."

"I know Unc, and now I don't think she's going take me back."

"You know she's the best thing to ever happen to you."

"I know, and that's why I'm buggin`."

"How did Quita react?"

"And what makes you think that she reacted at all?"

"I know her type."

"And what type is that?"

"She ain't got no class at all. She's what you youngins call a hood mouse."

Laughing, "Actually Unc, the term is hood rat."

"Mouse, rat, they all in the same family. They rodents, and they fuck shit up."

"You right, Unc."

"Well, if you knew she was a rat, why did you mess with her?"

"The sex was the bomb."

"So, Nia's sex is that bad?"

"Actually it's not, but..."

"If it's not bad, why did you cheat?"

"Well, Nia's real independent and she keeps busy without me."

"And?"

"And there were times I'd want to do something, but she had to do something for her business."

"So let me get this right, because she was trying to be a businesswoman, and make some money you chose a hood rodent to mess around with."

"Unc, a lot of these hood rats don't care if you have a woman as long as you lay the pipe right, feed em' and buy them something every now and then. So, yes Quita made it very easy."

"So, Quita never wanted a relationship?"

"I think she did because I lied to her and told her things were bad between Nia and I. Things with Nia and I were fine until I started messing around. Damn Unc what am I going to do?"

"I don't know what to tell you boy. You need to give her some time to sort things out. She may call you."

"So, you saying I shouldn't do anything?"

"Yep, that's what I'm saying, and if you're finished, I'm going to finish watching 'The Kings of Comedy.'

"Okay Unc, I'll talk to you soon. And thanks"

"Good luck boy and tell your mama I'll be over tomorrow."

Damn, talking to my Uncle James didn't help at all, but I got myself in this, and I'm the only one who can get me out of it. I know I'm not taking his advice about leaving Nia alone. That's not an option.

Nia

At this point we had collected most of his stuff, and the doorbell rang. After checking the peephole, and disengaging my alarm system, I let the locksmith in. He changed the lock on the front door, as well as the back door. Right after he arrived, the guy from ADT arrived, and within ten minutes, the code for the alarm was changed. All this cost me two hundred and sixty dollars and it was well worth it.

During the time we were packing the phone rang several times, but the caller would not leave a message, and the caller ID displayed a blocked number. It couldn't be anyone but Ben.

We pulled all his stuff into the garage, and by then we were hungry. "Lexy, I'm going into the kitchen to fry some wings and fries."

"Cool, I'm going to fix us some watermelon martinis. Where is your watermelon Pucker and Ciroc?"

"It's downstairs on the wine server."

Lexy was on her way downstairs, and she was singing 'You're getting in the way of what I'm feeling.'

"Nia, turn that up, that's my jam!"

"I know girl, Jill's CD is still the bomb! It's old but it still does it for me."

"Yes, it is still the bomb and it's been out for many years."

"Yeah, Jillie from Philly is doing the damn thing!"

Lexy came back upstairs with our drinks, "You know what Nia?"

"What crazy?"

"You're the crazy one, but anyway, we should take a trip. I heard Tom Joyner's cruise is off the chain! There aren't a lot of youngsters, and from what I've seen in different magazines, as well as what I've heard on the radio, they have a ball. After going through this with Ben, you deserve a vacation, and you know I can always get out of St. Louis. I'm going to check with Kenya and Alicia to see if they'd be interested. Damn these wings and fries are good."

"Girl, that sounds like a plan. I'm going to check to see if Collett would be interested. She can fly in from Atlanta to meet us. Girl, these are the same wings we serve when our clients request something spicy. You've never tasted them?"

"No, but they're good. I'll have to use Event Solutions at the funeral home. As for Collett, it will be cool to see her, I haven't seen her since her visit in November."

"I'm sure she'd be interested. She and I just discussed taking a trip together when I talked to her."

"I'll call Carla, the dependable travel agent, and ask her to check on the rates for the cruise. I heard it's expensive, but all the proceeds go to The United Negro Scholarship Fund."

"You know what? I'll call Carla from Dallas. I'd like for us to get nice cabins, and we can just split the cost between the five of us. We should be able to find something for ten thousand, and that would only be two thousand each. We want to get on it because I think the cruise is in two months and it normally sells out every year."

"We'll check and see what Carla says."

"That sounds like a winner. I priced different cruise lines and although it's more than a regular seven-day cruise, it's for a good cause and it's a black thang. Sending black kids to college is a great thing."

"Yes, it is, but Damn! Two thousand each?"

"Yeah, but where can you go and see several performances daily?"

"It still seems like a lot of money."

"Yeah, but it's for a good cause and we're worth it. Plus, we can see stars like, Patti LaBelle, Charlie Wilson, George Clinton and the P-Funk All Stars, Rachelle Ferrell, Midnight Star, D.L. Hughley, George Wallace and J. Anthony Brown from the Tom Joyner Morning Show will be in the house. Now, I've just named a few, and from what I've read there are performances all day, every day. So, it really is worth the money."

"All right, girl. I very seldom treat myself, so go ahead and have Carla hook us up."

"Cool. I'm on it like chocolate on Morris Chestnut."

Ben

I arrived home at two in the morning. I'd been driving around for the last three hours. The entire time I was driving, I kept hearing Oran Juice Jones singing, "I saw you...and him, walking in the rain", but my version was sung by Nia, "I saw you...and her kissing in the truck." I tried coming up with a lie, but after getting busted, I knew a lie would be a waste of time. I needed to come clean. Damn I hate I ever got mixed up with ol' girl. When I saw her in the club, shakin' her ass like it was her profession, I should've left her there. Damn! Why didn't I listen to Mystikal when he said, 'Danger', because that's what she is. I knew it wasn't going to be easy, but Nia was worth the effort. I arrived at the townhouse and the lights were on, so Nia and her girls were probably having a niggas-ain't-shit Soiree. (Sighing) It's going to be a long night. Here goes nothing.

Nia

After cleaning the kitchen, we heard Ben trying to enter. It was two in the morning, and it startled us. He tried his key but had no success. I'm sure he was shocked, but at least now he knows how fed up I am. He's here early for a Saturday night. Before his triflin' ass was caught, he wouldn't have come home until five or six. I guess he wants to talk but no one cares about what his tired ass wants anymore. He rang the doorbell and I answered.

"Your stuff is in the garage. I'll open it for you."

"I can't believe you changed the locks. Can I come in? We need to talk."

"Why wouldn't I change the locks when you've made the choice to live elsewhere?"

"I didn't decide, you did."

"All right Gomer Pyle."

"Nia, can we please talk?'

"Talk! Nigga please! Talk about what? You've been playing me like the Final Four for the last few months, staying out until the sun rises. I didn't know where you were, and you never bothered to offer any information. Now I know why. You were with your new boo-"

"She is not my woman, you are Boo, and I know what I did was wrong and I'm sorry. I don't want to lose you."

"Don't give me that Boo shit, I haven't been Boo in months, but now you're caught, and BAM! I'm Boo again." Tsk... "I must look like Boo Boo the fool, but like Ice Cube said, "I ain't the one". Did you think about losing me when you were doing what you were doing?"

"She was just-"

"What? Just a fuck, a friend, a what?"

"She's just a friend."

"Okay Biz Markie! I saw the kiss, and it was not a friendship on the lips kiss. It was tongue." I threw my hands up! "Fuck It! It's irrelevant now, you made your choice."

"Baby, don't do this, I don't want to lose you. I'll do anything to get you back."

"You are crazy. You fuck around on me with some project-hood-rat-ghetto-gangsta-bitch, and you want me to forget it happened? How do you propose I do that?"

"I don't know, but I'll do anything. We can try couples counseling."

"Couples counseling? You're the only crazy one, I don't need counseling."

"Boo, why are you trippin`?"

Totally ignoring his crazy ass! I took a step back into the house and gave Lexy some directions.

29

"Alexis, open the garage door, be sure to lock the door between the garage, and the kitchen."

I turned back to him, "As for you Mr. Jones, Alexis and I boxed all your stuff up and it's in the garage. You can load it into your truck, it should fit. If I find anything else, I'll send it to your mama's house, or if you'd like, I can have it delivered to the address down on Hunt."

"I don't live with her."

"That's a shame, you threw our relationship and your home away for nothing."

"Boo, I know I messed up and no one realizes how sorry I am more than me but I'm asking for another chance. I love you."

"Chance. As in second?"

"Yes, please."

"NOT!" In my Rose Royce voice, I sang, "Just a vacancy, love don't live here anymore." Literally!

As I closed the door, Ben was saying something, but I wasn't trying to hear it. What did we have to talk about? Nothing. Nada. Zilch. I was done. Like a T-bone steak. Once he left, Lexy and I were too sleepy, so she crashed in the guest room, and I climbed into my bed. Thirty minutes later, the phone began ringing. Of course, it was Ben. I went through the house and turned off every single ringer. Voice mail could deal with Mr. Jones tonight.

Last night wore us out, Alexis and I slept until ten, which is late for us. I got up, showered, laid my clothes out for my trip, and began breakfast. I prepared bacon, rice, scrambled eggs with cheese, and biscuits. I guess the aroma woke Lexy up. She entered the kitchen. I greeted her. "Hey girl, how are you?"

"I'm fine. The question is, how are you? And why are you impersonating a cook, again?"

"Actually, I'm fine. I slept so well last night, and my heart feels much lighter. I got on my knees and thanked God for His mercy and grace. I know I'll be all right. I am so blessed! No, I don't have a man, but I have wonderful friends and family who are hella supportive. As for my cooking, you know I can burn in the kitchen. Alexis, I know I said-

"Nia, you don't have to thank me, we're sisters."

"I know but let me finish. You have always been there for me. I want you to know I love you and I thank God daily for your friendship."

Embracing with tears in our eyes, "You are so welcome, and I love you too."

"All right, enough of the mushy friendship stuff, let's eat! I'll turn the ringers on after we eat."

"Nia, this food is so good. You fried my bacon crispy just like I like it, and my eggs are nice and fluffy. It's almost as good as Goody Goody, and you know they have the best breakfast in St. Louis."

Laughing, "I told you I could burn in the kitchen, Ms. Thang."

We both cleaned our plates and the kitchen. I turned the ringer on, and you know it rang immediately. I answered.

30

Ben

Nia answered the phone, "Hello."

"Boo, are you still mad at me? I want us to talk. I need to explain what happened."

"There is nothing for you to explain. I saw what I needed to see with my two eyes."

"Boo, I know what you saw, but I really can explain."

"Any so-called explanation would be a lie, and I'm not in the mood. Alicia and I leave for Dallas tonight."

"Can we talk before you leave?"

"What part of NO don't you understand? The N, or the O? I don't have time to deal with this shit! It is imperative I focus on my presentation."

"I know, but I want to be the one to celebrate with you."

"Sorry, but I'll be doing my celebrating with those who really care for me. Those would be my family and friends. Gladly, it does not include you. I'm not going to worry about you, or this situation. You created this shit. I will tell you this, I am not changing my number or blocking your number, but I am telling you to stop calling me after we end this conversation. IF, and that's a big IF, I have the desire to speak with you, I will call you. If I were you, I wouldn't sit around waiting. I love you, but that's not enough anymore. It's over, and there is no chance of reconciliation. We will not be doing the Peaches & Herb thang. No reuniting here. I love Nia, and she must be my priority. Ben is no longer part of the equation. So, take care!" With all that said and done, she hung up on my ass. CLICK!

Nia

High fiving me, Alexis said, "You go girl! I am so proud of you. I honestly thought you would give in."

"Give in to what? Without trust there's nothing, and right now that's what Ben and I have....nothing. One thing's for sure, when a woman's fed up...."
The phone began ringing again. I was getting my money's worth from AT&T's voice mail.

"I normally would've given in, but prayer is a powerful thing. Now you know I'm not a holy roller, but I do believe. I told God if He delivered me from Ben, I would leave him alone unequivocally. Well, He answered my prayer, and I intend to follow through on my end of the deal. I'm sure there will be times when I miss Ben, hell, I may even shed a tear or two, but it's definitely over. Anyway, crying cleanses. I am so tired of meeting brothas, and giving them all of me, literally. I am not a whore, but I sometimes feel like one with all the so-called relationships I've had, and all of the coochie I've shared. I know

31

there had to be a sign on my forehead that reads, 'COOCHIE WITHOUT COMMITMENT!'

You meet someone, you all click, you become acquainted, and you both want the same things out of life. You later find out he was lying. All he wanted was some coochie, and a place to watch ESPN on a sixty-five inch television. All sistahs get is another signature on the vaginal wall. If I could peek inside, I would see that it probably resembles the veteran wall in D.C."

"You know you are too silly, but I know what you mean. Take my parents for instance, they've been married forty-two years, and my daddy is the only man my mama has ever been with. Unfortunately, we've missed the only had-one-man-era. If I could do it over, I'd still be a virgin. The dick has been good, but obviously their dicks, nor my coochie has found their soulmate."

"Relationships are hard and it's not just black men. White women, as well as Hispanic women are complaining about their men also. Hell, white men are baby daddies too, just like some of these brothas, instead of being fathers. The other day, I was changing channels, and I came across crazy ass Maury Povich. There were three women on. One black. One white. And you guessed it, one Hispanic. They were all crying and whining about the same thing, "My man did me wrong", "What I'm gone do?" My crazy ass was yelling at the TV, "Leave him alone! He doesn't know what he wants!"

Laughing Alexis responded, "Nia, you are crazy! I can see your ass in your family room yelling like you're talking to someone in your house. I never did understand why these women go on TV and tell all they business. That's what your girls are for."

"Hello! What would we do without our friends? I would rather be by my damn self, than go through all the mess some relationships endure. After a relationship, I try to allow myself sufficient time to regroup. The time varies and it rarely works because I open myself up to another failed relationship with another fool."

"I feel you, I used to take a year. Girl, I stopped doing the year thing because it didn't work. Niggas don't wait, so I'm not waiting either."

"Don't we need to try and do better than these brothas out here acting like dogs in heat?"

"I guess, but the times I gave myself one year of solitude, it didn't make a difference."

"I see your point. Shit, with all the knicks my vagina has endured, forget HIV, I'm afraid that my coochie may just fall out. Girl, this may sound crazy, but I've envisioned myself being asleep, and I have to pee. I went into the bathroom, but I realize my vagina is gone. I panic, but my urge to pee is so strong that my bladder bursts and I die." Lexy was looking at me like I'd lost my mind.

"Crazy? You're past crazy. Girl, you're getting a little too deep and dark for me. I understand where you're coming from, but you put way too much thought into this but that's only my opinion. Yes, you've had sex with more than one man, most sistahs have, but in your heart each one was special."

"Yeah, they were special, but I want the ONE! I want til' death do us part. I want special and sincere love, not the bullshit I've been getting. I want what my parents had before my daddy passed, and what your parents still have."

"I feel you girl but all I can say is hold on, it's coming. You're too good of a person to not experience the love you desire."

"Thanks for the vote of confidence, but do you know how many black women there are with no husband, and no children?"

"Too many."

"You're damn right, and I don't wanna be one of them. One of my girls in Houston called me the other day, and she said she's accepting the fact she may be one of those women."

"Girl, fuck that! I will not be forty and a less woman. Husband-less and child-less."

"You know Lexy, it's almost as if sistahs gotta lose themselves to have a successful relationship. We give up so much, most of which we never get back. I know relationships are just experiences we must endure before we get to our mate, but I am so tired."

"I know what you mean about being tired, I feel the same way, but what do you mean when you say we lose ourselves?"

"In my opinion, we give up a lot to make ourselves available to those interested in us. They don't really give up anything. What happened to sacrificing and compromising to get what you want? I'll tell you what happened, we're the ones doing all the sacrificing and compromising. If he plays ball on Saturdays, he'll continue to visit the courts. If he hangs out with the fellas on Friday, he'll continue to be "In Da Club", with his boys and 50Cent. Sistahs on the other hand, stop hangin' with the girls for the weekly happy hour or book club meeting. The only time she sees her girls is at the hair salon. Phone conversations may have occurred three to four times a week diminish to two times a month, and that's a good month."

"Isn't it the choice we as women make?"

"Yes, it is, but unconsciously. I feel like brothas expect it. God forbid, you are not available when he wants you. We turn into SWM's (sistahs with men), and we tend to neglect our sistahs without men. When will the madness stop? For your girl, the madness stops right here, right now. I will not allow a man to belittle my friendships or stop me from spending time with my girls. Other than our parents, true friends are our backbone."

"I hear ya' girl. Friendship's a spiritual thang. It's like you're the yin to my yang. The alpha to my omega."

"I feel the same way, that's why it's so important to hold onto true friends, and not neglect them. The older we get, the more desperate we become. I'm beginning to think being in your thirties is synonymous to desperation."

33

"Girl, I know that's right. I want to get married as much as the next sistah who has entered the DECADE OF DOOM. Over thirty or not, I'm not willing to settle just to say I got a husband."

"Yeah, because the minute you become comfortable saying my husband, you'll have to begin looking for a divorce attorney. So many people wed for the wrong reasons."

"You always have the option of getting a ghetto divorce?"

"A ghetto divorce....What the hell is a ghetto divorce?"

"Girl, you know what a ghetto divorce is. Those couples who have been married for ten years or more, but they've been separated seven of those years."

Laughing, "Girl, you are ignorant! I do agree with you though. Why do they stay married? He got a woman, has always had a woman. Neither will file for divorce. I know some sistahs who never date other men because she's honoring her vows. It doesn't matter what his trifling ass is doing. He has a different woman every six months."

"Those sistahs are crazy."

"Amen. I believe in working out your problems. If his dick tastes a different flavor every six months, it's time to divorce and move on. Divorces only cost five hundred dollars, and that's the maximum without a lawyer. If neither of them can come up with $500 in 7 years, then they shouldn't have gotten married in the first place."

"Amen to that. I think some couples who marry now don't really understand what being together through thick and thin means because when things get thick, one of them thins the hell out."

"I heard that girl. We could talk all day, but Becky and Lisa are waiting for me. I've got to get my hair and nails done before I leave tonight."

"Are you going to get your usual?"

"Since we have a business meeting, I'm going to stick with the usual because it's conservative, and it's going to go with my account-winning suit."

"Well, let me get out of here. I know you and Alicia will be fine tomorrow. Mr. Wells won't know what hit him when the two of you finish your presentation."

"Thanks for the vote of confidence, I'll call you from Dallas. Again, Lexy, thanks for everything."

"That's what friends are for."

"Love you."

"Love you too."

After Lexy left, I turned on the TV in the family room and cleaned up. The 76ers were playing the Heat. My appointment was an hour away, and I only lived ten minutes from the shop. Just as I was getting into the game, the phone rang. I grabbed the cordless, the one without caller id.

"Hello."

"Hey Boo, whatcha doin'?"

Immediately, I recognized his voice, and my voice reflected my disdain. "Ben, what do you want?"

"You."

"Well, I'm no longer yours for the taking. I advise you to go back to the poster child for Ghetto America you were swapping spit with less than twenty-four hours ago."

"Aw baby, that was noth-

"Don't do that."

"What? Don't do what?"

"Do not insult my intelligence by telling me it was nothing. I may love you, but I'm not stupid. Our, whatever you wanted to call it is painfully over. I advise you to deal with it and move on. I have."

"But Nia-

"But Nia nothing, this discussion is over. I have a presentation to prepare for."

"I know baby, and I want to wish you good luck."

"Oh...so now you want to wish me good luck. You have never displayed any interest in my business, nor have you shown me any support. You're interested and supportive now....Yea' right, good-bye Mr. Jones."

CLICK. The phone began ringing again, voice mail answered.

After talking to Ben, I only had twenty minutes to get to the shop, and I planned on stopping for gas. I hopped in my Accord coupe and began pulling out of the garage. As I'm closing the garage, in my rear-view mirror I see a Tahoe. Yes, it was that Tahoe! This fool is crazy!

Ben

I know Nia thinks I'm crazy, but I'm going to do whatever I have to do to get her back in my life. I even tried calling her girl Alexis, but she wasn't trying to hear anything I had to say. I was determined Nia was going to talk to me. Ghetto Queen was paging me like I was one of her baby daddies and someone needed pampers or milk. She doesn't have a clue; her stupid ass is yesterday's news. My boo is and was the only one who matters. She just didn't realize it yet. Damn! When a brotha fucks up. He really fucks up. And, I've fucked up.

Nia

When he called, it must've been from his cell. I've got to get a cordless with caller ID as soon as I get back in town. I acted as if he wasn't there and drove off. I stopped at the Amoco gas station on Delmar Blvd., filled up, and five minutes later I arrived at *Rezults* Salon on Olive Blvd. My girl chose the right name for the shop. The results you receive from her, or any of her stylists, are phenomenal.

As I emerged from my car, I noticed the Tahoe again. This is crazy, why is he following me? I walked over to confront him, and crazy let the window down with an I-just-won-the-power-ball-grin on his face. I had to ask, "What the fuck is wrong with you?"

"What are you talking about Boo?"

I hate a dumb ass, or even worse, someone who acts as if they don't have a clue. He was really trying my patience.

"Why are you following me? I gave you all your shit this morning, and I requested, no I demanded you stop calling, so there's no need for you to be at my townhouse, or the hair salon, or any other place I frequent. So, what do you want?"

"I want to talk. I know I fucked up but-"

"Yes, you did fuck up, and there's nothing to say. Our relationship has been rocky, for the last six months, and we would've eventually gone our separate ways. Ending is for the best."

"But Boo, I love you."

"I know Boo, me and the Ghetto Poster child."

"No, she was just a-"

"What? Just a fuck? You had around the clock cookie and blow jobs, but no more! Professional black athletes will all marry black women before I, Nia Witherspoon suck your dick again. Please leave me alone. Maybe one day we can be associates, but right now I can't deal with you or your bruised ego."

"Bruised ego, call it what you want. I just want my woman back."

"Not your woman. Don't have time, and while you're trying to kiss up, kiss the flattest part of my black ass! See ya' when I see ya'." I proceeded to my mother's to drop off Sheba and then headed to the hair salon. Crazy yelled out the window. "Nia, it's not over." It's not over in your sick mind, but Mr. Jones, it's over. Nia deserves something better.

Ben

She ain't trying to hear shit I'm saying. Her girls won't talk to me, but I really need a female point-of-view. I may have to call my mama. When I tell her what happened she's going to give me an ear full. She really likes Nia, but she knows I ain't right. She'll help me, and if all else fails, flowers, candy and of course diamonds are a girl's best friend

Nia

Becky Sheffield greeted me at the door. The girl is fierce with hair styling, and she's been a friend since middle school. She has not changed at all since the sixth grade, and she runs a very professional shop. *Rezults* is her salon, and she's owned it for years now. It is one of the nicest African American owned shops in the St. Louis area.

Hugging each other. "Hey girl, sorry I'm late."

"Girl, it's cool, I just finished up Keisha."

"How's Keisha, I haven't seen her in a while?"

"She's fine, and she asked about you as well. So, what's up? How is Mr. Fine-ass-Ben Jones?"

Before answering her, I greeted everyone in the shop. "Hey ya'll. How ya doin'?" My greeting was followed with "Hey Nia" Then I answered Becky's question. "I traded Ben's ass in for a peace of mind."

"Uh-oh, is there trouble in paradise?"

"No trouble at all, I'm just through with him. I don't know why men cheat, they're no good at it."

"You serious? You caught him cheating?"

"Yes girl, with the poster child for ghetto America. Lexy and I did some I Spy shit on his ass. Men will never realize sistahs have detective instincts embedded in them. Aren't you glad you're no longer single?"

Laughing. "I am very glad I'm not single, I see what my single friends go through and all I can do is thank God for my nine years of marriage."

"It's been nine years?"

"It will be this summer."

"Time flies. How is your family?"

"Girl they're fine."

"Business is good at Sheffield Construction?"

"Yeah girl, we're blessed."

"That is a blessing. So, what's up?"

"What's up is you catching Ben's cheating butt. What would you have done if he came to you and admitted he was cheating?"

"It would've still hurt but at least I would've respected him for being a man and telling the truth."

"But would you have stayed with him? People do make mistakes you know."

"I know but Ben's ass is a massive mistake waiting to happen. He's the only man I know who can find new coochie every other month to fall on his dick."

"Girl, you are crazy, you got my sides hurting. You know you did the right thing. If they cheat once, more than likely, they'll do it again."

"So many women settle. I refuse to do that. My daddy was a good man, so I know they're out there. I may sound idealistic comparing these men to my daddy, but he was my example. He wasn't perfect, but he was a good father, husband, and provider."

"Your daddy was a sweetheart. Well, let me take your coat. Can I offer you something to drink?

"Actually, I'd like a glass of Sauvignon Blanc if you have some. I want something calming."

"A glass of your choice it is."

Rezults is a classy shop. As a matter of fact, Essence magazine did an article listing different cities, and the salons to visit. Rezults was one of the shops listed for St. Louis. I'm so proud of her. The location is not far from where we grew up. Your stylist always greets you at the door, takes your coat, and offers you something to drink. It wasn't the typical black salon. You know, loud talking, Shenika's kids running around, and music so loud you think you're in a club. They specialize in healthy and stylish hair, as well as pedicures, manicures, and makeovers. The shop's colors are black and silver. It was stylishly decorated with a beautiful chandelier. The counters and the stylist's stations were black trimmed in silver, and all the seating was black. In the reception area there was a white leather tufted couch. Becky had speakers installed throughout the shop, and she always played a variety of jazz and rhythm and blues. The music was played softly throughout the shop, and occasionally they'd tune into a movie. There was also complimentary water with lemon, if you didn't want any of the other beverages she always kept onsite. Other than herself, there were six stylists, and one nail technician. Other stylists always approached her about working in the shop, but she always had a full shop, and unfortunately had to turn people away. At this time, she felt she could give her clients the best service if she kept it small, so she wasn't interested in expanding. Her reputation was one of excellence. She and the other stylists were booked for at least two months. I kept a standing appointment, but I sometimes needed to come on a different day and/or time and fortunately for me, she always worked around my schedule.

She led me to her station and caped me.

"What would you like today?"

"I need a dandruff treatment, and you can wrap it. I'd also like to get my eyebrows waxed."

"All right let's get started, you've got a plane to catch."

"Your memory is good girl. I can't believe you remembered?"

"You're my client and friend, of course I remembered."

We went to the shampoo bowl, where she shampooed and conditioned my hair. She gave my head a good scrubbing. I like her because she takes really good care of my hair. I've found a lot of stylists can really style your hair but know nothing about healthy hair. These young women can style a woman's baldhead, but eventually, even the baldhead wants some hair growth. I think a lot of these young stylists are wearing short haircuts, but not by choice. Becky keeps it healthy, as well as stylish.

"Girl, you know you can shampoo."

"No problem, you're the only client I have who gets my fingers hurting. If my other clients knew I shampooed your hair four times, they'd request the same, and I'd have carpal tunnel."

Laughing. "I know, I'll keep it on the low low. I appreciate the special care you give."

"As long as you've been patronizing me, it's the least I can do. Remember when I would do your hair in my parent's kitchen?"

"Girl, yes! Back then I could get a relaxer and a cut for twenty dollars. Now both of those services are ninety-five dollars. You've come a long way baby."

"I know girl, God has been so good. I have been successful, but it can be overwhelming at times. Who knew that little skinny Becky from U. City High would be a successful stylist?"

"Girl don't sell yourself short, you were fly in high school and you're still the bomb. You were cutting, relaxing, and styling then, before you even thought about entering cosmetology school. You, baby girl were destined for success."

"I appreciate it girl. I'm going to wax your eyebrows before I put you under the dryer."

"That's fine, just shape them but not too thin."

"Don't worry, I got you."

She completed waxing my eyebrows, and then wrapped my hair. "Nia, sit here a minute, I want to turn a dryer on so it will be warm when you get under it."

"Thanks Beck."

About three minutes later she returned with a fresh glass of Sauvignon Blanc for me.

"Would you like something to read? Or did you bring your presentation information?"

"I am so tired of the presentation information. I know it's important to our futures, but I really need a break. I just purchased 'The Other Woman' by Eric Jerome Dickey. That man must've been born with a Mont Blanc pen in his hand. The way he expresses himself is unbelievable."

"You're a big fan of his, is it good?"

"I'm sure it is, you know I love EJD, but I haven't started it yet."

"Well, come on, your dryer awaits you."

"Is there someplace I can leave my handbag?"

"Sure, I'll put it in my office."

I was under the dryer, sipping' on my wine, laughing aloud at Charles in The Other Woman. After forty-five minutes of being under the dryer, Becky tapped me on the leg to tell me there was a delivery up front for me.

"Are you sure it's for me?"

"Well, he asked for Nia Witherspoon, and you're the only Nia Witherspoon I know."

I got up and went to the front of the salon. Ben had his goofy ass up there with a bouquet of yellow and peach tulips (my favorites). I took the flowers from him and pulled him aside.

"What are you trying to do, embarrass yourself? The flower trick won't work."

"I just want you to know how sorry I am."

Gritting my teeth I mumbled, "Believe me, I know how sorry you are. Sorry ass should be your middle name. I'm sorry too. Sorry I put up with your cheating-community-dick-sharing-ass as long as I did. But I am now free. I'm sure Harriet Tubman didn't feel half as good after freeing her first group of slaves, as I feel now."

"Damn Boo, why you trippin? So, I made a mistake! What happened to forgiving a brotha?"

"I do forgive you, but I don't want you! I've moved on and you should do the same. I'm going back to the dryer."

"Yeah okay.....just know this, a brotha ain't giving up."

"Hey, if a brotha's got time to waste, waste away."

I left the flowers at the receptionist's desk and went back to the dryer. After a total of two hours under the dryer, my hair was finally dry. Thick hair had its advantages, as well as its disadvantages. Long dryer time was the latter. Becky combed my hair out and used a flat iron to give it some extra body. As usual, she did a beautiful job.

I then moved to Lisa's chair. She was the only ghetto element in the entire shop. She was ghetto and classy if those could be mixed. Her clients loved her, and the girl could do some nails. Her pedicures were the best I've ever experienced. I wasn't in to patronizing the Asians, although they have two nail shops on every corner, it seems in every city. On every corner in ghetto America there is normally an Asian nail shop, a liquor store, a church, and a chicken fast food joint. African American nail technicians were like Great White whales, almost extinct. I had found one I was going to stick with. I do a basic manicure. I don't care for sculptured nails. I wore them once and they messed up my nail bed. Of the services Lisa offers, the pedicures were my favorite. She really knows how to massage your feet, as well as your legs. I always doze off when's she's giving me a pedicure.

"Hey Nia."

"What's up girl?"

"What was up with your man earlier? Those flowers are beautiful."

"You know how these men can be. If you want, you can have the flowers."

"It's like that?"

"And that's the way it is."

"All right Run DMC". Laughing she said, "Thank you, I'll take the flowers. Are you sure?"

"I leave town tonight, and I am more than sure."

"Girl thanks. I appreciate it. I'll take them home and maybe Andre will be jealous."

"Are you and Andre all right?"

"Yeah, just typical male behavior. We've been together for two years, and I guess the thrill is gone. He hasn't sent me flowers since Valentine's Day. Maybe the flowers will rouse him a little."

"Well, go for it girl. A sistahs gotta do what a sistahs gotta do."

"Nia, thanks, I'll see you in two weeks at your standing appointment. Oh, before I forget, Good Luck!"

"Thanks girl."

40

"No problem."
On my nails I got the American manicure, and on my toes, I got a pretty plum color.
Then I proceeded to pay for my services, giving them both a twenty-dollar tip. I headed home to pack. Our flight was leaving in two hours. We would only be in Dallas for two days. For that reason, I didn't set out a lot. I prepared outfits for the presentation and a celebration night.

Count Down to Success

After I arrived home, I turned on some jazz. I prepared myself a small chicken Caesar salad. I can't do airline food unless I'm flying first class. On this trip we decided to fly coach. On our flight back, we'll upgrade to first class in recognition of our victory.
I ate the salad, drank a large glass of water with lemon, and cleaned the kitchen. The phone began to ring, I started to ignore it, but I remembered it could be Alicia. I hadn't spoken with her all day.
"Hello."
"What's up, baby girl?"
"Hey Jake!"
"What's up baby?"
"Nothing much, I just wanted to wish you good luck for tomorrow. I tried calling your cell, but I think it was turned off."
"Yeah, it was off. I'll have to call you from Dallas and explain what's going on."
"Aw shit, this doesn't sound good."
"It's cool believe me, but I don't have time to talk about it now. I promise to call tomorrow, after the presentation."
"All right baby girl, if you're sure you're okay I'll let it go until tomorrow."
"Okay I'll call you tomorrow, and Jake?"
"Yeah, babe."
"Thanks for everything."
"No need for that, that's what brothers are for."
"All right. Love you."
"Love you, too. And Nia, good luck."
"Thanks baby!"
My call waiting beeped in. "Well, that's probably Alicia so I'll call you tomorrow."
"All right."
"Hello."
"Boo- CLICK! I'm tired of Ben and not in the mood for his shit.

41

Jake McFarlin is the brother my parents never gave me. He and I have been friends since the eighth grade. He's the first boy I ever kissed. We realized, during our one and only kiss, all we could ever be is friends. In our case, friendship was better than a relationship. He is the best friend/brother a sister could want. If I had a blood brother, we probably wouldn't be this close. He's compassionate, loving, understanding, giving and down to earth. He's also handsome, successful, thirty-nine and childless. He's what most women in their thirties are looking for. Unfortunately, he's not available, like most men who have his attributes. His fiancée is Kayla, she's cool, but there's something about her that doesn't feel right to me. Because we're so close, we've had problems in the past with our relationships. His women had a problem with me, and my men had a problem with him. Our relationship has always been platonic. Kayla doesn't like me and the jury's still out on her. If I could clone him, I would. Women would be better off with more Jakes in the world. I sometimes wish we could be in a relationship because he's such a good person, but that's too much like incest. A relationship would mess our friendship up, and neither of us is willing to risk it. Knowing he always has my back is more than enough for me.

Ben

No, she didn't hang up on me. How am I supposed to talk to her if she hangs up on me when I call? I don't want to keep calling, but I know if I just pop up over there, she's not going to let me in. She got all the locks changed so I know she's serious. I've done some shit in the past, but she's never done this. Normally we'd just argue, she'd go to bed mad, but she'd wake up okay. I guess I've pushed her to the limit. My mother warned me she wasn't going to keep putting up with me, and my bullshit. I'm going to call mama for some guidance. "Hello."

"Hey mama, how are you?"

"Hey Ben baby, I'm fine. How are you?"

"Can't complain."

"Well, you don't sound all right. You wanna tell me what's wrong?"

"It's me and Nia, I-"

"Boy, please don't tell me you done messed that up."

"Uh...well...

"No need for stuttering now, you done messed up. Lawd have mercy, I told you to leave that gal alone if you weren't going to be true to her. What happened?"

"I was messing' with this girl named Quita and Nia caught us together."

"Boy don't tell me you had the skank in Nia's beautiful home?"

"Naw, Ma, I ain't that stupid."

"Well, the judge and jury's still deliberating."

"Ma, I'm feeling bad enough."

Totally ignoring my misery, "So, how did she catch ya?"

"I don't know, she told me her and Alexis were going to Landry's, and the next thing I knew, an hour later she pulled up behind me right after I arrived at Quita's."

"She must've suspected something."

"I guess so, but I was being real careful."

"Ain't no such thing as being careful when you involve someone else. You stopped being careful the minute you took up with Carla, Cita or whatever her name is. I guess you wanted one of those things. I think it's called, aw hell I don't know what it's called but it involves three people. How many times have I told you you ain't no playa? If you do people wrong, it always comes back on ya."

"I know Ma, what goes around...."

"Well, you reap what you sow. So, whatcha gone do?"

"That's why I'm calling you. I want some guidance."

"Why didn't you call me before you made the decision to take up with the jezebel?"

"Ma, I didn't think I was gone get caught."

"I'm sure you didn't. What you want me to do?"

"Would you call Nia?"

"And say what? My son a damn fool, he sorry he had relations with the jezebel, but if you take him back, he promises to be faithful. You think she gone believe me?"

"Well, Ma what should I do?"

"I guess you can start by apologizing."

"Ma, what do you think you raised?"

"I didn't think I raised a cheat, but your cheating ass got caught."

"Ma, you don't have to keep reminding me. I know the mess I've made better than anyone."

"Well, it sounds like you are thinking straight now, why couldn't you before you got caught?"

"Ma, are you going to continue to dog me or are you going to help me? I know I messed up, but I love Nia."

"I can call her, but you know I can't make any promises."

"I know Ma, but I'd appreciate anything you can do."

"Now, if she decides to take your sorry ass back, do not mess up again."

"I won't, I've definitely learned my lesson."

"Well, we'll see."

"Thanks Ma, I really appreciate this."

"I'm only doing this cause I know she's the best thing to ever happen to you."

"She leaves for Dallas this evening."

"That's right, she got the presentation with the black owned company. I hope she does okay considering she has to deal with this. You know she told me you never supported her business. Why?"

"I don't know Ma, I think I'm a little jealous."

"Jealous! Of what?"

"Her being more successful than me."

"Let me let you in on a secret."

"Yes ma'am'?"

"She's already more successful than you, but she still loved your ass. You didn't buy anything in her house, and she has some nice stuff."

"Ma, I know, but she's going to make a lot of money, especially once she gets this new account."

"So what! Has she ever said anything about the money you make?"

"No ma'am, but"

"But nothing. Why are you trippin? Black men need to get over themselves. A lot of these young black gals make more than these young black men. As long as the women ain't making a fuss about it, and they allow you to be the man in the relationship, ya'll need to get over it."

"Yes ma'am, I understand what you're saying."

"All right then, I'll call Nia a little later."

"Again, thanks Ma."

Nia

The phone began ringing again. This time I got up and checked the caller id in the bedroom, it was Alicia. "Hey girl!"

"Hey! Where have you been? Did you check your messages?"

"No, I didn't check my messages, or my caller ID until just now. I was at Becky's. The other news of the day is Ben's mission."

"What's up?"

"I'll tell you during the flight."

"All right, what time do you want to leave? It's five-fifteen now."

"Well, my toiletries are already packed, and my clothes are laid out. All I have to do is put everything into my garment bag and hop in the shower. I can be ready at six."

"Six it is, I'll meet you at your place. Do you want to go over the presentation during the flight?"

"Can we wait until tomorrow morning? We've been over this stuff for the last six weeks. I just want to read my book and chill."

"That's cool. I just purchased 'Just Too Good To Be True', E. Lynn Harris' last novel. I can get my read on too."

"I was thinking we could meet in my suite tomorrow morning at ten, have breakfast, and then go over our notes because our meeting isn't until two in the afternoon with Mr. Wells."

44

"That will give us plenty of time to go over everything right before the presentation."

"That sounds like a plan, let me get off of the phone, and into the shower. I'll see you at six."

After disconnecting with Alicia, I went into my bedroom, and loaded my stuff in my garment bag. Thank God, I'd set out everything earlier. I wrapped my hair and hopped in the shower. I used my Chance shower gel by Chanel. I dried off, put on my Victoria's Secret underwear, and put on my Polo Jeans and my Pepsi sweatshirt. I found my Nike Air Max Plus and put them on. I was looking for something comfortable. A sistah will put on a suit and get clean when she needs to. When she has to. Other than those times, I'm a blue-jean-tee-shirt and tennis shoe gal. Alicia is more of the corporate type. After I dressed, and combed my hair, I took my luggage downstairs. I made sure everything was locked up and I set the timers on my lamps. It was five-fifty and I had ten minutes to call my mother.

"Hello"

"Hey Ma."

"Hey baby, how you doing? I called you earlier."

"I'm sorry Ma, it's been a busy day, and I haven't checked my messages yet. I wanted to call before I left."

"I was hoping you would, I've been thinking about you and Alicia. I know you girls are going to knock that DEO off his feet."

Laughing. "Yes ma`am` we're going to try. Ma, it's CEO.

"Whatever DEO, CEO, you know what I mean."

"Okay Ma. I really appreciate all the support you always give me. You have always been there for me. I wish Daddy could see me now."

"I know baby. He'd be so proud of you but always remember he's with you in spirit."

"I know he is. Well, Ma, I gotta go. I'll call you when I get back. Oh, before I forget, will you please use the new key code and collect my mail. You can leave it on the island in the kitchen, or in the office. I'll text the code to you."

"Why can't Ben's lazy ass get it? Wait! New code?" She was concerned.

"Ma, he no longer lives here."

"What do you mean he no longer lives there?" Silence......

"Nia!"

"Ma`am?"

"Do you want to explain?"

"Yes ma`am`, but not right now, I really have to go."

"Okay, but I do expect an explanation when you return. Take care. Good luck. I love you."

"Thanks, I love you too."

I hung up with my mother and went to place my garment bag and small tote in the trunk of my car.

I decided I'd better check my voice mail before leaving, but before I could, the phone rang. I hope it's not Ben.

"Hello."

"Hi Nia baby, how are you?"

"Hey Mama Jones, I'm fine. How are you?"

"I'm good. My sugar hasn't been acting' up so I can't complain."

"Well, that's good to hear. You must take care of yourself."

"I know I do baby and I appreciate your concern."

"No problem, Mama Jones. I don't mean to rush off the phone, but I was about to leave. I have a plane to catch and Ben's not here."

"Baby, I know Ben's not there. He told me what happened."

"Oh, did he? I'm surprised because I thought he'd be too embarrassed to tell anyone. Especially you."

"Well, more than anything he's sorry. He realizes he made a big mistake."

"Mama Jones, I don't mean no disrespect, but what happened is between Ben and I. I will say this, it's officially over, but if you need me for anything, please call. I love you, and Ben and I not being together won't change that."

"I love you too, baby. Let me say this, and I won't say another word about it. Ben's sorry, but more than that I'm sorry. I've been telling him for years what goes around.....comes around. I hate this had to happen to you, I was hoping you were going to be my daughter-in-law. I want you to keep in touch."

"I will Mama Jones, I promise. I was hoping you'd be my in-law as well, but I guess it wasn't meant to be. I also told him what goes around......"

"I guess not baby. He learned a lesson this time. Well, good luck on your business in Dallas and have a safe trip."

"Yes ma`am, thank you."

"Please call me to tell me how your business went."

"Yes ma`am I will. I'll talk to you soon."

"Okay baby."

No, that Negro didn't have his mama call me. He has some nerve, trying to play the mama card. I love his mama, but she ain't the one who tried to play me like Jenga. The game's over, and all the pieces fell, just like my relationship with him. It was time to check my voice mail. I dialed my number and entered my pin number.

"You have twelve new messages. Press one to play. Press two to save. Press three to delete. I'm either hella popular, which I am not, or Ben's crazy ass is in his begging mode. You know, the famous Spike Lee line, 'Please Baby Please', well he's taken the line and perfected it.

Message #1- "Baby-Delete

Message #2- "Just listen-Delete

Message #3- "This is your mother, call me." Delete

Message #4- "Nia, please- Delete

46

Message #5- "Boo, I promise- Delete

Message #6- "If you'll take me- Delete

Message #7- "Nia, it's me. When you get in, call me we need to discuss what time we're leaving."- Delete

Message #8- Silence....Delete

Message #9- "I know I - Delete

Message #10- "Nia, it's Lexy. I know you're preparing for your trip, but I wanted to check on you, and wish you good luck. If you need me, you know where I am 24/7. Smooches." Delete

Message #11- "I hope you liked the flowers. I really am sorry."- Delete

Message #12- "Nia please- Delete

He doesn't realize it is over. I do not want to be with him. He's two days late and about fifty dollars short. Just as I was finishing up the retrieval of my messages, the doorbell rang. I checked the peephole. It was Alicia. She lives three doors from me. She was with me when I viewed my townhouse. She was so impressed she decided to purchase a unit as well. Another deciding factor was the option of customizing your townhouse. Although they appear to be identical externally, each unit is uniquely designed per the buyer's specific requests. I opened the door.

"Hey you ready?"

"As ready as I'll be. You can go into the garage and load your stuff. I'm driving the Accord. I'm going to grab my handbag and briefcase, and then set the alarm."

"Okay, I'll wait in the car."

I made sure the stove was turned off. I punched in my code and headed to the garage. We were on our way.

"Damn!"

"What's wrong?"

"I forgot my cell phone, but I'll leave it. I really don't need any distractions."

Fortunately, we only lived about ten minutes from the airport. Our ritual prior to boarding a plane for business is to listen to 'Stand', it is sung by Ron Winans and Friends. It's very inspirational. It says when you've done all you can, just stand on God's word. This song was appropriate for this situation. We're prepared, we just need to stand on God's word. And our faith. And our experience and expertise.

We arrived at Lambert Airport, parked in short-term parking, and caught a shuttle to the main terminal, which is where Delta Airlines is. When we arrived at the gate, they were already boarding. Alicia and I found our seats, placed our luggage in the overhead compartment and prepared for take-off. Holding each other's hands, we prayed; "Heavenly Father, please get us to Dallas safely. We ask this in the name of Jesus, Amen."

"Amen. All right girl, we should be good to go."

"Watch out Mr. Wells, and Wells Communications! We're coming, we're coming, we're coming. We're coming, we're coming, we're coming. We're There!"

"Girl, that was the jam back in the day."

"Don't I know it," laughing.

I began reading my book, and Alicia began her novel by E. Lynn Harris. I dozed off several times. I did get through the first four chapters before I fell asleep. I awoke upon our arrival in Dallas at nine o'clock. We gathered our luggage from the overhead compartment and went to retrieve our rental car. Alicia reserved a Maxima, but they only had them with manual transmissions, so I was the designated driver. Alicia never wanted to learn how to drive a stick shift. Mr. Wells' office was in Addison, Texas, a suburb of Dallas. He was kind enough to reserve two suites for us at Inter-Continental, a really nice hotel in the Dallas area. We arrived at the hotel in approximately thirty minutes. Once we checked into our rooms and got settled, I called Alicia to say good night. We had a long day ahead of us. No one in St. Louis was aware of which hotel we were staying in, so I was guaranteed a night of rest without Ben-I'm-Sorry-Give-Me-Another-Chance-Jones distracting me. The suites were supplied with cable, so I caught the last fifteen minutes of a Martin rerun on the USA channel, before I fell into dreamland.

We're On.....

The following morning, I woke up at nine a.m., and called Alicia to make sure she was up. I hung up with her, and did my normal morning ritual, I prayed. I don't consider myself a religious person, but I am very spiritual. I don't attend church as often as I should, but I'm going to do better. God has been too good to me for me to not give him some time in return. I knew God would be with us during our presentation.

I then proceeded to the shower to do what all well-groomed people do, shit, shave, and shower. I decided to wait on dressing, so I put on the robe the hotel supplied me to lounge in. I turned on MSNBC to catch the world news. I was about to sit on the couch when I heard a knock at the door. It had to be Alicia's always prompt ass.

"Hey girl, how are you?"

"I'm fine."

"I'm just ready for this presentation to be over. Are you ready to go over the information for the last time?"

"I'll be ready after I eat. I'm about to call room service and order. What do you want?"

"I'll take two slices of bacon, one slice of toast and two eggs over easy."

"Do you want something to drink?"

"Yes, I'll take a glass of Cranberry juice."

I ordered two scrambled eggs with cheese, two slices of toast, two slices of bacon and a glass of cranberry juice.

"Okay, the food is ordered."

Alicia said, "Great, let me get my briefcase. During the presentation, remember our main purpose is to give as many benefits for hiring us as possible. Also, we must stay focused."

"In other words, we must keep our eyes on the prize!"

"And you know this.....man!"

"Keep me laughing, because I'm nervous as hell."

"There's no need to be nervous, we're ready."

For the next forty-five minutes we ate, and went over our information, and prepared for our presentation. We were ready. As ready as we were going to be. It's now eleven-fifteen, and our meeting isn't until two.

"Alicia since we have at least two hours before the meeting, I'm going to take a nap."

"A nap! Girl no! Let's do something else."

"Something else like what? It's not like we have the time to get into anything."

"Well, I was reading through the hotel's brochure, and they have a masseuse on staff."

"Hmm…sounds like a plan. A massage would do a sistah good. How much is it?"

"The brochure didn't have a price list."

"Aw, shit, no price means pull out the platinum card."

"Well, let me call and see."

"That's cool with me. I haven't had a massage in a minute."

Alicia called and was able to schedule us for eleven-forty-five. We lounged until he arrived. At that point I decided to call Colett to see if she'd be interested in going on the cruise with us.

"Hello."

"Hey girl, what's up?"

"Hey Nia, nothing's up. Nothing at all."

"You don't sound like yourself. What's wrong?'

"Girl, I just found out Kenny has been recording my conversations."

"What? Why?"

"I don't know why, I guess his ass is crazy."

"Well, what happened?"

"Okay, you know we broke up about three weeks ago, things just weren't going well, and I figured it was best to just leave it alone."

"Okay, I remember you telling me that, but what's happened since then?"

"He's been calling saying he wants to talk about us reconciling, but I wasn't really trying to be bothered. So, he called yesterday and asked me to come over to talk. I knew I didn't want to hear anything he had to say, but I had

49

some stuff at his apartment I needed to get. So, I agreed to go over there."

"Okay, I'm with you so far."

"When I got there, I made it clear all I wanted was my stuff, but he kept trying to talk anyway. I ignored him. He obviously wasn't pleased with the way I was acting and when I got ready to leave, he handed me a large manila envelope. When I asked what it was, he wouldn't say, he just told me to open it when I got home."

"What was in it?"

"Hold up girl, I'm getting to that part. I was curious so I opened it in my car. Inside there was a four-page two-sided letter and a cassette. My curiosity was getting the best of me, but my car doesn't have a cassette player, only a CD player. So, I drove faster. I couldn't wait to hear what was on the cassette. I arrived at my condo and popped in the cassette. I remembered where my old cassette player was; I was glad I held on to it. In an instant I began to hear phone conversations I'd had while I was staying at his condo."

"What was his reason for doing this?"

"Who knows? Insecure. Crazy. Take your pick."

"He didn't find anything incriminating, did he?"

"Nope, because I was faithful to his no-faith-having-insecure-like-a-bitch-ass!
He recorded me checking my messages, so of course, he heard when Tyler called, but so what! I broke up with Tyler's commitment phobic ass eighteen months before I even met Kenny, so, I don't know why he felt the need to record the conversations."

"He tripped."

"Yes, he did. There are conversations I had with you, my mother and some of my girls here in Atlanta. Two can play his game. I went to get a restraining order today, and while there the judge told me, him recording my conversations was against the law."

"Oh well, you commit the crime, you must do the time. That's what his busted ass gets."

"All right girl, enough about me and my problems, are you nervous about the presentation?"

"Yes, I am but I'll be all right. I was actually calling because Kenya, Alicia, Alexis and I are planning to go on Tom Joyner's cruise. We want to get two large cabins with balconies, and we can split the cost between the five of us. I wanted to know would you be interested?"

"Hell yes, I need a vacation and after this shit with Kenny, I'm really going to need to get away. So, count me in.

"I knew you'd be interested."

"When is it normally?"

"Normally they sail out the Sunday before Memorial Day, but I'm going to do some research and find out for sure."

"Just keep me posted."

"I'll do that, I'm going to call Carla and make the reservations now. I'll call you tomorrow to check on you."

"Well, thanks for calling. I'll talk to you soon."

"All right."

I had a few minutes before the masseuse was due to arrive. I decided to call Carla so she could go ahead and start checking on our travel arrangements.

"Thank you for calling 'Destinations For You'. This is Ann, how may I help you?"

"Ann, this is Nia Witherspoon calling for Carla Southerland."

"Okay Nia, let me try Carla's extension for you. Hold on a moment."

"Thank you."

"You're welcome."

After a brief holding period, she answered, "Thank you for calling, this is Carla."

"Hey girl, how are you?"

"I'm well, you?"

"Can't complain."

"Where do you want to go now?"

"You know me too well."

"Tell me about it. What's the destination for this month?"

"In fact, it's not for this month but for May. Me, Kenya, Alicia, and Alexis want to attend Tom Joyner's cruise. We'd like two large cabins with balconies."

"So, it's for the four of you?"

"In fact, there will be five of us. Colett would like to join us, remember she's in Atlanta?"

"I remember Colett, how is she?"

"She's making it girl, just like the rest of us. Carla, do you think it's possible to book our flight so we have a layover in Atlanta, and Colett will be able to fly down with us."

"I'll see if I can arrange that."

"Well, I'm in Dallas now, I'll call you in two days once I'm back in St. Louis."

"That should give me plenty of time to find something."

"All right, I'll talk to you in two days."

The masseuse arrived at eleven-thirty-five. "Hello ladies."

In unison we responded with, "Hello."

"My name is Rafael, and I'm here to rub your worries away."

Damn, he's fine! He was about six feet four inches tall, caramel, had a slick head, and a perfectly chiseled body. He could rub on me anytime.

Alicia said, "Well rub on baby!"

"I second that."

Laughing, Rafael said, "You ladies are feisty, I like that. Which of you would like to go first?"

We raised our hands like we were in school, and Rafael was the sexy ass professor. In unison, we answered. "I would."

"Unfortunately, I can only do one at a time. No menage a trois massages."

Alicia said, "All right, I'll be the first volunteer."

"Yeah, all right with your volunteering ass! I'll go next only because I know Rafael is saving the best for last." I gave both a wink.

Since we were pressed for time, he gave each of us a thirty-minute massage. His hands were so gentle yet very thorough. Anything longer than thirty minutes, I'd be no good for the presentation. The massages were one hundred and fifty dollars for the two of us, and we gave him a fifty-dollar tip.

"Thank you, ladies, your generosity is greatly appreciated. If you're back in Dallas, look me up. I can hook you up in more ways than one." He gave each of us a business card and we reciprocated.

Alicia said, "All right Mr. Massage-Me-Right, we'll call you the next time we visit."

Rafael said, "You do that."

I said, "Mr. Rafael, we've got to go, our presentation is in an hour and fifteen minutes."

"Bye ladies, good luck on your presentation."

In unison, "Bye, and thank you."

Alicia left for her room, and I proceeded to shower, again, and get ready. I packed my Ralph Lauren black wool crepe single button pant suit. The pants had a full leg. I wore a gray silk mock turtleneck with my suit. I didn't want my 36D's taking over the meeting. My accessories were black sheer Hanes hose, Gucci pumps, and my Gucci briefcase. Sistahs are naturally colorful and beautiful. Makeup only enhances what we already have. I don't do much, but I wanted to look good. So, I first powdered my face with a pressed powder by Mac. Then I lined and filled my lips with Mac's chestnut liner and plum colored lip gloss. After preparing myself I called downstairs for them to have our car ready. As I was hanging the phone up, Alicia knocked at the door.

Damn! My girl was clean. She was the epitome of corporate sistahood! She's itty bitty, but shapely. She's five feet one inch with much booty and size 36C breasts. She has light skin with freckles. Although dark sistahs were getting more play now, a lot of brothas still had a thing for light sistahs with long hair, and her natural hair was down her back. Alicia wore a Donna Karan single button navy suit. Her skirt was two and half inches above her knees to display her shapely legs, and she wore her navy Coach pumps. She complimented her suit with a gray silk blouse with French cuff sleeves, and her navy Coach briefcase. We were dressed for success. It was one-thirty-five, and Mr. Wells' building was only ten to fifteen minutes away. The valet had our car waiting, we tipped him and were on our way. Fifteen minutes later we arrived at Wells Communications and were greeted by Ms. Mattie, his very efficient secretary. She greeted us and informed us Mr. Wells was ready when we were. She walked us to the conference room, but before she opened the door, we asked for two minutes to pray. She granted our wish and agreed to pray with us. We bowed our heads, held hands, and I began.

"Heavenly Father we come to You giving You praise, glory and honor! We give You reverence in our lives, and we thank You for Your presence. We also thank You for Ms. Mattie, she is our personal angel in our time of need, and we thank You for her."

"Father, Alicia and I ask You guide us during our meeting with Mr. Wells. We have prepared ourselves for this meeting, therefore we claim the victory in the name of Jesus. Philippians 4:13 states that we can do all things through Christ who gives us strength, so Father, we'll take your strength with us."

"Father, should we become weary, energize us. If we lose focus, put us back on track. If we become nervous, soothe our nerves. If Satan tries to cast shadows of doubt, together we demand he loose the situation in the name of Jesus. Your power is the only power. We rebuke Satan and his satanic powers in the MIGHTY name of Jesus."

"Again, we're prepared. So, Father thank You for the victory. We give You thanks, praise, glory, and honor! In the name of Your son, our Savior, Jesus Christ. AMEN!

Alicia was overwhelmed and shared her feelings, "Girl, you've been holding out on me, I didn't know you could pray like that. You took us to church; it was so powerful. It gave me chills. Thank you so much for that."

"It gave me chills too, but they are good chills. I have a really good feeling about this."

"Well, Nia this is it! No matter what happens, I love you."

"I love you too. God has truly blessed me with a great business partner and an even better friend."

Mattie said, "That was a powerful prayer, you girls are going to succeed. You've got God on your side. I can feel your success. Mr. Wells is a smart man, so he's not going to let this opportunity pass by."

For the next two hours, Alicia and I eagerly expressed to Mr. Wells and his associates' reasons for hiring Event Solutions, to plan, decorate, and cater for all their company functions. Alicia and I supplied them with figures displaying how Event Solutions compares to the competition, and how we can benefit Wells Communications.

Unfortunately, Mr. Wells didn't show any emotion, so we had no idea what his decision was going to be. He sat in his chair at the head of the table, thinking but not speaking. Alicia and I sat next to one another holding hands and silently praying. After approximately ten minutes, Mr. Wells began to speak.

"Ladies, your presentation was excellent. The way you've presented yourselves was creative, concise, professional, as well as informative. I remember starting my company fifteen years ago. It was a struggle, but I've

53

been blessed. I was given an opportunity to prove myself, and I want to be the one granting you the same opportunity. Normally the company wouldn't go with a small company, but I have a good feeling about this. I think this is going to be a great partnership. Now, my attorney will give you the details." At that time, Mr. Michael Stephens, his attorney spoke.

"Mr. Wells is willing to offer you ladies a two-year, four-million-dollar contract with an extension clause if the partnership is a successful one. Of course, we would suggest both of you read over the contract, as well as your attorney."

In unison we said while trying to maintain our excitement, "Of course."

We were trying to remain composed. It was a difficult task.

Alicia spoke first, "Actually our attorney, Michelle Gaffney is waiting on our call. Is there an office with a fax machine we can use?"

"Sure, you can use my office, Mattie will lead the way."

"Again ladies, welcome aboard."

We shook his hand and Alicia said, "Thank you so much for the opportunity, Mr. Wells we won't let you down."

"I know you won't. I've made a lot of decisions throughout my career, and this one was a wise choice. I'll be here when you return from talking with Miss Gaffney, and then we can begin our celebration."

Mattie led us to Mr. Wells' office, and once the door was closed, she said.

"I know you girls want to have a private celebration. For your information, this office is soundproof. See you in a little while. Again, congratulations and welcome to the family."

Nia said, "Thank you, Ms. Mattie."

"Yes, Ms. Mattie, thank you for everything."

"Don't you babies mention it. You all are the same age as my Kimberly. It does my heart proud to see young people progressing in the business world. It also shows our ancestors didn't suffer in vain. Mr. Wells is a good man to be associated with. Now you all go ahead and call your attorney."

"Thank you, Ms. Mattie."

Success is Sweet

Alicia and I entered Mr. Wells' office, closed the door, and both of us screamed, jumped, and hugged. Both of us had tears in our eyes.

"Girl, we did it!"

"I know, my Daddy's not here, but he'd be so proud."

"He's watching us from Heaven, so he's here. I'm proud of you girl."

"And I'm proud of you. God is good."

"All the time."

"We really did it."

"Yes, we did."

54

"Now we have to make sure we cross all of our T's and dot all of our I's. Mr. Wells is giving us the opportunity of a lifetime.

"I agree with you, we can't let him down. Let me call Michelle." Michelle went to high school with Alicia, Kenya, and I. She was always a cool white girl, and I always liked her because I could be myself with her. She never tried to be anyone but Michelle, and that's one of the main reasons I like her. Sure, we'd given her a crash course in Negrology 101 so she wouldn't get lost when we spoke slang, but she kept it real. Her family was very wealthy, but always treated us like family. After high school, we stayed in touch.

She went away to the University of Georgia for her BA, but she returned home to attend St. Louis University's Law School where she graduated with honors.

Although she hung out with sistahs, she never dated one black man. They tried, but she wasn't having it. We once had a conversation about it because she understood my feelings on the interracial dating thing.

Brothas without question noticed. For a white girl she was hooked up. Hell, her ass was bigger than mine. I often teased her we must've been related, both of us had to be of mixed heritage. I got the white ass and way down the line there had to be someone black in her family, and that's how she got the ass.

Michelle was five feet six inches tall with an onion shaped ass, skinny legs, a small waist and size 34C breasts. She has naturally curly dark brown hair, hair with natural reddish-brown streaks. She wears her hair in a chin length Bob. Her skin is olive colored, and she has Brooke Shields' eyebrows. She's very well-groomed. She lives in a two thousand five hundred square foot loft in the central west end. She's a partner in her father's law firm. She has it going on. The conversation we had while having lunch at Caleco's will never be forgotten.

"Michelle, you know it's weird you've never dated a brotha."

Eating a chicken wing she asked, "Why?"

"It seems like most white women, and yes, I'm being stereotypical right now, hanging around black women date black men."

"I would agree with you although I'm not aware of the actual percentages."

"Do you find black men attractive?"

"Yes, I do, but so are white men. Do you find white men attractive?"

"Honestly, very few. Brad Pitt, Matthew McConaghey, and Matt Damon, and when I was younger, I liked Rob Lowe. I personally find black men beautiful."

"I feel the same way about white men, those you mentioned as well as Ben Affleck, the Jonas Brothers, Chris Pratt, Orlando Bloom and the list could go on. There are several reasons why I've never dated a black man. The number one reason is society. I don't think society will ever accept interracial dating. I don't want to deal with the stares or comments. Also, as much as my parents love you, Kenya, and Alicia, they'd have a fit if I brought a black man home as my boyfriend. It's different when you have friends who are black, but honestly most parents don't want their son or daughter to date outside of their race. That doesn't make them racist, it's just their preference."

"I agree with you, I don't think my parents would be too keen on the idea either. Hell, my daddy would probably flip in his grave."

"They say love conquers all."

"Yeah, but you and I both know that's bullshit."

"I hear you girl. There's just too much mess to deal with in interracial dating. Like there are not enough problems in white-on-white or black-on-black relationships. I have enough stress dealing with clients, and trying to prepare my cases, I don't need added stress. Relationships should be drama free, and for the most part stress free. I see how you look at interracial couples, and I know you're not the only black woman giving those looks."

"You noticed that?"

"Girl, how long have I known you?"

"Too long I guess."

"Exactly, and I don't want to deal with those stares. The stares come from white men as well. They hate to see white women with black men. I really don't have time to fight throughout my relationship. How can you enjoy your relationship if you are constantly fighting and on the defense?"

"I understand what you're saying. It's wild, our views are the same. White men have approached me, I guess they see the flat ass and assume I'm down with D.W.B. (dating white boys). I think the worst thing is a bi-racial child who grows up confused, but America will tell you what group you belong to. In elementary school, kids are terrible. A white boy called me a nigger every day in the second grade. At the time I didn't know what a nigger was, but when I told my Daddy, he made sure I understood, as well as the principal. My first bout with racism occurred in the second grade. Bi-racial children deal with racism on both ends, white kids call them niggers, and black kids call them whitey. It's a no-win situation, and it's too much for a child to deal with."

"That's a really good point Nia, but no need to worry, I'm with Brett all the way. I think he's the one."

"Well, you go girl! You know me, I'll stick with the brothas."

"Don't I know it; you love your chocolate."

The conversation shed some light on our personalities, as well as our friendship. I feel like we're closer since we were honest and vulnerable with one another. I dialed the number to Michelle's office.

"Gaffney, Smith, Rosenblum, Gaffney and Associates, this is Patricia and how may I direct your call?"

"Hey Patricia, this is Nia."

"Hey Nia, how did the meeting go?"

"CHA-CHING! Need I say more?"

"Congratulations girl! You and Alicia are women on the move, and you all deserve it."

"Thanks Patricia. Hey, is Michelle available?"

"In her office waiting on this call."

"Send me through, but don't tell her the news."

"All right, again, congratulations!

"You're very welcome. Hold on while I connect you with Michelle."

Patricia rang Michelle's office.

"Yeah Tricia, what's up?"

"Nia Witherspoon of Event Solutions is on the line, and I know you've been waiting on her call."

"Yes, I have. How does she sound?"

"Normal. Same as always."

"Really? That's not good. All right, send her through."

"Hey Nia, what's up?"

Sounding solemn, "Nothing, girl".

"How did the meeting go?"

"It was all right, not as well as we expected."

"Oh really?...........What happened?" Concern reflected in her voice.

"Nothing much, we gave our presentation, and Mr. Wells offered us a two-year contract for four million dollars. Alicia and I think-

"What! Wait a minute. You come on the line sounding like you lost one of your best friends, but we got the account?"

"Yes girl, we got the account. Also, the contract has an extension clause as long as the partnership is a successful one."

"Where are you?"

"We're in Mr. Wells' office. Why?"

"Does he have a speaker phone?"

Looking at the business phone with many buttons on it. "Let me see, this phone has a lot of buttons.........Okay, here it is, let me lay the handset down."

"Make sure Licia can hear this as well."

"She's right here with a wide ass grin on her face."

"I want to congratulate both of you. I am so proud. Damn, I've got tears in my eyes, I'm so proud."

Alicia said, "Michelle, thank you for being a wonderful friend, and the best attorney in the Midwest."   .

"I second cond that, your support means everything."

"Well, fax over the contract, and I'll look it over. Inform Mr. Wells as long as there aren't any problems, he should have it back by Wednesday."

"Again, Chelle thanks, and we love you."

"I love both of you too. Are you all celebrating tonight?"

"Mr. Wells has invited us to a celebration", Alicia informed Michelle.

"Is that it?"

"What do you mean?"

"Aren't you going out after the celebration?"

"It depends on how we feel."

"Go and celebrate, you both deserve it!"

57

In unison we answered, "All right."
After speaking with Michelle, we returned to the conference room.

Mr. Wells said, "Welcome back ladies, I asked Mattie to get a bottle of black label Moet to toast with." Mattie distributed the glasses.

Mr. Wells gave the first toast, "To new relationships, as well as good business."

Alicia toasted, "To Mr. Wells, and Wells Communications for the opportunity of a lifetime."

I toasted, "To African American business owners sticking together, and helping each other."

Mr. Wells said, "Amen to that. I'd like you ladies to join my staff, my wife and I for dinner at Houston's. I've reserved a banquet room."

Alicia responded, "Mr. Wells, we'd love that, and we'd be honored. What time should we be there?"

Mr. Wells said, "It's ten after four now, would six o'clock be all right?"

"Nia, is six o'clock good for you?"

"Six is fine with me."

Alicia said, "Well, Mr. Wells, six o'clock is fine. Where is Houston's?"

"It's ten minutes down the tollway. I'm sure the Concierge at the hotel can give you accurate directions from the hotel."

"Great, we'll see you at six."

"Okay ladies, six it is. My wife is looking forward to meeting you."

"We look forward to meeting her as well."

Alicia and I left the Wells Communications Building to return to our hotel. Our drive to the hotel was a silent one. I know my silence was due to me just thinking about what just transpired. I speculated Alicia's silence was for the same reason.

Let The Celebrating Begin

After arriving at the hotel, we had about an hour to get ready, so we departed to our rooms. I called the Concierge and got directions to Houston's. Then I decided to call my mother, Jake, and Lexy and check my messages at home.

"Hello."

"Hey Ma, how are you?"

"I'm fine, how was the meeting?"

"The meeting was great; we got the contract."

"Congratulations baby! That's wonderful. Be sure to tell Alicia I said congratulations."

"I will and thank you."

"Do you want to tell me about Ben now?"

"All I have to say about that situation is it's over. Things have been shaky awhile, and it was best to just end it."

"I know there has to be more to it than that."

"Yes, there is, and I don't mean any disrespect, but it's none of your business. It's between Ben and I."

"I'll respect your wishes although I don't like it."

Laughing, "I know you don't because you've gotten nosey in your old age."

"You watch who you're talking to young lady, I'm still your mother."

I countered with, "I know Ma. Again, I don't mean any disrespect. I will call you when I return tomorrow."

"What time does your flight come in, and do you need a ride from the airport?"

"Our flight comes in at three-thirty-five, and I left my car in a parking garage. Also, how is Sheba?"

"Spoiled. You have her rotten. Well, call me when you get home. I may cook fried chicken, collard greens, and sweet potatoes for dinner. If so, then I'll leave a message on your machine."

"She is spoiled but she's, my baby. The menu sounds good, you know I love your collard greens. So, I'll talk to you tomorrow."

"Okay, have a safe trip."

"We will."

After I hung up from my mother, I kicked my shoes off and grabbed a bottle of water. Then I called Lexy, but I received her voice mail.

"You've reached the Knight residence, no one is available to answer your call, please leave a message after the tone. God Bless."

"Hey Lexy, it's me girl and we did it! We got the contract! We'll have to celebrate when Alicia and I return. We're going out tonight, so I'll call tomorrow when I return. And Lexy, thanks for what you did this weekend." I then called Jake.

"Hello."

"Hey Jake, what's up?"

"Hey baby girl, how are you?"

"I'm good. What are you doing?"

"I'm just chillin' right now, about to make some dinner."

"Kayla's cooking?"

"No, she's not here."

"What? Is something wrong? She's always there."

"I asked her to give me some space."

"Space? Normally when men ask for space, they really mean the relationship is at the end."

"I'm having doubts."

"Doubts, about what?"

"About marrying her. I'm not sure if she's sincere. I'd hate to marry her if she's only after my money, and what I can do for her. Hell, what can she do for me?"

"Damn! I had no idea you felt this way. You know I don't really care for her, but I'd never tell you to leave her."

59

"What about her, don't you like?

"She doesn't seem sincere, and she doesn't like me."

"She doesn't like you because she thinks you like me."

"I do like you, hell, I love you, and if she can't accept our friendship, that's her problem."

"I really don't know what to do. She knows how I feel about you, and I will not give up our friendship."

"You shouldn't have to."

"Those are my feelings as well."

"Well, you asked her to marry you, so you need to really, really think about it. You don't want to marry her, and then six months later, have regrets about your decision. More than anything, I want you to be happy, whether it be with Kayla or someone else."

"I know, I know, but enough about me, how was the presentation?"

"The presentation was good, so good we were offered a two-year, four-million-dollar contract."

"Uh...did you say four million dollars?"

"Uh....yes I did!"

"Damn....CHA CHING! You go girl! You and Alicia are on your way. All of the hard work has paid off."

"Yes, we're definitely on our way. Now, I can get the Mercedes I've been wanting."

"Yes, you can. As a matter of fact, we can go to Plaza Motors when you get home."

"A friend of mine works at Tri-Star Mercedes, so we can go there too."

"Cool."

"I'm looking forward to it."

"So, what's up with you and bitch ass Ben?"

"Ain't nothing up, I caught his ass cheating with a hood rat, and it's over. No excuse will be a good one, so it's over. Love is not enough to sustain the relationship, but what's love got to do with it anyway?"

"I knew the nigga wasn't shit, but you loved him, so I didn't say anything."

"You should've said something."

"Think about it Nia, would it have mattered? You would've stayed with him until you were ready to leave him alone."

"I guess you're right. I feel the same about Kayla, but I know how you felt about her."

"Well, the jury's still out on her and our situation. I've got some more soul searching to do."

"Well, I think you can do better. And I know the perfect woman for you."

"And who would that be?"

"You and Lexy would be great together."

"Lexy! I've known her almost as long as I've known you."

60

"I know, but have you really looked at her?"

"I looked at her every day in college, and at your house during each break. For a minute I thought she was your other sister. She was always at your house, and who knew when I decided to go to Howard, one of your best friends would also be there?"

"That was wild because we didn't become friends until the summer after high school. We met at a Kappa skating party at Saints."

"Yeah, we always had a good time back then. I remember the night we met her."

"Yeah, you stepped in when she was being disrespected."

"Yeah, I'm always trying to rescue someone."

"You just hate to see women disrespected. That's a good thing."

"I guess."

"Didn't you think she was cute then?"

"She was all right. She looked like an adolescent female with a nice figure."

"Yeah, but then she had pimples and braces. Now she's a beautiful black woman. She has her own business and therefore her own money. She's childless and she's available."

"I don't know Nia."

"Keep in mind, you've complained about the fact a lot of plans had to be canceled with Kayla because she couldn't find a babysitter. Lexy doesn't have children and won't be having any until she's married."

"I'll think about it."

"Yeah, you should. I promised Lexy I'd never tell you this but she's liked you since the summer we met her, but you were never interested."

"Is that right?"

"Yes, but don't tell her. I've got to go, we're having dinner with Mr.Wells, and his associates."

"Well enjoy, and again, congratulations! We'll look for the new ride next weekend."

"All right, have a good one."

"You too babe."

After I hung up with Jake, I laid down awhile and just thought about everything that had transpired within the last few days. Alicia and I were just blessed with the biggest contract of our careers thus far. I just caught my man cheating with a hood rat. I found out my best friend is not happy with his fiancée. A lot has transpired, and I had a lot to think about. First and foremost, I had to prepare for our celebration dinner. I didn't bring too many outfits with me, but I did bring one I think would be suitable for going out. I had a pair of charcoal gray and camel calf boots that I wore with a pair of charcoal tights, a charcoal mini skirt, a camel cashmere sweater, my camel leather coat, and my camel leather bag. That would be fine for this evening.

I was somewhat tired but for some reason, I couldn't sleep. I think I had too much on my mind. I kept thinking I should call Ben because for the last year or so, it was normal for me to call him and share my good news. But when I think about it, he never showed any enthusiasm with me. He never supported me regarding Event Solutions, although I supported him in whatever he did. He was funny like that, he wanted to benefit from the perks of my job, but not once did he congratulate me or encourage me. At the time I didn't notice it. It's funny what you notice when shit starts going bad. I guess that's why they say love is blind, you really don't see things while they're occurring. Reminiscing, I realize he had to be jealous of my success. My success was because of hard work and it ruining our relationship is crazy, but it shows me the kind of man and/or husband I don't want. If you can't support who you love, what's the purpose?

The more I thought about it, I began to feel depressed. Here I was in Dallas, Texas, the biggest night of my career, and the depression tried to sit in. Nope! Not! I was not having it. I got up, turned on the radio and Kendrick Lamar was rapping about being Humble, I bopped my head, and I hopped in the shower. I showered and drenched myself in my shower gel. I put on my robe, poured myself a glass of Zinfandel, and chilled on the couch bopping my head to Snoop Dogg while he rapped about women being beautiful. I did this until it was time to leave.

Alicia called at five-fifteen to tell me she was about to get dressed. She had already showered. So, I told her I'd get dressed as well and meet her in the hallway at five-thirty. I dressed and called the valet to have the car ready. At five-thirty we were ready to go. Alicia had changed into a pair of black suede capri pants, a white silk blouse with French cuff sleeves, a black-cropped suede jacket, and a pair of black suede mules and she carried a black Prada bag.

"Hey, you really look nice."

"Thank you, so do you."

"Nia, are you okay?"

"Yes, why wouldn't I be?"

"You just seem kind of quiet."

"I do have a lot on my mind, but I'm ready to celebrate."

"Me too. I'm thinking maybe we can go out afterwards."

"That's cool, one of my girls told me about a place called Sambuca's which is a jazz slash restaurant slash bar."

"That sounds like a winner."

"Did you get the directions?"

"Yeah, I called the concierge as soon as we got back to the hotel. He gave me directions to Houston's as well as Sambuca's."

"Well, let's go."

Celebrate Good Times..... But, Damn Who's The Cutie?

We made it to Houston's in twenty-five minutes. Being prompt is something we both pride ourselves in. We parked and headed into the restaurant. A very professional and cheerful hostess greeted us.

"Good evening Ladies. Welcome to Houston's. My name is Renee and how may I help you?"

Alicia spoke, "Good evening, Renee, we're here to join the Wells Communications Party."

"Oh, you must be Miss Fox and Miss Witherspoon?"

Alicia informed her, "You would be correct on both accounts."

"Mr. Wells informed me the two of you would be showing up. If you'd please follow me."

I said, "Thank you, Renee."

"You're welcome, right this way."

We followed Renee through Houston's, a dimly lit intimate restaurant with smells wafting under our noses and made our stomachs grumble. We both realized we hadn't eaten since breakfast. We were ready to fix that. Finally, we arrived at Houston's banquet room, and were greeted by approximately eight people. Mr. Wells spoke first.

"Welcome ladies, come in and make yourselves comfortable. I want to make the introductions."

"Yes, sir."

"Of course, you already know Mattie and my attorney, Mr. Stephens. In unison we replied, "Hello."

"I'd like for you to meet my lovely wife Shelby Wells. Like they say, 'behind every great man, is a greater woman', well here's my greater and most often better half."

Mrs. Wells spoke, "Girls as you can see, I've trained him well." Laughing. "It's a pleasure to finally meet the two of you, my husband has been talking about you all for the last two months. If you ladies are half as good as he says, our company is in great hands."

Alicia spoke first, "Mrs. Wells it's-

Mrs. Wells interrupted her, "Baby, call me Shelby, we're all family."

"Yes ma'am it's just a habit."

"I know baby. Obviously, your parents raised you right."

"Well, Mrs. Wells, I mean Shelby, it really is a pleasure to meet you. Mr. Wells has said some wonderful things about you."

"After thirty-five years of marriage he better say wonderful things." Laughing.

Mr. Wells stepped up to say, "Enough from Shelby, she'll talk you to death. I agree with her on one aspect, we are family. You don't have to address me as Mr. Wells, just call me James."

63

Alicia spoke, "Are you sure?"

"Of course, I'm sure."

"All right, you're the boss."

"That I am. Anyway, there are some others who would like to make your acquaintance. This handsome young man is my son James Richard Wells II, we just call him J.R., and he is the Vice President of Marketing. This is Nia Witherspoon, and the petite young lady is Alicia Fox."

I spoke first, "J.R. It's a pleasure to meet you. Your company has granted us a wonderful opportunity." I noticed the entire time he was shaking my hand; he was staring at Alicia. What was up with that?

Finally, J.R. Responded, "Nia, it's my pleasure, and I look forward to working with you."

"Thank you J.R., I look forward to us working together as well. This is my partner as well as my best friend, Alicia Fox."

"Yes. Hello Miss Fox or is it Mrs. Fox?"

"No J.R. it's Miss, and please call me Alicia. My mother is Mrs. Fox."

"Alicia it's my pleasure. And might I add, you truly are a fox."

J.R. was openly and blatantly flirting with Alicia and he is fine. He was a younger version of his father. He was about five feet ten inches tall, about 190 lbs., bald head, goatee, lips like L.L. Cool J, beautiful long eyelashes, hazel eyes, a dimpled chin, a beautiful smile, and skin the color of Hershey chocolate. Alicia was obviously interested as well because I'd never seen her bat her damn eyelashes like that.

"J.R., thank you for the compliment. You're a fox yourself."

Mr. Wells cut in to say, "J.R. You'll have plenty of time to become better acquainted with Alicia, but right now there are more people interested in meeting both of these young ladies."

At this point both J.R. and Alicia were blushing. Now for Alicia blushing was easy, because she has light skin, for J.R. it was a task because he was as dark as me.

"All right Dad, I'll wait until all of the introductions are made."

"Thank you, son. Ladies, this bright and beautiful young lady is Marissa Gonzales. She's our President of Public Relations, and she's been with me since she graduated from college, which was eight years ago."

Marissa spoke, "It's nice meeting both of you. James has said some great things about you."

I spoke, "Thank you Marissa, it's nice meeting you as well."

"The same goes for me Marissa," Alicia added.

"This is my daughter Brittany. She attends Prairie View A&M, but she was home, and I wanted her to meet both of you. She's interested in event planning."

Alicia spoke, "Brittany, it's great to meet you. If Nia or I can answer any questions regarding event planning, please don't hesitate to ask us. You look just like your mother."

"That's what everyone tells me. Thank you for offering your assistance, I may take you up on that while I'm at school."

I said, "Please do. We're sincere with our offer."

"Again, thank you both."

In unison we said, "You're welcome."

"Ladies, this old man is Mattie's husband, John. He and I are great friends, and I wanted him to be a part of our celebration."

I acknowledged John first, "John, it's nice to meet you. Your wife has been more than wonderful to Alicia and I."

"Well, my Mattie has said some wonderful things about the two of you. I had to meet the two ladies that made such a big impression on her." He patted her hand as he spoke.

"Again, thank you."

"Last but certainly not least, is next in charge of Wells Communications after me and J.R., his name is Scott Goldstein. We joke he's our token white employee," laughing.

Extending his hand for handshakes he said, "You've got to love James' sense of humor ladies. Seriously, I'm one of the few Caucasian faces here, but I'm here because this is where I want to be. James has built a great company from the ground up. Our revenue is more than one hundred million dollars annually. We are a family, and that's something we take pride in. A lot of these major corporations don't care about their employees. Well, we know we're different in that aspect."

Alicia said, "Really impressive. I agree most of the large corporations don't care about their employees, and it's refreshing to know there is a successful company talking the talk and walking the walk."

Mr. Wells spoke again, "Since the introductions have been made, let's order and enjoy."

Two waiters entered the room and began to take our orders. I ordered the Hawaiian steak, and Alicia ordered the rotisserie chicken. Mr. Wells ordered champagne for everyone, and the celebration began. Before dinner arrived, I left the banquet room to go to the restroom. On my way back to the banquet room, my eye caught a fine specimen. I hadn't dated or even met anyone who caught my eye since meeting Ben, which was two and a half years ago. I wasn't interested in anyone else and never allowed my eyes to scan any area men may have been in. But this brotha, this brotha had a lil' sumthin, sumthin'. He was sitting in a booth with three other fine male specimens. I love to see professional black men in a group. They emulate power, and don't even know it. Black men possess something no other race possesses. It can't be explained, and often they don't have a clue. Anyway, he was Hershey bar chocolate with shoulder length jet black locks, a well-groomed beard, light brown eyes, the deepest set of dimples I'd ever seen on a man, and a small mole above his lip. Damn! Damn! Diggity Damn! He was sexy and fine all rolled into one! He caught my eye, and I caught his. He was talking to his boys, and as I walked by, he stopped mid-sentence and looked up. I smiled.

He smiled. I continued to the banquet room. I'm not one to sweat a brotha, and as fine as he is, I'm sure sistahs can't help themselves. I wouldn't fall prey to his fine ass.

Malik

Rick said, "Earth to Malik. Nigga, what happened? You were telling us about your meeting, mid-sentence you stop, and now you're in la la land?"

Mike said, "Yeah nigga, what's up?"

"Ya'll didn't see her?"

In unison they replied, "See who?"

"Her."

Looking around to see who I was talking about, as if rehearsed they said, "Her who?"

"Her. The beautiful sistah who just glided by here."

Ray said, "Where is she now?"

"I don't know. She smiled, I smiled and went into a trance, and now she's gone."

Mike said, "Well, do you see her?"

Looking around, "Nope, I lost her."

Ray said, "Do you want to get up to look for her?"

"Naw, I ain't one to sweat a sistah."

Mike said, "What do you think you're doing now nigga? If staring off into la la land isn't sweatin' a woman, I don't know what is."

Rick said in his Chris Tucker Friday voice, "You're with your boys. You ain't got to lie Malik. You ain't got to lie."

Ray then intervened, "On the real Malik, we're too old to play these games. If you want the sistah....she was a sistah wasn't she?"

"Have you ever known me to date anything but?"

"I guess you've got a point there, but if you want her, go get her. Nothing is handed to a black man on a silver platter."

Mike said, "All jokes aside, Ray's right. You haven't dated anyone since Melina. Remember she was the I-don't-know-if-I-fuck-men-or-women confused one. All women aren't like her."

"Man, I know that, but I don't want to open myself up for disappointment. Sistahs talk about brothas being dawgs, but some of them are just as scandalous, if not worse."

Rick said, "Everything's a gamble, you just have to decipher what's worth the gamble, and what's not."

"All right, all right, I'll walk around the restaurant and see if she's still here."

Mike said, "That's right man, you can do it. If Trump's racist and sorry ass can steal the right to be president, you can steal, well not steal, but you can at least find and meet this mystery woman."

66

I got up in search of the mystery woman.

Ray said, "Nigga what kind of analogy was that? Trump's trifling-thieving ass ain't got nothing to do with Malik meeting ol' girl. You need to be quiet."

"Man, fuck you! You be quiet."

Rick said, "Mike, the analogy didn't make sense, but we'll excuse your ignorant ass this time."

Ray said, "While Malik is up looking for the mystery lady, there's something I want to discuss with both of you."

Rick said, "Shouldn't we wait on Malik?"

"No, because it's about Malik."

Mike said, "It sounds serious. What's up?"

"I'm worried about Malik."

Rick and Mike looked at one another and they both said, "Why?"

"He doesn't seem like himself. He's real leery of women."

Mike said, "What do you expect? His woman was fucking another woman. Some brothas don't have a problem with that, but Malik ain't the threesome type of guy."

Rick said, "Ray does have a point, Malik ain't had none since Melina let herself into his house and seduced him."

Mike said, "Damn, two months is a long time to go without?"

Rick said, "I guess, I don't keep count, but sex isn't the issue."

Ray said, "Oh really, what is?"

Rick said, "All you have on the brain is booty. Nigga you are forty, and there are more important things in life than gettin' your freak on."

"Besides money, what's more important than getting some ass."

Mike said, "It's a shame you're literally responsible for a little girl. We'll see if you have the same views once Rae starts fucking."

Ray said, "What does this have to do with my daughter?"

Rick said, "Everything. One day Rae will be a young lady, and some nigga who's just like you will be pushing up on her."

"And?"

"And? Do you want some little nigga after her for the ass and nothing else?"

Ray said, "Man this is different."

"How? To somebody, she's going to be a piece of ass."

Mike said, "Man change the subject before there's a fight."

Rick said, "Man I love Ray like a brother, but he can be foul at times. I just want him to look at things in a different perspective."

Reluctantly Ray said, "I feel you man. Since you put Rae into the equation, I understand."

"Cool, I just wanted you to really understand. All these women, they're someone's daughter. At least respect that."

Mike said, "Back to the original subject at hand, our boy Malik. What should we do?"

Rick said, "I don't think we should do anything. Sex obviously isn't as important to him, as it is to us. Hell, for all we know, he could be chokin' his chicken."

Right then I re-appeared. "Damn, who's chokin' their chicken?"

Lying, Mike said, "Nobody you know man, just this guy who works with me."

Ray said, "How did your search go?"

"Unfortunately, not good at all. I walked around twice, and even stood by the door to the ladies room. No queens in sight."

Rick said, "Well, at least you tried."

"Yes, I did. Well, let's finish our drinks."

Mike said, "You all still want to go to Sambuca's?"

Ray said, "Hell yeah! Honeys, booze, and jazz. That's my kind of mixture."

Rick said, "Oh snap! Before I forget, I was surfing the net last night, and one of my co-workers told me to check out Tom Joyner's website."

Mike said, "I didn't know he had a website. Is he touring?"

Rick said, "No, he isn't, but you know he's been doing the Fantastic Voyage cruise every year and the proceeds go to the United Negro College fund."

Ray said, "All right nigga, and?"

"Well, we had to cancel our trip to the St. Lucia Jazz Festival last year, so I think we should do Tom Joyner's cruise."

I said, "Sounds like a plan."

Ray said, "I'm impressed. You came up with a decent suggestion? I'm down with it."

Rick said, "I'm down. Just let me know how much and when I should be ready."

"Cool, I'll get on the details tomorrow."

"If it's all right with you all, I want to invite Gerald," Mike suggested.

"Gerald who plays ball with us on Saturday?" Ray asked.

"Yeah, he's a cool guy and since he's not from Dallas he doesn't have many friends. I think he'd enjoy the trip and he's cool to hang out with," explained Mike.

"Man, you ain't got to sell us on Gerald, he's cool, and as far as I'm concerned, he's more than welcome to join us," Ray said.

"Are all of you cool with this?"

Everyone answered with yes.

Malik said, "All right, let's toast."

Ray looking puzzled, said, "Toast? To what?"

"To friendship, honeys and the baddest cruise sailing the Caribbean Sea."

Mike said, "I'll drink to that."

Malik, Ray, and Rick said in unison, "Nigga you'll drink to anything!"

Laughing he replied, "Ya'll do have a point."

68

We stayed at Houston's another twenty to twenty-five minutes before we left, piled into my Yukon, and headed to Sambuca's.

Nia

As soon as I arrived in the banquet room, Alicia questioned me. "Nia, where have you been?"

"Why are you whispering?"

"You've got this silly grin on your face."

"I do not. You must be imagining things."

"What was in the restroom?"

"Uh...toilets, sinks, soap and paper towels."

"Ha Ha funny Miss Witherspoon, but toilets, sinks, soap, and paper towels don't have you grinning."

"I didn't realize I was grinning."

"So, tell me what's up?"

"What's up with what?"

"Girl, you ain't slick! I've known your ass since the fifth grade. I know when you're up to something."

"Don't trip, go get your flirt on with Mr. J.R." My suggestion to flirt with J.R. obviously got her mind off me because she quickly changed the subject. I wanted to have the opportunity to bask in the glow of Mr. Mystery man's smile. All by myself.

"Girl, can you believe he was blatantly flirting?"

"Yeah, I can believe it, you got it goin' on baby."

"And you are silly."

"I may be silly, but you are the bomb!"

From out of nowhere we heard, "I second that." We both looked up as J.R. arrived. He was really diggin' Alicia. I decided to give them some time alone.

"I'm going to leave the two of you alone while I get me a glass of champagne."

"All right, girl."

"The food should be here in a minute. Dad said the waiter told him another ten minutes, which was approximately five minutes ago," J.R. offered.

"Good, cause I'm starving."

Alicia

"So, Miss Fox, what's up with you?"

"Nothing much Mr. Wells the II, you?"

"I'm just interested in us becoming better acquainted."

"Is that right? You don't look like the lonely type."

"You know what they say, looks can be deceiving. I was a nerd because I was smart."

69

"Really? Me too, until Nia and I began to hang out."

"Oh, so you all weren't always friends?"

"Actually, we've been friends since fifth grade, but I never went out. Nia would always invite me, but I was shy, had braces and I wore glasses. Thick glasses. We met at recess. Our class was playing kickball, and I didn't catch the ball. So, the other kids began to talk about my kickball skills, or lack thereof. Nia stood up for me and we've been friends since then."

"I can't imagine you being shy. You exude confidence."

"Now I am, and a lot of the new me, is because of Nia and our friendship. The other kids would tease me, but like I mentioned earlier, Nia always stood up for me, even fought a few times."

"Nia, fighting? Now I can't even see that. She exudes professionalism."

"Nia has dual personalities, she is the epitome of professionalism, but she will get ghetto if she must. Back in the day she'd fight anyone who stepped to her, boys included."

"What? She fought boys. Did she win?"

"I won't say she won, but she didn't lose either. Her dad taught her to fight because as he said, she didn't have a brother, and he couldn't protect her twenty-four-seven."

"To look at her now, I would've never guessed that."

"Well, she's matured, but she still doesn't put up with any craziness."

"Damn, I'm amazed. She's not big at all."

"No, she's not, but she's not to be messed with. Believe that."

"It's wild what you can learn by talking to someone, and it proves looks are definitely deceiving."

"You're right about that."

"So, Miss Fox, are you seeing someone in St. Louis?"

"Actually, I'm currently single, have been for about nine months."

"Really? And why is that?"

"My ex and I realized after two years together we want different things out of life."

"And what do you want?"

"I want a successful business as well as a family. Tony was driven by money, nothing else mattered to him. He always had to have the newest in everything. He leases a different car each year, last year it was an E Class Mercedes, and this year it's a Lexus ES 350 and BMW X7 SUV."

"He's got it like that?"

"He makes really good money, he's an attorney at his father's law firm."

"Well, if he can afford it."

"Don't get me wrong, I like nice things also, I just purchased the new Jaguar, but I also want a family."

"Well, why do you think he didn't want these things?"

"His father was obsessed with building his law firm so much it drove his wife, Tony's mother out of their lives. Tony has the same obsession, and I think it's why he shies away from committed relationships."

"So, you all weren't committed?"

"Actually, we were, and we were happy, but when I began to talk about marriage, you know the true commitment, he would always become evasive. So, finally one day I asked him where we were headed."

"And?"

"And he said in his opinion, we were fine and there was no reason to ruin it by getting married. To him, we could have a baby together without being married, as well as live together."

"I take it you weren't down with that?"

"Not at all, and because I don't believe in giving ultimatums, I left him alone."

"Why not give the ultimatum after two years of being together?"

"To me ultimatums are useless. If a man really wants to marry you, they'll ask without coercion. Ultimatums force the other person's hand, and I don't want to get married because he feels like he's being forced to."

"Do you think he regrets his decision?"

"I really don't know. We're still platonic friends, but I've never brought it up and neither has he."

"Do you regret your decision?"

"Not at all. I love Tony, but I love myself more, and the thought of having a family."

"Still had to be a hard decision after two years of loving someone."

"It was, but why should I miss out on having a family to stay with him? Hell, if he loved me like he claims he does, he would've at least considered it."

"So, with him it was a resonating NO."

"Yes, it was not open for discussion."

"Well, it sounds like you definitely made the right decision."

"I think so."

"Well, I'm sure you can tell I'm interested."

"Hmm-mmm."

"I'm not going to pressure you, but I'd like to see you the next time you visit Dallas. Also, keep in mind, I'm not opposed to visiting St. Louis."

"I appreciate you not pressuring me, and yes, I will go out with you the next time I'm visiting Dallas."

"Are you sure?"

"Yes, I'm sure, and I'm looking forward to it."

"Cool. Do you want to exchange numbers?"

"Sure, we can do that."

So, J.R. and I exchanged numbers, and I was actually excited about us becoming acquainted with each other. I hadn't been this excited since first meeting Tony.

71

Nia

On the other side of the room, I was getting more acquainted with Mrs. Wells and daughter, I mean Shelby and Brittany.

"So Brittany how's Prairie View A&M?"

"It's all right considering I spend seventy-five percent of my time studying."

"Well, that's good."

"I'm committed to keeping my grades up, but a sistah would like to get her party on every once in a while."

"Brittany, I know what you mean, but honestly, the party doesn't start until you turn twenty-one, and by then, school will be just about completed. I'll even take you out for your twenty-first birthday."

"Nia, I know what you're saying is true, and I'm going to hold you to my twenty-first birthday celebration."

"That's fine, I keep my promises."

"Cool. I've always wanted an older sister, so consider yourself adopted."

"Well, that's makes two of us. I always wanted an older sister also, but I'm the oldest."

"What does your sibling do?"

"Nandi is a Pediatrician in Montgomery, Alabama, and she's happily married with twins."

"Nandi, what a beautiful name," Shelby commented.

"Thank you, Shelby. She was named after King Shaka Zulu's mother."

"Well, both of your names are beautiful. I wanted to give Brittany an African name, but James wouldn't allow it."

"Thank you for the compliment. I don't know if my parents set out to give us African names, but they wanted us to have names with meaning and it didn't hurt being beautiful."

"They succeeded. Sometimes I wish Daddy would've allowed Mama to give me a different name, but I've grown into Brittany now."

"It fits you, and although you don't have an ethnic name, it's a beautiful name."

Hugging me, Brittany said, "Thank you, adopting you is good for my ego."

Just then the waiters appeared with our salads, so we sat down and began to eat. As I ate, I thought about the cutie I saw. Damn he was sex-fine, but so was Ben, and we know how it turned out. I used to think dating an unattractive man would guarantee no heartache, but some of them are foul as well. I've dated the cousins, Ug and Lee and I even dated their distant cousin, Fatty. Men are out there because sistahs are desperate and tired of dealing with their bullshit every day. So, no I don't look for fine brothas like the one sitting in Houston's main dining room, but I don't shy away from them either. On the other hand, I don't look for Ug, Lee or Fatty, but I may shy away depending on

72

how ugly or how fat they are. Right now, I'm going to put the beautiful brotha out of my mind and concentrate on eating and celebrating. Our party went on to celebrate our new union with good food, and good drinks. It was a little after nine when we decided to call it a night. Mr. Wells said, "Well, everyone, Shelby, Brittany, J.R. and I are about to leave. We all have an early morning ahead of us, and I know Nia and Alicia have a flight to catch tomorrow. I want to thank all of you for joining in on our celebration. Wells Communications and Event Solutions have a bright future. So, if you'll excuse us."

Nia said, "Before everyone leaves, I'd like to say something."

Mr. Wells, "You go right ahead young lady."

"Thank you, sir. Alicia and I are overwhelmed with gratefulness. This is such a blessing for both of us. We look at this as a business opportunity as well as the adoption of an extended family. All of you have made us feel like family, and we sincerely appreciate it. I know I speak for both of us when I say we plan to do the very best for you, and we look forward to working with each of you. We have immensely enjoyed ourselves this evening and we thank all of you."

Shelby said, "Nia, you are more than welcome. I read people every day, and after meeting you and Alicia I know James made the right decision."

In unison we responded with, "Thank you."

Mr. Wells said, "All right ladies, I'll talk to you soon, and I'll be looking for your signed contract."

Alicia said, "Yes sir, we will get it to you immediately."

Shelby hugged us and said, "It was a pleasure meeting both of you. The next time you're in town have James bring you to the house. I'll cook a New Orleans style meal. New Orleans is my hometown."

I said, "I'm looking forward to it already. I love Cajun food."

"Then it's a date. You all have a safe trip."

We said, "We will."

Alicia said, "Goodnight, everyone."

Alicia

At that time, everyone began to depart. Prior to the Wells family departing, J.R. pulled me aside.

"Well, Miss Fox, it was definitely a pleasure meeting you, and I'm sorry the evening's ending so fast, but we'll see each other soon, and talk to each other even sooner."

"Yes, we will J.R. and meeting you was a pleasant surprise. I knew Mr. Wells had a son, but I didn't expect you."

"Oh, what did you expect?"

"I don't know really. I guess I expected you to be younger because I thought your father was in his forties."

73

"Pops will love to hear that, but that's just black folks aging gracefully. He's damned near sixty, and so is Mama."

"Really? They both look great."

"I'll give you a call tomorrow, if that's all right."

"That will be fine. I should be home after seven, I have some errands to run when I get back in town."

"I'll talk to you then. Enjoy your private celebration with Nia because I know you all aren't finished."

"You're right."

"I won't even ask where you're going because if I know, I'll be compelled to join you."

"Not that I would have a problem with you joining me any other night, but tonight belongs to Nia and me. This is a tremendous night for our careers."

"I know, and I totally understand. Enjoy, and you and I will celebrate during your next visit."

"Sounds like a plan."

"You all be careful."

"We will and thank you."

"Again, you're welcome."

J.R. and I hugged, and he kissed me on the cheek. We were the last to leave. After we got into our rental, Nia followed the Concierge's directions to Sambuca's.

Sambuca

There we found a stylish and what appeared to be a young black professional crowd enjoying good jazz, good food and from the looks of it, good conversation. The club was very chic and modern. We were fortunate enough to find a booth, so that's where we planted our asses. As soon as we sat down, I could feel someone staring at me, but I didn't know anyone in Dallas, so I ignored the feeling. Alicia ordered an Apple Martini. I was celebrating so I ordered a bottle of Moet. After Alicia finishes her Martini, she can help drink the Moet.

Alicia said, "Girl, this place is nice. Who told you about it?"

"You remember Karen?"

"Karen, Karen who?"

"Karen Lacey, she went to high school with us?"

"Karen Lacey with the gorgeous smile and the mole above her lip?"

"Yes, that Karen. Why do black people always describe each other by a body part?"

"I don't know girl, that's just what we do."

"You don't know how many times I've heard, "You know Nia?" "You mean Nia with the flat ass and the big breasts?"

Laughing. "Shit, I always get short Alicia with the freckles."

"Black folks, we gotta love our people, we are definitely one of a kind."

"Give me some dap girlfriend."

74

"Girl, c'mon and drink some of this Moet` with me. Anyway, Karen lived here for a minute, and she fell in love with this place, so she suggested we come here during our visit."

"Well, great suggestion. We need one of these in St. Louis."

"I second that. Hell, let's drink to that."

"Your ass is drinking to everything tonight."

"Like the fellas would say, "true dat."

Malik

The fellas and I decided to chill out at Sambuca's after we left Houston's. I still had the hottie I saw on my mind, but I figured I should let it go. I doubt I'll ever see her again. I'll just have to continue to see her in my dreams because I know she's going to appear there. Or would I see her sooner? Here's to wishful thinking. I decided to head to the restroom before joining the fellas. On my way to the table, there she was. The mystery woman had reappeared. I was stunned. Frozen in place. She never saw me and therefore never saw the look in my eyes or on my face. I must've stood there for five minutes totally blown away. I decided to head to the table to report my findings to my boys.

"Niggas, this must be my lucky night."

Ray said, "Why, what's up? Did you find out Melina's crazy ass is moving to Zimbabwe?"

"Man, fuck Melina. Anyway, the honey I saw at Houston's but couldn't find during my search is in the house!"

Mike said, "Aw shit, where is she?"

"She's sitting in a booth on the other side with one of her girlfriends, who's fine in her own right as well."

Mike said, "Only one friend? There are three of us."

"You niggas will figure it out."

Ten more minutes had passed, and I hadn't got up to go to Ms. Mystery.

Rick said, "Malik, you announced almost ten minutes ago that Miss Thang is here, but you're still here sitting with us."

"Nigga, don't you think I know I'm sittin' here? She and her girl are kickin' it, and I don't want to interrupt them."

Mike said, "Man, you better get your ass up. You may not see her again, and I don't want you whining to us about the one who got away."

"Whateva nigga, I don't whine."

Ray said, "Mike's right Malik, you may not whine, but you're going to coulda, woulda, shoulda us to death. Man, I just ain't up for the bullshit. Go find the girl."

"Aight, I'm going. You niggas are a pain in my ass."

"Well, then you know you're a pain to each and every one of ours too," Mike admitted.

I mentally grabbed my balls and proceeded to meet the mystery woman, with her fine ass. When I arrived at their table, no one looked up. They were laughing and didn't notice they had company. After an awkward minute, sexy's friend looked up.

Alicia said, "Hello, may I help you?"

Before I could respond, she looked up, and we just stared at one another while her friend watched us as if she were watching the Williams' sisters playing a game of tennis. Sexy from Houston's stared at me, and I boldly stared back at her. She was sexy as hell with a beautiful smile. I couldn't help but blush.

Alicia spoke again, "Do you two know one another?"

Finally, the goddess spoke, "No, we don't but we saw each other at Houston's."

"Oh, that's what you were-Nia kicked Alicia under the table to get her to shut up.

"Excuse my friend, she's somewhat intoxicated."

"I am not."

"Anyway, may I help you?"

"I don't run bullshit lines, but I wanted to tell you my name is Malik Black and I think....no I know you're beautiful."

Nia

"Well, Mr. Black thank you for the compliment." You aren't too shabby yourself with those deep ass dimples, pretty ass lips and the sexy mole above your lip which I'd like to kiss. Of course, I didn't express those sentiments to him but to myself. I've never been attracted to brothas with locks, but this brotha's entire package was top rate, from his Ralph Lauren suit to his Gucci loafers, to his very well groomed beard, to his neat head of locks. Damn! "My name is Nia Witherspoon, and this is my girl Alicia Fox."

"Ladies, it's a pleasure to meet both of you. Would you mind if my friends and I joined you?"

Alicia said, "How many friends?"

"My three best friends are with me."

Looking at Alicia I said, "It's up to you, Alicia."

"Three's cool, bring them on over."

"All right, ladies, I'll be right back."

"We'll be here, waiting." Once Malik walked away Alicia began her third degree.

"Nia, you've got two minutes and two seconds to explain that fine specimen to me."

"Okay, you remember when I went to the restroom at Houston's?"

"Yeah?"

"Well, on my way back to the banquet room I passed a table with four fine ass black men, Malik looked up, our eyes locked, we smiled, and I kept walking."

"So that's what the mischievous grin was about?"

"I guess so."

"I knew it! You can't hold back from your girl."

"Alicia, ain't nothing up, hell, I just broke up with Ben."

"Not trying to be negative, but I told you he was not the one. He constantly tried to bring you down. That is not support."

"I know you're right, but it's still too soon to be thinking about a relationship."

"Why? For the last two years, your relationship with Ben has been strictly sexual. His intentions were to live off you and never marry you. Please don't give me the bullshit about him proposing because he did it after you caught him cheating. He has never supported Event Solutions, even when it was just an idea."

"I know everything you say is true, but I need time. It wasn't intentional, but with Ben, I was careless with my heart. That is no longer an option."

"All right, but Malik is super fine. Hell, he's almost Morris Chestnut fine and you know he's one of God's gifts to black women."

"Amen to that. Morris is extra fine."

"I know right and gets better as he ages."

"I'll be nice to Malik, and enjoy his company, but we will not be exchanging numbers."

"We'll see."

"We'll see my ass. It ain't happening. I'm just trying to have a good time, and if Malik and his boys can enhance our fun, then so be it."

Malik

When I arrived back at the table, the fellas were talking about some big booty girl who was dancing with a nerd.

Rick said, "What is she doing with him? With an ass like that, she needs to be with me."

Laughing so hard he spit some of his beer out, Mike said, "Boy, you would not know what to do with all that ass."

"Well, get her over here and I'll show you."

"I will not assist in your embarrassment."

Just then they finally noticed I had appeared.

Rick said, "Nigga please don't tell us she got away again."

Mike said, "I'm with Rick, you've been thinking about this sistah all night long, if you let her get away..."

"Fuck you niggas I ain't thinking about you or Rick. Anyway, I found them, and they're waiting for all of us to return."

Ray said, "All of us?"

Mike said, "What makes you think we want to meet her or her friend?"

"I don't want to be the third wheel, and her girl is fine. I don't care for red bone sistahs but I give props when they're due, and she is fine."

Rick said, "Yeah she's fine, but there's only one friend, where you've got three."

"Nigga whateva, we're going to go over there, listen to some music, enjoy some good conversation and have a good time. All the booger bears I've entertained for you all. All of you owe me one. I'm collecting my debt tonight. Let's go."

Mike said, "Damn fellas, he got us on that one, so let's go."

Reluctantly, Ray, Mike and Rick followed me to Nia and Alicia's booth, and the fun began.

The Meeting

As Malik and his boys approached our booth, I locked eyes with Malik. At that moment, there was no one in Sambuca's except the two of us. We both had silly ass grins on their faces. "Nia, Alicia, these are my boys, my best friends. This is Rick, that's Ray, and this is Mike."

In unison they said, "Hello."

"I'm Alicia."

"And I'm Nia."

Mike said, "Well, it's nice to meet both of you."

I said, "C'mon sit down. I just ordered another bottle of Moet."

Ray said, "What? Are we celebrating something?"

I said, "As a matter of fact we are."

Rick said, "And what are we celebrating?"

"We're celebrating our meeting tonight. New friendships, and whatever other shit we got going on in our lives."

Ray said, "Oh, that's cool, and I already like you. There is nothing like a down-to-earth sistah."

"Well, thank you. It's Ray, right?"

"That's right."

"I'll have all of your names together before we leave."

Malik said jokingly, "Don't worry about learning their names, just call them Curly, Mo, and Larry."

Ray said, "Aw, so a nigga got jokes n' shit? You don't want to go there! You just met Nia, but I could embarrass yo ass right now."

"A'ight nigga, chill."

Laughing, Alicia asked, "How long have you all been friends?"

Mike said, "Too damn long. I've been friends with these clowns since kindergarten, and I just can't get rid of them."

Rick said, "Nigga, you the one we trying to get rid of."

"Whateva nigga, I'm the cream of the crop when it comes to being a friend."

Malik, Rick, and Ray all looked at each other, gave a funny grin and each gave the same response, "True dat."

I said, "Ya'll are extra silly! My girls and I have been friends since the fifth grade, but we don't have issues like ya'll."

Malik said, "Fifth grade, huh? Most women fall out over something and don't remain friends that long."

78

Alicia said, "I agree, women can be silly and trivial like that, but one thing I've learned, true friends, the operative word being 'true', stick around. Nia and I occasionally disagree, but we're adult enough to deal with the situation and move on. There's also the unwritten rule, and we know to respect that."

Ray asked, "What's the unwritten rule?"

Alicia explained the rule, "We would never consider being involved with each other's man. Our friendship means too much. As a matter of fact, if I meet someone and he's ever had any relations with Nia, or any of my other girls, he's off limits."

I said, "We've never had to deal with those types of situations, and anyway, we're attracted to different types of men."

Alicia added this, "Whew! Not that Nia picks bad men, but they're just not for me. I won't say they aren't my type because I don't have a type."

I said, "I've had my share of so-called friends. Some tried to fuck my men, others just fucked the friendship. Now since I'm older I can see who's real and who isn't, and I choose to not deal with those who can't give one hundred percent to the friendship. It amazes me what some women will put up with in a relationship, but they wanna put their friends down. Quick, fast, and in a hurry. People need to realize friendships are merely relationships you have with friends and should be treated as such. Relationships have to be worked at, and so do friendships."

Ray said, "I think brothas have it easier because we don't trip off the shit women do."

Alicia said, "What do you mean?"

"Well, sistahs fight over niggas, and most brothas won't allow a woman to come between them."

Rick said, "It depends on what kinda man he is. Is he low caliber, or high caliber?"

Mike said, "True dat. See, we've been boys since kindergarten, and we've seen each other through a lot, so no female could ruin what we have."

I said, "What if one of you were dating a woman who didn't like the friendship you've cultivated over the years?"

The four of them gave that look again, and then in unison Mike, Ray and Rick said, "Malik."

Malik said, "Well first of all-"

I had to ask, "Wait a minute. What's up with this look, and you becoming the speaker of the house for the majority?"

Malik said, "Well, I'm the designated speaker on subjects the fellas and I agree one hundred percent on." By this time, we were on our third bottle of Moet and Alicia, and I were getting a little loose with our tongues.

Alicia said, "I hear you bruh."

I added, "Is that right? Well, speak on my brotha."

Malik said, "Thank you very much my sistah. First of all, I have to address the word cultivate, it's strictly a female's word, brothas would never

79

use the term 'cultivate the friendship.' Secondly, if one of us is dating a woman who doesn't like the brotherhood, because we're more than friends, then she gotta get some gone. We love each other, and we respect each other. Each of us is intelligent, funny, ambitious, and responsible; there's no reason for any animosity."

I had to play devil's advocate and ask, "Okay, okay, but what if one of you disrespects her?"

Mike said, "It'll never happen because of the love we have for each other. We're not in high school, we're 40, and unlike a lot of brothas out here we act our age."

In unison, and with snaps of our fingers, Alicia and I said, "I heard that!"

Alicia said, "Hmmm...."

Mike said, "And what does hmmm mean?"

She elaborated, "Hmmm means it's nice to meet a group of mature brothas who truly have a bond. So many brothas in their thirties and forties are so immature, and sistahs are tired of brothas and their bullshit."
Throughout the time we spent with Malik and his boys, he just sat and stared at me whenever he wasn't talking. Up until the time this particular subject came up, he didn't have much to say.
That soon ended.

"Is that right?"

Alicia said, "Actually I feel-"

Malik said, "No disrespect Alicia, but I'm quite interested in what Nia has to say on the subject matter."

Not paying much attention I said, "Excuse me, did you say something?"

"Yes, I did, I'm interested in your opinion on the subject."

"I'm sorry, but what subject is that?"

"Sistahs being tired of brothas and their bullshit."

"Oh, that subject?"

"Yes, ma'am."

"Well, I don't know if we have enough time to get into it."

Looking at his watch, Mike said, "It's still early, and even if it wasn't, we're all grown."

"All right, I'll give my opinion."

The fellas began to look at me with an inquisitive look and Malik said, "Please bless us with your dissertation."

"Okay, here goes. Other than a child created by a black man and a black woman, black men are our greatest gift. The same goes for us, being your greatest gift. You all possess a strength even if you don't recognize it. Our people have endured a lot, and you all have had to deal with the brunt of it, but through it all, we've been by your side. Also, through it all, our people have maintained and prospered."

"There was nothing negative in that. So, what are you sick of?" Ray asked.

"Oh, I wasn't finished. What am I sick of? I'm sick of black men blaming the man for their downfalls. Now, don't get me wrong, I understand what they've done to you and us. What I can't seem to grasp is the fact a lot of you are still holding onto and using it as a crutch to not succeed. If anything-

Ray attempted to interject, "A crutch. What the-"

"Ray let me finish."

"I'll let you finish, but don't dis the bruhs."

"It may sound like I'm dissing men, but allow me to finish, and you will understand."

"Okay, go ahead."

"Now, where was I?" With a snap of my fingers, I remembered and continued, "I remember now. A strong and proud African American man raised me, and I saw how the system worked on beating him down daily. I'm not saying it's easy, but he persevered. He didn't allow the system to categorize him, like it does to so many of our men."

Rick said, "So your father was one of the lucky ones?"

"No, he wasn't. Luck had nothing to do with it, but God had everything to do with it. My father never knew his biological father and therefore he didn't have a good example of being a father. His experience became his motivation for being a good father. So, what he did was set goals for himself. He set professional goals, as well as personal goals, and he did everything he could to achieve those goals. I think my father, rest his soul is a great example of what a black man can achieve. So basically, it's a mind thing if you think great things, you'll achieve great things."

Laughing, Mike said, "So, this is the garbage you feed men? No disrespect to your father."

"You can say what you want Mike, but people who desire great things, achieve great things. If we as a people succumb to the things said to us, and about us, we'd never achieve greatness. Talk about a slap in the face to Sojourner Truth, Malcolm X, Harriet Tubman, and all our ancestors who lead the way for us."

"Nia, I see your point, but this is my point."

"Mike?"

"Yeah?"

"Get to the point," laughing.

Laughing. "I'm getting there. I totally understand the think-it-so-you-can-be-it advice but for us as a people, actions speaking louder than words works better. It's our responsibility to go back to our neighborhoods, take a lost soul by the hand, and lead them out of poverty."

"I agree with you."

"You agree with me, but we're not doing it."

"Some of us are. As a matter of fact, a lot of us are."

"Yeah, but not enough of us. That's the main reason the fellas and I volunteer to help the youth. Sometimes these young cats just need guidance and a light shone down the correct path."

"My parents taught me the importance of giving back, but I still think black men should stop blaming the white man."

"I agree, and when I say this, I know I'm speaking for thousands of men. Who should we blame?"

"Why do you have to blame anyone?"

"It's a man thing."

"Well, if it's a man thing, men need to start acting as such instead of blaming others, they need to blame their lack of drive and ambition on themselves. Look at all of you. You all didn't become statistics. You're hardworking men and you give back to the community."

Malik began to express himself which shut Mike down, "Yeah, but a lot of these brothas don't know any other way. Their grandfather was a hustler, their father was a hustler and it's all they know. Some brothas can get out no matter their situation, but some can't. All they see is the fast money, and they want it."

"So, you're condoning their profession?"

"No, not at all. I don't believe in racial genocide, but I also don't believe in a society where the educational system is unfair. Like it or not, this is America. I was raised to believe knowledge is power and therefore I would always strive for excellence, and I achieved that. I'm a black man with a bachelor's from Hampton University and a master's from Stanford. That's one of their finest schools. It didn't help though. I still had a hard time finding a job. My degrees didn't change the color of my skin. My only choice was to start my own business."

"So, are you telling me they're a product of their environment? That's another excuse I'm tired of hearing. One of my classmates from high school grew up without a father, and a mother who struggled. He survived, without selling drugs. Hell, he wore hand-me-downs and got talked about, but he made it." By this time, Alicia, Ray, Mike, and Rick were no longer listening. They got bored with what we were talking about. I guess they weren't interested in hearing about what I'm sick of.

"Well, their environment has something to do with it."

"I disagree and I am not a snob. I think it has to do with a yearning inside of you. My name means "purpose" in Swahili, and my parents instilled in me the significance to succeed; I felt compelled to do just that."

"See, that's what I'm talking about, you had parents. A lot of these young men who have chosen to sell drugs, don't have parents. If they do, they have just one and they're cracked out, or working too much to provide for their child, or spend quality time. They don't make time to nurture their child. I come from a two-parent family, and I made it, but I sometimes wonder if the results would've been the same if I didn't. Another obstacle is funding for college or lack thereof, and with the Republican party stopping all strides by the Democrats, African Americans don't have a chance."

"Okay, now since you put it that way, I understand. I know children with two parents have a better chance. I also know I can't fully understand what it's like to be impoverished, but I would hope growing up this way would push one to want more out of life. I guess I just don't understand it."

"Well, it's a difficult situation, but to them, selling drugs allows them more material things. America associates success with 'things', so in their eyes they are successful."

"There's nothing wrong with things, hell, I like nice things, but I also like getting them legally."

"True dat. That's one of the reasons I volunteer. I talk to the youth, and I stress to them selling drugs to our people is not success, and neither is fast money. I make them aware of their other options. I also try to equate success with hard work, empowerment, and education. Every time I leave the youth center, I pray I've touched one of their lives."

"That's admirable, and I'm sure you're touching their lives. So many times, we as a people succeed and become Republicans and therefore forget where we come from. You're passionate about giving back so I know one of those young men or women are taking heed."

"I hope you're right. My parents always stressed the significance of giving back. For me it's not a choice, it's mandatory."

"Hey, how did we get off the subject? We were talking about what I'm sick of."

"Yeah, we did get off the subject. So, other than blame-it-on-the-man brothas what else are you sick of?"

"I'm sick of brothas fighting sistahs."

"Fighting, as in fist fighting?"

"No. I wish a nigga would put his hands on me. I'm talking about the emotional war black-on-black love endures. We all have issues and baggage, but if we work together, I really think our relationships would flourish."

"So, you don't think there's enough effort?"

"Not at all. People get married now with the notion if things don't work out, they'll just go to divorce court. No way, not me, I'm in it to win it."

"Marriage is crazy now. They lack loyalty and sincerity. When our parent's generation married, and those preceding theirs married, they took their vows literally."

"The missing ingredient to a successful union is spirituality."

"That's true. My parents say keeping God first is what keeps them together."

"Now I definitely agree with that. No one can survive without God in their life."

"I agree."

Just then Alicia sat her glass on the table with a loud thud, which got our attention. I could tell she was a little tipsy, so there was no telling what

83

would come out of her mouth. Slurring her words, she said, "Could y'all shut the fuck up about giving back to the community. We know what we sposed to do. We're supposed to be celebrating new friendships and shit, not talking about serious stuff."

We all looked at Alicia like she'd lost her damn mind and laughed wildly at her. That's my girl. "Baby, are you okay?" I inquired.

"I'm fine, why do you ask?" She began to look at each of us and noticed we were giving her this you-must-be-crazy look. "What's wrong? And what the hell is so funny?"

Ray said, "Well, you did go off on us about a minute ago."

"Did I really?"

Jokingly Mike said, "You'll probably deny it to your grave. We'll just let it pass."

Right then the band began to play 'Gina' by Najee, which is a favorite of mine. "Ooh, that's my jam. I love Najee."

Malik said, "He's one of my favorite artists as well. Would you like to dance?"

"As a matter of fact, I would."

Malik offered me his hand and led me to the dance floor. As I walked behind him, I noticed he was taller than I thought, and had a nice ass. I also noticed Mr. Black was bow legged, and sistahs know there's nothing sexier than a bow legged brotha. His body was muscular, but not too much to be a turn-off. Because of his height, I wrapped my arms around his waist, instead of his neck. He held me in his arms as we swayed back and forth to the beat of Najee's soothing horn playing. I could smell his mint mixed with Moet breath. While we danced, I wanted to touch his hair. I wondered if it was soft. A friend once told me people with locs aren't clean because they don't wash their hair. Unfortunately, I believed her. Now I'd met a brotha with dreads, I wanted to see for myself. He looked clean, and standing this close to him I could smell him, and he didn't stink. People had been wrong before. I gently touched his hair, and it was so soft. They were truly wrong about this one. He was so sexy, it was evident I wanted him, but I couldn't and wouldn't go there. Ben had left a deep scar. I needed to heal completely before venturing off into the relationship ring again. I also needed to get me a new set of boxing gloves so I could be an appropriate contender in my next bout with love. Yes, it had come to that. Women viewing love as if it were a boxing match. I swing and you swing back. Tit for tat. This for that. There's nothing wrong with tit for tat, it's what we're swinging that makes the difference. Instead of swinging with monogamy and love, brothas and sistahs are swinging deception, lies, and lust. At this point, I'm worn out from my last bout, but damn how I'd like to be a contender with Malik's sexy ass.

Malik

Damn this girl has much sex appeal. She doesn't have much in the ass department, but other than that, she's all that. She fits into my embrace like it's where she belongs. She smells delectable. Her breasts are full, and right now her nipples are hard as pebbles and massaging a brotha's chest. I just hope I don't get a woody. I don't want her to think all a brotha wants is some ass, but damn if her nipples don't stop, she may experience the wrath of my second head! Bada Boom, Bada Bing, it's a thick and long thing!

Just then the band went right into a jazzy rendition of 'Maria Maria' by Carlos Santana.

"Nia, would you like to keep dancing?"

"If you're up to it, sure."

"Do you know how to step?"

"You live in Texas; the question is do you know how to step?"

"Yes, I do."

"I'm not talking about that dosi-do shit."

Laughing heartily, he responded with, "You are silly. I may live in Texas, but a cowboy I'm not. I'm talking about the kind of stepping they do in Chicago."

"Ninety percent of my family lives in Chicago, so stepping is in my blood. How would a country boy livin' in Texas know about that?"

"I won't tell you how I know, I'll just show you." I felt a hard on coming on, so fortunately the change of music saved me.

We began to step, and I must admit she's good, real good as a matter of fact, but I was not going to be outdone. If my ex was good for anything, it was teaching me to step since she was from Chicago. No one would guess this was our first meeting. Our moves were synchronized so well. She knew when to dip, and she felt so right in my arms. Nia and I danced for at least fifteen minutes, I guess they were playing the R. Kelly extended remix, but I didn't mind at all, I like her in my arms. After the Carlos Santana jam, they played the stepper's anthem. Everyone knew 'Step For Love' and Nia and I continued to do our thang. The band obviously enjoyed seeing all the couples dancing because they continued to play upbeat jams. They played 'After the Dance' by Marvin Gaye, and then followed it with one of my old school jams by the Isley Brothers, 'Harvest for the World'.

"You wanna keep dancing?"

"Yeah, I love the Isley Brothers, especially this song."

"We have too much in common."

"Is that right?"

"I know you don't want to admit the attraction, but it's there."

"Okay, I'll admit to it, but now what?"

"Nothing, we'll just go with the flow."

85

I wanted to say we should see where we could go together, but I knew her frame of mind was somewhere else. I was determined I was going to make this woman mine. I had to get to know her, mind, body, and soul.

Nia

Why do I feel like his arms should be home to me? Why can he dance like he took dance lessons? I'm talking about really dancing. Why did I just go through hell with Ben? If I met Malik first, he'd be mine, but that's not how it happened. We always meet the right one after we've fallen in love with Mr. I'm-wrong-for-you-but-I'll-do-for-right-now. Unfortunately, I can't even think about getting involved with him, until I've healed from Ben's crazy-ghetto-girl-lovin'-ass, but I want to. I want to throw caution to the wind and get with this sexy specimen. He's really turning me on, and all he's doing is holding me. The chemistry between us is undeniable. My body could mask my attraction, but his couldn't. I felt his erection before we moved away from each other to begin stepping. I know his arousal was partially the reason why he suggested we step. Sambuca's was crowded, but I only had eyes for Malik. I'd even lost sight of Alicia, Ray, Rick, and Mike. I heard myself moan during one of the times we were chest to chest. I know if I heard it, he heard it as well. Yep my body couldn't mask my attraction. My nipples were as hard as icicles, and I was pretty sure he was aware of this fact as well. I hate it when I meet a man, and although he's not touching me intimately, he's turning me on. This doesn't happen often, but it always happens when I don't want to get involved, but I, like most sistahs give in, but not this time. This time it would be easy because we live in different cities. This time walking away would be as easy as breathing. Or so I thought. And hoped. Abruptly, I stopped dancing, "Can we go back to the table?"
Looking bewildered he replied with "Sure, you okay?"
"Yes, why do you ask?"
"Well, we were getting our groove on when you just stopped."
Lying through my teeth I said, "I'm sorry, I didn't mean to make you think there was something wrong, I'm just thirsty."
"Yeah, okay. Let's get you something to drink."

Malik

I didn't want to stop dancing, but I could tell Nia had something on her mind and that's why she backed away. I did as she requested. As we were walking back to the table, I had to readjust my penis because I still had that problem, and it wasn't going away anytime soon. I'd be taking a cold shower when I arrived home.
I think Nia pulled away because she felt the electricity between us, she had to feel it. It was too strong to ignore, but I think her intentions were just that, to

86

ignore what was happening between us. I would play along with her, but I am not giving up.

Nia

When Malik and I got back to the table, the peanut gallery had a lot to say. Rick was the first to comment. "What's up, Ginger and Fred?"
Alicia said, "You mean Sonny and Cher?"
Ray said, "You all are much too generous, because to me they look like Dorothy and the Scarecrow from 'The Wiz'.
Laughing, Rick said, "Man, not Michael Jackson and Diana Ross?"
Mike said, "Man, fuck what they talking about, you all were getting your swerve on. You looked like Nia and Larenz from that scene in 'Love Jones'.
Malik explained, "Thanks Mike, obviously these other Negroes don't know much about real dancing, all they're accustomed to is bumpin' and grindin'."
"You all are too silly. If I was dancing like one of these video hoes, then you'd have something to say too. You all just need some of your own business."
Licia said, "Oh, is that it?"
"That would be the answer."
"Mmmm…Hmmmm."
"Girl, whatever. I'm thirsty as hell, is there any Moet left?"
"No, but I can-"
"Actually, I think I'll just get me a glass of water."
Malik said, "I'll have the waiter get it. Do you want tap water or bottled water?"
"I'll take Evian if they have it."
"I'll check with the waiter."
"Thank you, Mr. Black."
"No problem, Miss Witherspoon."
Rick said, "Damn! Enough with all the Leave it to Beaver bullshit. Thank you, no problem. I know you all just met but damn! In six months, the conversation will be more like this, "Your ass want some water? Cause if you do, you better get your ass up and get it yourself, and then Nia will say something like, "Nigga, fuck you. I can get my own water."
Laughing Malik said, "Your ass is ignorant. Only you would come up with that shit."
Mike said, "You know how you women change? You act this way one-"
Alicia quickly interjected, "Hold up!"
Of course, I had to add my ten cents, "Wait a minute!"
"Nia, thank you for having my back cause I'm about to blow these clowns away."
Mike said, "Is that right?"
"Yes sir! Yes sir! I'm about to-"
"Hold up, let-"
Ray shouted, "Wait a minute." Of course, laughter erupted.

Alicia continued, "I need to break something down for you brothas because-"

The fellas looked at each other, began smiling, and screamed, "These are the breaks!"

"You all are so silly, but right now I want you to calm your silly asses down, so I can explain something to you. You must think it's nineteen eighty-nine and you're at a Kurtis Blow concert."

Mike said, "Okay, okay we'll stop being silly."

"Thank you, Mike, you're the only sane one I see. Anyway, women change, but only after ya'll change. Keep in mind in the beginning both parties make the relationship a priority, they spend all their spare time together, but once the man achieves a certain level of comfort, he changes. They normally spent Saturday mornings in the bed but that quickly becomes a thing of the past."

Ray tried interrupting, "But sis-"

"Let me finish, then you can have your say. Anyway, she's still in bed hoping she can persuade him to stay. He chose the basketball court instead. Those Saturday nights they spent together listening to jazz, and enjoying each other's company, those nights turn into his night with the boys and the NBA, or the NFL. So, yes sistahs do change, but their change is justified. Brothas should start like they plan to finish, but they don't. In other words, don't act a certain way to get her, and then flip the script after you have her."

Ray said, "May I speak now?"

"Sure, Ray, go ahead, but you know what I said is true."

"Alicia, I understand your point, and I partially agree. Brothas should not start something they can't, nor want to finish. That is the main reason why I don't stop hanging with the fellas because if I do, the minute I want to hang, I'll have to hear her whining and complaining. Honestly, I ain't tryin' to hear it, but sistahs do change."

Malik said, "Bruh, please explain to these lovely ladies how they change."

"Gladly."

I said, "Yes, I'd be interested in hearing this."

Ray was eager to elaborate, "Okay, in the beginning, you all cook, clean, and do all the other domestic shit, but you all reach a certain comfort level as well. When you do, the full course home cooked meals turn into Popeye's chicken you picked up on the way home from work. The sexy underwear turns into period panties with holes in them."

Alicia said with much attitude, "You did not have to go there."

"But I did and felt the need to because you're turning this into a BB session."

"What the hell does BB stand for?"

"Brotha bashing, as if you didn't know."

I said, "I get tired of guys complaining we are always bashing brothas. If ya'll would start acting more like men, and less like little boys maybe we would cool out on the bashing."

Mike said, "Little boys? I'm tired of women always blaming brothas, but some out here don't respect themselves."

Alicia said, "What makes you think that?"

"They dress like hoochies but get mad when you make a crude comment and they fuck any nigga that's willing to spend his money on Prada, Gucci, Coach or any other designer. Why should I respect women acting like that?"

I said, "Mike, I agree with you, but all sistahs aren't like that, especially the ones our age. There's also a flip side to that because sistahs like me who don't wear the come-fuck-me-dress get no play. Niggas say they don't want the women wearing tight dresses revealing a lot, but that's a damn lie. I swear men say one thing but do another."

"So, you're saying the two of you don't get hollered at?"

"Let me put it this way, one of my girls has a bad ass body but I'm deficient in the ass department and if we go out, I don't get any play. It doesn't matter I'm intelligent, ambitious, hardworking, and if I must say so myself, I'm easy on the eyes. Those pertinent qualities don't matter, but a fat ass does."

Malik said, "I can attest to that. You're so easy on the eyes."

"Thank you, sir. Doesn't matter though, what does matter is I'm not walking around in revealing clothing, with a fat ass."

Rick said, "I guess brothas can be shallow, but what does it say about women who will have sex with a man to get an outfit, a bill paid or a piece of jewelry?"

I shared my observation. "It's bad situation for men and women. Everyone is looking for the superficial, instead of really focusing on what's real. How big a woman's ass is should be of no relevance, and the same goes for how big a man's wallet or dick is."

Laughing and looking at Alicia and I, Ray said, "Oh, so now size doesn't matter?"

Alicia stated, "It matters, but it's not the only thing."

Mike stated, "The size of our wallets shouldn't matter either."

Malik said, "If that could only that was true."

I asked, "Please don't tell me you all have been meeting the wrong women as well?"

Malik said, "You know what they say."

I commented, "Yeah you know what they say."

Mike said, "Actually, we don't know, but I'm sure you're gonna tell us."

Snapping her fingers, Alicia smacked her lips and began, "Yes I am, the wrong people tend to find their way to one another, and it's very seldom two right people come together."

I said, "What are two right people?"

"Two people with a lot of the same views, beliefs, and morals. An example would be my beliefs in raising my children the same way my parents raised me, but my ex believed in that 'time out' bullshit. When I say time out, it'll be a time out for me beating some ass."

I said, "I heard that! Spare the rod and you spoil the child! My Daddy used to tear my ass up, but now because I'm older, I appreciate the path my parents chose to raise me as well as discipline me. I feared both of my parents. All I had to do was get the look, and you know what look I'm talking about."

Rick said, "Oh yeah, we definitely know the look. We work with a group of youth in our church, and we're trying to guide them down the right path. We don't discipline them, but we let them know how they should treat their parents and any elderly person. So many of these children crave discipline, but for whatever reason their parents aren't giving them any."

I said, "That's true, but they get mad if their teachers try to discipline them."

Ray said, "I couldn't be a teacher, they don't pay enough, nor do I have the patience for BeBe's kids."

Malik said, "Things have just changed since we were in school."

Alicia said, "Yes, they have. I remember the time Mr.Witherspoon came up to-"

"Licia, no you ain't talking about my grade school years. You better tell them about the time, Raymond Sutter pulled your hair."

"I'll get to that, but I have to tell them about your daddy first."

"No you-"

Malik said, "C'mon Nia, let her tell the story, we all have embarrassing moments from our childhood years."

"That may be true, but I don't know if anyone has a story as embarrassing as mine."

Sure, he could outdo me, Malik shared his story. "Shit! Let me share a story with you. When I was in the sixth grade, my parents were out of town for a weekend, so we-"

"Who is we?"

"The four of us, of course. Anyway, we were at my house and Ray was talking to fine ass Kim Gold. She was the prettiest girl in the sixth grade, and all her friends were cute too. Ray, being the big pimp he was back in the day talked her into coming for a visit and bringing her friends. After he got off the phone with her and told us what was about to go down, we began putting on deodorant, using mouthwash and we used my older brother's cologne. So, we're waiting, and the doorbell rings. Since Ray was the coolest one, he answered the door. Along with Kim was, Marie, Shellie and Angie, all grinning. Ray let them in, and we all went downstairs. Once downstairs, we paired up. I'd had a crush on Shellie because she had the prettiest dimples, and-"

Mike finished Malik's sentence, "That nigga's got dimples, so he thought if he got with Shellie, they'd end up married and all of their kids would have dimples too."

At that time everybody was laughing, even Malik.

"Anyway, Mike was with Marie, Ray was with Kim and Rick was with Angie. We were all shy, so instead of starting a conversation, we began to watch Ben, and-"

Alicia said, "Ben, the movie with Michael Jackson?"

"Exactly. So, you know y'all loved some MJ back in the day when he was black, so I figured it would help break the ice. What I didn't anticipate is the movie would frighten them and have them in our laps, but I guess it worked out in our favor. So, they're in our laps and since we were only in the sixth grade, any and everything excited us. I had an erection, and I knew Shellie could feel it, but she never said anything, she just smiled. We continued to watch the movie, and halfway into it I heard my mother yell my name. We all looked at each other stunned because they weren't supposed to be back until Sunday. It was only Saturday. I had to answer because if I didn't, my daddy was coming downstairs. I answered by saying "Ma`am?"

"What are you doing?"

"Nothing."

"Come upstairs for a minute."

"Yes, Ma'am, just a minute. I couldn't go upstairs because I had a woody, and it wasn't going away. Mike, Ray and Rick jumped up and began to fumble around and one of them caused an ashtray to fall on the floor."

My daddy spoke, "Malik, what the hell are you doing down there?"

"Nothing."

"What was that noise?"

"The ashtray fell on the floor."

"Didn't your mama call you?"

"Yes, sir."

"Well, then get your little ass up here."

"Yes, sir."

Rick whispering, "Whatcha gone do?"

"I'm going upstairs, you know my daddy don't play.'

My daddy must have known something was going on because as I was walking up the stairs, he was coming down.

"Now why can't you come when your mama calls you?'

"Daddy, I was on my way upstairs."

"Boy, your mama called you two minutes ago. What did I tell you?"

"That if either of you call me to come fast."

"Okay, so what's going on downstairs where you can't come upstairs?"

"Nothing daddy, I'm coming upstairs now."

"Boy, just turn around. I want to see what's keeping you down here. Me, and your mama weren't due back until tomorrow, so you being a typical boy, you got yourself into something."

91

"No sir, no I didn't, let's just go upstairs."

"Now I know I'm going downstairs." Of course, at this point, I couldn't do anything except follow him.

Grinning. "I knew there was something keeping you down here. What's up fellas?"

In unison they replied, "Hello, Mr. Black."

"Hello, ladies."

"Hello, Mr. Black."

"Malik, aren't you going to introduce me to your new friends."

At that point I was about to piss on myself because I knew I was in trouble, so I didn't even hear my daddy call my name.

"Boy, did you hear me?"

"Huh, sir, what did you say?"

"Are you going to introduce your new friends?"

"Yes, sir." Pointing I said, "That's Angie, Shellie, Kim and Marie."

"Ladies, it's nice to meet you."

In unison again they said, "Hello, Mr. Black."

"Daddy, they just came over to watch a movie with us."

"What movie?"

"We just finished looking at Ben."

Grinning, my daddy said, "Hmm...Is that right?

"Yes, sir. Daddy?"

"Yeah?"

"Why are you looking like that?"

"No particular reason."

"Daddy, do I still have to go upstairs?"

"Naw son, your mama just wanted to talk to you about the stains in your drawers."

"Daddeeeee...." Everyone began to laugh like a bunch of hyenas, everybody except me of course. My father had just embarrassed the shit out of me. I could get with my parents yelling at me in front of my friends, I had even become accustomed to them popping me every now and then in front of them, but this, this was unforgivable. "How you gon' bust me out in front of everybody?"

"The same way you tried to hold out on me and your mama with your company."

"Daddy, it wasn't like that, you and mama weren't due back until tomorrow."

"Aw, so you were trying to be slick?"

"No sir, I was just having company. Shemar knew I was having company."

"And who is Shemar?"

"My older brother who you left in charge."

"Well, I guess I made a mistake. You don't think your big brother would allow you to get into trouble?"

"I would hope not."

92

"Well, he allowed it." Then my father just started laughing. I damn near pissed on myself and everyone was laughing at me. I couldn't believe this shit. At that moment, my brother and mother came downstairs, and they were laughing as well. I guess it was have-a-joke-on-Malik-day, but I didn't find anything funny. Nothing at all. So, everyone laughed at me for like five minutes, and I was pissed. I couldn't believe my family would do that to me, and in front of Shellie. It really hurt, and it's something I haven't forgotten.

Laughing hysterically, I said, "You poor baby. It scarred you for life, didn't it?"

"I wouldn't say I'm scarred but, I haven't forgotten it."

"Do your parents remember the incident?"

"As if it were yesterday. They get their laugh on every time they bring it up."

"Well, my moment wasn't as embarrassing, but it was embarrassing nonetheless."

At this time, Alicia was cracking up like the shit just happened a minute ago.

"Well, it's obvious that Alicia finds it extremely hilarious, so let me share it with you all. In the fifth grade, well, first let me explain the scenario. Our fifth-grade teacher had us in check, and I don't mean in a bad way because we had the utmost respect for her. She was an excellent teacher, but at the same time she was a strict disciplinarian. She didn't take any shit, and she demanded respect from us at all times, even when she wasn't there."

Looking bewildered, Ray asked, "Even when she wasn't there? What kind of shit is that?"

"Like I said, she was no joke and she had us in check. I remember when I was in grade school how we'd cut up whenever we had a substitute teacher. Well, our fifth-grade teacher didn't play that. She-"

Mike replied, "How would she know, if she was absent?"

"That's what I'm sayin', we feared her, so we didn't even try her."

"She had ya'll in check for real," Malik offered.

"Yes, she did."

Rick's inquiring mind wanted to know, "So, what made her an exemplary teacher?"

"Her number one priority was academic excellence, and-

"Well, wasn't that every teacher's top priority?" Malik inquired.

"Back in our day, I'd say yes, but it was her style more than anything. First of all, she was dressed to impress daily. As I previously mentioned, she demanded respect from us, and I honestly think her demands embedded self-respect in all of us. Another plus was that she made learning fun. I remember one of our assignments was to read Huckleberry Finn. Once the assignment was finished, we went on a field trip to Hannibal, MO where the story took place. Something else that stands out is the World Food Day we had, where each of us had to choose a country and bring a dish which originated in our chosen country. I remember I chose Germany, and my choice was a German chocolate cake."

Agitated, Alicia said, "Damn Nia, get to the point, all of this reminiscing is not necessary."

93

"Well, is the pot calling the kettle black? You're the one who wanted to share my fifth-grade story. Anyway, I was a hardheaded little girl and I always wanted to be heard, so one day in class I ran my mouth, and when Ms. Lewis asked me to keep quiet, I rolled my eyes at her. I didn't think much of it because she didn't say anything about it. Once I arrived at home, I realized why she didn't say much. She had called Mr. Witherspoon. So, when I arrived at home, I went through my normal ritual of changing from my school clothes to my play clothes and then I got ready to do my homework. Just as I was about to sit at my desk in my room, my daddy called my name."

"Nia?"

"Sir?"

"Come here for a minute."

So, I get up and go into the kitchen where my mother and father are sitting. "Yes, sir."

"Have a seat." So, I sat down and patiently waited. At this point my father began to play the you-should-tell-on-yourself game.

"What kind of game is that?" Rick inquired.

"We've all unknowingly played the game, and you'll soon know. So, the games begin, and keep in mind my mother doesn't say a word, but she knows it's game time, and my daddy initiates it."

He asks the first of many questions, "Nia, is there something you want to tell us?"

"About what daddy?"

He was really vague. "Oh, anything."

So, I looked from one to the other, and I gave my mother this please-help-me look, and she totally ignored it. So, I started thinking to myself and trying to remember if I'd done something which needed to be brought to their attention. I didn't even think about the eye rolling incident which occurred earlier because Ms. Lewis never said anything to me about it., I don't know what I'm supposed to tell you."

"Well, maybe I can refresh your memory baby girl."

"Uh...okay."

"Did you do something in school today you shouldn't have done?"

"Uh....well...I don't-"

"Something wrong with your memory baby girl?"

"No, sir. Today I was talking in class, Ms. Lewis asked me to be quiet and I rolled my eyes at her, and-"

"You rolled your eyes at her?"

"Yyyes sir," I replied with a shaky voice.

"You rolled the eyes God blessed you with?"

Again, I replied with my shaky voice, "Yyyes, sir."

"And you didn't think it was important enough to mention to your mother and I?"

"Well...."

"C'mon girl, speak up, we taught you better."

"No, sir, I didn't think it was important."

"Or is it because, you didn't think she'd call us, and you were trying to be slick?"

"No, sir....I wasn't trying to be slick."

"Well, what do you call it, because you had to know your mother and I would not approve?"

"Yes, sir, I knew you wouldn't approve, and although I wasn't trying to be slick, I didn't feel the need to mention what happened."

"Okay, I'll accept that, but you know you're going to be punished, so how would you like to be punished?"

"I can pick my own punishment?"

"If your mother and I feel it fits the crime, then yes, you can pick it."

I was happy to offer a suggestion, "Well...Alicia's having a party this weekend, and I really want to go, but I'll stay home. I think that's a fair punishment."

My daddy started laughing like Bernie Mac had just told the joke of his career. "Daddy, what's funny?"

"What's funny is, you roll your ten-year-old eyes at an authority figure, but you didn't feel the need to tell your parents, and then you stand here and tell me us not allowing you to go to Alicia's party is your punishment."

With a shaky voice, I said, "Well, yes, sir. You know how much I want to go to Licia's party, and if I can't go, it's punishment."

"Well, it's not satisfactory to your mother and I, but I'm sure we'll come up with something."

Teary eyed I said, "Okay. Daddy, may I go back to my room?"

"Yeah, baby girl, you can go back, your mother will call you when dinner is ready."

"Yes, sir." So I went back to my room and-

"And what happened?" Ray inquired.

"Well, when I arrived in my room, I couldn't concentrate on my Pre-Algebra homework. My only thoughts were of my pending punishment. It was evident my parents were going to torture me, and not tell me anything. The family sat down to a dinner of smothered fried chicken, mashed potatoes n' gravy and fried cabbage. It's wild because I can still remember what we ate, it's one meal I won't forget. After dinner, I cleaned the kitchen, and my parents allowed me to talk to Alicia. I knew I was going to get it because I was never allowed to use the phone when I was in trouble, but they allowed me to talk to one of my friends. As the night progressed, there was still nothing, so I went to sleep. It was a fitful sleep, but sleep, nonetheless. The next morning, I got up, showered, dressed, and ate breakfast with my family. Shortly thereafter, I prepared to leave for school.

My mother instructed me to bundle up, "Nia, it's cold outside so be sure to put your hat and mittens on."

"Yes, ma'am."

"Baby girl?"

95

"Yes, Daddy."

"Have a good day at school."

"I will Daddy, and I'm sorry for not telling you and mama about me rolling my eyes at Miss Lewis."

"It's okay baby girl, but don't let it happen again. Daddy loves you and I'll see you later."

"I love you too, Daddy, and I won't let it happen again."

I kissed them both goodbye and left so I could meet Alicia at our meeting spot. I met up with her, and of course she was interested in what my punishment would be.

"Hey, Nia."

"Hey, Licia." I replied sounding sad.

"What's wrong?"

"The stuff with Ms. Lewis, and my punishment."

"So, what did you choose for your punishment?"

"I suggested I not attend your party."

"What? You not come to my party? That's ridiculous. I can't have a party without you."

"Whoa! Slow down Alicia. Let me ex-"

"There's nothing to explain, me having a party without you is like Batman without Robin."

"I know but again, let me explain. I suggested it because I knew my parents wouldn't agree to it, and I was hoping they would just forget it."

"Well?"

"I think it may have worked."

"Why do you say that?"

"Well, neither of them said anything this morning. I apologized and my Daddy kissed and hugged me after telling me he loved me."

"So you think that's it?"

"Honestly Licia, I don't know, but I'm sure I'll find out in due time."

"Well, keep me posted."

"I'm sure you'll hear about it, if not from me, your parents will tell you."

We completed our walk to school, and around fourth period, I was called to the office. When I arrived at the office, I saw my father. For some reason, the theme to 'Shaft' began to play in my head. I don't know where that came from, or what it meant, but it continued to play, nonetheless. My father's face replaced Richard Roundtree's and I kept hearing "He's a bad mutha...shut yo mouth!"

"Hi, Daddy."

"Hey, baby-girl."

"Why are you here?"

"You'll see soon enough. Let's go to your class."

We proceeded to my class where everyone was in the middle of a reading assignment. A few heads popped up as we entered the room, but Ms. Lewis rules with a firm hand, so they knew to get back to their lesson. Ms. Lewis would call on us at any time, and she expected us to be able to pick up where the previous student left off. Ms. Lewis saw us enter and greeted my father.

"Hello Mr. Witherspoon."

"Ms. Lewis, as always it's a pleasure."

"Is there something I can help you with?"

"Yes, may I please see you in the hall?"

"Sure, class you can continue to read silently. Is Nia stepping into the hall with us?"

"No, she isn't. Baby girl, sit down in the chair next to Ms. Lewis' desk."

"Yes, sir."

I began to get nervous because I didn't know what was going on, but knowing Ralph Witherspoon, I'd know very soon. I sat for about five minutes, and then they re-entered the room. Ms. Lewis spoke first. "Class, Nia's father, Mr. Witherspoon would like to address the class so please extend him your undivided attention."

The class responded by saying, "Yes, ma`am'."

My father stood at the front of the class and began to speak.

"For those of you who don't know me. I'm Mr. Witherspoon, Nia's father. The other day I received a disturbing phone call from Ms. Lewis regarding Nia. Now, I know a lot of your parents because we attend the same church, so I know you all receive discipline at home. Being Nia's father, I know her mother and I have taught her right from wrong, and I assure you she's disciplined with a firm hand. So, it came as a shock to me when Ms. Lewis informed me my very well-mannered daughter rolled her ten-year-old eyes at Ms. Lewis, an authority figure, an adult, her teacher. Can you imagine my surprise? Nia knows better. I know it. Ms. Lewis knows it. Most importantly, Nia knows it." At this time, my classmates began to look at me. Some with sympathy, some with foolish grins, but Alicia, she looked at me with such sincerity. Now I realize the sincerity in her eyes was there because she knew my father. I mean she really knew him. She knew he didn't play. She knew he'd beat my ass in a heartbeat. Hell, in less than a heartbeat. I appreciated her empathy. That was the difference in her look, versus my other classmates. They sympathized with me. They may have taunted me if my father weren't there. That's what kids do at that age, although they know their parents would react the same way if they were the ones who had rolled their eyes. Licia empathized with me. He'd beat her ass a few times, so she felt my pain and truly understood my dilemma. My father continued his mini speech. "Nia's mother and I will not tolerate disrespectful behavior from our children, especially Nia because she's the oldest. Last night we gave her the option of choosing her own punishment, but we weren't satisfied with her suggestion. So, this morning we decided on her punishment. It wasn't easy because she's a daddy's girl and although I know raising her requires discipline, it's sometimes hard to reinforce. I'm sure your parents feel the same at times. Our decision was solely based on embarrassment. My wife and I were embarrassed when we received Ms. Lewis' call because again, Nia knows

97

better. So, as childish as this sounds, since she embarrassed us, we decided what's good for the goose, is also good for the gander."

Everyone in the class began to look at me and some of them began to snicker. Ms. Lewis quickly put an end to that. "Ladies and gentlemen, calm down or suffer the consequences." The class rapidly took heed because they knew Ms. Lewis was no joke. My father proceeded.

"This was a difficult decision for us, me more so than my wife because as I previously mentioned, Nia is a daddy's girl. Anyway, whenever she or her sister has done something that warrants punishment, my wife and I try to think of something they won't forget. So, since Miss Witherspoon embarrassed us, we figured if she received a spanking in front of her classmates, that would be the ultimate embarrassing moment for her. It would be a moment in her childhood she'd never forget."

My classmates began to stare at me, and I stared back with a smile on my face. It had to be evident I was in shock because my father had just announced to my entire class, he was going to beat my ass in front of all of them. I snapped out of it when Alicia looked at me with horror and empathy. I couldn't believe my parents had decided on me getting my ass beat as my punishment. Well, they wanted something I'd never forget. They succeeded. As if rehearsed, Ms. Lewis placed a chair at the front of the class. Tears began to roll down my cheeks like the water that runs down Niagara Falls, and the smile that seconds ago graced my face was quickly replaced with a solemn expression. Reality had sunk in. My father was about to beat my ass in front of my teacher, and my classmates. I wasn't really concerned about Alicia, because she'd witnessed the wrath of Mr. Witherspoon before, so this was nothing to her, but no one else knew what my father was capable of. Well, they were about to find out.

My father sat in the chair Ms. Lewis provided. He politely laid me across his lap, and he commenced to beating my ten-year-old ass. He labeled it as a spanking, but you all know that's a white term. Black parents didn't spank, they beat ass. I was too embarrassed to feel the pain but by the look on my classmate's faces, I knew the sight was horrific to them. In the sea of horrific faces there was an angel. My angel. God had blessed me with her, and I knew from that moment, Alicia Fox and I would always remain friends. When I saw her, she had tears in her eyes, and she mouthed the words 'It-will-be-okay'. I continued to look at her as I took my beating like a champ. By that point, my father had been beating my ass a good ten minutes. That's what my ten-year-old mind thought anyway. He'd only been at it two, maybe three minutes, but of course it felt like an eternity to me.

As if my father could read my mind, the torture finally ended. My father had completed what he came to do. His reason for stopping so soon, I don't know. Exhaustion? Sympathy? Empathy? Love? I didn't know and I really didn't care. I was just happy as hell he'd stopped. I stood up with a river of tears still in my eyes and I stared at Alicia. My friend. My angel. My rock. She was so many things to me. For all those things, I'd be forever grateful. She

98

stared back at me and rose out of her chair with her question asking hand up. Ms. Lewis acknowledged Alicia by asking her if there was something she needed. With tears in her eyes, she asked Ms. Lewis if she could ask my father a question.

Ms. Lewis quickly answered by saying, "Sure, as long as Mr. Witherspoon doesn't oppose."

"Of course, I don't, I love Alicia as if she were one of my own, " my father offered. Looking directly into Alicia's eyes, he asked, "What is it Alicia?"

Nervously stuttering Alicia answered with, "Mmm, Mmm, Mr. Witherspoon, is it okay if I take Nia into the restroom and help her clean herself up?"

My father looked at me, and then Ms. Lewis before he answered Alicia, "As long as it's okay with Ms. Lewis." All eyes were on Ms. Lewis, but she didn't hesitate when she said, "Sure you can, Alicia. It is sweet for you to offer, but I know how close you two are."

"Yes ma'am, we are close and thank you."

"You're welcome."

Alicia began her descent toward my desk, which was on the other side of the class. Ms. Lewis had separated our desks some time ago. On her way over, my father stopped her.

"Alicia, if you don't mind, please wait a minute."

"Of course, Mr. Witherspoon."

"I'd like to address the class again." Alicia returned to her desk. My father began with his boring ass never-disrespect-your-elders-stay-in-school lecture.

"I want you all to know Nia receives a lot of love from her family and we're a strong family unit with deep-rooted Christian values. As a matter of fact, discipline is a part of those values. The Bible clearly states sparing the rod will spoil the child. I will admit, spanking her in class was a little over the top but it was done for shock purposes. You all must respect and obey your elders. I know your parents have stressed this point to each of you. Ms. Lewis has a job to do and it's pertinent to your future. Therefore, it is always imperative you all respect her. I hope I won't have to revisit your class to inflict more discipline, but I will."

Everyone in the class looked at each other with fear in their eyes. My father made his mark. From that day on, everyone at Daniel Boone Elementary knew that Mr. Ralph Witherspoon was no joke.

He continued. "I know how kids are, especially the boys, but I'm going to ask something of you anyway. Please don't taunt Nia about what occurred today. I won't be held responsible for any of her actions. You all enjoy your day." Directing this comment to Alicia, he said, "You may now accompany Nia to the rest room."

Licia got up from her desk again, so I got up as well and began the long walk to the door. The room was so quiet you could hear a feather fall. I felt like Tupac because all eyes were on me. I was slightly embarrassed, nope

99

I can't lie, I was extremely embarrassed, but my parents raised me to be proud no matter what. So, I held my head high and with my tear ducts overflowing, I looked each of my classmates in their faces and smiled. Then I found the courage to look at my daddy. He also had tears in his eyes, but he smiled at me. I couldn't stay mad at him. I could only smile back. After all was said and done; he was my daddy, and I was a daddy's girl. He then mouthed I-love-you and I did the same. At the same time, my heart smiled. Everything would be all right. He had given me a lesson in respect, and I'd take heed.

After I finished telling my story, everyone was silent. Malik broke that silence.

"Nia, that was embarrassing, but we've all been there."

"Yeah, cause I could tell you a lot of shit that happened to me in my childhood, but it definitely makes you stronger," Ray offered.

"I agree but it was still embarrassing nonetheless."

"Do you all like rap?" Rick asked this question to change the subject. Alicia and I looked at each other as if to say. "Is he serious?" We masked our feelings, and Alicia replied, "As in music?"

"Well, I'm not talking about gift wrap."

As if we had rehearsed, Alicia and I said in unison, "Hell yeah, we grew up on rap."

I added, "We were in the seventh grade when Sugar Hill Gang's 'Rapper's Delight' came out, and Alicia and I would walk down the halls rapping along."

"And yes, we knew all the words, although Nia had a problem with the bang bang boogie line."

Malik said, "Not the, "To the bang bang boogie, say up jump the boogie, to the rhythm of the boogity beat."

"Yep, she messed that line up because she said it too fast."

"That may be true, but I got it together. I had it together so well when Sequence came out with 'Funk You Up', and they sang, 'We gon' funk you right on up, we gon' funk you right on up, I say get up, get up, get up, get up, get up, get up, get up, get up, get up, sit back down', I could sing right along with them. I knew all the words and didn't mess it up."

Ray said, "Today the kids know all the words to Drake, Jay Z, 50Cent and Gucci Mane."

"And every other rapper," Ray added.

Alicia was bopping her head like she was at a LL Cool J concert back in the day when she said, "Yeah, but the difference is our schoolwork wasn't a factor. It wasn't in jeopardy, like the children today. Some of today's children know the latest rap songs, but they can't break down a sentence or conjugate a verb."

"Enough of that, we could talk about our failing school systems as well as our failing children all night, but shit is depressing." This was Ray expressing his opinion of our conversation.

Rick said, "True dat. We are here to relax and have a good time, not talk about world events because that shit, doesn't coincide with fun."

"Let's not bring up the fact we're at odds with other countries, but isn't that the case whenever Republican are up in arms and not getting their way?" Malik asked.

"We are not going to talk about any of the depressing shit occurring in the world today," Mike stated.

As if we had practiced together, we said, "Agreed." With that said, the depressing subjects were laid to rest.

"So, Ray why did you ask about rap? You a rapper?" After asking Ray if he was a rapper, Alicia began to giggle like a hyena.

Ray being silly as well, replies, "Yep, did you see my video on YouTube?"

Shaking his head, Malik looked at Ray, then Alicia before he said, "A rapper! That nigga ain't no rapper, and he ain't got no rap."

"No rap! Ain't that a bitch. I go home to a woman; you go home to an empty ass king size bed."

"Nigga that's by choice."

"Whatever. All I know is most brothas would prefer to lay next to curves."

"That may be true, but some of the curves we lay next to are from a dog."

"How is a brotha who ain't had no coo-"

Mike quickly interjected, "Whoa, whoa. We need to send the conversation in a different direction. Let's go to Dreamz?"

I said, "Dreamz? What is that?"

Ray said, "A club here in Dallas. They play ol' school and new school, and it's a mature crowd."

Alicia said, "Mmm, I don't know. We don't do clubs in St. Louis."

Rick said, "Why is that?"

"We did the club thing all through our twenties, but we just stopped going out in our early 30's. Now, we're just in a chill mode."

Malik said, "We don't go out much, but we like this club because of the music they play."

"What kind of old school?" Alicia inquired.

"What kind of old school?" Malik asked as if we knew exactly what he was talking about when he opened his mouth.

"Yeah, what do you mean, old school?"

"I mean, old school like Vaughn, Mason & Crew."

Ray began to bop his head and snap his fingers, "Nigga, no you didn't go there. Bounce, Rocccccck, Skate, Roooooll, Bounce."

Alicia looked at me, "Nia, we haven't been out in a while and knowing us, we won't be going out anytime soon, so I think we should join the fellas."

"Yeah, okay, we can show them how to party STL style."

101

"What, don't you think brothas in Dallas can get their party on?
Laughing I added, "You all are going to show us how to line dance?"
Ray said, "You really got jokes, don't you? If you want to see how Texas men get their party on, follow us to the club."
"All right, we'll follow you but if they start clapping, line dancing, and yelling Hee-Haw! We're going back to our hotel."

Kickin' It Would be All Right.....Wouldn't It?

So, we decided to leave with the 'foolish foursome' and head to the club. Alicia and I were parked out front, so we waited until they pulled up to us and then we followed. Dreamz wasn't far from Sambuca's.
When we arrived, we valet parked and entered the club. The first song rumbling through my eardrums was "*The Show*" by Slick Rick and Dougie Fresh. I began doing the prep. "That's my jam."
Mike was also bopping his head when he invited me to party, "Well, let's not waste that energy, let's get on the dance floor."
"I can't pass up that invite, let's go." Looking over my shoulder, I looked back at the peanut gallery and said, "Find us somewhere to sit. Licia take my handbag for me please."
"No problem. Get your party on old school style."
We found a spot on the dance floor and began to get our groove on. We danced through '*The Show*', '*Paul Revere*' by the Beastie Boys, '*Dowhatchalike*' by Digital Underground and '*I'm Bad*' by LL Cool J. The deejay wasn't letting up, but he decided to slow it down. He played '*Fire & Desire*' by Rick James and Teena Marie. Mike and I made our way to the table.
As we approached, Alicia said, "Did you all get your party on or what?"
Mike and I looked at one another and replied together, "Hell yeah!"
Snapping his fingers and bopping his head, Mike said, "This music takes me back to middle school and high school."
"Like I said, rap is in our blood. We were raised on it," I reiterated.
Agreeing, Rick said, "I hear you."
Alicia stated, "It's funny some people think because we're professional women we're not supposed to like rap."
"Well, it's just wild to see sistahs rappin' along with artists like Eminem, DMX and Jay Z." Malik said.
Alicia said, "Why? Because they use profanity?"
"Well...to be honest, yeah." Malik said.
"Well, sistahs like the beat and sometimes we even like what they're saying."
"Is that right? Give me an example." Ray requested.
"An example of what?" Alicia said.

"A song where you like the lyrics, and another song where you like the beat." Ray said.

Preparing myself to answer his question, I took a sip of the frozen Midori sour Licia ordered for me and began to explain, "All right that should be pretty easy. I love *H.O.V.A.* by Jay Z. The beat is fierce."

"In my opinion, all of Jigga's shit is tight. Blueprint 3 isn't as good as Blueprint, but it's tight. The Black Album was good too," Ray informed us.

"I agree, Roc-A-Fella Records held it down. I remember when that nigga got a shoe endorsement deal with Reebok. The very first rapper to have a shoe deal." Rick said.

"I personally love the American Gangster album?" Mike asked.

"Yeah, the movie was tight too." Ray commented.

"I love him and Bey together," Rick said.

"They have a love jones for each other. I think they're good for each other," I stated.

"Straight power couple," Alicia stated.

"She's bad! The blonde hair looks good on her but it's not my thing," Rick commented.

"My boys and I like women who look like sistahs," Malik voiced.

"With a body like hers, Beyonce looks like no one but a black woman," I said.

"Yeah, the body is definitely a sistahs but what Ray meant is we like our women with their natural hair color, no hair weaves, and not a lot of make-up," Rick explained to us.

"Aw, so you all like your women au naturel?" Alicia wanted to know.

Looking directly at me Malik answered, "Yes, we do, women who look like you all."

Laughing I asked, "Really?"

The fellas all answered in unison with laughter, "Damn right!"

"Y'all silly, but back to Jigga. So proud of his grind. He's a multi-millionaire," Alicia inquired.

"Yep, brotha's grind is real," Ray announced.

"I agree, he's a great example of what hard work can achieve. I won't be surprised if he reaches billionaire status." Everyone shook their heads in agreement.

"Anyway, I love DMX; I'm a huge fan of his. I used to love Juvenile, but he wasn't talking about anything positive. Although the prayer DMX did on each of his albums was very positive. I know all rap doesn't have to be positive, but it seems like none of it is. That's one of the reasons I love rap from the late 80's to the early 2000's. Groups like Boogie Down Productions, Public Enemy and X-Clan all had something to say, and they said it to a good beat. X-Clan used a lot of George Clinton's music."

"Damn! You went way back! Malik, you remember that shit?" Rick asked.

103

"Damn right, to the east black wards sissy! Their beats always made me move," Malik informed us.

"True dat. X-Clan was on some serious shit, but KRS-One was my cat. Bruh kicked knowledge twenty-four-seven," Ray added.

"That's what I'm talking about. I like the rap today, but I also like the brothas who held it down while also sharing some knowledge", I stated.

"Nia, I agree with everything you've said but understand the rappers of the nineties and the new millennium rappers rap about shit they can relate to. Like-"

"Like bitches and hoes and-"

"Those are two examples, but they rap about the streets because that's what most of them know, and yes, terms like bitches and hoes happen to be a part of that. That's probably what they heard at home, and it's what they hear now," Malik informed us.

"I understand, really I do, and honestly, the bitches and hoes don't bother me because I know I'm neither, but it bothers a lot of women," Alicia offered.

"I'm in total agreement with you, but you can't please everybody all the time. There are going to be people who dislike what you do, with or without profanity, but as artists they must do what makes them happy," Mike indicated.

"Mike, I guess you're right because no matter how many people speak out against rappers, they're still going multi-platinum," I said.

Malik said, "All right, enough about those rich ass niggas, I wanna party."

At that moment the DJ began to play *Me and my Girlfriend'* by Jigga and I began to bop my head because that's my shit. "I loved the original version of this."

"Yeah Tupac's version was tight." Ray added.

"Since you like Jigga and this is obviously your jam, you wanna dance?" Malik asked.

"Oh yeah, let's go. Y'all need to get up and shake your ass before your old asses dry up."

"Don't worry Nia, Alicia and I are right behind you and Malik." Rick stated.

On the dance floor, we got our party on to *'Me and my Girlfriend'*, and the DJ gave us a double dose of Jigga. He played *'Jigga, Jigga....That Nigga Jigga!'* Mike and Ray found some sistahs to dance with and the party was on. He began to mix the old school with the new school. He blessed us with what in my opinion is the best R&B/Rap duo ever. That would be Method Man's sexy ass with Mary J. Singing *'You're all I Need.'* He also gave us some *'Southern Hospitality'* mixed in with *'Move Bitch'* and *'Stand Up'* by Ludacris who's one of my favorites. The DJ must've been inside my head because he was playing all my jams. Next through the speakers was DMX and Sisqo asking the question, *"What these bitches want?"* Yep, the DJ was clearly in my head. We stayed with the crowd, continuing to shake our asses, and enjoy ourselves. He then played one of Alicia's favorites from way back, *'I'm a Ho'* by Whodini.

"Aw shit, that's my cut." She announced it to everyone, as if I didn't already know. She threw her hands up and proceeded to shake her ass as if this would be her last time doing so. The DJ decided to slow it down, and we decided to sit it down. We made our way back to the table and Mike began asking all of us what we wanted to drink. Everyone except Ray and Alicia wanted water. Mike went in search of a waitress, while we cooled off at the table.

"Now that was cool. I haven't partied like that in a long time," I announced.

Wiping sweat from his forehead, Rick said, "Neither have I. That was all right. I'll be glad when Mike finds that waitress cause I'm thirsty as hell."

Malik had been searching the club for something or someone. Which I didn't know, and I didn't want him to know I'd noticed him looking around. Pointing across the room, Malik stated to Rick, "There he is, and he found the waitress. We should have our drinks shortly." I'd gotten my answer to the question of what or who Malik was looking for without any investigating. It's funny how you can meet someone and although you've only known them for a few hours, the chemistry is so strong it's as if you've known them for years. That is what was happening with Malik and I. How I wished I hadn't gone through what I'd just gone through with Ben. The chemistry I have with Malik is even stronger than what I had with Ben during our initial meeting, but the pain still lingered, and my shield of caution stood its ground like the American Troops during wars. I just couldn't go there, not right now. It was time to move on before the feelings began to grow and I couldn't walk away. Looking at my watch, I said, "Well, fellas it's two-fifteen and we have a nine o'clock flight. We need to pack and try and get some rest. We really need to leave."

Everyone looked at Malik, and he looked at me with this sad look in his eyes but said nothing. Mike took it upon himself to say something since Malik had chosen to be silent. "C'mon Nia, I know it's late but at least stay to have one last drink with us. The waitress is on her way over and I promise we'll drink fast." Holding his hands up with the scout sign, he said, "Scout's honor."

I looked at Alicia with my Is-this-all-right-look, and she replied by saying, "It's cool."
"All right fellas, one last drink and then we really have to leave."

The waitress arrived with our drinks, and the DJ began to play *'I'd Rather'* by Luther. I loved that song, and voiced my appreciation, "Oh, that is such a beautiful song, Malik would you like to dance?"

Without any hesitation, he said, "With you, of course I would." He stood up and held his hand out to me. I gently placed my hand in his and we glided to the dance floor. He took me in his arms, I placed my head on his chest, and we swayed to the music. It seemed to me his embrace was tighter, but it was okay because this time, I wanted to be held. Tightly. This would be our last time together. After playing one of Luther's jams, he decided to play

105

'*Whenever, Wherever*, Whatever' by Maxwell. Although, it was an older song, it was still the jam. It was evident either this was Malik's jam as well, or he really didn't want to let me go. We remained on the dance floor until Maxwell was done crooning' for us. After blessing us with his falsetto, we returned to the table. Everyone was quiet I guess because our great evening was about to end. I drank my glass of water and while doing so I'd decided there was no reason to prolong our good-bye.

The Departure

"Licia, are you ready?"

"If you are."

"Fellas we hate to cut out on you, but we really need to go."

Mike replied with, "We understand, and we've got to be going ourselves. Tomorrow is a workday." Everyone grabbed their belongings, and Malik grabbed my hand, but I never looked at him. I could feel his eyes on me. I know he wants my number, but I can't give it to him. The attraction is undeniable, but Ben is still a factor. Plus, I'm in my I'm-tired-of-black-men mode and would like to remain there for a little bit. I'm not ready to take the risk and/or gamble of being hurt again.

Lord knows I'd never allow a black man this fine, this intelligent, this successful and most importantly this into me, get away. He was undeniably a keeper, but I couldn't.

Right now, my frame of mind isn't where it should be to begin a relationship, and I know that's what Malik would eventually want.

So, the fellas walked us to our rental car. Malik never let go of my hand. I looked at my watch and was surprised by the time. It was two forty-seven. I hadn't seen this hour in a very long time, and I doubted I would see it again any time soon. Although the hour was obviously late, I can say I had a really good time.

"Well ladies, I hope you enjoyed your evening as well as your overall visit to Dallas. I know, I speak for the fellas when I say it was definitely a pleasure meeting both of you, and if you're ever in Dallas we must do this again," Mike stated.

Ray added, "Yeah, this was cool. It's seldom we meet down-to-earth women, most of the time they're stuck up."

"We definitely enjoyed ourselves and believe me when I say the pleasure was all ours," Alicia announced.

The entire time, Malik was still holding onto my hand. The fellas hugged Alicia, and then me. The fellas noticed Malik's reluctance to let go, so after they said their good-byes, they went to his vehicle. "Malik, I have your keys. We'll wait in the truck," Mike said.

"That's cool. I'll be there in a minute."

With that, the fellas left, and Alicia got into our rental car. There was a solemn look on his face when he asked, "So, I guess this is good-bye?"

"Yeah, I guess it is."

"I'd really like us to keep in touch."

Silence enveloped the moment. I didn't know what to say because as attracted as I am to him, I can't seem to forget or let go of what Mr. Jones had just taken me through. That damn song by Billy Paul kept going through my head, but of course I had changed the lyrics. "Me and Mr. Jones. Ain't got shit going on."

"Nia?"

"Huh..Oh I'm sorry. What did you say?"

With sincerity in his eyes, he said, "I asked if we could keep in touch?"

"Malik, I'm very attracted to you, I'd be lying' If I said I wasn't but I just got out of a bad relationship, and I'm just not ready for another."

"I'd like to be your friend. Can we be friends?"

"Malik, you and I both know you want more than friendship, but I can't give you what you want right now."

"Okay, you got me. I won't lie, I do want more, but I'm willing to accept your friendship."

"Honestly, I think we'd be good friends, but-"

"I know we'd be good friends."

"We agree on that, but the fact remains I just got out of a bad relationship and my feelings aren't resolved and because I am attracted to you, a simple friendship would not work."

"So, when you say your feelings aren't resolved so you're considering reconciling?"

I looked at him as if he'd lost his mind.

"Why are you looking at me like that?"

Shaking my head, I replied, "I'm looking at you like you're crazy because you must be. To answer your question, Hell to the No! It's not just no, but hell no to the tenth power. I know beyond a shadow of a doubt I don't want to be with him, but it doesn't mean my feelings are resolved."

"I understand what you're saying, but I just want to be your friend."

Laughing, I said, "You lie."

"I guess you're right, but what's a brotha to do? I'm not the one to feed a sistahs ego, but I very seldom come across ladies of your caliber."

"Thank you for the compliment although I know there are some ladies in Dallas with the same if not better qualities than what I possess."

"That may be true, but I haven't run across any."

"I'm not going to argue the point, but a friendship wouldn't be fair to you."

"Shouldn't I be the judge of that?"

"I guess so...maybe...but I wouldn't feel right since I know what you want."

"Why not?"

"The first reason is that I will never knowingly lead someone on. It's not right and it's not me. Secondly, although I'm not getting back with him, I need to resolve my feelings. There's nothing worse than someone with too much baggage. That shit can get to be too heavy."

"Okay, I can respect that."

"Thank you for not trying to pressure me, most men would."

"It's cool. I'd like to give you my number, and although you probably won't use it, I'd like you to have it just in case."

"Just in case?"

Laughing he said, "Yeah, like insurance. You get it just in case something happens. I want to give you my number just in case you want to call."

Joining in on his laughter, I said, "That's original. I won't make any promises, but I'll accept your number, just in case."

"That's cool."

He found a small piece of paper in his wallet and wrote his number on it. As he handed me the piece of paper, he held onto my hand. I slowly lifted my eyes and in doing so, I could see the look he was giving me. It was so intense and sincere it melted my heart.

"What?"

"What?"

"Why are you looking at me like that?"

"Like what?"

"Like I'm a lollipop waiting to be licked."

Laughing he said, "Guilty as charged."

"And you want us to be friends?"

"You're right. I'll stop."

"Remember you said no pressure."

"I did, didn't I?"

"Yes, so stop."

"Other than the lollipop comment, what did I do?"

"You keep looking at me with those eyes."

"I'm sorry, but I can't get another set of eyes and as for looking at you, I can't help it."

"You can't help it? What does that mean and before you explain, please don't give me a line about me being so beautiful you can't help but stare. I know-"

"Well since-"

"No, let me finish."

"Okay but I will have my say."

"Somehow I don't doubt that."

"Exactly. As the old adage says, "Ladies first."

"To my parents and friends, I'm beautiful but they know me inside and out. Brothas are so shallow because the exterior is all that matters."

"That's not-"

108

"It's still my turn, Mr. Black."

"You're right, I'm sorry."

"Now would you still call me beautiful without any make up, in a pair of sweats with holes in them with a raggedy tee shirt on? Or better yet, would I be beautiful in my flannel pj's with my hair wrapped and a hair net on? Probably not. Brothas expect sistahs to always look glamorous and that's not reality."

There was silence for about twenty seconds. I assumed maybe Malik didn't know I was done. "Malik, I'm done." The silence stayed like a nagging headache. I pressed on, "What, cat got your tongue?"

"No, I'm just getting my thoughts together."

"That's good because-"

"I know if I said the wrong thing, you'd get with me."

"You know it."

"Okay, let me start by saying I have always been a good judge of character, and although physical beauty is important-"

"I told you."

"Hey, I'm just keepin' it real. Initially I don't know you as a person, but there needs to be something that attracts me but also understand physical beauty means absolutely nothing without inner beauty.

"Yeah whateva! That's what all men say."

"Miss Witherspoon, you've had your say so-"

"Okay, okay. I apologize for the interruption. Go ahead and finish." I replied while impatiently tapping my foot.

"Thank you, ma'am. As I was saying...(clearing his throat) I think you're probably as beautiful inside as you are outside. If given the opportunity, I'd like to find out if my assumption is correct. Before you say anything, I know you hear this from other men, but I can only prove I'm different if given the chance. I am tired. Tired of superficial beautiful sistahs who don't have a brain or a personality. I want a woman who is first and foremost God fearing, intelligent, independent, ambitious and if she happens to be beautiful, I won't complain, but I-"

Sarcastically, I commented, "Oh, it's okay if she's beautiful?"

"Nia, understand me and what I'm about to say. I'll date a woman who isn't beautiful if she possesses all the qualities I'm looking for in a woman. No, she can't have a third eye in the middle of her forehead or be toothless, but she doesn't have to be as beautiful as you either."

"Is that right?" I was blushing like a schoolgirl.

"Yeah, that's right. You see, you've been blessed with the whole package, and everyone isn't as blessed. There are some with exterior beauty, but their personality is foul. Then there are those who have great personalities but they're hard on the eyes."

"So, are you insinuating I possess both?"

"Yes, that's what I'm saying or should I say assuming. From what I've seen tonight, I know I want to see if my assumptions are correct."

"I'm just not ready for this."

"I understand but let me just leave you with this."

"And what's that?"

"Very seldom will we meet someone with the chemistry you and I had tonight. Sure, we've met and will meet people we're attracted to but nothing this strong. The chemistry between us is deep and strong. So much so, it's scary. I'll admit because I've never been this drawn to anyone, and I have a feeling neither have you. You can deny it if you want, but if you really think about it, you'll agree with me."

"I'll think about everything you've said tonight and just in case, I have the insurance you provided me with, and I can call you."

"I'd like that."

"Well Mr. Black, I'm tired and our friends are waiting on us."

"Yes, I guess they are. I just hate to see you go."

"Look at it this way, if it's meant for us to see one another again, we will."

"I can live with that. I guess I have no choice. If, or should I say when we see one another again, I guess fate will be our guide."

"I guess so Mr. Black."

"Well, can I get a hug?"

"Of course." At that time, he stepped forward and we embraced. For a long time, we held one another. Our bodies fit together like a jigsaw puzzle. Neither of us wanted to let go, but we both knew we had to. Surprisingly, he was the one to relent first, but he continued to hold my hands. I looked into his eyes, and I could see his yearning. I wondered if my eyes reflected the same yearning because I did want him. He leaned forward and kissed me on my cheek. "I hope I wasn't out of line."

"For what?"

"Kissing you on the cheek."

Yawning I said "Naw, it's cool."

"Well, I see you're tired, so I'll let you go."

Yawning again I replied, "Thank you and I'm sorry for all the yawning."

"It's okay. I know you're tired."

"I am, but I have to say this."

"What's that?"

"No matter what happens between us, I want you to know I'm glad we met. Under different circumstances, I'd be willing to put forth the effort a relationship requires, but right now I can't. I want to but I can't, and I need you to understand that."

"Believe it or not, I do understand."

"Also know it's not you, it's me."

"I know the scenario."

"And what's that?"

"Bad man, your ex, messes it up for the good man, me."

"Unfortunately, that's true and I wish things were different, but they aren't."

"Nia, I could talk to you all night, but I know you need your rest."

"I appreciate that. So, I guess I'll see you later, if fate chooses that route."

While still holding hands, he leaned in and gave me a brief, but endearing hug. He also kissed my forehead. "I hope to talk to you soon. You and Alicia have a safe trip back to St. Louis."

"I'm sure we will and Malik."

"Yes?"

"Take good care of yourself."

"I will, and you do the same." I got into the rental with Alicia and before I could start the car, there was a tapping on the car window. I started the engine so I could let the window down. "Yes, Malik?"

"Do you need directions to your hotel?"

"No, the concierge gave them to me, but thank you for offering."

"Okay, I just didn't want you all getting lost at this late hour."

"Again, thank you for your concern, but we'll be fine."

"Okay, be safe."

"You too."

I let the window up, waved good-bye and pulled off. As I looked in the rear-view mirror, I could see Malik walking his sexy bow-legged ass to his SUV. Mmmm...Mmmm...Mmmm....It's not going to be easy to forget him. As I run my fingers over the piece of paper, he wrote his number on, I'm contemplating if I even want to try to forget him. Mr. Black has absolutely made an impression on me.

Nia

When I got into the car, I was extremely quiet. There was a lot going through my head, but I knew I'd have to have this conversation with Alicia. It was inevitable.

"So, girl what was he talking about?" Silence encompassed the car. I guess I was in another world because I didn't hear Alicia. She hates to be ignored, so of course she repeated herself. "Nia, what was he talking about?" Before I could answer, her frustration took over. "Damn girl, don't you hear me talking to you? Are you ignoring me?"

"Huh...No, girl. I am not ignoring you, I just-"

"You just what?"

"Nothing, never mind."

"Never mind what?"

"Nothing at all."

"Are you going to tell me what he was talking about?"

111

"Yeah, sure, I'll tell you," But I didn't say anything. My mind was reeling, and as strange as it may sound, there was a funny feeling in my heart. I didn't know what was going on.

"Nia, snap out of it. Tell me what he said."

"You are really getting on my nerves."

"What's new?"

"You're right. Anyway, he talked about the usual."

"Don't play with me."

"Play with you how?"

"You better tell me what he said."

"Girl, get your panties out your ass. I'm going to tell you, but-."

"It's about time."

"Let me finish. Can I tell you tomorrow? It's late and I'm tired."

"I'm tired too, but you better give up the details. Now!"

"Damn Licia! You need some dick in your life, that's what you need, dick in your life."

"And why is that?"

"Cause you ain't had none in six months."

"By choice."

"Choice, huh? Well, you need to choose some dick."

"I'm cool."

"No, you're not cause you're all up in mine. Not getting any may be by choice but women have needs. And for the record, you trying to vicariously live through my love life is tiresome."

She began laughing like a hyena while I'm trying to remember how to get back to the hotel. "What the hell is so funny?"

"Your vicarious ass! I can question your love life and anything else, that's what friends are for. You better tell me what fine ass Malik said."

I couldn't help but to join in on her laughter, "Your ass is so pathetic, you know that?"

"Yeah, whatever! You've been putting up with my pathetic ass for the last thirty years, so give it up!"

"Okay, okay. Basically, he asked if we could keep in touch and-"

Cutting me off completely, "And what did your pitiful ass say?"

"If you allow me to finish, I can tell you."

"All right. I'll be quiet."

"I doubt that, but anyway, he asked me if we could keep in touch."

"Well, what did you say?"

"Girl, you are something else."

"Is that right?"

"And you know it. As I was saying, I briefly explained to Malik without going into too much detail, the situation with sorry ass."

"So, in other words you told him you all couldn't keep in touch?"

"What do you think Alicia? I just got out of a relationship!"

"Nia, I understand your pain, but I also know men like Malik are rare."

With a lot of reluctance, I said, "I know Licia, but I can't."

"Sweetie, I know it's hard and I know you're hurting but men like Malik are so hard to come by. I think you should reconsider."

"Licia, just drop the subject. I don't want to talk about it. It's my problem and I'll deal with it." We continued our drive to the hotel in silence. Alicia eventually drifted off to sleep, but only for a few minutes. She woke up and I knew she'd start in on me again.

"I fell asleep for a short time, but you know I'm not done."

Sighing, "I know, so speak your peace."

"Why won't you at least try? If it works, fine, if it doesn't then close the chapter and move on."

"Hello? Didn't I just get out of a relationship?"

"Yeah. And?"

"And? Hell, that should be enough."

"Okay, but you could've explained to him what was going on. He may be willing to wait."

"I couldn't ask him to do that."

"He's grown, it would've been his choice."

"I did tell him, and he still wanted to try, but damn! I'm scared."

"Of what?"

"No you didn't just ask me that dumb ass question, but I'll answer it anyway. I don't know if my heart can take another blow."

"Baby, I know you don't want to go through-"

"Then why can't you drop it?"

"Because I can't. God will never give us something we can't handle, and you know this. You're stronger than you think you are."

"I know and I appreciate your effort, but knowing my strength doesn't ease my pain. Yes, I know I'll get through it and over it. Yes, I know I'll love again, but right now the pain is fresh. As fresh as the collard greens in your mother's garden."

"I understand."

"In fact, you don't. Only God and I really know how I feel and how much pain I've endured."

"Okay, that's fair. Why didn't you just tell Malik you needed time?"

"Number one, I just met him and therefore I don't really know him. I don't owe him anything, especially an explanation. Secondly, he doesn't need to get personal with me."

"Nia, I'll leave it alone after I say this."

"Yeah right, but what is it?"

"I will not be the one to say I-told-you-so when he slips through your fingers."

"Licia, let me explain something to you. If that happens, then so be it. If it's meant for us to see each other or, begin a relationship, then it will happen. It's called fate for your information."

113

Laughing. "Girl, I know what it's called, and I believe in it, but I also believe when a situation like this arises, one must act on it."

"Well if I miss out, then that's life. Cest la vie!"

"Sometimes I can't stand you with your nonchalant attitude."

"Girl, it's me. You know this and should be accustomed to my ways."

"I'm accustomed, doesn't mean I agree or like it. I accept you as you are because I love you and you're my girl."

"If that's the case and I know it is, please do not wig out on me regarding Malik Black."

"Okay, I'm done."

"I doubt that."

"Well, I'm done for now."

"Now, that's more like it."

Malik

I was tired, stressed and somewhat depressed when I climbed into my truck with the fellas. I knew they'd be ready to question me, and I wouldn't be able to hide my disappointment. I've known my boys most of my life and I can't lie to them. They would see straight through it. If I remain quiet, I can possibly miss out on the Q & A session. I was silent as I started my vehicle and pulled off. I could tell there was something holding Nia back from me, and I kinda figured it was some tired ass nigga that is now her ex. Her ex obviously didn't know a good thing when she was naked in front of him. What I can't understand is if he's her ex and she doesn't want to reconcile, why won't she give me a chance? I didn't dog her, he did! I'll admit, in my former life, I was that same kinda dude, but I grew up. My father raised a man, not a boy. I'd also realized I'd messed over too many women and as the saying goes, "What goes around....well, I'm sure you know the rest, and eventually I knew I'd want to settle down. Monogamy was difficult to achieve, especially with the ratio of men to women, but I was faithful to my ex. She was the unfaithful one, but I was overdue. Like I said, "What goes around....

Nia's in a class by herself. I recognize I want a woman like her. I don't care about the miles separating us, all I know is I want Miss Witherspoon. And what Malik wants, Malik gets.

"Malik, what's up?" Mike inquired. I knew I couldn't hold off the inquisition for long. Before I could answer Mike and Rick asked, "Yeah nigga, did she give up the digits?"

"Yeah, did she give up-" Ray

Solemnly, I replied, "Naw."

"I know she gave em' up, Malik's the charming one. Wait a minute. Did you just say no?" Ray asked.

"Yeah, that's what I said."

"What the hell? All of us could feel the chemistry, so what the fuck happened?" Mike wanted to know.

"A game-playin'-lying-still-a-boy-not-quite-a-man-cheatin' ass nigga is what happened."

"Aw, so she's got baggage?" Mike questioned.

"And not just a few pieces, but an entire set." Ray stated.

"A set of Louis Vuitton at that, not just any ol' luggage." Rick added.

"Sistahs do have baggage but hell, so do we." Mike stated matter of factly.

"Mike that may be true, but we check ours," Ray communicated,

"Not all brothas. Not every time." Mike said.

"Well, to speak up for sistahs, I think they have so much baggage they can't let go of all of it. Sistahs have to deal with cheating more than men. I think it would be hard for me if I constantly had to deal with the same bullshit over and over."

"You've got a point, but just because her loser ex did her wrong doesn't mean you're going to mistreat her," Ray said.

"Yeah, she doesn't know you well enough to assume you won't treat her right. Southern men are from a different breed than those clowns she's obviously dealt with," Mike expressed.

"True dat, but can you blame a sistah for being reluctant? I mean look at it, she's probably our age, probably been dating for the last sixteen to eighteen years and probably been cheated on at least six to seven times. Man, you know women. Sex for them is emotional, but for us it's a N-U-T. Nothing more, nothing less!" I explained.

"Damn Malik! You wanna get with her or join her crusade? Sounds like the latter to me," Ray joked.

"You all are my boys, so let me keep it real with you."

"Yeah, you do that," Mike stated.

"We're all aware of the shit Melina did and-"

"Malik, I still don't see the problem with that, you should've just joined the party," Rick's freaky ass commented.

"Nigga, fuck you, I ain't into the menage a' trois thing. I want my lady to myself."

Laughing Rick asked, "What about Kim, and Delinda?"

"Kim and Delinda? Man, you mean freshmen year in college? Those two freaks gave it up to every brown brotha on campus: African-American, Puerto-Rican, and Mexican. They probably fucked some white boys too."

Still laughing Rick reiterated, "Man the point is, you had sex with two women at one time and that's a menage a' trois, college or not. Melina offered that shit on a silver platter, but you chose to ignore it."

"Hell yeah, I chose to ignore it. I'm forty and not just looking for pussy. I want a meaningful relationship. I want the shit my parents have. It's time to settle down and bonin' two women, at one time is not my idea of settling down. Melina knew what I wanted, but she disregarded my feelings. She claims she was curious, but she was in a committed relationship. If she was curious, she should've shown me respect and ended what we had."

Ray added, "Bruh understand, most sistahs who go both ways assume we're down for it because most of the time we are. I'm sure Melina didn't think her actions would warrant your breakup."

"You know what? She literally said the exact thing. In my opinion, I couldn't stay with her. She broke our commitment, which made it easier to break up with her. I needed something, and her infidelity was my way out. It was the straw that broke the camel's back."

"No one knows what you can put up with better than you. We all have different tolerance levels and yours was apparently at the limit," Mike offered.

"I really appreciate you understanding."

"We're your boys, it's our duty to be there for you and we'll do that 'til the day we die," Ray offered emphatically.

A chorus of "yeah mans" followed from everyone else. I continued to drive hoping the conversation would not get back to Nia, but of course I wouldn't be so lucky. Rick made sure of that. "So, what are you going to do about Nia?"

"What can I do? Do you all have any suggestions?"

"I suggest you go after her," Ray stated.

"And how do you propose I do that?"

"We need to come up with a game plan cause it's obvious like Usher, you got it bad," Mike said.

"As much as I want her, and believe me I do want her, she's made it clear she's not ready for what I want. On the other hand, I understand her pain. She didn't come right out and say it, but I got the feeling she just broke up with him, like within the last few days. Like I said, I want her but when I get her, I want her to have feelings for me and me alone."

"I see your point man, but what if you don't see her again? Then what?" Mike's inquiring ass wanted to know.

"Well, that's the chance I'm willing to take, but as strong as our chemistry was, I think I will see her again. Our meeting was fate."

"Nigga whateva! Fate is seldom on a black man's side, you better keep that in mind," Rick reminded me.

"Fate? You meet a beautiful woman with big round breasts and you're talking that fate shit," Ray laughed.

"Man, she is fine, but she ain't got no ass!" Mike shared his observation.

"Nigga, I got eyes. I do like a fat ass-"

Cutting me off to list his favorite asses was Ray, "Like fine ass Sheree Whitfield, Kenya Moore, Sanaa Lathan and Beyonce. Just to name a few."

"What about J-Lo?" Rick inquired.

"What about her?" Mike asked.

Rick was voicing his appreciation of Jennifer Lopez, "Last time I looked she had a fat ass."

Mike had other thoughts and he voiced them, "J-Lo's ass is cool but, in my opinion, everyone is only making the hoopla over her ass because she's

116

not a black woman. Hell, black women have had asses like that and better since the beginning of time. Look at Trina. Now that's an ass sculpted by God."

"As I was saying, I like a fat ass but I'm looking for more. I want a woman with real substance and Nia appears to have that. Because she seems to have the other characteristics that I want, I'm willing to overlook the flat ass."

"If you say so. That's on you, but a fat ass is a prerequisite. As for this fate issue, good luck." Ray said.

"Bruh that's what you don't understand, I don't need luck, I've got fate."

"If you say so," replied Rick.

"You niggas will see. Fate is on my side and with that said, this conversation is over."

Nia

By the time we arrived at the hotel, it was approximately three twenty-five. Alicia was fast asleep after holding her inquisition. I pulled into valet parking. While waiting on an attendant, I woke Alicia up by nudging her shoulder. "Licia, wake up." I had to nudge her again. "Licia, get up we're here."

Slowly she woke up, "Nia, I'm sorry I fell asleep, but I'm sleepier than I thought."

"It's cool, but I'm not sleepy at all."

Wearing a funny smirk Alicia asked with sarcasm, "Why is that?" Grabbing my handbag to retrieve money to tip the attendant, I answered, "I have a lot on my mind."

"I'm sure Malik, I mean a lot is on your mind."

"Alicia-" Just then the valet attendant arrived, I tipped him, and we exited the car to enter the hotel. I continued talking to Alicia, "As I was saying, I have a lot on my mind. I came to Dallas on business, not to meet anyone."

"I understand that, but-"

"No, you don't Licia. You and Tony had a mutual breakup and you're still friends. Ben and I broke up because that muthafucka cheated on me. In other words, he endangered my health and my life. AIDS is real in the African American community and no matter what he tried to tell me; I know he fucked that bitch without a condom. Nia Witherspoon may be a lot of things, but stupid ain't one of em."

"Nia, I didn't mean-"

"Licia, it's okay. I know you have my best interest at heart, and you think Malik would be good for me. You know what?"

Pushing the up button on the elevator "What's that?"

"Your assumption may be correct about Malik, but I can't. I just can't. I wish I could, but I can't."

"Okay Nia, I'm going to drop the subject."

"Thank you for understanding."

117

"I don't understand but I'm your girl and I can't make you do anything you don't want to do."

Stepping off the elevator, "Well whatever the reason, thank you." Before Licia could do more talking, I walked in the direction of our rooms. It was three thirty-five and our flight was due to leave at nine a.m. "Good night Licia, I'll call you at six. We need to leave no later than six forty-five, so if you feel up to it, get your stuff ready tonight."

"All right girl, good night."

When I arrived in my room, I wasn't sleepy at all, so I packed my clothes and took a shower. I began to reminisce about our evening and all I could think of was Malik Black and Ben Jones. Had I never met Ben's pitiful ass, I'd be more receptive to Malik. Damn! Damn! Damn! I can't erase my past because if I could Ben would be no part of it. I'm a firm believer in things happening for a reason. Everything went down between Ben, and it was supposed to happen just the way it did. I don't know anything personal about Malik. I tried to keep the conversation as general as possible. I'd succeeded. I can look at him and know he's got it going on, but when Alicia mentioned it and harassed me about it only confirmed what I knew was true. I may have let a good one get away. Oh well, I must live with my decision. I mean the brotha had on Gucci loafers. Since I like nice things, I noticed. Don't get me wrong I know just as the Lord giveth, He will taketh away. I like nice things, but I don't idolize them. God is first and foremost in my life, but for a man to put care into his appearance says a lot about himself.

Anyway, I like a man who appreciates nice things and can purchase them, for himself. Ben appreciated nice things, but his ass didn't want to work for them. He'd rather have somebody buy them for him. He thinks that someone owes him something. Thinking about it, I think I do owe him something. A good ol' ass kicking, but he's not even worth the effort.

Malik on the other hand appears to have money, but that means nothing. Black folk are good at appearing this way or that way but being broke as hell. I know I've been there. Perpetrator. I just want a man with his own stuff. What did Billie Holiday say, "God bless the child that's got its own." I'm tired of taking care of Negroes. Beyonce and her crew sang about independent women, but they should've been singing about independent men. Singing about somebody throwing their damn hands up. These men need to throw their hands in their pockets and try to line their wallets. Truth be told, the independent men need to throw their hands up so the independent women won't have such a hard time finding them. It's like trying to find a brotha or sistah at a Metallica concert. They may be there, but they're hard as hell to find. A needle in a damn haystack.

I know, I'm talking about finding a man, but turning away what could be a good one. I can be honest, I'm scared. I know life's a gamble and so is love. You must be willing to put forth an effort, but right now I'm not. Why couldn't I meet Malik first? For some reason, I had to meet Ben's trifling ass first, but it was obviously God's plan. I realize God brought him into my life for a reason. I honestly believe God's reason was to show me the kind of man I don't want. Everyone comes into our lives for a reason, sometimes a season. There are always lessons to be learned. It's up to us to accept the lesson and after acceptance comes understanding. Nia Witherspoon took heed; I got the message. He brought Ben into my life but, He also brought Malik into my life. We didn't cross paths by coincidence. Although I feel God has a plan, there's a lot of resistance on my part. I know it has a lot to do with my recent break up with Ben as well as my existing insecurities and fears. Starting over is another reason. I'm tired of the cycle. To me, it's the worst thing about dating. You meet someone. There's mutual attraction. You start to spend time together. Sex may or may not be discussed. When you're both in agreement, you begin to develop a sexual relationship. You're both tested for HIV. The results. Negative. The relationship has progressed to the next level. Things go well for one, two, maybe even three years. Then the inevitable occurs, you fuck up. He fucks up. Or. You both decide the relationship is not progressing the way either of you would like it to. Sistahs may not blame the brotha but more often than not, she feels as if she's put more into the relationship. Giving is a woman's nature. When we're really diggin' our guy, we give. Time. Money. Our bodies. We give. Whatever it takes to maintain the relationship. That's just what we do.

Well, I guess that's enough about Malik, I gotta try and get some sleep. Sleep was not coming easily. I even tried counting shit, but nothing was doing the trick. Counting sheep. Counting Gucci bags. Counting whatever I could to get my mind off a certain someone. Nothing was helping. The sheep I was counting all had Malik's face. I even counted dicks but that made me horny. I stopped counting and allowed my thoughts to do as they pleased. Suffice it to say; I got no sleep. No sleep at all.

The Morning After

Six in the morning came as fast as a tornado. I called Alicia and surprisingly she was up. The shuttle was due to take us to the airport at seven, so we agreed to meet in the hallway at six forty-five. I'd arranged to have the rental picked up from the hotel.

After wrapping up my conversation with Alicia, I sat up in the bed. On the nightstand was his number. I picked the piece of paper up and ran my fingers over it. While my mind lingered on the night I'd spent with him, I picked the phone up and began dialing his number and after four digits, I hung up. I couldn't do it. I wanted to, but the bars around my heart wouldn't loosen. I was being held captive by fear.

Nia

After meeting Malik in Dallas and returning to St. Louis, my life returned to some normalcy. Whatever normal is. After meeting Mr. Black, I knew my life wouldn't be the same. He was worth the gamble. Wasn't he? So why wasn't I willing to place my bet? Isn't that what life and love are? Aren't they both gambles? In life, tomorrow isn't promised, but we get up every day and live our lives. In love, it's never guaranteed, but we, men, and women, yearn for it. My girls and I want to get married, although the divorce statistics are outrageous. It's all a gamble. There's a fifty-fifty chance it will or won't work, but you never know unless you try. Normally I try, and try again, but I'm tired. There's no need in listing what I'm tired of because I'm sure most single women are tired of the same things. I'm also sure although we normally try repeatedly, fear finally creeps into our inner being. This fear causes us to erect walls. Walls that protect us. Walls we think will protect us anyway.

After arriving home and gaining the normalcy I just talked about, I hooked up with Jake and we headed to Plaza Motors. That's the luxury car dealership in St. Louis. Jake promised to accompany me to ensure that I got a good deal on the car I wanted. I'd decided to give my cousin Jenise the Honda. It would be a surprise for her. She was enrolled in Washington University's Pre-med program. She's done well in school, and she'd made it through without any pregnancy scares. I wanted her to have reliable transportation. Although we were cousins, I treated her like my little sister. Anyway, we left Plaza Motors about three hours later and I was the proud owner of a two thousand eighteen Mercedes Benz E450. She was beautiful. She was a deep navy blue with peanut butter interior. It had all the standard Benz features which included supple leather seats with seat warmers and coolers, a sunroof, premium stereo system, wood grain and a navigation system.

As for Ben, his crazy ass was still crazy. Calling me at home, on my cell, and at the office. You'd think he'd be tired of me hanging up on him. The Negro even had the nerve to call Diane Witherspoon's house. My mama. Yes, he went there, or tried to. He won't be revisiting that option again. My mother informed him that in no uncertain terms should he ever call her home looking for me. He was calling twenty-four seven like my house was 7-11. Always open for service. He was begging like Keith Sweat. Me? I was ignoring him. Ignoring him like the SARS epidemic and I was vacationing in China. I didn't want to hear anything he had to say. What he said came across loud and clear in front of ol' girl's house. Not only did I hear it, but I also understood it. He was a part of my past and that's where I wanted him to stay.

Malik on the other hand, popped into my thoughts constantly. I had fingered the sheet of paper that he wrote his numbers on while contemplating if I was going to call him. Deep down I knew I wasn't going to call him, but I wanted to. Damn, how I wanted to.

His face kept appearing in my dreams as well as my thoughts. And to think I thought this would be easy. I honestly thought when I said, "good-bye" outside of Dreamz that would be it. Boy, was I wrong. It's so evident to me now how strong our chemistry was. The fact that I'm thinking about a man I spent approximately four hours with, is evident of my interest. Two hundred and forty minutes and I'm thinking about him like we spent years, months, and days together. I think about him more than I think about Ben. I need to shake this off because I'm not calling him and therefore, I won't be seeing him. That's my final decision.

Post Nia

When my night with Nia ended, as crazy as it sounds, I was depressed. I was depressed over a woman I'd just met. She walked into my life and out of my life, all within a matter of hours.
I had a strong inkling we'd see one another again. I don't why I felt that way because she gave no indication, we'd be seeing each other. I guess it was my wishful thinking.
Nia Witherspoon had me second-guessing myself. Sistahs wanted a good man. Didn't they? I'm a good man. Aren't I? I'm not arrogant but I was aware of my assets. First and foremost, I love God and I keep Him first. I'm ambitious, hardworking, loyal, well groomed, a dapper dresser and a bruh's not too hard on the eyes. My most significant asset other than loving God is the fact that I'm settled and therefore I'm a one-woman-man.
Even with the second-guessing, my heart and mind tell me our meeting wasn't by chance. Fate had her hand in it. She was unquestionably involved in our meeting.

The fellas sensed my depression, but nothing they did changed my mood. They attempted to hook me up with different women, but I wasn't interested. I didn't want to hang out. I wanted to be by myself. Nothing could bring me out of this funk, nothing except Miss Witherspoon that is. Every day was the same. I hit the gym at five and worked out until six. I showered there, stopped every morning for coffee and a Danish at the local Starbucks and arrived in the office by seven. I began work at seven and my day was done by seven. I was the first in the office and the last to leave. I'd informed my secretary, Tanisha, to only pass through important calls. I'd given her a list and the list included my parents, any significant business associates, the fellas and of course Nia was on the list. Everyone on the list had called. Everyone except Nia. She didn't offer her number. The way we were vibin' she knew if she offered her digits, I would've used them, and she's scared. Scared because she was interested in me as well. Scared because my vibe was so strong, I knew deep down, she knew if given the chance, I'd treat her in the manner she deserves. She was scared to open and try again. In lieu of trying she opted to run away.

121

I'd once read an article in *Essence* Magazine which discussed black women and their low self-esteem. It talked about those with low self-esteem accepting a man respecting them. After being mistreated time and time again, some would sometimes shy away from a king treating her like a queen. I think that may be the case with Nia. I understand her reluctance, but you never know unless you try. I'm really trying to forget her, but it's not working. I keep myself busy, but it never fails. She occupies twenty-five percent of my days and the percentage increases during the weekend. I guess it didn't help I was spending my weekends watching every decent African American romantic comedy; 'Love Jones', 'Two Can Play that Game', 'Brown Sugar', 'Best Man' and 'Love & Basketball'. Nia Witherspoon. She was a character in all of them. My boys really thought I was trippin' and I guess some of it is due to the fact I'm used to getting what I want. I really want Nia, but unlike a lot of women I've dealt with in the past, she's not easy. Not in any sense of the word. There is life after Nia Witherspoon. I wanted her to be a part of my life but I'm strong. I will be all right and I still have my money on fate. Life until then would have to go back to normal. Whatever that is.

I-Need-Some

Malik was still on my mind. All the time. I couldn't shake it, but I ain't calling. Ben had been calling and pleading for the last month. I'd even received tulips on six different occasions. He was really getting on my nerves. He couldn't call and say he left something at the house because I made sure Lexy and I packed all his shit. The week after I ran across a few of his things. I found the zip code for the Hunt address and shipped his stuff there. After he received his package, I didn't hear from him for about two weeks. I knew his calling again was inevitable. When he finally got around to calling, I was feeling horny although I'd never tell him that, so I let him come over. He called on a Sunday evening around five-thirty, so I told him to be at my place at seven pm.

Ben

Damn! Nia finally gave in. I can't wait to see her. I miss her so much. I'll hop in the shower and prepare myself. I'll wear something casual because I don't want her to think I'm trying to impress her, although I am. I proceeded to shower, and I also decided to shave my head and trim my beard. Nia always did like my baldhead. She would kiss it whenever we made love. I used my D&G shower gel. After I dried off, I used the same lotion. I threw on my Levi's, a Polo shirt, and my Jordans. I used cocoa butter on my head so that it would be smooth. Just as I grabbed my keys, my cell phone rang. Without looking at the caller ID I answered.
    "What's up?"
    "Hey baby! You busy?"

"Who is this?"

"What do you mean who is this? How many women call your cell phone?"

"Who is this?"

"Damn! nigga it's Shaquita since you wanna act like you don't know my voice."

"Why are you calling me? I told you it's over."

"How many times have you told me that?"

"I mean it this time, I'm trying to progress in life with a progressive woman, and that is not you."

"Progressive? What does that mean?"

"See, that's what I'm talking about."

"Huh?"

"You don't even know what progressive means, so there's no chance you'll be progressing in life."

"And?"

"And? And you need to stop calling me, for real for real. I'm not the only man with a dick out there."

"What the fuck is that supposed to mean?"

"It means your ass is sweating me, although I've told you more than once the shit we had is over!"

"Aw baby, you still mad cause your 'Boo' caught us?"

"I ain't mad, but I'm through with your ass. Stop calling me."

"Then why did you call me last night?"

"You'd been calling my cell every day, ten times daily and paging me. I wanted to see what the hell you wanted."

"Well, you saw what I wanted and gave it to me."

Mumbling I said, "Easy."

"What did you say?"

"I said getting it was easy. You've got noncommittal coochie and that's why I keep coming back because I know I don't have to commit to you."

"I thought you loved me."

"And why in the fuck would you think that? I never told you I loved you."

"No, but you acted like you did."

"Why because I was nice to you, and we hung out?"

"Well, yeah."

"That's what I'm talking' about. A nigga's nice to you, and now you think I love you. You knew from the jump I had a woman and had no intentions of leaving her. My main purpose for being with you was to get some extra, easy sex, that's it. You know it's actually funny."

"What's funny?"

"Sistahs always bash brothas and call us dogs but sistahs allow us to fuck them without commitment. You sistahs aren't innocent, you-"

Cutting me off she proclaimed, "We never said we were innocent."

123

"No, you didn't, but you all are as bad as us, if not worse. I know sistahs that fuck several different men within a two-week period. They do everything to every one of them; suck their dicks, fuck without condoms and some even allow the brothas to fuck them in the ass, but brothas are dogs. We couldn't be dogs if you all didn't allow it. Hell, I told you about my lady up front, but did that matter? Nope. Your main concern was gettin' some of this dick. So, if we're dogs, it's only because tricks like you allow us to be."

"Is that right?"

"Ya damn skippy!"

"Well, you can still have some."

Damn, is she stupid or what? "Nope. No, thank you. Your shit caused me to lose my woman."

"Well, nigga you should have known when trying to creep, there was always a possibility you'd get caught. I think it's called consequences and repercussions."

"Ooh you used big words."

"Nigga fuck you."

"I already did that, remember?"

"Anyway, like I said you had to know there would be consequences if you got caught."

"Exactly, so why would I continue to deal with your skanky ass?"

"I care about you."

"I'm sorry to hear that."

"The feeling isn't mutual?"

"No."

"You don't want any more of this?"

"Nah, I'm good."

"Well, I want some more of that dick."

"I bet you do, but it ain't happening."

"Are you sure you don't want anymore?"

"Why would I want your stretched out coochie? Your shit is so big my dick entered a convention."

Her dumb ass had the nerve to be silent, like she didn't know what I was talking about, knowing she was the guest of honor at the convention, but I'll play dumb. Right along with her. As if a light bulb had gone off, she said, "A convention?"

"Yeah, all the men you'd freaked since junior high school were waiting in the wings. It had to be about five hundred of us."

"Nigga, fuck you!"

"Now isn't that ironic, that's what me and the fellas at the convention were discussing, how many times we'd freaked you and how easy it was."

"If I see you I'm-"

"That's just it, you won't be seeing me, like St. Louis' own Cedric the Entertainer would say, I'll holla." With that I disconnected the line. My phone

124

began to ring again. I knew I'd have to turn the ringer off when I arrived at Nia's.

Nia

I can't believe I just told Ben he can come over. What the hell was I thinking about? If my mama, or my girls knew, they would swear I needed to be committed. Or worse, they would think I'm about to catch a case. God rest my daddy's soul; he's probably turning flips in his grave. Unfortunately, I wasn't thinking about them right now. I know they meant well, but I'm horny. I'm having that tingling sensation. Women know what that means. So, forget them right now. Like Pac and Breed said, '*I gotta get mine*'. I hopped in the shower, used my smell good, dried off, and moisturized with lotion. I wanted to entice him, but I didn't want him to know those were my intentions. I put on my fringed cut off Levi's shorts with a cropped tee and a pair of flip-flops. I decided to put my hair into a ponytail. I'd prepared my dinner earlier, so I decided to eat before he arrived. I'd prepared pork loin roast, cornbread dressing, collard greens, and corn on the cob. I fixed myself a plate and then began watching Dateline in the family room. I loved this show. It was always so informative and never biased. That's why I enjoyed it. Anyway, they were doing a show on teens and plastic surgery. Just as I was really getting into my food and Dateline, the doorbell rang.

Ben

As I pulled up in my truck, I became nervous. I hadn't seen Nia since the hair salon, so it would be interesting to see what happens. I wanted to come over before now, but both my uncle and my mother asked me not to. They both said I should give Nia her space, and if I chose to go against what they suggested, more than likely it would push her farther away. She and my mother stayed in contact with each other, but my mother would never tell me what they talked about. She only told me to give Nia her space. It was hard to do, but I listened. More than anything, I wanted to run over there with flowers, candy, and anything else that I could think of that would assist her in making up with me, but I waited. Patience has never been one of my better qualities.

I kept looking around expecting something to be different, but it wasn't. I guess I was going through because this felt like my first visit. I didn't know what to expect. I pulled up and parked, and from the looks of it, she had company. There was a blue Mercedes in the driveway. Maybe she called one of her friends over for moral support. I didn't recognize the car, but I guess I'll find out about her visitor momentarily.
I parked my truck and turned my cell phone off. I couldn't chance Shaquita calling. Then I exited my truck.

Nia

Why are my palms sweaty? I don't have anything to be nervous about. This is the man I caught cheating on me. A man I loved for two years. A man I lived with. A man I gave my all to. We shared everything, or should I say, I shared everything. That's the way love goes. I guess. No need in waiting for the inevitable. I opened the door.

As I opened the door, Ben and I just stared at one another. It never fails, you break up with someone, you haven't seen him in a while, and Damn! if they don't look good! His bald head was shining, his facial hair was trimmed just right, and he looked good, but I was working with a lil' sumthin sumthin myself. He was casual, but I always did like him in casual clothes. I didn't know too many black men that didn't look good in suits, but I loved a brotha working casual clothes as well.

Ben

I knew when I saw her, she'd take my breath away again. I feel like this is my first time seeing her, and her beauty mesmerized me. The first time I saw her I thought she was the prettiest dark-skinned woman I'd ever seen. She was prettier than Iman and Naomi Campbell, and she had a pair of beautiful green eyes. And when she smiled, her dimples were so deep it looked like someone had tattooed the Grand Canyon onto her cheeks. I must've been crazy to let this one get away. Her allowing this visit is a step in the right direction because from this moment on, if she takes me back, I won't trip again. When she opened the door, I just stared. She had on a pair of tight cutoff jean shorts and a cropped tee that showed off her navel piercing and her six-pack. Of all the women I've dated, she had the prettiest and biggest breasts, and right now they were sitting up, all perky and shit and her nipples were jutting out and screaming my name. This night had to turn out right, I want my woman back and I'm willing to ger her by any means necessary.

Nia

Ben spoke first.
"Boo- I mean Nia, you're beautiful."
As my voice dripped with sarcasm, I replied, "It's funny what we don't notice when it's right in front of our face."
"You got me on that one."
"Well, come in." We stepped into the foyer. "You don't realize how long it's been since you complimented me."

126

"I complimented you all the time."

"Oh really? Where was I? Out of town on business? Let's go into the family room."

"I may not have complimented you as often as you thought I should, but I did compliment you nonetheless."

"I'm not going there with you."

"Seriously, I've always thought you were beautiful, and if I didn't always express myself, I apologize."

"Why couldn't you be this sweet and this sensitive when things were good between us?"

"Sometimes we lose sight of what's important."

"Is that what happens?" I questioned, as I began to walk around the family room. Being near him began to make me nervous. I still loved him, but I knew he was no good for me. Damn! Why did he have to come over here looking so good, and smelling good? I guess I should ask myself why I let him come over here? That's really the question of the hour.

"I'll answer your question in just a moment, but don't you have company?"

"No, why do you think that?"

"There's a blue Mercedes in the driveway."

"Oh, that?"

"Yeah, that. Rachel's from next door?"

"No, but if it was, why would Rachel's car be in my driveway? She has her own driveway."

"I don't know, I just wondered."

"Well, for your information, it's mine."

"Is that right? You didn't tell me you purchased a new car or were even thinking about it."

"Yep, I got it when I got back from Dallas. Jake helped me with the negotiations, and I didn't know I had to tell you."

"You don't but you normally would share something significant like this."

"Well, if my memory serves me correctly, you were never interested in anything I was doing not concerning you, so I figured you wouldn't be interested in the car."

"Well, the car is nice, it fits you. Also, just for the record, I wasn't as bad as you make me sound."

"Thank you, sir, and regarding you, yes, you were."

"Anyway, where's the Honda?"

"I gave it to Jenise. She's doing very well in school, and I wanted her to have a reliable car to get around, and I know she appreciates it."

"That's cool, but let's get back to what we were discussing. I know I messed up, but I miss you. Don't you miss me?"

He began to walk around the family room. I began to get chill bumps, so I knew he was behind me. This is going to be so hard.

Softening up I replied, "Yeah, I miss you a little, but you hurt me."

127

Now he was behind me rubbing my neck. "I know I hurt you, and I can't say how sorry I am, but I am, and I'll do anything to show how much I regret my actions."

I had to do something fast because if I didn't, we'd end up getting our swerve on. So, I did what came to mind first, I offered him some dinner.

"Would you like some dinner? I ate already, but there's plenty left."

"I thought I smelled something. What did you cook?"

"I prepared pork roast, collard greens, dressing, and corn on the cob."

"Damn! It's like that?"

"And that's the way it is."

"I'd love a plate. Is everything still warm?"

"It should be, but I'll make sure when I fix your plate."

"I can fix my plate and use the microwave if I need to."

Looking puzzled, "Are you sure?"

"Yeah. What? Why are you looking at me like that?"

"Nigga, you know why. When you lived here, I was your personal maid, but now you're trying to get back into my good graces and you can do shit for yourself."

Laughing. "I guess I was damned pathetic, but you're partially to blame."

"How can you blame me for your lazy, helpless ass?"

"You had a brotha spoiled."

"Well, a sistah should've been spoiled as well."

"True dat."

"Well, you go ahead and fix your plate, Insecure will be on in a minute."

"Aw shit, I know how you are when your shows come on."

"And you know this."

With that, Ben went into the kitchen to prepare his plate, and I went into the family room to tune into HBO.

"Can I have a glass of the raspberry lemonade?'

I said. "Sure."

"Thank you, I'll be right there."

He entered the family room and sat next to me on the sectional right as Insecure was beginning. As always, Issa Rae and company were clowning. My girls and I love this show. I guess because we're in our thirties and still single, we can relate to their characters.

After the show ended, I turned the TV off and played Jaguar Wright, her album was already chosen on my phone to play on my Echo Dot.

"Who is that?"

"Did you see Jay-Z's MTV Unplugged?"

"You know I did, Jigga is my dude. The rap game won't be the same when he retires."

"Well, she's the sistah singing with the Roots."

"Straight. She clowned on MTV."

128

"Yeah, she did, and this is her debut CD."

"Really? What's it called?"

"Denials, Delusions and Decisions."

"Well, Miss Wright is definitely talented."

"That's Mrs. Wright, she's married."

"Is that right? Well, married or not, she can blow."

"Now that's something we both agree on."

"I know something else we can agree on."

"What's that?"

"The food is delicious. I forgot how well you cooked."

"I guess you would, considering you were never home when I cooked."

"Baby, don't go there. I know the mistake I made better than anyone else."

"Anyway, selective memory is a mutha. You can remember everything except the fact you had a good woman who loved you."

"Do you want to argue, or enjoy each other's company?"

"Let me think about it."

"Ha Ha funny, I know you didn't agree to let me come over here to argue."

"No, I didn't, but it's hard to not bring shit up, considering."

"I know baby, but I'll make it up to you."

"Whateva!"

As the music played softly in the background, Ben and I began to talk. It was like old times when we could talk, laugh, and just enjoy each other.

"Would you like something to drink?"

"Sure. What do you have?"

"I'm going to get me a Corona with a lime."

"That's cool. If it's not a problem, could you grab one for me?"

"Sure, I'll be right back."

Ben

This is going better than expected, although she won't let up about my infidelity. I thought after Insecure went off, she'd want me to leave, but she doesn't seem to be in a hurry to see me go. Now, she's playing this new sistah Jaguar and she's putting me in the mood, not that I need anything to put me in the mood with my Boo.

Nia

"Here you are."

"Thank you."

"You're welcome."

I sat on the couch away from him, and we began discussing music. I noticed he began to inch toward me. After about twenty minutes, we were on our second beer, and he was sitting right next to me. The conversation continued to flow like the Coronas we were drinking. He began to massage my shoulders, and I allowed it because I'd had a hard week at work. Muscles were tense throughout my body. As he continued to massage my shoulders, I knew what would be next.

"Do you have any condoms?"

"For what?"

"What do you think?"

"We don't use condoms."

"We didn't when I thought you were being faithful, but now I know what I know, condoms will be used."

With this pleading look on his face he said, "Are you sure?"

"No protection, no affection."

"Well, do you have any condoms?"

"I do not, but even if I did, we're using yours."

He agreed to my terms, and we made love, or should I say we had sex. On my leather sectional, and on the floor. We never kissed and I liked it like that. Kissing always makes sex more emotional, and I didn't need that. Ben went south on me, and I really think he wanted me to do the same for him, but I wasn't trying to go there. For me it was a release. While having sex with him, I realized I was no longer in love with him. So much had transpired, and the trust was totally gone, and without trust we had nothing. Nothing from nothing leaves nothing. I got up to go shower because I didn't want to cuddle, but I did want to wash him off me as well as out of me.

"Boo, where are you going?"

"To the bathroom, I need to take a shower."

"Can't that wait, I wanna hold you."

"Ben, this was a mistake." Suddenly, I had to vomit. Fucking him had made me sick to my stomach. "Excuse me." I went into the bathroom to regurgitate my dinner. Afterwards, I brushed my teeth, rinsed my mouth, took a quick shower, and returned from the bathroom.

"Are you okay?"

"I'm fine now. Like I was saying, this was a mistake."

"No, it wasn't. We love each other."

"Love ain't got shit to do with it.

"What do you mean?"

"If we had love, you wouldn't have cheated. I can't be with a man I don't trust."

"Baby, do you think there will ever be a chance for us?"

"No. I'll probably always have feelings for you, but we are not reconciling."

"So, you can't forgive me?"

"Why should I forgive you?'

130

He had this I-lost-my-puppy-or-best-friend look on his face when he replied, "There are four reasons why you should forgive me. The first-"

"Hold up, you mean to tell me you can come up with four reasons on why I should take your community-dick-sharing-ass back, but you couldn't find one reason to be faithful?" This fool gave me this incredulous look like I'd said something ludicrous and continued to dismiss what I'd said.

"As I was saying, the first reason is I love you. The second reason is I realize I messed up and I want to make it up to you. Thirdly, I know I can be a good man, but I wasn't in the past because you and your success were intimidating. Lastly, I honestly don't think you'll find another brotha to love you more than I do."

I began laughing my ass off. What this fool said was damn funny. I couldn't stop laughing. Tears were flowing from my eyes. For once, I was crying, not tears of anguish or anger but I was crying because the shit was so funny. Hilariously funny, and for once, the joke was not on me.

Looking insulted, he asked, "Why are you laughing at me?"

Dabbing at the tears flowing from my eyes and attempting to muffle the laughter, I kept laughing. I couldn't help it. Anger flashed in his eyes like a flash of lightning, but my laughter did not stop. I allowed my banter to run its course and after my tears were dried, I broke him down.

"Now what were you saying?"

"I was interested in knowing why you were laughing."

"You want to know why I was laughing?"

"Yeah."

"I was laughing because you are not the sun and therefore, the earth does not revolve around you. The way you act, you obviously think you are something special."

"Nia, what kind of analogy is that?"

"Okay, let me give you the ghetto Oran-Juice-Jones analogy. You think this entire world is yours and revolves around Ben, and whatever Ben wants. In other words, it's your world and everyone else is just a squirrel trying to get a nut." I broke into the chorus of Nas and Lauryn Hill's rendition of 'If I Ruled the World.' I shook my head with pity written all over my face, and said, 'Imagine that, if you ruled the world.'

"For your information Miss Witherspoon, I don't think I'm all that."

"You don't say?"

"I'm just a regular brotha trying to get his woman back."

"Unfortunately, it's not going to happen?"

"Why not?"

With disdain I repeated what he just asked, "Why not?"

"Yeah, why not?"

"You could come up with four reasons on why I should take you back, but I came up with five on why I shouldn't."

"Oh, it's like that?"

"Unfortunately for you yes."

With a smirk on his face, he said, "What? You don't love me anymore?"

"Again, what's love got to do with it?"

"I thought everything."

"Naw, you couldn't have thought that with your cheatin' ass!"

"Damn! You can't let go, can you?"

"If I was the one cheatin', letting some other nigga hit it from the back, would you let it go?"

"As much as I love you, yes I would."

"That's bullshit, and you know it. Men expect sistahs to forgive them, but ya'll never forgive us."

"Baby, I didn't cheat because I don't love you. As a matter of fact, it had nothing to do with you, but everything to do with me."

I was clapping when I said, "Finally! You say something I agree with. One-hundred and ten percent. That's something your grown ass evidently doesn't understand.

"What are you talking about now?"

"Love."

There was a puzzled look on his face when he said, "Huh."

"Yes, fool, love. When you really and truly love someone, you don't cheat on them."

"I now understand, and I want to make it up to you."

"How do you propose we do that? You're going to allow me to have a 'Fuck-a-Thug-Day' since you fucked a hood rat?"

"Nia, don't play with me, I'd kill a nigga if he put his hands on you."

"See, that's what I'm saying, but you want me to forgive you. You don't even want to think about me having sex with someone else but-"

"I don't want to think about it."

"What about the thoughts going through my head with you and her ghettoness? Did you ever stop to think about me and how this would affect me?"

"I guess I didn't and again, I am so sorry."

"Only God knows how long you'd been sleeping with ol' girl, but you don't want me to sleep with anyone, just one time. Isn't that a crock of shit?"

Total silence enveloped the room. I guess I'd given him something to think about.

Solemnly he said, "Nia, I want you to know I see your point and with that realization, I want to again express how sorry I am. I never-"

I mumbled, "No one is disputing that fact."

"Disputing what fact?"

"The fact you're sorry. Sorry as hell."

"I'll take that because I know I fucked up, but our relationship won't progress if you can't let it go."

Giving him the ain't-that-about-a-bitch look, I asked, "Is that right?"

This fool responded by saying, "Yes Boo, and I really want us to work through this. I know we can."

"Actually, we can't and here are my five reasons why; you used me, you lied to me, you took me for granted, you disregarded my feelings and my health, and you cheated on me. I'll never trust you again and without trust, we have nothing. For these reasons, I won't even consider reconciling with you."

"There's nothing I can do?"

Shaking my head in a negative manner, "Other than kissing my ass, nope."

"Well, what just took place between us? What did we just do?"

"We, well, I can't speak for both of us, but I was horny."

"Yeah okay, you know that's bullshit."

"You can call it what you want, but I was horny, and I figured instead of trying to find some new dick, I could release my sexual tension inside of the condom on yours." I wanted to laugh because I had never said some bold shit like that, but I'd been given some newfound strength. Truth be told I felt like I'd grown balls, but I knew that wasn't the case because I'm all woman.

"You're full of it because for you to lay down with someone, you have to have feelings for them."

"I never said I don't have feelings for you. I'll always care about you, but to stay with you would be relationship suicide for me."
Looking at him as if he were a character on 'Lost in Space' I continued, "I dealt with your bullshit for two whole years! You have no idea how many brothas wanted who was committed to you."

"You tryin' to make me jealous?"

"No, I don't care enough about your feelings or our failed relationship to attempt to make you jealous. I was just stating facts. A lot of successful men approached me."

"What you trying to say?"

"I'm saying I was never the type of sistah to date a man based on his credentials."

"And what's wrong with my credentials?"

"Let's see...you've had the same position at UPS for four years, yet you complain daily. At one time you talked about starting your own business, but when I mentioned to you, I had the starting capital, you said you'd changed your mind. Your best asset is your dick, and in the end, it turned out to be your worst." He sat silent with this dumbfounded look on his face, so I continued.

"So, I never pushed the issue. I finally realized we want different things out of life. I want-"

"That's not true!'

"It's not. Well, tell me, what do you want out of life?"

"Nice things."

"And?"

"And that's it. I want a nice house and a nice ride."

" Figures."

133

"What the fu-, I mean what does that mean?"

"Ben, you had those things. You lived in a two hundred and seventy-five thousand tri-level town house in U. City bordering Clayton. You have a new Tahoe, and clothes galore. To top it off, you had a woman who loved you, but that wasn't enough for you."

"It was enough. Nia, can't you just forgive me? I made a mistake and I know it. I shouldn't have to pay for that mistake for the rest of my life."

"Why shouldn't you? You hurt me and you had to know if, and when I found out, I would be hurt. So, in my opinion, what you did, was deliberate."

"All I can do is apologize. I can't erase what happened, but I can try my best to right a wrong."

"Ben, it's too late. We don't even want the same things out of life."

"Well, what do you want out of life?"

"God's love. A strong African American man who loves God and therefore will love me the way I deserve to be loved. I want a man who is a lot like my Daddy. I want children and I want a man that's interested in being a wonderful father."

"You and I can have children."

"Oh, so now you want children?"

"Do you remember what you told me when we began dating?"

"I told you I didn't want children, but I've changed my mind."

"Why?"

"Why? Because God created women to reproduce, and family is important to me. I deserve total commitment."

"Total commitment, what's that?"

"Damn! Does everything have to be spelled out for you?"

"I guess so." He snapped.

"M-A-R-R-I-A-G-E. The total commitment is marriage. Us living together didn't mean shit. You-"

"It did to me."

"Oh really, I guess that's why you disrespected me every chance you got."

"Disrespected you, what are you talking about?"

"Staying out til the sun came up, every time you felt like it."

"I wasn't with Shaquita, I was just hanging."

"Ben, it didn't matter where you were or who you were with, all that mattered is in the beginning of our relationship we set rules, and you broke them."

"Rules. What rules?"

"Please don't play the I-don't-remember game with me. It's funny how men conveniently forget the shit they've done and the promises they've made. Selective memory is a trip!"

"Are you going to tell me about these rules?"

"Yeah, I'll tell you when we decided to put forth an effort to have a relationship, you and I together set a curfew."

134

Laughing, Ben said, "Curfew! What kind of curfew?"

"Aw shit, here I go spelling shit out again. If I'd known I had to say and spell everything out, I would've told you to bring your relationship 'See N' Say'. Anyway, the curfew we set was for two, no later than three in the morning and you broke it too many times to mention."

"But I called."

"Is Pinocchio in the room because lies are flowing from your mouth like water flows down the dirty Mississippi. For your information, calling twenty-four hours later don't mean shit, all it meant was fuck Nia, her feelings and this relationship."

"Nia, if it was that bad, why didn't you leave sooner?"

"Because like most women in love, we stay thinking it will get better, but then one day we realize the love is one sided, and we find the strength to let go. Sistahs can love themselves, by themselves."

"You saying I don't love you."

"I think in your sick perverted way you do."

"Who are you to judge my love? Who made you judge, jury, and Johnnie Cochran?"

"Who am I? I'm the one you were supposed to love for the last two years, but you fucked me like a bitch in heat."

"I love you very much. I've been sick without you."

"Unfortunately, your love isn't enough for me. "

"Damn! It's like that?"

"And that's the way it is."

"There's nothing else I can do?"

"NO!"

"Are you sure?"

"I'm very sure. You need to move one, I have."

"You're willing to throw away what we had?"

"Like a trash bag full of funky chitlins."

"Baby, I know I've done some foul shit, but I love you and if you give me the chance, I'll prove it to you. I'm willing to give you total commitment." At that point, he pulled a ring box out to show me a round cut one-carat diamond set in platinum. The ring was beautiful, but I was too through with him. "Oh, so now you're ready to be married? What are you going to tell your hood rat? Does she know you purchased a ring for me?"

"I'll do whatever it takes to keep you in my life, and I told you I don't deal with her anymore. Boo, I want you to be my wife."

"I had a feeling you'd be over here talking nonsense, so I went over to your other residence, and I saw your truck two weeks ago. The lies don't stop, do they?"

"Baby what was I supposed to do?"

"About what?"

"You wouldn't talk to me."

"So, you'd rather be with a rat?"

"No, my preference was to be with you, but you were playin' me at every turn."

"Playing you? Nigga you were wrong not me!"

"I just had a minor lapse in judgment. I was only there because she kept calling saying she needed to talk. I figured the only way I could get her to stop calling my cell phone, was to go by there and talk."

"Is that right? You fell for the bullshit?"

"I guess I did."

"So, you went over there, and she fell on your dick?"

Trying to look innocent, he responded with, "Now where did that come from?"

"You know where it came from, or are you going to lie to me and tell me she just wanted to talk to you? I know for a fact you were over there until one in the morning, and as you know it doesn't take all night to do anything, and it surely doesn't take long to tell someone you don't want to be with them."

"That's exactly what she wanted, she wanted to talk, but of course you're going to believe what you want to."

"So, you all didn't have sex?"

"No, we didn't", he adamantly replied.

"Yeah whateva! Well, you should've gotten with her, because this", licking my finger and running it across my shorts, "sugar shack is closed."

"So, there's nothing I can say to change your mind?"

"You had two years to prove your love, but all you could prove is you're a liar and a cheat."

"Baby, I am so sorry, but I know I can make it up to you if you just give me the opportunity."

"Ben, I love you, but we've lost too much, and it would never work."

"If we both put forth the effort, it can work."

"No, it can't, you cheated on me, and maybe that's nothing to you but it's a big fuckin' deal to me."

"It's a big deal to me also. I regret what I did, more than you'll know, but what happened to forgiveness?"

"I do forgive you, and there are no hard feelings, but I can't be in a relationship with you."

"What am I supposed to do?"

"You should've thought of that before you did what you did."

"Damn! Baby, I made a mistake. You just won't let it go, will you?"

"A mistake, is that what you call it?"

"Yes, it was a mistake, but given the opportunity, I could right the wrong."

"Righting a wrong, is that what you call it?"

"Yes, if you'll only allow it."

"You can call it what you want, but we are over."

"Again, you're willing to throw away what we had?"

"Ben, you obviously don't understand."

"Understand what?"

"You are the one throwing away what we had, not me."

"Boo, we can try again, and we can make it-"

"What, 'Make It Last Forever', like Keith Sweat? I don't think so."

"You know what Nia?"

"What, Ben?"

"Fuck you."

"Ahhh, the real Ben Jones has appeared. I was wondering where you were. I knew your foul ass would show up sooner than later. It's good to see you, although you weren't missed. You ain't-"

"Fuck you."

"Fuck me? You've fucked me for the last two years. I'm tired of being fucked, so fuck you, you bald-headed-hood-rat-lovin'-no-ambition-havin'-bastard! Now, get the fuck outta my house!"

Looking totally surprised. "Your house? This is my address as well."

"But whose name is on the deed? Nia Witherspoon." I began poking him in his big ass head. "That's me, not you. Who pays the fifteen-hundred-dollar mortgage? Nia! Not Ben! Who furnished this place? Again, the answer is Nia, not Ben! So, you really don't have anything to say. I own everything up in here, and you didn't bring shit to the table. You came to this relationship empty handed, and you're leaving it the same way." During our conversation, we ended up by the door, which would make it easier to put his funky ass out.

"I didn't bring anything to the table? What about my love?

"Love. Love shoulda kept your cheatin' ass faithful, but it didn't. So, love obviously don't mean shit to you so, don't try to use it as a crutch now." I began to snap my fingers and belt out Rose Royce's Love Don't Live Here Anymore! "Just a vacancy....love don't live here anymore."

"So, it's like that huh? Two years gone?"

"You threw it away. It wasn't me. I was faithful."

"I don't think you'll find anyone to treat you better."

"Better? Better than what? A liar. A cheater. A user. A thief. I think I'll take my chances."

"Thief? I don't take shit I don't own or get permission."

"My time. You stole and wasted my time."

Looking dumbfounded he said, "So, you really aren't going to give us another chance?"

"No!" I answered sternly. "If all I can get is a liar, thief, user, and cheater, then I'd rather be by myself."

"I'm so sorry."

"Again, that's something we'll always agree on. You are sorry."

"Well since I'm so sorry, I might as well fess up to the other crime I committed."

"For your information, there's nothing you can do or say to hurt me."

"Is that right? Well, let's try this."

137

"You know you're a sick bastard to come over here and because I won't do what you want, you're going to deliberately tell me something which should, in your opinion, hurt my feelings. So, go ahead."

With a nonchalant attitude he said, "You said we've been dating for two years, right?"

"Yeah, and?"

"Well, I've been fucking Amber for one year."

"Amber who?"

He had a silly ass grin on his face when he said, "You know Amber. You've known her eighteen years. I believe you dated her brother in high school, and you all called each other sisters."

"You know what, I haven't talked to her in over a year, but I always knew she'd do some foul shit like this. Granted, I never thought she'd do it to me, but it's okay. Does she know about your ghetto girl?"

"No, she doesn't, and she won't know. We love each other and even talked about marriage."

"Well, she ain't got shit. You're asking me to get married, but you're telling me the two of you discussed marriage. Don't the two of you know what you did to me will surely come back to you? What she did will also come back to her. What goes around...."

"Yeah, yeah I know the saying, but it won't haunt us. With nervousness in his voice, he asked, "Do you plan on telling her I was over here?"

"Fuck you and her. Hell, I hope she ends up with your foul ass, and the same goes for you ending up with her. I can't think of two foul-ass-twisted-sick-ass people who deserve each other more."

"I know you're hurting."

Laughter erupted inside of me and eventually, the laughter was external, "And I know you're crazy. I don't give five fucks about you or Amber. I sincerely mean it when I say you all deserve each other."

"Nia, you're right. I only told you about Amber to hurt you."

"I know, but it backfired, didn't it?"

"Yes it did, and I'm sorry."

"I know, really I do, but it's too late. My father raised me to expect better and more from a man, and if I really think about it, he would've never approved of you."

"Why is that?"

"Because, you are the weakest link...goodbye." With that, I opened the door, waiting for him to exit.

"I'll leave now, but I'll be back. You wanted me tonight; you'll want me again."

By this time, he was on the other side of the door. "Don't wait on it. Dicks come a dime a dozen, and unlike Amber and ghetto girl, sharing dick ain't in my DNA. You see she was the stupid one, because she knew she was sharing the dick. I had no knowledge of it. See, I can get dick."

"That may be true, but it won't be this dick."

138

"Your shit ain't that good. Community property normally ain't worth much including that sorry ass dick of yours. And take this ring with you, I'm sure Amber will be happy with it." With that I handed him his ring and slammed the door.

This motherfucka really got me fucked up. All the shit he's done, and he expects me to take him back, or treat him better than I'm treating him now. NOT! He has lied and cheated, probably throughout our fiasco because you can't label it as a relationship. In my opinion, relationships are based on two people who care about one another, and they're working toward a common goal. The goal should be building a successful relationship. That goal will hopefully and ultimately end in marriage. Ben and I didn't have that. Now that it's over, I really don't know how to label it. He should've just hit it and quit it because he never put forth an effort to have a successful relationship. Putting him out felt like a Master Card commercial.....Priceless.......

As for Amber, all I can do is shake my head. I know I was a good friend to her, and I know I would've never done some shit like this to her. All I can do is pray for her and dummy. They're both very sick. I am so tired of men tryin' to play women like the NFL, MLB, and the NBA. Why do the good women end up with the worthless men, and the decent guys end up with the gold-diggin' skanks? Is life lopsided or what? I don't consider myself a man basher, but if a man is foul, I will let it be known. The same goes for women who are foul. That's obvious from Amber's actions. There are some women who are worse than some of these dogs – I mean men. She's one of them. This news was going to blow my girls away. I'm so glad I showered earlier. I wanted his stench gone…forever. I had to call one of my girls. Alicia was the first on my list.
"Hey girl, what's up?"
"Nothing much."
"Are you busy?"
"Naw, why?"
"Are you sitting down?"
"C'mon Nia, you're scaring me. What's up?"
"Ben just left my house and-"
"What do you mean Ben just left your house? I thought you were done with his lousy cheatin' ass?"
"I am done with him, but I was horny. Anyway, let me tell you what I just found out."
"Okay girl, tell me what Ben's ignorant ass had to say."
"Okay here goes, Ben came over and he got my thing to stop tingling."
Alicia starts laughing but I keep talking, "After we were through, I got up to vomit and shower because I realized I'd just made a huge mistake. Mr. Jones had other plans, he-"
"Damn! You vomited? What plans?"
"Yes girl, he made me sick and if you stop being so jittery, I'll tell you."

139

"I'm sorry girl, I guess a lack of sex has me anxious."

"It's cool, I know the feeling. Anyway, this nigga pulls out a platinum round solitaire cut engagement ring and proposes. I almost-"

"Proposes?"

"Licia."

"Okay, I'll be quiet."

"Yes, he proposed, but he's full of shit. I was with him for two years, and now he wants to get married. Whateva!" There was silence on the line, but I know Alicia, and I know that she wanted to say something.

"Hello? Licia are you there?" There was still silence. "Licia?"

"Damn, I'm sorry Nia, but I'm in a daze. I can't believe he proposed. Well, that's what you've been waiting for, so how did it make you feel? When Phil proposed, it was a special moment for me. Although I didn't want to marry him."

"Aw girl, there's more to the story."

"More like what? He's decided he wants children now?"

"Damn, who are you? Miss Cleo's niece?"

"You are so silly. So, now he wants children although he swore, he'd never have children?"

"Yeah, ain't that a trip?"

"Niggas are a trip when they're caught."

"And let the congregation answer say AMEN."

"Amen. Seriously, what are you going to do?"

"I ain't gone do shit because not only is he fucking Shaquita's ghetto fabulous ass, but he's fucking Amber also."

"Amber. Amber who?"

"Amber Lewis."

"Dante's sister Amber?"

"Yes, Dante, the guy I dated in high school."

"Hold up, Nia. Are you talking about the Amber you loved like a sister? The Amber you've known since we were sixteen and she was twelve?"

"Yes, they are one in the same."

"The Amber who moved in with you rent free when she and her mother weren't getting along? Wasn't she the same girl your mother treated as a daughter? Didn't you help with the supplies for her apartment? As a matter of fact, your mother just bought a bunch of stuff for her place? Damn I just can't believe this. Is that the Amber you're referring to?"

"That would the one."

"What is her problem?"

"Well, per Ben, she's been upset with me over some things I said and did in the past."

From the way she sounded, I could tell Licia had that I-don't-believe-it-look on her face. "What things?"

"I have no idea, she never told me."

"When is the last time you talked to her?"

"We've been so busy with the business; I can't remember the exact time. It's been a while, but she hasn't called either."

"The last time you talked to her, how did she sound?"

"Normal. You know it's fucked up because when Ben and I had problems, ninety percent of the time, I would lean on her from time to time. During these times I'd call her. As a matter of fact, I found out one Sunday morning when I called her to complain about him not coming home, he was lying next to her."

"What! Nia, please tell me you're lying."

"Nope, I am not lying."

"That's low. Naw that's fucked up. No matter what you may have said or done, you didn't deserve that. Why didn't she come to you? None of us are perfect. We say and do things we don't mean all the time."

"Licia, that's what I don't understand. Why didn't she come to me? If I said or did things to hurt or upset her, why couldn't she just come to me and tell me? Instead, she chose to hurt me, or commit an act she thought would hurt me by fucking Ben. Hell, I feel sorry for her because he ain't shit, but now I see neither is she. A friend once told me the way you get a man, is the same way you lose him."

"That's something to think about."

"Yeah, it is, and if you really think about it, it's so true. I don't know how many women I know who have dated married men, he leaves his wife, marries her, and then he leaves her because someone else came along. It's a never-ending cycle."

"Well, these men, and women for that matter are grown, and that's the choice they make."

"Well, I ain't trying to share my man."

"A to the Men."

"As for the Amber deal, I hope it doesn't hurt too much. I know it hurts because you loved her and Ben, but it's their loss. He was your man, and she was the other woman. She had to hide and do everything on the low-low. No matter what you did, you didn't deserve this deceit."

"Girl, you know I appreciate you, and you know my motto."

In unison, we both said, "What goes around, comes around."

"That has always been your motto."

"I live by it because it's true. I know I'm not perfect, but I try my best to treat people the way I want to be treated."

"I agree with you. I still don't think you deserve what Amber and Ben did. I say this as a friend, and I'm aware of your faults."

"The shit they've done to me will definitely bite them in the ass."

"Yeah it will, but life goes on."

"Yeah it does, and I'll be blessed and they won't."

"A to the Men. I hate to beat a dead horse, but I can't believe she didn't call you."

"Call and say what? Hey girl, how you doing? Oh, by the way, I'm fuckin' your man."

141

"You've got a point."

"For real."

"Are you planning any revenge? If it were me, I would."

"Girl pulease, fuck em' both. Neither of them is worth the effort."

"True and God's revenge is greater than anything you could do."

"Exactly."

Alicia and I talked a little longer and during our conversation, I decided under no circumstances would I be seeing or talking to Ben again. Any dealing with him was over. Although he's going to ask Amber to marry him and he'll be engaged, I know I will hear from him.....again. He won't give up easily because I was his meal ticket. He may actually have feelings for Amber, but I'm certain even with her, he has an ulterior motive. He may marry her, but he'll use her up and by the time she realizes she's being used, she'll be too used up and he'll be on to his next victim.

Men and women must be accountable for their actions. It amazes me when people are in a dishonest relationship and they're mistreated, they act as if someone has committed a crime against them. They have the audacity to act appalled. Their "loved" one couldn't have done them wrong although both did someone wrong at some time or another without a second thought. Without considering anyone's feelings, they did what they wanted. When they wanted.

Cruisin'......

Time does fly fast. The trip the ladies and I planned, it seems yesterday, was now here. We leave in a few hours. Kenya decided to spend the night with me since she was the only one living out of the way in North County. "Kenya, hurry your slow ass up! Alexis and Alicia will be here in a minute. We need to be at the airport no later than seven a.m. Our flight leaves at nine and you know security is tight since 9/11. Why would you wait until the last minute to polish your ugly ass toenails? You were aware, two months ago, this was the day we were leaving. I should've known your procrastinating ass would not be ready-," she cut me off.

"Nia, I love you and you're my girl, but would you please shut the hell up so I can get ready?"

"I just want to know why you don't prepare yourself. Why? Why? Why? You've been moving in slow motion since eighth grade. Damn!"

"Girl, shut up! Knowing Alicia with her prompt ass, she'll be here at exactly six-thirty, so I have twenty-five minutes to finish. I can't concentrate while you're running your mouth."

"Had you prepared yourself, you wouldn't be worried about Alicia's prompt ass."

"Nia!"

"What?"

"Shut up!"

"Whatever! I'll leave your ass alone but if you're not ready! Alexis, Alicia, Colett and I will be singing, "Ain't no party like a Tom Joyner party cause a Tom Joyner party don't stop! And we'll be singing it without you!"

"Girl, whatever! If your flat-ass-big-titty having ass would leave me alone, I could finish."

"Yeah, okay but watch the flat ass comments. I may be shaped like a white girl, but I fight like a sistah."

Laughing she said, "Whateva, your ass is flat."

"And your mama's crazy."

"Okay, your point is?"

"No point, just facts. My ass is flat. Your mama is crazy. You talk about my ass. I talk about your mama."

"Nia."

"What?"

"Isn't there something else you can do besides, bother me?"

"I'm going to make some phone calls and place my luggage in the truck, please be ready when I return."

"If you leave me alone, I can get finished."

"Yeah, okay. Oh snap! I need to check my luggage to make sure I have all my swimsuits."

"How many are you taking?"

"I think I packed four, and I found one that makes me look like I have an ass."

"What? What is it, Wonder Panty?" Laughing.

"Make jokes if you want to but I will have an ass on this cruise."

"First time for everything."

"Don't hate, when all of the brothas are staring at my ass."

Laughing. "Girl, in your dreams. What? You'll have an ass during the day, but when we go out in the evenings your ass will be back flat. He's going to think your ass is playing hide and go seek."

I couldn't help but laugh, "You had your one minute of comic fame, but we'll see who's laughing when we arrive back in Florida. I'm going to check my luggage."

At that point I allowed her to finish, and I went to retrieve my luggage. I also made sure all the windows were closed, and the gas was off. I had already set the timers on my lamps. Sheba was at my mother's, and she'd agreed to get the mail. I called Colett to make sure she was up. Our layover was in Atlanta, where she'd be joining us.

"Hello."

"What's up, girl? You sleep?"

"Hey Nia no, I'm not asleep. Nothing's up, just ready to get my party on Tom Joyner style. Y'all ready?"

"I am, but of course slow-ass-wait-until-the-last-minute-to-paint-her-toe-nails Kenya isn't. She spent the night over here and still ain't ready."

143

"Girl, leave Kenya alone, she's been slow her entire life. It won't change."

"I know you're right, but it's frustrating as hell. Anyway, after I hang up with you, I'm going to put my luggage in the truck."

"You're driving instead of catching a cab?"

"Yeah, the four of us will split the charge for long-term parking."

"Well, be safe and I'll see you at the gate in Hartsfield."

"All right, I'll see you in a little bit. Hey, before I forget, have you heard from Kenny's ass since court?"

"Girl, I blocked his number day one, but I ran into him at Lennox."

"Did he see you?"

"Yeah, he saw me."

"Well, what did he say?"

"At first nothing because I ignored his stupid ass."

"I don't blame you."

"Girl, he then followed me into the BeBe store where I was looking for a pair of sandals for our trip, and just began talking like nothing negative had transpired between us."

"No, he didn't! Negroes are good for acting like nothing happened."

"I know! Anyway, he was saying how sorry he was for everything and if he could do it again, he'd do it differently. After he said that I tuned him out, all I heard him saying was, "Yada, yada, yada, blah, blah, blah.""

"He really has some nerve."

"Yes, he does. He had enough nerve to ask if he could call."

"What did you tell him?"

"I told him sure."

"Why? You know you don't want to be bothered."

"Because when he calls, he'll talk to an automated system, indicating his number has been blocked."

Laughing, "Oh well, you win some, you lose some, and he lost this one. He lost the best woman his crazy psycho ass would ever have."

"Oh well, his loss and another brotha's gain."

"I hear you. All right girl, I'll see you in a few hours and then cruise ship here we come."

"I need to check my luggage again."

"All right, girl, there's the doorbell, it must be Alicia and Alexis, be safe."

"All right, see you soon."

Answering the door, "What's up ladies?"

Alexis' crazy ass was singing and doing the 'prep', "Party over here, Party over there!"

Alicia said, "She was like this at my door also, and check out the dress."

I said, "Damn girl, you got it goin' on. Where did you get that dress, Hoochies R Us?"

"Nia, fuck you, you're just jealous you don't have any booty to fill out a dress like this."

"That may be true, but I've got the breasts to fill out this halter, you heifer!"

Laughter erupted from everyone.

Alexis said, "Where is Kenya?"

"You know her slow ass ain't ready."

Kenya came around the corner, "Wrong! I am ready."

Alicia said, "Damn, let me write this down and put it in my planner because this is definitely a first."

Kenya responded, "You can write it down, take a picture....I don't give a fuck!"

I said, "She's only ready because I got her ass up at five-forty-five. I knew the two of you would be on time."

Alexis said, "Girl, you've been up a long time."

"I know but I forgot to polish my toenails last night."

Laughing Alicia said, "I want to thank you."

With a confused look on her face, Kenya asked "Thank me for what?"

"For polishing those twin toes."

"Twins? What are you talking about?"

"The twins, Ug and Lee. You know ugly toes."

"Alicia?"

"What?"

"Fuck you!"

"I plan on doing just that, getting with somebody. I packed a big box of Magnum condoms," Alicia-never-give-up-booty said.

I asked, "You did what?'

"I packed a jumbo box of condoms because I knew you all wouldn't, but if any of us meet Dexter St. Jacque, we need to be prepared."

Alexis began walking around Alicia and giving her a strange look. Then she began lifting her top.

I said, "I ain't giving none of those foreign niggas none."

Alexis said while lifting Alicia's clothing, "Where is Alicia Marie Fox? You know the sistah that makes a brotha wait two to three months before she gives up the ill na na. The Alicia I know does not give strangers the ill na na!"

"Well, when I reach Florida soil, I will no longer be Alicia."

I had to ask, "Who are you going to be? Monique?"

"Thanks Nia, Monique will work. You all should practice calling me that now because I won't be Alicia on Florida soil."

Kenya said, "Whatever girl, I don't need no condoms because ain't nobody gettin' nothing."

Alexis, Alicia, and I looked at each other, shook our heads, and said, "Yeah, right."

"What does that mean?"

145

Alicia said, "That means you can't seem to say no to dick. It calls your name, and you willingly submit."

"I just like spice."

I said, "Well, you've definitely sampled enough spices."

Alexis said, "We're all grown so do what you want. It's your life and your body."

With an attitude Kenya replied, "That it is. So, let's go."

I said, "Yeah, let's. My luggage is already in my truck, and it's unlocked. I have my passport; I hope you all remembered to bring yours."

Kenya said, "I have mine."

Alicia said, "I just checked my wallet, and it's there."

Alexis said, " I gave mine to you, remember?"

"Yeah, I got you covered. I guess we're ATL bound."

Smiling Kenya said, "Let's roll."

They loaded their luggage in the back of the truck. I activated the alarm, and we were on our way. We arrived at the airport about fifteen minutes later and found a spot in long-term parking.

I said, "Do we have everything?"

Kenya said, "If we don't, we'll buy it. Let's go."

We went to the ticketing counter, got our boarding passes, and proceeded to the assigned gate with our luggage. Fortunately, our wait wasn't long. They began boarding fifteen minutes after we arrived at the gate. Alexis and I sat together, and Alicia and Kenya sat together. Alexis led us in prayer.

"C'mon ya'll, hold hands so we can pray, and I can go to sleep."

I said, "Amen to that."

"Heavenly Father, we come to you giving you praise, glory, and honor. Father, as we embark on this adventure, we ask you to guide us as well as watch over us. We also ask your Angels to help guide the pilot to ensure us and all the passengers a safe arrival. We ask this in the name of your son, our savior Jesus Christ. Amen."

In unison, "Amen."

Our flight was a little under two hours, and we all slept. We arrived in Atlanta at eight twenty-seven, and waiting at the gate was Colett. She began to get her sing on as soon as she saw us.

"Ain't no party like a Tom Joyner party, cause a Tom Joyner party don't stop." The seas won't ever be the same, constant parties and beach games. My girls and I shall emerge. Getting our party on is a splurge. Cauuuuuse....Ain't no party like a Tom Joyner party, cause a Tom Joyner party don't stop."

After hugging her, I said, "No, your crazy ass didn't make up a rhyme. Are you ready to party, or what?"

Kenya mumbled, "That shit sounded more like a nursery rhyme."

Colett said, "Kenya shut your hatin' ass up! What? You're just mad because you didn't come up with it first? It's obvious that instead of drinking orange juice this morning, you drank a large glass of HATERADE?"

146

Kenya said, "Whatever!"

Alicia decided to referee, "Ladies, ladies we're vacationing, not arguing. Stop trippin'."

I always knew Kenya was a bit envious of my friendship with Colett, but she's never been this obvious. I love Kenya but she talks too damn much, as a matter of fact, she's the only friend of mine whose mouth runs as fast as a stray dog. For this reason, I can't tell her anything intended to remain on the down low. She's not envious of Alicia or Lexy because we've all been close since high school, but Colett and I have only known each other for ten years. One would think she and I have been friends for at least twenty years. We're very close, and unlike Kenya, I trust her totally. There's a certain level of trust I have with Kenya, but I must watch what I say, or it will be on BET, MSNBC, CNN, and CSPAN. I know Kenya likes Colett, but there is a definite jealous streak.

Alicia said, "I agree, I am not up for any BS."

I said, "Licia's right. If you all are going to keep it up, both of you can go home."

Colett said, "And whose mama, are you?"

"Nobody's but I know we paid too much for this cruise to deal with any nonsense."

They just looked at each other and I looked at them. Kenya finally broke the silence.

"Damn! Okay, I'll stop trippin'."

"Yeah girl, don't trip, there's enough of me to go around and I love all of my girls."

Alicia said, "Okay, we have a thirty-minute layover, and I'm hungry, and I don't do airplane food."

Alexis said, "Now you're talking. Arguing over Nia's no booty having ass!"

"All right heifer, watch the ass jokes. Let's go because I don't care for airplane food either."

Laughing, we proceeded to Burger King for breakfast. After everyone received their orders, we made it back to our gate. Again, our wait wasn't long. Thirty minutes after arriving at the gate, we began boarding. Lexy, Licia, and Kenya sat together while Colett and I sat together across from them. Who I sat by was unimportant because I planned on being knocked out.

I said, "Is everyone buckled in?"

Lexy spoke, "Everyone except Kenya's crazy ass. Girl suck in that gut and fasten the belt."

"Lexy, kiss my ass, I don't have a gut."

"Oh, I forgot, you're the pill-popping queen."

"Whatever keeps the six-pack tight."

Lexy's fit ass said, "Girl, try a milkshake and a platinum card."

"What! What does that have to do with staying fit?"

147

"The milkshake as in Slim Fast, and the platinum card as in membership to a gym."

Licia spoke, "Damn, that was a good one. Lexy, you're getting witty in your old age."

"Old? W
ho you calling old?"

Colett said, "Y'all stop! Please shut up so Nia can say the prayer." We knew what time it was; we automatically grabbed hands and bowed our heads. The prayer from Atlanta to Florida was the same as the prayer we said earlier. The flight crew went through their normal information regarding safety. We listened and patiently waited until they were done so we could sleep.

Kenya asked, "Nia, this is a straight flight, isn't it?"

"Yeah, the only layover was the one in Atlanta."

"How long is the flight?"

"Damn Kenya, do I have travel agent written on my forehead?"

"No, but you did make the arrangements."

"No, I didn't, Carla did, and you have a copy of your travel documents. I suggest you read them because I'm about to go to sleep." With that, I was out. I know I was asleep before we left Atlanta. There's something about flying that lulls me into a deep sleep.

We arrived in Miami two hours later at eleven fifteen. We were amazed at all the melanin traveling. Of course, we were more intrigued with the men, but we were glad to see such a large turnout. None of us checked bags, so we proceeded to the transportation area. Carla had hooked us up with a limo to take us to embarkation. She said it was the least she could do considering all the money my girls and I spent with her. Our driver was holding a sign with the name Witherspoon, N. on it, so we'd found our ride. He greeted us with an accent although he was as black as your grandmother's skillet.

"Hello, ladies."

In unison, we replied, "Hello."

"My name is Abdul, and I am your driver. Which one of you is Miss Witherspoon?"

"That would be me, do you need the transportation voucher?"

He replied, "Yes, ma'am, I do."

Pulling my travel documents out of my tote, "Here you are, Abdul."

"Thank you, Miss Witherspoon."

"If I can call you Abdul, you can call me Nia, and I guess I should introduce my friends. This is Colett, Alicia, Kenya and Alexis."

"Ladies, it is my pleasure. You all are very beautiful."

Lexy's flirty ass had to comment, "Well, you're black and beautiful too." His black ass turned red from blushing.

"Do you ladies have all of your luggage?"

Alicia stepped in, "Yes, sir we do. None of us checked any luggage."

"All right then, I'm going to load everything on this luggage carrier and then we'll proceed to the limo."

148

"Yes, sir."

Abdul loaded our luggage onto the carrier, and we proceeded to where the limo was parked.

"Ladies, here we are."

I asked, "In the white limo, or the stretch gator?"

Laughing, Abdul replied, "The stretch gator."

With a hand on my hip, "Why are you laughing at me?"

"Stretch gator is a term rarely heard outside of Florida."

"Well, you know me, I keep up with the sayings."

"I guess you do."

"Well, Carla definitely took care of us on this trip."

Alexis commented, "She sure did."

I said, "Let's roll. We'll take care of Carla when we get back in St. Louis."

We climbed into the luxury the Lincoln Navigator offered and settled in to enjoy the ride. Abdul instructed us to help ourselves to the bar. That was an order we all obeyed.

Lexy, evidently thirsty asked, "Licia, since you're sitting next to the bar, would you open it up and tell me what's in there."

"Yeah girl, let me get comfy and I'll see what's inside." Alicia laid her purse down and found a comfortable position, and then proceeded to look in the bar to study its contents. "Let's see what they have. I-"

Lexy voiced what she wanted, "I know we're on vacation but it's still early and I'm not interested in the alcoholic beverages they have."

"Girl, I got you covered. I know you're not the alcoholic, Kenya is."

Kenya quickly acknowledged the comment by responding, "And what the hell does that mean?"

"I saw you taking a sip this morning and-"

"That was for the flight. I always take a sip before I fly. It helps to ease my nerves." Kenya explained.

"Anyway, there's Pepsi, 7UP, fruit punch, cranberry juice, and your favorite Nia, Evian."

"I'll take an Evian, please," I requested and Licia handed it to me. "Thanks girl."

"You're welcome."

"Aren't you going to hand the rest of us something?" Kenya boldly asked.

Lexy snapped back with, "Aren't you the one who owns the maid service?"

"What does that have to do with anything?"

"Alicia is not a maid and-"

"All right, everybody just chill! Damn, we're supposed to be the exception to what they say about women not being able to hang out without arguing. We're on vacation, and I'm really not up for the bullshit, so please

149

stop all of this petty shit, and stop acting like bitches." This was Colett's calm, cool and collected ass.

At this point, Alexis began to laugh so hard she was bent over and holding her stomach.

"Alexis Marie Knight, what is so funny?" Alicia wanted to know.

"No, you didn't say my whole name."

"Yes, I did because I knew I'd get your attention, but I'd really like to know what's so funny."

"What's funny is the fact that Colett is right, we're on vacation and we're supposed to be enjoying ourselves, but you heifers are arguing and that's a damn shame."

Kenya interjected, "All right, let's make a pact right now."

"Kenya, we don't need a pact. Ya'll just need to act like grown ass women." Alexis added.

I said, "True dat! I'll definitely do my part."

Kenya added, "I'm down with that as well."

Once we went through the embarkation process, (you know proving we're US citizens), we were given our identification cards, and given directions to our staterooms. After inquiring about our luggage and being informed they would be delivered to our staterooms, we proceeded to go through the maze, also known as a cruise ship.

Prior to leaving, we decided as a group who would bunk with whom. Since there are five of us, three of us would occupy one stateroom, and the other two would occupy the other.

We decided on Kenya and Alicia staying in one stateroom, while Alexis, Colett and I would occupy the other. Since our staterooms weren't the same size, they weren't adjacent. There were approximately ten cabins separating them.

The entourage arrived at the larger stateroom first, and I opened the door.

The stateroom was huge, well larger than my last cruise anyway. The colors were soft, and the interior was very plush. I was certain we'd made the best possible choice. Kenya was the first to display her satisfaction. "Girl, this is bad! I hope our stateroom is this nice."

Colett said, "This is nice. Once again, Carla has hooked us up."

"I'm sure yours is just as nice although it's not as large. Remember, there are three of us and only two of you," I replied.

Alicia stated, "I'm sure ours isn't as large, but I did some research on cruise lines and Royal Carribbean's staterooms are fifty percent larger than the other cruise lines."

"I can believe that my mother and I have been on different cruise lines."

Alexis added, "Well, whatever the case may be, we're good to go."

Colett said, "Yes, we are, and I am ready to get my drink on, so let's go."

"That's cool, but we need to put our belongings in our safe first because I don't want to carry any of this unnecessary stuff with me."

150

I located the safe in the closet. Colett, Aexis and I put our stuff in our safe before going with Kenya and Alicia to their stateroom.

Upon entering their stateroom, we saw theirs was decorated in the same colors, it was just a little smaller.

"Oh, this is nice," Kenya observed.

"I told you it would be. Again, ours is larger because there's three of us."

"Girl don't listen to Kenya's hatin' ass! You know she wouldn't be Kenya if she didn't complain about something," Alicia commented.

Kenya rolled her eyes and gave us her famous silly grin, and we couldn't do anything but laugh at her crazy ass!

"I guess that's why we're friends, we're all crazy." While still laughing, this is the comment Colett made.

"Anyway, we've seen where we're going to lay our heads, and now it's time to check out the scenery on this lovely ship!" Alexis anxiously expressed.

"Amen to that," Colett enthusiastically agreed.

"I thought we came on this ship to enjoy ourselves and the entertainment Tom Joyner and crew are providing us." With a straight face, I made that comment knowing that along with enjoying ourselves we would also be flirting our asses off.

"That's partially true, but you know we're hot blooded, single, and might I add beautiful black women who have entered into an oasis of black men. So, you know we got to check out the peep show," Kenya's hot ass explained.

"For once Kenya has a legitimate explanation," jokingly Alicia added.

With that said, Alicia and Kenya placed their personal belongings in the safe and we went to explore.

It was just past two o'clock, but I was ready for a cold one.

"Let's go get a drink." That was my suggestion, but of course Licia's holier than thou ass acted as if she was appalled.

"Drink! As in alcohol?" Licia delved.

"Naw, drink as in milk doing a body good. Damn right, I'm talking about alcohol."

"Isn't it kind of early? It's just a little past two."

"I don't know Licia, but one thing I do know is that Diane Witherspoon is in the STL, and God rest his soul, but Ralph Witherspoon is now my angel in heaven, so my parents aren't here to provide parental guidance, but shit the last time I checked, my ass was grown."

"I'm just sayin'-"

"What are you saying? I can't have a drink because of the time of day. We aren't the designated drivers so why not indulge? I just-"

"Shit! I'll drive this big bitch." Kenya's crazy ass had to add her two cents to the conversation.

"Drive! Girl, you can barely drive that country girl bama ass Ford F-250 you have. How in the H-E-L-L are you going to direct a big ass ship?"

151

"Do ya'll remember when Kenya stole her daddy's eighty-four Monte Carlo and drove it into Alicia's yard? Or should I say Mr. and Mrs. Fox's yard? Licia's parents were pissed." Alexis remembered.

Laughing Kenya said, "Mr. and Mrs. Fox never let me forget, they remind me once a year, but I can drive now."

"Is that what you call it?" jokingly I asked.

Kenya said, "What does that mean?"

Ignoring her question, I replied, "Anyway, getting back to the original subject at hand, which was alcohol and me getting some. As I was saying, we're on vacation, so why not? Plus, it's 5 o'clock somewhere in the world."

Again, Licia's self-righteous ass had to comment, "It's just kind of early."

"I'll tell you what Licia, you can order a virgin daiquiri, papaya juice or milk, but I'm about to order an extra-large frozen Midori Sour. You, Miss Thang, can be like Digital Underground and Dowutchyalike." Once that was said and done, we made our way to the pool area.

"Damn, it's warm up here." That was Lexy's wanna be naked ass.

"Warm as in the weather, or warm as in, you see all of these men, and you want them to see the skin you're in?"

Laughing, Alexis replied, "You can call it what you want but I am a single black woman with a body that's like that, so don't hate because I want to show it off."

"Oh, I'm not hating, I'm participating because as soon as our luggage arrives, I'm getting suited up as well."

"Yeah, okay Nia, but that was a hater move!"

"All right, maybe it was, but don't mind me. I got nothing' but love for you."

"All right, let's go to the bar and order our drinks," Colett stated.
It was evident everyone on the ship had the same idea as us. The bar was packed. While we were in line waiting our turn, we enjoyed the view, and what a view it was. There was a sea of chocolate.
There was every kind of chocolate available. There was white chocolate, café' au lait chocolate, caramel chocolate, milk chocolate, and of course my favorite, dark chocolate. Why we feel the need to date outside of our race, when we have every color of the spectrum amongst ourselves, is beyond me. I guess to each its own. Anyway, we were waiting in line, and just observing our surroundings, and I felt someone tapping on my arm like an anxious, and very worrisome child. When I turned around, I saw that Alicia was the culprit. I looked at her with what I'm sure was an irritated look.

"Damn, Nia you probably won't believe this, but that sexy-chocolate-bow-legged-mole-over the-lip brotha from Dallas is here."

My heart began to race. "For real? Did he see you?"

"I don't think so?"

"So, what is he doing?"

"He's talking to some fine ass fellas. Never mind girl it's just Ray, Rick and Mike, but there's some caramel candy over there too."

"Caramel candy?"

Licking her lips Alicia replied with, "Yeah this brotha with them is the color of caramel candy, and by his looks, I bet he's tasty."

"Girl, keep me informed,"

"Oops! The-"

"What?

"The fellas just looked over here."

"Is that right?"

"Uh-oh, he must've – oh shit he just spotted you because he's on his way over here."

Colett was on my other side and informed me of another surprise. Muffling her voice so she couldn't be overheard, she said, "Girl, Ben's on his way over here as well." Alicia stood there with a dumbfounded look on her face, and didn't have anything to say, which was not the norm for her at all. I was thinking to myself what did I do to deserve this? And where was the cat holding her tongue hostage?

Alexis was in shock also but she, Colett, and Kenya were coherent enough to help me out. I asked Kenya to run interference while I got rid of Ben's fatal ass. Alicia came around at the last minute and was going to introduce Colett and Alexis to Malik, so they could keep him occupied while I talked to Ben's crazy ass!

With as much finesse as I could muster, without trying to look sly, I turned to the left to greet Ben, and my posse turned to the right to converse with fine ass Malik. We couldn't have done it better if Debbie Allen had choreographed it herself.

Malik

The fellas and I went through with our plan to take Tom Joyner's cruise benefitting the United Negro College Fund. We arrived and were ready to enjoy ourselves. We were lounging' out by the pool, and just observing all the sistahs when I saw a familiar face, or so I thought. I couldn't really tell because four women surrounded her. Her hair looked like Nia's, and her style of dress reminded me of Nia. This woman had on a peach-colored wrap halter-top and a multicolored ankle length skirt, and that was Nia's style. As I continued to stare, I guess I stared so hard it willed her to turn around. As she turned around, I saw her large perky breasts and her shoulder length curly hair. I saw her smile and I knew. In that instant. Yep, I'm talking about the infamous Nia Witherspoon from the STL. I didn't think I'd ever see her again although I wished I would, and here she was. As beautiful as I remember. I was caught up in a daze. Caught up in her rapture. I couldn't believe she was here. I knew fate was on my side. The fellas noticed I'd become quiet, and wanted to know what was up. Mike was the first to inquire.

"Malik!" I didn't respond, so he said my name again. "Malik!"

153

Ray said, "Oh shit, this nigga has found something, or should I say someone to look at, and she really has his attention."

"Malik!" Rick yelled.

"Huh?"

"Nigga who is she?" Rick inquired.

"Yeah, who'd you see? Nia Long? Halle Berry? Naw you like your women a little thicker than Halle and Nia, although Halle and Nia are both fine as hell. Who is it? Regina Hall? Sanaa Lathan?" Ray inquired.

"Or maybe it's my baby Angela Bassett?" Mike added.

"Man don't play, you know Angela's my woman," Gerald commented.

"It's Nia." I quietly answered.

Mike said, "Really. You've always given her props, but she's not your type. You've never freaked out before when you saw her. Is it because she's here in person?"

Ray said, "Mike, you have a point, why all of the interest in Nia Long?"

"On snap! I figured it out! It's not Nia Long, but that honey named Nia he met at home. Ya'll remember her? She was from St. Louis." Mike's know-it-all-ass replied.

"Dawg, is that who you saw?" Rick asked.

I didn't respond. I couldn't. I still couldn't believe she was here.

"Earth to Malik! Earth to Malik!" Ray's crazy ass was yelling, and people were beginning to look. I had to respond. The fellas wouldn't allow me to have my moment.

"Yeah, it's her," I replied, and kept staring. The fellas were staring as well. Mike went from silly to serious within seconds and said, "Nigga, you met her in March, it's May and you're still talking about her. I know it's been a while since you had some, and although I know you want more with Nia, you need to hurry up and get some or we'll have to present you with the Dusty Dick Trophy. "

Laughing Ray said, "Mike's silly as hell, but on the real Malik, there's obviously something about this woman which has you trippin'. It looks like she's found a place in your heart."

"That's not-" I tried to interject, but Mike wouldn't allow it.

"Nigga be quiet, and just listen. I've known you ninety percent of my life, and no woman has ever affected you like Nia, not even Melina's trifling ass. So, please talk to her, get her number, and start something."

"Mike's right man! We ride you about this obvious infatuation, but you really are digging her, and as your boys we say GO FOR IT!" Rick insisted.

Ray added, "We got your back."

"A'ight, aight! I will aggressively pursue her this week."

"Cool! You can start now, there she is. I guess those are her girls with her, and they are fine." Mike informed us.

"Yes, they are," Gerald cheerfully said.

"All right, all right, give me a minute. I need to gather my thoughts."

154

"Yeah okay, but if you take too long, I will play Cupid", Mike announced.

We continued to hang out and observe all the women. Sistahs were representing in every hue God created us in, as well as every size and shape. I checked out Nia's girls, and Mike's right, they are fine, but Nia stands out the most. That's my opinion anyway. I guess I'm going to take my shot now. "Fellas, I'll be back."

I began my, what seemed like a long walk in the direction of Miss Witherspoon. One of her girls looked my way, but it wasn't Alicia, so I don't know if it was coincidental or what. I continued my descent.

Ben

I knew Nia and her girls would be on this cruise, so I'm hoping I can finally get through to her. I even exchanged the ring I got her for a bigger diamond. I've put Amber on hold until I find out what can happen between Nia and I. My boy and I checked into our stateroom and now we're mingling. There are some fine ass sistahs on this ship! Damn! I see why men cheat. We really have too much to choose from. Anyway, we were just walking around socializing, and I spotted her. I expected to see her, but not this soon. Of course, she was with her scandalous ass friends. I know I have to deal with them since I want to be with her.

I know they want me, and that's why they talk badly about me to her. I've seen the way they look at me, especially Alexis with that fat ass of hers. I'd never date any of them because they talk too damn much, but I'd fuck the shit out of Alexis. Don't confuse it, I love Nia and her pancake ass, but I'm a black man and a fat ass makes me teary eyed. Like most good onions do. Her girl is definitely working with a lil' sumthin' sumthin'. Anyway, enough about those skanks, I'm going to see my Boo.

"Rob, I'm going to see my woman, I'll be back in a minute."

"Dawg, where is she?"

"Follow me, I'll introduce you to the wifey to be."

Rob and I made our way through the crowd to meet my queen. Colett sees me first and frowns.

"Damn, why is baby girl frowning?" Rob questioned.

"Man fuck her, just ignore her. Her girls can be so silly at times."

Rob and I reached our destination and fortunately Alexis, Alicia and Kenya were talking to some black nigga with dread locks. I really don't see what sistahs see in that shit. It's nappy and in my opinion, it looks dirty. But these niggas think they're Eric Benet or Bob Marley. I expect them to start singing No Woman No Cry. A brotha like me doesn't need extra shit. I just got it like that. Anyway, one of them must be trying to get their mack on. I won't have to worry about them getting up in my business. Nia sees me and frowns.

Rob inquires, "Man is that her?"

155

"Yeah, that's her."

"She's beautiful."

"I know."

"She favors the Sistah, on Real Housewives, I think her name is Kenya."

"I know."

"Hey baby, how you doing?"

"I'm fine Ben. You?"

"I'm good baby, real good."

Rob cleared his throat, so I wouldn't forget him.

"Well, what do you want?"

"I wanted to say hello and introduce my boy to you."

"Your what?"

"My boy, Rob."

"Your boy? You don't have any friends."

I ignored her observation, "Rob works with me, and we just hit it off, so we decided to take this trip together."

"Is that right?" Nia questioned, with much sarcasm.

"Yeah, we're cool, and I told him all about you."

"And why would you do that?"

I gave her a pleading look before I said, "You're all I talk about, and he wants to meet the woman who has my heart."

"Ben, I'm not going there with you, I'll meet your boy, but afterwards leave me alone. I don't want to look up for the next seven days and have you up in my face all day and all night. There are plenty of big booty, beautiful black women on this ship. Please find yourself one and enjoy. Keep in mind I am single and for that reason, don't approach me if you see me talking to one of these fine ass black men. If you do, as you know, I can and will clown."

"Damn! It's like that?"

"And that's the way it is."

After that was said, with a smile on her face, she turned to Rob with an outstretched hand.

"Hello, I'm Nia, Ben's ex."

"It's nice to meet you, I've heard a lot about you."

"Now that's interesting, but I won't even go there."

"Aw baby, you know I'm always talking about you."

"Why? We aren't together."

"It ain't because a brotha ain't trying."

Nia

Ben's new friend, and I use the term loosely, was looking at Ben and I as if we'd lost our minds, but I wasn't going to stand there and put on a show for him. Ben had him believe things were A-okay with us, but now he'd know the

156

truth. I wasn't about to get into it with Ben. There were too many people around to be arguing with him in public. So, I let it go.

"Rob, it was nice to meet you, and I hope you enjoy yourself this week. Ben, I hope you enjoy yourself as well."

"Nia, it was nice meeting you as well, I hope to see you again."

"All right Rob, take care."

After holding that conversation, I turned around and those dimples were smiling at me.

And So We Meet Again

"Nia, guess who's here?" Alicia asked.

Smiling I replied, "I see who it is."

It was happening again. Although the ship was packed, it was as if there was no one here.

It was Bill Withers singing one of my favorite songs, while Grover (God rest their souls) was doing what he did best. It was just the two of us.

Grabbing my hand he exclaimed, "Hey there Miss Witherspoon. Fancy meeting you here," Malik greeted me. I allowed him to hold my hand because it felt so natural.

"Hey Mr. Black, how are you?"

"Pretty good, but I think things are about to get better."

"Is that right?"

"Yeah, I think so."

"All right where are they?" I asked, while looking from side to side.

"Who?"

"Aw, so now you're an owl?"

Laughing, "Who are you looking for?"

"I know the fellas are with you."

"Is that right?"

"Yep."

"A brotha may have come solo."

"Yeah, okay. Not only are they here with you, but they've already checked my girls out."

Chuckling, he said, "You know the fellas too well."

"So, where are they?"

Looking around, he found them and waved them over.

"What's up, fellas!"

"What's up with you? How are things in the STL?" Mike inquired.

"Things are good at home, and the city continues to progress."

"It's good to see you, Nia." Looking over at Malik, Ray added, "Real good."

"It's good to see you all as well. Hey Rick!"

"Hey, Miss Lady."

Mike introduced the guy with them I didn't know, "Nia this is one of our boys. He came along for the ride."

157

"Is that right?"

"Yeah. Nia. Gerald. Gerald. Nia."

With an outstretched hand I said, "Gerald, it's nice to meet you. If you are hanging with these clowns, you must be all right."

"It's my pleasure Nia," he said while looking at Colett. I guess he saw something he liked. "I want you all to meet my girls." As soon as I made my announcement, they turned around to meet, and greet.

"Nia, I've already had the pleasure, Alicia introduced me already." Malik informed me.

"Cool. You know Alicia. This is Alexis, Kenya and my girl from the ATL, Colett." In unison, my girls waved and said, "Hello."

"Ladies, these are Malik's partners in crime. That's Curly, Mo, Larry and Laurel. I don't know where Hardy is. They probably locked him in the stateroom. Laughing I added, "Just joking! This is Mike, Ray, Gerald and Rick."

In unison, they replied, "What's up, ladies?"

There was a moment of awkward silence, but Lexy broke it. "So, you're the four who had my girls hanging out in Dallas until three in the morning?"

Mike replied, "Yeah, we're the guilty ones, but we kicked it."

"You may have kicked it, but they were dead tired when they got back, Shit, we don't stay up past midnight."

"I feel ya'. We very seldom do the late-night thing unless we're chillin' at one of our houses," Ray added.

"We sometimes do that as well. A couple of weeks ago we had a slumber party at Kenya's, and we had a really good time," Alicia informed the fellas.

"Straight! So, you all had a 'Waiting to Exhale' party?" Rick inquired. Before any of us could answer, Mike said, "C'mon now, let's call it what it really is."

"And what would that be?" Alexis wanted to know.

"A brother bashing bonanza!" Mike added.

Malik, Ray, Gerald, and Rick looked at each other, and then at Mike and in unison they said, "Nigga what?"

Laughter erupted from all of us, and Malik began to delve to find out what the hell Mike was talking about. "Did you hear what you just said? A brother bashing bonanza? Bonanza? Nigga, brothas don't use words like bonanza. What's up with that?"

"For real Mike, bruhs don't use the word bonanza!" Ray said.

We were all looking at Mike and waiting for an answer. We didn't know if he was serious or not.

"Why are all of you staring at me?" Mike inquired.

Rick said, with a strange look on his face, "Why are we staring at you? Nigga, when you start using words like bonanza, you better be glad we're just staring at you, and not kickin' your ass."

158

"You'd kick my ass for using the word bonanza? What kind of shit is that?" Mike wanted to know.

"It's some suspect shit, that's what it is." Ray replied.

"Now you know that's some bullshit, the way I talk has nothing to do with my sexuality."

Alicia stepped in, to calm things down before they got out of hand, "All right fellas, we are on vacation, and this is not the time to be arguing over some nonsense. Mike used the word bonanza, oh well, that was his choice. So, you all need to chill the fuck out!"

"You're right Alicia, and I'm sorry for trippin." Malik indicated.

"I think we should grab a table and get better acquainted." Alexis suggested.

"Now that sounds like a plan." Rick said.

Again, looking at Colett, Gerald said, "It sure does."

We were able to find an oblong table to seat all of us, so we began to talk about general things. The fellas talked about Dallas. We talked about St. Louis, and the need for a vacation. Malik tried to mention work, but Alexis cut him off informing him we agreed we would not mention work while on vacation. He and the fellas agreed to this as well. It wasn't surprising to me my girls got along with the fellas. I knew they'd like them when Licia and I met them in Dallas. They're hella cool and real. They're a group of down to earth black men who enjoy a good time and good conversation. Yep, the conversation flowed as well as our drinks. I hate to talk about people, but our people are so colorful. Tom Joyner and crew attract ages from the early twenties to the mid-seventies, so there was an array of black folks on the ship. This brotha walked on deck with his seventies gear on, and of course he was the center of attention. He had on navy polyester shorts, a floral shirt, a straw hat with the same floral print as the shirt and last but not least, he had on a pair of silk socks. Bruh had on some gators, but the rest of the fit was so out there the gators were easily overlooked. He was downright country and outdated. He even had the nerve to smile. Why was his mouth full of gold? Why was the word S-M-I-L-E-Y spelled out in his teeth? Why do we do this to ourselves? Why? Also, I know we come in all shapes, sizes and colors but why would a three-hundred-pound woman wear a bikini? Or a better question is, why would a clothing manufacturer make a bikini that large? My answer to both questions is 'I don't know.' After two hours of people watching with the fellas, the captain of the ship announced over the P.A. system we'd be sailing within the next half hour. The girls and I decided this would be our chance to return to our rooms. We could check on the arrival of our luggage and take a nap.

Alicia stood up and announced, "Fellas we hate to cut it short, but it's our nap time."

With a-no-she-didn't-say-nap-time-cuz-they-grown looks on their faces the fellas asked together, "Nap time?"

"Yes, nap time. How do you think we keep ourselves so beautiful? So youthful?"

"You know black don't crack." Ray offered.

"True. You got a good point Ray." Gerald was still staring at Colett.

"You make a good point, but adequate rest has a lot to do with it as well."

I interjected. "I could actually use a nap as well. A sistah's been up since five and I plan on getting my groove on tonight. Isn't the Gap Band performing tonight?"

Mike answered. "Yeah, I think they are."

"Oh it's on! *"You dropped the Bomb on Me"*, and you know Charlie Wilson's going to sing '*Without You*' off of his first solo album," Snapping her fingers Kenya said. Ray began to snap his fingers also. "Aw shit, that's my joint!"

"Yeah, that song is tight!" Malik said while looking at me with yearning in those eyes of his. I looked away because I knew if I didn't, he'd see my eyes mirrored his. I couldn't allow him to see that.

Colett began yawning. "Well, fellas we're about to head to our rooms."

Malik asked, "Speaking of what are your room numbers?"

Alexis gave up the information. "Nia, Colett and I are sharing a room and the stateroom number is eleven-hundred-sixty-three. Kenya and Alicia are right down the hall in stateroom number eleven-hundred-fifty-one."

"Cool, I'll put that in my memory bank. We have connecting rooms; I think on the same floor as you. Our stateroom numbers are one-thousand-seventeen and one thousand-nineteen."

Ray asked, "Which dinner seating are you all scheduled for?"

Kenya replied. "The second, which I believe is at eight."

"Cool. So are we."

"Why is it cool? We won't be able to sit together."

Malik explained. "It's okay Kenya, you just met us and therefore you don't know what we're capable of. Believe me when I say we will be sitting together."

This I found amusing. Grinning like a toothless fool, I asked, "Is that right?"

"Oh yeah, I'm going to make sure we're sitting together every night. That is unless you ladies don't approve," Malik replied while giving me that look.

I decided to play with him, so I batted my eyelashes and seductively asked, "How do you plan on doing that, Mr. Black?"

"A brotha has his ways and that's all I'm going to say."

Snapping her fingers in that he-told-you-manner, Colett said, "I guess we'll have to wait and see then."

Looking Colett up and down Gerald said, "I guess you will."

By this time, everyone was yawning. We were ready to lay it down but evidently Alicia was impatient and ready to go now. "All right fellas, we'll see you then."

"Yeah, we should be going. We'll just see you all at dinner," I informed them.

160

"Dinner it is. We'll see you there," Gerald stated while still looking at Colett.

Throughout the week, we hung out with Malik and his boys. Everyone had matched up and we did the couple thing during the cruise. It was no surprise Colett and Gerald ended up hanging considering the looks he'd been giving her since day one. Also because of Gerald's looks, I knew Colett wouldn't pass him up. He was fine. He favored Boris Kodjoe so much. He was the color of caramel candy. He wears a baldhead and a goatee. He's a construction worker and I'm sure his profession contributed to his physique. He had arms like LL, and he had a few tattoos. Other than Ray, he was the only one with a child. One of his tattoos was of his son's name, Gerald Jr.

Alexis was with Mike; Kenya was with Rick and Alicia was with Ray. Our hanging together wasn't planned but after the initial meeting on the first day, we clicked, and the rest is history. I'm sure one of the main reasons the ladies went along with it is because they were trying to play Cupid. Whatever the reason, we were all having a great time.

Malik had been attentive and a gentleman so far. I don't know if he's always affectionate, but he was pulling out all the stops. I do like affectionate men, but most men are only affectionate in the beginning. I, like most women like men who are affectionate all the time. Unfortunately, when this cruise is over, I won't be able to find out about his on-going tendencies because I wouldn't see him again.

Ben hasn't approached me since the first day, but he'd become a borderline stalker. Everywhere we went. He was there. Looking. Lurking. I thought Malik would say something about him lurking around, but he hasn't. I guess it doesn't matter to him who's looking and/or lurking because all my time was spent with him.

When boarding a cruise ship you have to present a credit card or a cash deposit for any purchases made aboard. The cruise line takes the deposit and applies it to a cruise line credit card for you to use on any purchases. Food and beverages are included but alcohol isn't. Neither are purchases made at any of the boutiques on the ship, or at the various ports of call. I purchased a Movado watch on the ship but other than that, I hadn't spent any money. Malik had purchased all my drinks. He offered to pay for the watch, but I refused his offer. Remember I'm not a gold digger, a goal digger maybe but not a gold digger; I can do for myself. He also purchased this African print sarong we saw while sightseeing in Antigua. He was the perfect gentleman. It was nice to be treated this way. It had been so long since a man treated me like a queen. I could get used to this. My girls weren't spending much of their money either; the fellas were also being perfect gentlemen. To sum it up, we had a great

161

time. On the days we were at sea, we hung out at the pool or in the casino losing their money. I'm not much of a gambler but if someone gives me money to lose, I will play the slots. Of course, we made it our business to indulge in as many concerts as we could. We'd seen The Gap Band, After 7, Rachelle Ferrell, and a slew of others. My favorite concert had to be the Parliament/Funkadelic featuring George Clinton. I got a serious groove on that night. I also thoroughly enjoyed the Dougie Fresh/MC Lyte concert. I just love ol' school. We were eating lunch on deck when Gerald asked about us attending the Lyte concert. All my girls looked at me. This caused the fellas to look puzzled. I know Gerald was taken aback but he was also curious. "Excuse me ladies, but why are you all looking at Nia? When I asked that question, it was meant for everyone."

Colett took it upon herself to explain, "Gerald let me explain something. We're all in our thirties, well they are. I'm only one year from thirty so we appreciate the old school era, but Nia loves this era. I know this about her after only knowing her for a short time." Alexis jumped in and added, "When we were about twenty-one, we would go to this club in East St. Louis, Illinois called the Wiz and Nia thought she was MC Lyte."

I began rolling my eyes because I hated when my girls, or the women posing as my girls told personal shit about me. It could be so embarrassing at times. This conversation obviously piqued Malik's interest because he asked, "What do you mean she thought she was MC Lyte?"

Alexis continued, "On Thursdays at the club they did The Gong Show and-" At that point, Kenya eagerly jumped in, "I forgot about that. I remember Nia speeding down I-70, going across the Poplar Street Bridge into Illinois to make it to the club before midnight."

"Yeah, Ladies Night on Thursdays." Alicia commented with a faraway look on her face. She must've been reminiscing.

Alexis jumped back in. "Before I was interrupted by Kenya, I was going to say I remember Cedric performing."

Alicia wanted to comment on the good ol' days, and she did. "I remember Cedric performing too. I also remember him winning. Look at him now. That shit paid off."

With a confused look on his face Ray asked, "Cedric? Cedric who?"

With my hands on my hips doing my best Lovita Alizay Jenkins-Robinson imitation, I said, "Cedric Jackie Robinson, that's who."

Mumbling to himself, Ray repeated what I said, "Cedric Jackie Robinson. Who the hell is that?"

Kenya, Alexis, Alicia, and I looked at Ray as if he was a Martian. Cedric was a household name by now. Black households especially. Colett saw the look we gave Ray and decided to check Ray for us. "Who is Cedric? I'm not from the STL but my girls are so proud of St. Louis' own, Cedric the Entertainer."

"Damn! I forgot he was from the STL."

Alexis continued. "He used to perform at this club. Well, one night Nia decided she was going to perform. Jake egged her on and she found the courage. So-."

"Excuse me, Alexis, but who is Jake?" Gerald questioned.

"Jake is like a brother to us. Kenya, Alicia and Nia have known him since elementary school and he and I attended Howard University together." Alexis went on to finish her tale about me. "So, since Jake got her confidence up, she added her name to the list of people to perform. When it was her turn, we heard the first few beats of "Cha, Cha, Cha" and she began to flow like MC Lyte. Cedric won, but Nia did a damn good job and ever since then, she thinks she's Lyte; it's her alter ego."

"Lexy, you know I'm going to get you right?"

"Girl, I ain't thinking about you, I just wanted the fellas to know why we have to attend the concert."

As the days and the ship rolled on, we continued to enjoy ourselves. I'd seen Ben's crazy ass still lurking around like a nerd with a high school crush. Of course, we were all ignoring him. He couldn't grasp the concept he is old news.

The cruise was ending, and we were all looking forward to the captain's dinner. Black folks never pass up the chance to get jazzy and look good. It's what we do.

The last night of the cruise, which is also the captain's dinner, we told the fellas we'd meet them in the dining room, instead of them coming to our rooms. We wanted to WOW them in our formal wear. We were scheduled for dinner at eight, so we left the fellas to return to our staterooms at four-thirty.

Kenya could clean the hell out of a house, but she could also do hair. I'd been wearing my hair naturally all week, but for this dinner I wanted my hair straightened. In the elevator on the way to our rooms, I asked Kenya, "After I shower, would you please blow dry my hair?"

"Yeah, I'll hook you up, but let me take a nap first. Can you come to our room at six-thirty?"

"Sure, you're doing me a favor and I appreciate it."

This fool began to sing, 'That's what friends are for'. Everyone else joined in the singing. As we got off the elevator, still singing mind you, and hugging, people were looking at us as if we'd totally lost our minds. We didn't care because they didn't understand our bond. Our friendship was a special one. After we finished our rendition of Dionne, Elton, Stevie, and Gladys' song, we went to our rooms.

I showered first and made sure to shampoo my hair to get rid of the chlorine. Colett showered after me, and then Alexis. I was determined to sleep for at least one hour. I think my girls were thinking the same thing. After their bathroom ritual, they climbed into their beds as well.

Our nap time ended up being one and a half hours. I woke up at six-fifteen and the rest had done me good. I felt refreshed. I got up, woke Alexis and Colett up, brushed my teeth and headed to Kenya and Alicia's room.

163

After shampooing my hair, I allowed it to air dry so by the time I arrived at their door, I had a curly bush on my head.

Kenya opened the door, "Girl, what's wrong with your hair?"

Touching my hair I said, "I let it air dry."

"Well, I'm glad you're not tender headed. Come on in so we can get started."

I followed Kenya. Alicia had just gotten up and was heading for the shower. Kenya set up everything on her nightstand. I sat on the floor, and she began using the blow dryer. She was right. It was good I wasn't tender headed because she was working my bush out. How my mother dealt with this hair when I was a little girl was a miracle to me.

"Nia, do you want me to curl your hair?"

"Do we have time?"

"I turned the curling iron on, and I can give you some big wavy curls."

"Hmmmm.....I was thinking about wearing it up."

"You still can if you want to."

"Okay." Kenya proceeded to curl my hair and Lexy began to get ready. Once Kenya was done, I returned to my stateroom. Colett and Alexis were putting their lotion on. I began to emulate their actions because time was winding down. After applying my lotion, I retrieved my dress, my hosiery, my shoes and my handbag. "Lex, when I'm done with my makeup, will you put my hair up using my silver sequined hairpin?"

"Of course. Let me know when you're ready."

"I will. Thank you."

"You're welcome." We both sprang into action to complete our preparation. I decided to make my face up before I put my dress on. I applied a light coat of silver eye shadow and lined my upper and lower eyelid with black eye liner. As usual, I utilized my MAC chestnut lip liner and applied a light plum shimmery colored gloss. I drenched my curves in Chance by Chanel. I chose my two-carat white gold princess cut diamond studs to adorn my earlobes. Following the inspection of my makeup, I informed Alicia I was ready to have my hair put up. She brushed my hair to loosen the curls and pulled all of it up into the hairpin. She left some bangs out on the right side, which she swooped up. She left tendrils around the perimeter of my head. The effect was breathtaking.

I had a lot of formal dresses to choose from, but I decided on a sage green halter gown that draped in the front to show a hint of my assets. It was also draped in the back and possessed a high slit on the left side of the dress to expose a hint of leg and thigh. I teamed the dress with silver glimmer hose and my silver sequined Stuart Weitzman sling back pumps and the matching clutch.

Alexis was hot in her red. Her makeup, as always, was flawless. Her dress was form-fitting, off the shoulder and short with a side slit. She decided to go bare-legged. She wore red suede strappy sandals with a matching red clutch.

Colett wore a silver one-armed gown. Her dress was formal but short. The hem of the dress was adorned with silver beads. She opted to not wear pantyhose and go bare-legged like Alicia. She wore silver stiletto sling-back sandals and carried her silver beaded clutch. She

"Nia, call Alicia and Kenya and tell them we're ready. Ask them to meet us in the hall," Colett said. called and they met us.

I must admit we clean up well. We all looked beautiful. "Ladies, I know I'm biased, but you all look beautiful. We set out to WOW the fellas and I know we've achieved that."

Kenya and Alicia were dressed to the nines as well. Alicia had on a black dress which crisscrossed the front, as well as in the back. The back of the dress dipped to the crack of her ass, and it hugged her body like a second skin. She wore a pair of black satin four-inch stiletto pumps with jet-black hosiery. The dress was definitely made for her figure.

Finally, there was Kenya, and her gown was navy. It was strapless and hit right below the knee with a slit that came up mid-thigh. It was form fitting and gorgeous on her. Her strappy navy sandals were the perfect fit for the dress. We headed in the direction of the elevator. We could see all the passengers were dressed to the nines. Some even had on African garb and it almost reminded me of the annual 'Unity Ball' we have in St. Louis. There we celebrated African Americans who'd had a positive effect on the community and the attire was black tie or African garb. We arrived on the dining room floor and as we emerged from the elevator, we heard whistles. The fellas had already arrived. Since the attention was on us, we began to walk the hallway as if it were a Paris runway. Other passengers were getting a kick out of our antics, so they stopped, looked, and laughed.

After a few minutes, we stopped and joined our dates. Mike was the first to say something, "You ladies look awesome."

Malik, Gerald, Rick, and Ray agreed with, "Yeahs" and "He's right."

Malik pulled me to the side to say, "You look amazing, I mean absolutely breathtaking."

"Thank you so much. You look pretty dapper in your tux." Malik had on a black Sean John tux with silk lapels. With it he had on a light gray silk shirt with a matching tie.

Bowing he replied with, "Thank you ma'am, I try."

"Well, from the looks of it, you don't have to try too hard."

"Again, thank you for the compliment."

"No problem, but I'm sure you get compliments all the time."

"That may be true, but your compliment is the only important one."

"Awww, Mr. Black you're so charming."

"Not trying to be charming, just speaking the truth."

"Okay then. I'm hungry so let's eat."

"Yeah, let's." We returned to everyone, and they'd already matched up. They followed Malik and I into the dining room to our table. After being seated, the conversation began to flow freely. After a week with the fellas, it was safe to say our comfort level with them had grown by leaps and bounds. They were like old friends. Our server served us, and we got our eat on. During our last evening together, we immensely enjoyed each other's company. After eating, we danced the night away in one of the ship's clubs before retiring. The ship was set to dock at seven in the morning and when he was ready to walk me to the cabin, it was five. I suggested we watch the sun rise together.

"Malik, since it's so late what do you say to us watching the sun rise?"
"If you're up for it?"
"I'm cool."
"Okay, but I should probably grab a blanket."
"Since we're here at my door, I'll grab one. Wait here for me. I don't know if the girls are decent."
"I'll be waiting." I entered our stateroom to find Colett and Alicia in the bed and they were wide-awake. Colett spoke first.
"Girl we were wondering when you and Mr. Black were going to find your way back. The rest of us left the club an hour ago."
"We were having such a good time we decided to stay."
"Well, you better get some sleep, it's late."
Grabbing the blanket off my bed I said, "Actually I just came to get this blanket. Malik and I are going to watch the sun rise."
Alicia sat up straight, "Whaaaat? You're going where? With whom?"
At the same time Colett and I said, "Alicia, go to sleep."
"Colett, I'll be back in about two hours."
"All right girl, enjoy yourself. You deserve some happiness."
"See you in a few." I stepped back into the hallway. He was leaning against the wall with his tie loosened   looking as sexy as ever.
"I'm sorry it took so long. I had to be chastised by Alicia's crazy ass."
"That's cool." Offering me his hand he asked, "You ready?"
Accepting his hand, I replied with, "Yes, I am." We made our way onto the Lido deck and found two beach chairs.
"Here we are. Which chair would you like?"
Looking at him like he'd lost his mind, "We're going to share a chair."
"Aw okay. I didn't want to assume."
"I appreciate that, but there's only one blanket. So, this is what I propose. You sit first and then I'll sit between your legs and cover us with the blanket."
"Okay." We did just what I proposed and gazed into the sky. It was a beautiful and peaceful night. We sat in each other's embrace enjoying the moment because it would most likely be our last. We remained there in total silence until the sun rose. The view was breathtaking. This moment. This memory. I would be able to hold onto forever. Although this felt so right, I

honestly was not ready for this. It was going to be hard to leave him behind, but I didn't have a choice. Did I?

"Malik?" Silence ensued the moment. I repeated his name.

"Malik?"

"Yeah baby?"

"I want to thank you for showing me a great time this week. I really enjoyed myself and-" He cut me off.

"I want to-" I cut him off.

"No let me say this. This time spent with you was great. I never thought I'd see you again, but I am glad I did. Honestly, our being together feels normal, but I still am not ready for a relationship. I didn't mean to lead you on by spending time with you, it just felt right but once we leave to go to our stateroom that's it."

"That's it, just like that?"

"Yeah, it has to be."

"Why Nia?"

"I just told you Malik, I'm not ready."

"You don't think you're going to regret this decision?"

"I don't know. Maybe. Probably. Damn, Malik this is hard enough without these questions."

"If it's that hard Nia, then there are some obvious feelings there."

With anguish in my voice I said, "I'm not denying there are feelings, but I just can't."

"Okay Nia, I won't pressure you. I gave you my number in Dallas so if you change your mind, call me." He got up and left. No goodbye kiss, no hug or anything. I guess I couldn't blame him. If the tables were turned, I'd probably feel the same way. Anyway, I got up and carried my now depressed ass to my stateroom to get ready to leave. When I arrived in the room Colett and Alexis were both up shoving their belongings into their luggage. Alexis informed me she'd already called Kenya and Alicia. They were getting their stuff ready also. I decided to shower before I began packing my stuff. So far neither of them had asked me about my night but I knew it was only a matter of time. After dressing I began packing and the questions began. Colett was the first to say something.

"So, Nia how was your evening?" I decided to just answer their questions.

"It was fine until it was time to say good-bye."

"What happened?" Before I could answer Lexy's witty ass answered for me.

"I'll tell you what happened. She gave him the I'm-not-ready-for-this line."

"You think you know me so well."

"Well, am I right or wrong?"

"All right heifer you know me. I told him I'm not ready and I'm not. Remember, I just broke up with pitiful ass two, maybe three months ago."

"That's true but men like Malik don't come around too often."
Colett felt the need to respond to this line of conversation, "Alexis is right, Nia. Men like Malik are not grown too often in America. Not now anyway."

"I know, but I can't."

"Yeah, he's surely from an old school breed. He's like our fathers and that's what we want but I understand if you're not ready."
Looking at Colett I said, "Thank you for understanding, Colett."
Holding her hands in the surrender position, Alexis said, "Hey, I'm just looking out for you. I don't want you to end up back in Ben's bed or another stranger."
Colett and I looked at each other and then at Alexis. I don't know where that comment came from, but she was out of line.

"You don't have to worry about that Lex and whose bed I end up in is really none of your business."

"I'm sorry. I'm just looking out for you, and I was joking. I know better than err body, you and Ben are a threw piece!"
Again, Colett and I looked at each other, faintly laughed, but this time I decided not to say a word. I continued packing. The phone rang and I answered.

"Hello."

"Hey Nia." It was Alicia. "Did you enjoy your evening with Malik?"

"We will talk later."

"Who pissed you off?"

"How did you know?"

"Girl, I just know. I can hear it in your voice. We'll be down there in a minute. We're packed and ready to go."

"Okay, we'll be ready."
By the time they reached our stateroom, we were pulling our luggage into the hallway. They stood and waited while we joined them.
I asked everyone, "Do you all have everything?"
Everyone replied with, "Yeah."

We proceeded downstairs to leave the ship. There was a huge crowd of people waiting to leave and within the crowd we were able to locate Abdul. He was right on time like he said he'd be. Walking toward Abdul, I felt someone to the right staring at me, so I looked in that direction. The eyes looking at me were Ben's. I shook my head and rolled my eyes. This fatal attraction shit had quickly become tiring. I looked past him and into the golden-brown eyes of Malik. He had a sad look in his eyes and I'm certain my eyes had the same look, but I still couldn't go there with him. I looked at him for what I was sure would be the last time. I was trying to etch his face into my memory. After staring, we proceeded outside. Abdul dropped us at the airport where we boarded our plane. Since I was sleep deprived, I slept on the flight. We arrived in Atlanta and said our good-byes to Colett. She hugged the girls first and then me.

168

"Nia, thank you for including me. I had a wonderful time."

"I'm glad you agreed to come. It wouldn't have been the same without you."

"Well, let me go, call me when you get home tonight."

Hugging her, "I will girl. I love you."

"I love you, too."

We walked away in different directions. We had another plane to catch, and she had to get home.

Nia

The week after arriving home from the cruise I settled back into my normal routine. Getting him off my mind was difficult, but I did it. I was chilling in my townhouse that following Sunday evening, watching 'Insecure, and preparing myself for the workweek. I was laughing my ass off at Molly's sassy ass, and the phone rang. I peeked at my caller ID and it displayed a number with a Dallas area code. One of my girls lived there, but she moved back two years ago, so I didn't know who this was and calling on a Sunday night. Evidently, they didn't know me well because they weren't familiar with my-don't-call-my-house during any of my shows. So, I decided to answer the phone to see who it was. Inquiring minds wanted to know....

Agitated, I answered, "Hello"!

"Uh..yes, may I speak with Nia?

Now, I would know his voice anywhere, but I can't believe it's at the opposite end of my phone line. I vividly recall not giving him my number although he was quite persistent in pursuing it.

Agitated, I replied, "This is she."

"Did I catch you at a bad time?"

I couldn't let him know I knew his voice. That since leaving Florida, he was all I thought about. Yes, it's a game. A significant part of the dating game.

"Who is this?"

"This is Malik."

"Oh yeah...how did you get my number?"

Thinking to himself, 'Damn, is this the same sistah I met in Dallas first, then on the cruise?'

"Your girl Alexis gave it to me. I hope that was all right".

"I guess it has to be all right, you've got the number".

"I mean if it's a problem, I can let you go".

"No, no, that's all right. I apologize for being so abrupt, but I had a rough week, and I was watching 'Insecure'.

Laughing, "Well, excuse me!" Sistahs love them some 'Insecure'
Damn! That was a close call, I thought she was going to keep the attitude and not carry on the conversation.

"Yeah, the show is the bomb!"

"It's a great show for bruhs too."

169

"Oh, you watch?"

"Yep, when I have time, or I can stay awake!"

"So, tell me Malik, why did you want my number?"

"Now Nia, don't play crazy with me. I was very honest with you in Dallas, and on the cruise. I must've asked for your number ten times, and if my memory serves me correctly, I gave you my number in Dallas."

"You did, didn't you?"

"Yep, but you never called, and I don't even want to hear the excuse."

"Okay, no excuses. I recall you saying you were interested in us possibly pursuing something together."

"Well, you are right in your recollection."

"As I told you in Dallas and on the cruise, I'm not interested. Been there. Done that. Gotta therapist to prove it!"

"Well, I'm not giving up that easy. It's been a long time since I met a woman as down to earth as you, and not into the material bullshit like so many are".

"Me and my girls had a great time with you and the fellas on the cruise, but that was strictly us vacationing. I also appreciate the compliment, but that doesn't change my mind, or the way I feel. I've been happy by myself since I caught my ex-cheating. Although I had to endure that, I am not bitter, nor have I given up on black men, but I'm not up for any bullshit. You say you're bullshitless, but how many of us, men, and women, would admit to being bullshitters. I'm sorry, but I choose not to deal".

"Nia, I see your point, and I feel the same. I've had a starring role in Bullshitters R US, and I'm tired as well. I won't pressure you, but I'd like your friendship."

"Okay, then friends it is."

"Friends for now, but I'm not giving up. So, did you have a good time on the cruise?"

"Hell yes! Ain't no party like a Tom Joyner party cause a Tom Joyner party don't stop! We got our party on. Other than the Essence Music Festival in New Orleans and Sinbad's Seventies Music Festival in Aruba, that's the most fun I've ever had on a trip. Doing the Electric Slide in the ocean during our stop in Antigua, and the Soul Train Line on the beach was too much fun. It's always good to get away."

"I agree! We also had a great time. I couldn't believe Tom Joyner, Myra J., and Sybil! They straight got their party on! And J. Anthony Brown, he's a damn fool for real. I hated to return home."

"When a vacation is good, you never want to return home, but at least the weather's warm in Dallas. We left ninety-degree weather to return to forty-degree weather and rain. It's unseasonably cold for this time of the year, but you never know in St. Louis. The weather is so unpredictable."

He responded with, "It's eighty degrees down here, but we also have rain." Just as I was about to answer, the call waiting informed me there was another call on the line. "Malik, can you hold on for a minute?"

170

"Sure."

Without glancing at the caller id, I pushed the flash button on my phone and answered, "Hello."

"Hey Girl, what are you doing?"

"I've got a bone to pick with you Miss Knight, but it will have to wait because I'm on the other line."

Sighing, "What did I do now?"

"You know what you did, you-number-giving-traitor!"

"Who did I-oops, I know."

"I thought you would. I'll call you back."

"Wait a minute, what are you all talking about?"

"None of your business." Then I hung up on her.

"Malik I'm sorry about that. That was nosey ass Alexis."

"It's cool."

"As I was saying before she interrupted us, your weather is better than what we have."

"It may be warm, but it's raining niggas and chicken wings."

"Raining niggas and chicken wings? That is what you just said, isn't it?"

Laughing. "Yeah, that's what I said, it's the ghetto version of, raining cats and dogs."

"And you say I'm silly? That's all you!"

"Now, there may be some truth in that."

"Mr. Black, there's so much truth in that."

"Well, don't you think its fate we met in Dallas, and then on the cruise?"

"Why, do you?"

"I know it was fate."

"If you say so."

"How else can it be explained?"

"I don't know."

"I think Alexis thinks it was fate as well and that's why she gave me your number. She threatened me if I didn't treat you like a queen. Now, I just have to convince you of the same."

"We'll see about that."

"You'll come around lady."

"Now back to what we were discussing. I guess us meeting was fate considering we live hundreds of miles apart."

"I thought you'd see it my way."

"You're crazy."

"So, you say."

"Anyway, while we were on the cruise, we didn't discuss anything personal-

"Not for a lack of trying on my part."

171

"Touche. Tell me a lil' sumthin' sumthin' about yourself. You know how many baby mamas do you have? What do you do for a living? Do you respect your mammy? Do you disregard black women and date white women? Are you an Atheist? You know personal shit like that."

"I'll be more than happy to give you my personal history, but before I get into that, I have a personal question for you?"

"What's up?"

"Who was the man sweating you on the cruise?"

Laughing I responded, "That fool was my cheating ex. We broke up about two, three months ago."

"Really? From the sound of it, you kicked him to the curb. He was on you, like white on rice."

"I didn't really have a choice. I caught him cheating. Before you say anything, or think something negative about me, yes, me, and one of my girls did some I Spy shit! If a man won't be man enough by being honest, it's my duty to investigate. I did and we're no longer together. I had to check his ass on the cruise. I was not down there to vacation with him. I was with my girls. He only planned on going after we broke up and he found out I was going."

"Nia, who am I to judge you? I've done some things I'm not proud of. I can't blame the brotha for wanting you back, you are fine!"

"Awww….thank you! Men are so quick to call some women crazy, and if that's how you want to label me, then so be it. When I love, I give my all and then some, and I expect the same in return. I realize loving someone does not guarantee they'll love you back, but once the three words are spoken, I expect him to be a man, and act accordingly. He did not. If he was bored, or I wasn't enough for him, he should've just walked away. I'm a big girl, I could've handled it."

"From what I can tell, it was his loss. Nia, all men aren't like him, some of us can be sincere. You being vulnerable is a good thing, a lot of sistahs have been through so much they don't want to share any part of their lives with brothas. Sistahs seem to bounce back faster than men once they've been hurt, but I have noticed they always hold onto their heart a little tighter."

"Malik, deep inside I know what you've said is true, but it's just really hard now. I know why we hold onto their hearts. It can only break so many times, and it's such a deep pain. I agree, we do bounce back faster, but that's because no matter how many times we hurt, ultimately, we want that special kind of love."

"That's deep, but I feel you. Do you want to talk about what happened with you and your ex; I mean the details?"

"I prefer to not discuss details of previous relationships. I know we agreed to be friends, but you have an agenda that includes me, and us. I guess at this point you're going to tell me you don't have a woman?"

"I respect your privacy regarding your past, and no I don't have a woman. My last relationship ended approximately nine months ago."

"So, are you still in relationship rehab?"

"My rehab lasted about six months, but for the last three months I've been in relationship recovery."

"Is that right? So, you all aren't fucking anymore?"

"Damn, let's get straight to the point."

"Let's.We're grown, why beat around the bush?"

"I respect that, but no, we're done having sexual relations. She seduced me about six months ago."

"How does someone seduce you if you don't want to be seduced?"

"Well, I still had feelings for her, and a brotha hadn't had any in a while."

"Well, what happened?"

"I hadn't changed my locks, and she still had a key. One night I came home, and she was here wearing next to nothing. Let me be real, she was butt ass naked."

"Is that right? So, she was coochie up for you?"

"I guess you could say that."

"So, what happened after that? No reconciliation."

"None of that. I immediately regretted it afterwards, asked her to leave and had my locks changed the next day."

"That had to hurt her feelings."

"I'm sure it did, but it would've been worse if I wasn't honest with myself or her. I had a temporary lust moment, but I overcame it."

"No other episodes since then?"

"Nope. Never. Part of the past."

"Whatever. All right, it's your turn to answer my questions."

"Let me see if I can remember. Not only do I respect my mammy, I love her. She and my father have been married forty-two years, and they live in Orlando, Florida. As for what I do for a living, I'm the sole proprietor of Black Consultants, which is a computer programmer and analyst company. We set up systems, maintain them, and train people how to use them. I am not an Atheist; I believe in God, and I give Him praise. I don't attend church like I should, but I definitely know Him. Is that it?"

"Now, Mr. Black, you forgot two of the most important questions. How you forgot those are beyond me. The first was about how many baby mamas you have, and the second was about you dating white women."

"Oh, those questions?"

"Yes, those questions."

"I have three children, one is in Dallas with me, one is in Orlando where my parents are, and I also have one in DC."

"Damn! You've been slinging it."

Laughing, "Why does a forty-year-old black man have to have children? Did I just assume that you have children?"

"You're one of the first to not assume. So, I guess the answer is, no?"

"Now, that would be the correct assumption. Malik ain't having no babies without a wife."

173

"Hold up, that's me and my girl's motto. No babies, without husbands."

"That's the best way to be. There are so many African American children who only have one parent and it isn't fair to them. It's not guaranteed the parents will stay together, but it's good to know their intentions were good."

"It's a good foundation to start with. Your parents have been married forty-two years, and more than likely once you marry yours will be lasting as well. Prior to my father passing away, my parents were married for thirty-three years, and I'm sure that if he were still living, they would've just celebrated their forty-year anniversary."

"I'm sorry to hear about your father."

"No one is sorrier than me. We were very close, and I was a definite daddy's girl. I think it's why I haven't married."

"What do you mean?"

"I want someone like my father."

"And how was he?"

I lovingly replied, "He was God-fearing, hardworking, affectionate, supportive, loving, understanding, a great listener, and he had the best sense of humor. He always had my mother, my sister and I laughing. I miss him so much."

"I can hear the pain in your voice, and that saddens me. In your heart know he's in a much better place."

"Thank you. It's nice to see a man that's compassionate."

"I understand because I love my parents dearly, and the thought of losing them is a thought I'd rather not think about."

"It's hard, but time, and God ease the pain. Now when I find someone that's half the man he was, I'll open my heart to love again. Right now, it's closed for renovations."

"I feel you; I've had my share of disappointing relationships."

"So, to get off the sad subject, you can now answer the million-dollar question of the day?"

"What would that be?"

"How soon we forget or are you trying to avoid it?"

"Me, avoid something? Not in me, I face everything."

"Is that right?"

"Yes, it is Miss Witherspoon and to answer your last question, no, I do not disregard sistahs by dating white women.First let me explain something to you. A strong black woman raised me. She happens to be the descendant of strong black men and women. My grandmothers and aunts are black women, and in my opinion to date any women other than a black one would be a slap in their faces, and if you know black women like I know black women, they ain't havin' it."

"I heard that, and I respect that, but what about those people who say you can't help who you fall in love with?"

"Bullshit! I can say without a doubt I will never fall for a white woman, because I will never date one. Black women were made just for black men, and I plan to accept my prize with pride."

"You just earned mega points for that, but I'm sure white girls push up on you."

"Yes, they do, professionally and personally, but I let them know up front I am not the one. I like my coffee black and my meat dark. I like chocolate ice cream, not vanilla. I like soul food, not gourmet food. I like-"

Laughing, "Okay, okay! I get the point. You are too silly, but I like that in you."

"And remember...my last name is Black."

"Touché ."

"I just don't want there to be any confusion."

"Like I said, I got it. I hate to see brothas with "them". I look at my girls and I; we're educated, successful, independent, and good-looking but we're single. I see these white girls with these brothas and it pisses me off. I feel like black women should have first dibs on black men. Now, if "they" want our leftovers, well so be it, but we should have first choice at choosing our men."

"I feel ya. I know a lot of men who have slept with white women, and I know a slew of them who used them while in college, but I can say I've never dated one or slept with one. My mama would've disowned me."

"Well, that's admirable, and I have a lot of respect for you. Our attorney is a white girl who attended high school with us, and although she hangs out with us, she's never dated a black man. I respect her for that."

"That interracial thing has too many negative aspects."

"I agree. So, do any of your friends have children?"

"I have three friends who are like brothers to me, but you know that. Gerald and I are cool, but we've only known each other for about two years. He has a son who he takes care of but that's all I know."

"So, of your three close friends?"

"We're all the same age, but only one of them has a child."

"Father or baby daddy?"

"Definitely a father, our parents raised us right. It's my friend Ray, and his daughter is Rae. She was named after her daddy, but her name is spelled R-A-E"

"That's sweet. How old is Rae, and is Ray with Rae's mom?"

"Rae is three, and adorable. She has all of us wrapped around her little finger. And, no, Ray's not with Sabrina. They dated for years, broke up, but they were still sampling the goods when Rae was conceived."

"So, why not reconcile?"

"When they parted it was on good terms, but they had grown apart and neither of them wanted to reconcile. They did agree they would be the best parents they could be to Rae. They have a great friendship, and Rae has greatly benefitted from that."

"Wait one second, that's the brotha who was ogling Lexy's ass the whole time we were cruising?"

"Yep, that's him I didn't say he was perfect, just a great father."

Laughing, "True dat!"

"I also have a female friend who has a son. Her name is Brenda, and his name is Brandon. He's my Godson."

"Uh-oh, female friend drama. What? You all dated at one time?"

"NOT! We've been friends since second grade, but we've never been anything more. She had a crush on me in high school, but I was not interested. In fact, I've never been interested, not on that level. She respects it because she'd never want to lose our friendship. She's married to Brandon's father. His name is also Brandon, he's a wonderful man and he treats her like a queen."

"Well, Brenda sounds like she has a great family."

"She does. Are you opposed to opposite sex friendships? I know some women have a problem with that."

"If it is a problem, would it matter?"

"In this case, yes, Brenda's like family to me."

"You just got points for that. It's obvious friendship is important to you, and you should never give your true friends up for anything or anyone."

"Do you have any male friends?"

"Actually one of my best friends is a male, his name is Jake and we've been friends since the eighth grade. He's the brother I never had."

"Now, it's only fair I ask you the same thing you asked me."

"Go for it."

"Have you and Jake been intimate?"

"Jake is the first boy I kissed, and I realized then we could only be friends."

"Did he feel the same way?"

"As far as I know he did."

"Well, that's cool."

"Sometimes I wish I could turn the friendship love I have for him into romantic love."

"Why is that?"

"He's a great person, and from what I've seen, he's good to his women. He's what I'm looking for but can't seem to get my hands on."

"Your time will come."

"I keep hearing that, but it ain't happened yet."

"You have to be patient."

"Yeah, I know. Anyway, I'm trying to hook up Lexy and Jake, but it's a hard task."

"Why?"

"They just don't see each other that way, but they'd be perfect for each other. I think they're fighting it."

"Jake's not involved with anyone?"

"Yeah, no. Not really."

176

"Which one is it?"

"He had a fiancée, but she wasn't the one for him. She only wants him for his money."

"Have you told him this?"

"Yes, and he's starting to see for himself. Her true colors are shining through."

"It sounds like you've got his back."

"Since eighth grade until forever."

"I'll have to meet this brotha."

"I may be able to arrange that."

"So, can you answer the same questions that you asked me?"

"Sure. I already told you no babies without the husband. I own Event Solutions with Alicia. It's an event planning company, and we do all the decorating and catering."

"Is that why you all were in town the night we met?"

"Yep, it is."

"That sounds interesting."

"It is and we love it."

"My mother and I are very close. Although I was daddy's girl, she and I have always been close. Like you, I know God and I try to honor him. I don't attend church regularly, but I try to live right. Last but not least, I do not date white men. This queen can only be happy with a king and in my opinion brothas are the true kings."

"Now that's what I'm talking about. I like your way of thinking."

"I'm just speaking from my heart, and my heart belongs to black men."

"That ex of yours was a damn fool!"

"Yeah, well you know how that is."

"It's definitely my gain."

"Well, Mr. Black, my time is up. I have an early meeting in the morning, so I must retire. A sistahs got to get her beauty sleep."

"I understand. Do you mind if I call you again?"

"Not at all friend. As a matter of a fact, I'll get your number also, if that's all right. I actually enjoyed our conversation."

"Damn skippy it's all right. I enjoyed our conversation as well. Do you have something to write with?"

"Hold on just a moment, and Mr. Black?"

"What's up?"

"No office numbers only."

"Yes, ma'am. Just remember, I don't have anything to hide."

I wrote the numbers down, He gave me his home number, as well as his office, and cell. There was no way I wouldn't be able to contact him.

"What time do you work?"

"Normally I go in around six, I try to beat this Dallas traffic, and I get home around six."

"Damn, that's a long day."

177

"That's how it is when you have your own business. What time do you work?"

"I normally go in at nine and I'm home by three or four, unless of course we have something planned and if that's the case, we're working all day long."

"Nine to four huh? That's pretty good."

"It's cool but believe me when I say that on those thirteen-to-fourteen-hour days I'm worn out. My short days mixed with long days even themselves out to about forty-five hours a week. Our calendar is pretty full."

"That's a blessing."

"Yes, it is. If you're working as long as you do, you're pretty blessed as well."

"Yes, I am. I knew I had to get my own right after college. Corporate America can suck the life out of you."

"Yes, it can."

"I do respect brothas and sistahs that survive within corporate America and not lose their identity."

"Me too. That's an accomplishment within itself."

"Yes, it is, but I'm going to let you go now."

"All right Mr. Black, I'll talk to you soon."

"Baby, you'll talk to me tomorrow."

No, this Negro didn't call me baby. He's being a bit presumptuous, but I'll let it ride and see what's up. Normally I give myself a year of solitude, but I'm a little intrigued by Mr. Black. Like my girl Alexis always says, "Nothing gets you over a man, but another man." I wasn't tripping off my breakup with Ben nor was I considering getting back with him, but I have to admit I still love him. Unfortunately, you fall in love much faster than you fall out of it. I'll just take it one day at a time and see what's up with Malik, with his sexy ass.

I got off the phone and began to prepare for my day. I showered and then watched "Insecure" on HBOWest since Malik interrupted me. It was midnight when it went off. I played my quiet storm mix on Pandora and relaxed. Just as I was about to doze off the phone rang. Oops! I was supposed to call Alexis back, I was sure she was calling so I didn't look at the caller ID.

"Alexis Marie Knight, why are you calling me after midnight?"

A male voice came over the telephone line, "Hello." Oh shit, it's him calling. Again. Why is he calling back? What could he possibly have forgotten? He spoke again and this time he said my name. "Hello Nia."

"Uh, hello."

"Hey, did I wake you?"

"Malik?"

"Yeah, it's me and I can't sleep."

"So, you figured you'd keep me from sleeping as well?"

"I'm sorry. I didn't mean to wake you, but I can't get you off of my mind."

178

Yeah right. He's full of shit already. I'll play along. Dating is a game, right? Whoa. Did I just say dating? Has my mind decided that I'll be dating Mr. Black?

"I wasn't deep into my sleep yet. From the way I answered the phone you can see I was expecting Lexy. I should've called her back, but I forgot. Or maybe I didn't want to talk to her nosey ass."

"You don't want to fill her in on our conversation?"

"Eventually, but not right now."

"I understand."

"No. No, you don't. Women are different than men. Sure, the fellas will want to know what we talked about, but my girls, especially Lexy will turn into bugaboos. They'll call me at home, at the office, at my mama's and on my cell until they hear what they think they want to hear."

"And what do you think that is?"

"We're madly in love and getting married." Laughter spread across the line like AT&T's dial tone. "You think it's funny, but you don't know my girls."

"Well, I won't say I'd be opposed to you having those type of feelings for me, but it's kinda soon. Dontcha think?"

"They don't care about how long it's been. They'll say some shit like we're meant to be."

"Is that right?"

"Oh yeah."

"Baby, I'm sure your friends mean well." *Baby, did he just call me baby again? No, this Negro didn't call me baby. Anyway, I'll overlook it for now.*

"Yeah, they mean well, but that doesn't mean they don't get on my nerves."

"You know how friends are."

"Yeah whateva."

Malik thought to himself, 'Damn does she have a smart-ass mouth or what?' He decided to voice his opinion, "You have a smart mouth."

"I do, don't I?"

"Girl, you're a trip."

"I've heard worse."

"I'm sure."

"I'm one of those sistahs who speaks her mind. Some people say I have a smart mouth, but if I never said anything I'd be passive. My parents didn't raise me to be passive. My lineage is strong and it's all I know."

"I understand that."

"Do you?"

"Of course."

"How do you know?"

"Well, it's like this-

Yawning, "It's not that I don't want to know how you know, but I'm so sleepy. Can we please finish this conversation tomorrow?"

"That's cool. I'm sorry to keep you up so late."

179

"It's not a problem."

"I'll call you after I get home from work."

"I'll be waiting. Until then good night."

"Peace."

Just like that, the conversation ceased. I rolled over to get a full night of rest. Malik was a man of his word. He called the next day and every day after that. Our conversations became a part of our daily routine. For me it was an expectation. I expected him to call and fortunately my expectations never failed me. We have become friends and so far, no games have been played. This man had stepped up to the plate for the real black men of America. He was quickly changing my mind about black men. He began to talk about us seeing each other. I wanted to spend some time, but I was honestly scared. Scared of the what ifs.

Malik

After a lot of coercion, she gave in and agreed to me visiting. I wanted her to visit me in Dallas, but I thought she'd feel more comfortable on her stomping ground. During my visit she'd planned on working but I believed she tried to design an itinerary that would keep me busy and we'd both be guaranteed a good time. The weekend she agreed upon had some festivities she thought I'd be interested in, but she was saving that information as a surprise. She shortened her hours at the office so we could spend some quality time together. She informed me she enlisted David, Lexy's cousin, and Jake to hang out with me during her weekday work hours. Coincidentally, all of them were working nights so it worked out fine. I informed her I take daily trips to the gym, and she thought I could hang with them. They're on someone's court shooting hoops by mid-afternoon so she figured I would fit right on in. Yep, I was certain this trip would be a good one.

Nia

I arrived at Lambert International Airport early to pick up Malik. This was his first visit, but not his last, I was certain of that. He was due to arrive at the main terminal at twelve-thirty. Our first time seeing one another since the cruise, which was a month ago, although we'd been talking on the phone two to four times daily. The brotha was calling everyday but I cannot be available to a man twenty-four seven. They only take you for granted when you're available to them. I know the games we play. Anyway, he was arriving on an American Airlines flight but since we can no longer meet at the gate, I advised him to follow the exit to terminal signs. Unfortunately, our airport isn't the easiest to get around in if you're not familiar with it. Since my intentions were to arrive early, I bought some of my work stuff to go over. Things have been so busy since we acquired the Wells Communications account, but a blessing for us.

After about twenty minutes, the attendant announced the flight had landed, and the passengers would be embarking upon our city. I gathered my belongings and nervously awaited Mr. Black, while my conscience taunted me.

"Why am I nervous?" "Why are you nervous? What kind of question is that? Malik is fine and that's why you're nervous. No one has made your stuff quiver like him since Ben's trifling ass. He may be the "ONE". That Miss Witherspoon is why you're nervous, but get over it because ready or not, here he comes." My damn conscience gets on my damned nerves.

I dressed casually because I knew we'd be hanging out doing the sightseeing thing. This morning when I talked to him, I told him to dress casually as well. I had on a pair of Levi's, a Nike tee shirt, and my Air Max Plus. My hair was pulled into a ponytail. Malik had never seen me this casual and I hope he recognizes me.

I bent over to place my work materials in my briefcase, and I saw a pair of Air Jordan encased feet, and two pieces of luggage were in front of me. Upon looking up I was greeted by the deepest dimples ever, those sexy ass dreads, and those supple lips which were turned up into an inviting smile just for me. I guess I didn't have to worry about him recognizing me.
My nervousness went into the background like the Pips to Gladys Knight. He spoke first.
"Hey you!"
"Hey back at you. Welcome to St. Louis, Mr. Black."
"Thank you for having me, Miss Witherspoon."
"You're very welcome. How was your flight?"
"Good considering, I slept the entire time."
"Do we need to go to baggage claim?"
"No, everything's in my duffle bag and my garment bag. Although I would like to go to the rest room to brush my teeth."
"That's cool, I hate going to baggage claim."
"Me too. I learned my lesson. My luggage has been lost one time too many."
"I experienced lost luggage two times, so I never check my luggage. An acquaintance of mine lost her luggage, and they never found it."
"Live and learn." We both said it simultaneously and then smiled at one another.
We came across a restroom, so I waited while Malik brushed his teeth.
After leaving the rest room, I asked, "You get rid of the sleepy breath?"
"I think so, but if you like you can be the judge of that."
"And how would you propose I do that?"
Staring at me as if he was in a trance, he said, "You're beautiful."
Blushing, "Thank you. I guess you like my au natural face. I didn't think you'd recognize me without the makeup."
"You're proof sistahs really don't need makeup, or in some cases, war paint. You didn't have much makeup on when I met you in Dallas or on the cruise ship."

"Again, thank you. I don't wear a lot of makeup because my mother always told me black women don't need it."

"Well, I can't argue with your mother over that point."

"Mr. Black?"

"Yes, ma`am`."

"Are you evading my question?"

"Not at all, we'll discuss that later."

"If you say so."

"Can a brotha get a hug?"

I was trying to keep my distance because just seeing him is turning me on, but I guess I should go ahead and indulge in bodily contact.

"After that compliment, how could I deny you? Of course, you can have a hug." We were joined hip-to-chest because he's much taller than me. He had to bend down since there were six inches between us. Our hug lasted fifteen seconds, but it felt like fifteen minutes. I backed away first.

"Let's go, my truck is in the garage."

Picking up his luggage, "Truck, did you say truck? As in SUV?"

"Yes. Is there a problem?"

"No, no problem at all, I just never thought you'd be driving an SUV. You look like a BMW or Mercedes driver."

Laughing, "Is that right?"

"Yep."

"Well, I don't like BMW's, but I love my Toyota 4Runner."

"Cool. Just lead the way."

"Let's go. So, are you hungry?"

"As a matter of fact, I am. What do you have in mind?"

"Well, you can't visit St. Louis and not sample a steak from the *Best Steak House*."

"What about *White Castle's*?"

"What about it?"

"My boy from Chicago said I should try it."

"You will, another day."

"All right but don't we need to change?"

"Change what?"

"Our clothes."

Looking at him with my puzzled look, "No, why?"

"Well, you stated the name of the restaurant is, *The Best Steak House*, so shouldn't we look our best?"

Laughing I said, "Let me explain the Best Steak House. It's not a hole in the wall but it's not five stars either. It's an older establishment and what's different about it is that you stand in line, and one of the cook's yells "Next", and depending on where you fall in line, you yell out your order."

"Excuse me?"

"You heard me. You yell your order and by the time you reach the cashier your order is ready."

182

"And their food is good?"

"It's delicious. The steaks are always cooked just the way you order them, and their bread is so good, you've got to get an extra slice."

"Since you're giving them rave reviews, let's do it. Not that I know St. Louis but where are they located?"

"They're located in midtown. Also located in the area are St. Louis University, Jazz at the Bistro, the Fox Theater, Powell Symphony Hall and the Grandel Theater which used to be home to St. Louis' Black Repertory Theater."

"It sounds like a busy area."

"It is, but it's safe and parking is inexpensive."

We arrived at my truck, Malik put his bags in the back of the truck, and we were on our way. While driving down I-70 east bound I gave Malik some St. Louis facts.

"You know St. Louis is home to Red Foxx, Arthur Ashe, Cedric the Entertainer, Chingy, Nelly, and the St. Lunatics. What some don't know, Maya Angelou and Josephine Baker were born here, and Tina Turner moved here at the age of 16 and attended Sumner high school, which has a rich history within the city."

"I know Nelly's from here because he talks about St. Louis in his music, as well as his interviews."

"He and I actually went to the same high school, but I'm older than he is."

"Really?"

"Yep. Anyway, St. Louis has three major interstates. They are I-70, I-40/64 and I-44, and three bypasses 370, 270 and 170. You can reach any destination in St. Louis city or St. Louis County within twenty-five to thirty minutes."

"Reaching a destination within twenty-five minutes is unheard of in Dallas."

"Well, Dallas is a much larger city. St. Louis is growing and becoming more diverse. Nelly and Cedric have given the city so much publicity."

"How are the race relations?"

"For a long time, St. Louis was very segregated."

"Race relations are better?"

"They seem to be although you'll always have your bigots."

"Is St. Louis' mayor African American?"

"We go back and forth.....black...then white....white then black. We have also had men and women."

"So, diversity is being practiced?"

"If that's what you want to call it. St. Louis' first black mayor was Freeman Bosley Jr., and he did an excellent job."

"What did he do so special?"

"St. Louis city is divided into several communities but as a whole, there's North St. Louis and South St. Louis. Most of the white people that reside in the city of St. Louis reside in south St. Louis. Although a lot of them

183

are now moving back to the city."

"So, North St. Louis is the black side?"

"Basically, yes and for years no one cared about north St. Louis, or its residents."

"Until this Bosley guy comes along?"

"Exactly and he did basic stuff, but it indicated he cared."

"Basic stuff like what?"

"There's a street that runs through north and south St. Louis called Kingshighway and in south St. Louis the street was always well paved, and tree lined. In north St. Louis it was one of the most run down streets and was known to tear a car up because of the potholes."

"Potholes. What is a pothole?"

"When it snows our transportation department lines the street with salt."

"Salt? We use sand."

"Sand? Does it help?"

"Not really, people in Dallas can't drive in snow, we're not accustomed to it."

"It very seldom snows there so that's understandable, but we sometimes get hit pretty hard. The salt melts the snow and ice, but it also eats away at the asphalt causing potholes."

"A lesson in winter driving."

"It may come in handy if you ever visit in the winter."

"That's a good sign, we're already discussing future visits."

"Anyway Mr. Black, Mr. Bosley paved Kingshighway on the north side and new homes were built in St. Louis city."

"North and south?"

"Yes, and that's a good thing because more people are moving back to the city. More businesses are going up in downtown St. Louis and thanks to Mr. Bosley, we had the Rams."

"So, he's the one that got the Rams?"

"He had a hand in it, although they're now gone. He's also the one who made sure when the new dome was being built, minority owned construction companies weren't excluded."

"It sounds like the brotha's interest in the city is genuine."

"Definitely, he was born and raised here."

"How many urban radio stations are there in St. Louis?"

"Hmm...Let me think. There's 100.3 The Beat, 104.1 WHHL and 96.3 which is home to the Rickey Smiley Morning Show."

By this time, we'd exited off I-70 and we were driving south on Grand Blvd.

"No matter how many cities I visit, the 'ghetto' always looks the same. Boarded up houses and buildings, and every corner has a business, and most of them aren't owned by us, a nail shop, a liquor store, a convenience store, and a beauty supply store. We really need to reclaim our neighborhoods."

184

"Those of us who are making money and have families, or plan on starting a family don't want to live in a neighborhood with dilapidated housing."

"I agree but if the entire community works together, it can be done."

"It has to be a collective effort but unfortunately, it seems like the number of people who don't care outnumber those who do."

"That seems to be the same in a majority of black neighborhoods, across the country."

"I agree."

We parked on Washington Blvd., fed the meter change, and walked around the corner to the steak house. There were about twelve people in line ahead of us so Malik would be able to get the full 'Best Steak House', experience, a St. Louis tradition.

"Malik, I can yell out your order, or you can do it by yourself."

"You were serious?"

"Very."

"I guess I can do it."

"Okay, do you know what you want?"

"Not yet, what are you getting?"

"The chicken plate with tip potatoes, and an extra piece of toast."

"Is that what you normally get? And what are tip potatoes?"

"That or the steak and chicken. Tip potatoes are fried potatoes with cheese and/or onions. The expectation is the cook will get a tip when he prepares them."

"How often do you eat here?"

"Oh, about every six weeks, or whenever I'm in the area. If we're attending something at the Fox, we go. Alicia loves this place."

"I think I'm going to try the steak and chicken with the tip potatoes. A brotha could eat both of those every day."

"I'm sure you'll be pleased."

Soon thereafter the cook began yelling 'Next'. I stood in front of Malik so when it was my turn, I yelled my order. "Chicken plate with tip potatoes with light onions and cheese, and an extra slice of toast."

Malik followed suit. "Steak and chicken, medium-well with tip potatoes, with cheese and onions."

Those in line behind us continued to place their orders as we moved through the line, retrieving our silverware, salads, and our drinks. I got ready to pay the cashier, but Malik wanted to pay.

"Nia, I'll take care of this."

"No, that's all right. The bill won't be more than thirty dollars."

"No matter how much it is I want to pay."

"That's kind of you, but you're my guest."

"Are you sure?"

"Yes, I'm sure."

"I don't want you telling your friends tonight at your place I didn't want to feed you."

185

Laughing, "They know better."

I paid the cashier, and our plates were ready. We found a booth and began to eat.

"Damn, this is good."

I remained silent and gave him an I-told-you-so look.

"Don't give me that look. How was I supposed to know a restaurant where you literally serve yourself and yell out your order, was going to be good? And this good? I would've never imagined."

"Well, you're supposed to trust me."

"Yeah okay, but when you described the restaurant, it sounded raggedy."

"Raggedy, huh?"

"Well, maybe not raggedy, but definitely different, and not what I'm accustomed to."

"Different I can agree on. I was shocked on my first visit, and I live in St. Louis, but the food remains to be delicious."

"You were right about the bread."

"Told ya!"

We completed our meal and headed back outside to my truck.

"So, what do you want to do next?"

"Do you all have a Saks Fifth Avenue here?"

"Of course, would you like to go?"

"If you don't mind."

"Your wish is my command."

"Is that right?"

"Within reason Mr. Black, within reason."

His laughter filled the interior of my truck. I found myself laughing along with him. His laughter was infectious. Down I-40 west bound, Plaza Frontenac was only twenty minutes with no traffic from the steak house. I exited onto Lindbergh Avenue, made a right on Clayton Avenue and then I turned into the parking lot of Plaza Frontenac. It houses Saks Fifth Avenue, Neiman Marcus, Coach, Louis Vuitton and other expensive as well as exclusive stores. We had other malls, but if someone wanted to purchase Gucci, Ferragamo, Prada, D&G, or any other expensive designer, Plaza Frontenac is where they'd have to go.

"After we leave Plaza Frontenac, we need to go to my townhouse. I need to prepare dinner and feed Sheba."

"Sheba's the Rottweiler, right?"

"Yep, that's my baby."

"Does she bite?"

"I bite if provoked."

"Really? That may be interesting."

"Anyway, anyone or anything with teeth can and will bite, but she's not a vicious dog."

"Most in her breed are."

186

"Actually, they're not, they just get a bad rap. It's really based on how they're raised. I raised Sheba to be a good watch dog and she will attack if she has to."

"I'll keep that in mind."

"You'll be fine because you'll be with me. Once she sniffs you, you won't have to worry about her."

"If you say so."

"Are you afraid of dogs?"

"No, I love dogs. If I had family in Dallas, I'd have a dog, but I travel too much."

"I travel a lot also, but my mother watches Sheba, and if she's unavailable normally Kenya will watch her. Lexy's allergic to dogs."

"It's good you have family support."

"Yes, I'm very blessed in that aspect."

"Yes, you are. Do you come to this mall frequently?"

"No because I'd be broke."

"Why is that?"

"I love Gucci."

"I totally understand. I just purchased some Gucci loafers."

"I have five pair of Gucci shoes, five handbags, five pair of sunglasses, a watch and a belt."

"Damn! You do have it bad."

"Yes, I do, so you have to help me control myself."

Laughing, "I'll do that."

I parked in the underground garage, and we entered through the Saks Fifth Avenue entrance.

"Are you looking for anything in particular?"

"Not really, I just enjoy shopping."

"That's something we have in common."

"Yeah, that's something else we have in common."

"Most men hate shopping."

"I guess."

"My ex didn't like shopping, but my friend Jake loves to shop. The two of us are always in the Galleria or West County Mall."

"We have a Galleria in Dallas."

"Yes, I know. Alicia and I've been there. Our Galleria isn't as large as the one in Dallas."

"Yeah, the one in Dallas doesn't compare to the one in Houston."

"I've been there, and I agree. That mall is huge."

"Jake's the friend that's like a brother to you?"

"Yep, that's my boy."

"Did he and Lexy hook up yet?"

"Not yet. He just got rid of what's-her-name."

"You really don't like her, do you?"

"I don't like people who take advantage of people."

187

"She was that bad?"

"She was all right, but she is not the one for Jake."

"He wasn't happy with her?"

"Not really but he went out of his way to make her happy because that's the kind of man he is."

"I bet she's trippin' now."

"Oh yeah, now she says she wants to change, but like Luther sang, "It's over now! He realized his happiness had to be his priority because it wasn't hers."

"She sounds selfish."

"She is and that's why she's manless."

"So, Miss Witherspoon, why are you manless?"

Just then my cell phone rang. Grinning at Malik, I said, "Saved by the bell. Hello?"

Kenya's voice came across the digital line, "Hey Nia."

"Hey Kenya, what's up?"

"Nothing girl, whatcha doin'?"

"I'm at Plaza Frontenac."

"Really, with who? If you would've waited, I would've gone with you."

"Your memory is terrible."

"What did I forget this time?"

"Malik came in town today."

"The sexy-dread-lock-wearing-mole-above-the-lip-bow-legged-Malik who I've been hearing about for the last two months?"

"Yes, that would be the one."

"I finally get to meet him?"

"Meet him? You met him in on the cruise."

"Yeah, but you all are trying to work on a lil' sumthin' sumthin' now."

"Anyway, did you forget you; Lexy, Alicia, and Jake are coming over tonight for dinner?"

"Damn! I did forget but I don't have anything planned so I'll be there."

"Your ass needs some Ginkoba with your forgetful ass!"

"I'm too young to take that shit."

"You're also too young to be as forgetful as you are."

"Anywho, do you need me to bring anything?"

"Yes, it's B.Y.O.B."

"Damn Nia, I gotta bring my own drank?"

"Damn girl, B.Y.O.B. – bring your own boo! You don't have to bring a date, but Lexy will be with Jake I think.I'll be with Malik, and I think Alicia's bringing someone."

"I thought Alicia was kicking it with J.R.?"

"Kenya?"

"What?"

"Stay out of grown folks' business. Are you going to bring someone?"

"If I can find someone. This is last minute."

188

"Actually, it isn't, but you and your Alzheimer's having ass can't remember the day of the week."

"Yo mama has Alzheimer's."

"That's fine, but at least she remembers to change her Depends diaper. Yo mama wears the same diaper for seven damn days because she don't know any better and your forgetful ass forgets to check on her."

Laughing she said, "Your ass is silly."

I was also laughing, "No sillier than your ass. I'll see you tonight."

"Yeah okay, I'll bring my ol' stand by."

"Who? Craig?"

"That would be the one."

"Okay, dinner will start at six-thirty sharp."

"What's on the menu?"

"All of Malik's favorites."

"Tell Malik hello, and what are his favorites?"

To Malik I said, "Kenya said hello."

He responded with, "Tell her I said hello, and I'm looking forward to seeing her this evening."

"Kenya, you hear that?"

"Yes."

"The menu consists of T-bone steaks, shrimp scampi, baked potatoes, and mixed vegetables."

"Damn if Malik gets us a meal like that, we may have to keep him."

"Whateva nigga, see you at six."

"All right girl."

When I got off of the phone, Malik was giving me a you're crazy look but also smiling.

"What?"

"B.Y.O.B. – bring your own boo? I like the sound of that Miss WItherspoon and, did you and Kenya just have a yo mama session?"

"We did."

"And you called her nigga?"

"Yes, I did, me and my girls keep it real, and we joke with one another."

"You all are off the chain! I can honestly say I've never met anyone like you."

"Is that a compliment?"

"Yes, it is."

"Well in that case, thank you. I just feel like I should be able to be Nia every day, and people should be willing to accept that."

"I can get with that. Before I forget, I want to say thank you."

"For what?"

"For preparing my favorite foods. It shows how thoughtful you are and how well you remember things. I wondered if I'd get the chance to sample your culinary talents."

189

"You don't know if I'm talented yet. Let me know what you think after the fact."

"I'll do that, but if Wells Communications hired you, you've got to be very good."

"Well, thank you for the compliment and I hope you enjoy it. Do you see anything you like?"

Staring into my eyes Malik said, "Most definitely."

"I'm talking about clothes man."

"Oh, in that case I saw a D&G belt I want."

"You wear a lot of D&G?"

"Not really, but if I see something that I like, I'll pick it up."

"I own a pair of their jeans. They fit sistahs so well, even those of us that have been cursed with no-ass-at-all."

Laughing, "You make jokes about your disease."

"Of course, I've heard every flat ass joke there is, but it doesn't bother me. It did when I was younger, but I realized I didn't need a big onion booty to get what I want out of life."

"There's more to women than asses anyway. My ex had a fat ass, but she was diseased with no-sense-at-all. I think your disease is better."

"If you say so Mr. Black. Let me see the belt you're interested in buying."

"I didn't offend you, did I?"

"Not at all, I've been without an ass for quite some time now. Forty years to be exact. I have other assets which will make a brotha forget I'm suffering from no-ass-at-all."

"Is that right?"

"Without a doubt."

"I can't wait to find out what those assets are."

"Maybe you'll find out, maybe you won't."

"Well, I'm intrigued nonetheless."

Lowering my eyelids and giving him what I know was one of my sexy looks, I responded by saying, "Yeah, I'm sure you are."

Malik showed me the D&G belt he liked, and he purchased it. We left Plaza Frontenac without any Gucci incidents on my part. He tried luring me into that department, but I was strong. They have gotten enough of my money this year. My Saks Fifth Avenue account was full of Gucci purchases. It was almost four o'clock by this time and I had to get home to prepare dinner. I'd already prepared the scampi sauce for the shrimp, and the shrimp had been cleaned and de-veined. I had also prepared the dough for the rolls.

Malik

Nia drove down Lindbergh to Olive Street Road which she headed east on. She then made a right onto North and South, which is her street. As we pulled up, she announced, "This is home sweet home."

I inquired, "Are these town homes?"

"Yeah, they've been here about two years. There were some older homes here the city purchased, tore down and built these. Alicia and I are both happy with our purchase."

"I do remember you saying Alicia lived a few doors down from you." She opened the garage and pulled in next to her Mercedes E450.

"Nice car, and it suits you."

"Thank you. I just purchased it. As a matter of fact, I got it after my first trip to Dallas. Jake helped me pick it out and made sure I got a good deal. I had a Honda Accord Coupe, but I gave it to my cousin when I decided to buy the Mercedes. She's in medical school and I wanted her to have something reliable to get around in."

"You gave it to her? You didn't sell it to her?"

"Yes, I gave it to her. You can't be blessed if you don't bless others."

"That's a nice sentiment."

"It's the truth."

I grabbed my bags from the truck, and we entered her humble abode. She removed her shoes but didn't request I do the same.

She yelled for her pet, "Sheba!"

"My moment of truth."

"There's no need to worry, she'll love you as long as she doesn't sense any fear from you."

"Is that the secret?"

"Well, it's not a secret. Dogs normally will attack if fear is present. That's no secret but a known fact."

Sheba walked up to Nia, she rubbed her head and behind her ears and then she headed to me. She looked up, tilted her head to the side like dogs do and she studied me. I took that as my cue.

"Hi Sheba! How are you girl? Nia, she's beautiful," I stated as she allowed me to rub her head. Sheba then went to her corner in the kitchen to lie down on her mat.

"She is, isn't she? She's the Queen of the house."

"Somehow I doubt that."

"I think she likes you."

"How do you know?"

"She sniffed you, licked you, allowed you to rub her head and went to lie down. If she didn't like you, she'd be growling or showing some teeth."

"Well, that's good to know."

"Go ahead and make yourself at home. When you're ready to go upstairs, I'll show you to your room."

"Are there any rules I should know about?"

"I'm glad you asked. I prefer no shoes be worn in the house."

"No problem. I thought it was odd when you removed your shoes but didn't request, I do the same."

"It's your first visit."

"Can I get a tour?"

191

"Sure. Follow me," I removed my shoes and followed her to her gourmet kitchen.

"This of course is the kitchen."

"Very state of the art."

"Thank you. It's the cook in me."

We left the kitchen and made a left from the hall.

"This is the dining room, as you can see it seats eight people."

"The table's unique."

"There was a store here called Dolnick's and they carried lots of unique pieces."

"It's nice, you have great taste."

"Thank you. This is the living room, but it's very seldom used. I entertain in the family room or the basement."

"Basements aren't prevalent in Dallas."

"Really? Here in St. Louis, don't quote me because I don't know the actual percentage, but I would guess that ninety-eight percent of the homes here have basements."

We went back into the kitchen, through another hall which led to the family room.

"This is my favorite room in the house, the family room."

"Damn! This is nice. Did you have someone decorate?"

"No, I did everything myself."

"Really? I really like this room, and I love the sculpture."

"Well, thank you. This is where we'll spend most of our time during your visit."

The back of the house was all glass and there were steps going upstairs as well as downstairs.

"We can go downstairs first, since your room will be upstairs."

"That's cool."

"Follow me."

"I'll follow you anywhere you want. How many rooms are in the basement?"

"There is a sitting/rec room for the entertaining, a library, an exercise room, and a bathroom."

"You actually have a library?"

"I love to read, and I've been collecting books for the last ten years, so when I had my place built, I asked the builder if one of the rooms in the basement could be a library."

"Did the builder build the bookshelves?"

"Yes, they did, but I did the decorating."

Before we got to the library, we passed through the rec room, which included a Ms. Pac-Man machine, a pool table, a large pinball machine, an electronic dartboard, and a huge flat screen TV that has Playstation 4 and XBOX connected to it.

"This is a child's paradise."

192

"Well, I'm just a kid at heart."

"I see. You have everything. This is really nice, and I'm very impressed."

"I'm not trying to impress you, I just wanted to show my home."

"Well, I'm still impressed nonetheless."

"Thank you, I'm very happy with the decorating."

"You should be. I'm ready to see this library now."

"All right, it's to the left."

The library was painted black and tan. Big bold pinstripes, with tan colored bookshelves. The floors were hardwood. In one corner, there was mahogany shelving with African artifacts, specifically Thomas Blackshear's Ebony Visions. On the only wall without shelving, there was a collage of pictures of important African Americans, male and female. There was a black leather couch, a tan leather lazy boy chair and a tan coffee and end-table. Under the coffee table was a black area rug with African designs.

"These are all your books?"

"Yep. I told you I love to read."

"You read all of these?"

"Yep."

"Damn! There has to be about four hundred books here."

"Actually, there are six hundred."

"You've got some great authors here, James Baldwin, Nikki Giovanni, Alice Walker, Phyllis Wheatley and Toni Morrison. I see you also have some of the new authors, Terri McMillan, E. Lynn Harris, Sheneska Jackson, Kimberla Lawson Roby, Eric Jerome Dickey, Michael Baisden and Sister Souljah. I see you also have all of Zane's books. She is the queen of black eroticism."

"Yes, she was. I loved her last book, 'Nervous'."

"You really read all of these books?"

"I have. Reading relaxes me."

"Maybe I'll read to you some time."

"You know how to read?"

"You got jokes? Let me call Comic View."

"Ha-Ha Mr. Black."

"Anyway, I noticed all of your books are by African American authors."

"Those are the ones I relate to. Just think, they said we as a people didn't read. I guess we've made them out to be liars once again."

"Yes, we have. I read a little, but nothing like this."

"Oh really, who do you like?"

"Michael Baisden is pretty tight with his writing."

"Yeah, he is."

"So, you really decorated this room?"

"Right again."

"You're talented."

"Another compliment, I could get used to this."

"So where's the exercise room?"

193

"The bathroom sits between the library and the exercise room."

"Let me see what kind of equipment you have."

"Actually, I don't have much, just an elliptical machine, a tread mill, some free weights and a TV to tune into several gurus who I access via YouTube."

"How often do you work out?"

"At least three times a week. Do you work out?"

"Every morning before I go into the office."

"Really?"

"Yeah, it's just a part of my daily routine now."

"Now I'm the one that's impressed."

"Why?"

"Because I hate working out and there are some days when I don't want to, but I know I have to."

"It is something you have to get used to."

"Would you like to go upstairs now?"

"Sure. How many rooms are up there?"

"My bedroom of course, the guestroom, the main bathroom and my office."

"Lead the way."

We went upstairs to her office first.

I complimented her office. "My office is never this neat."

"Did I mention one of my girls owns a cleaning company?"

"No, you didn't."

"Well, Kenya owns Kenya's Kwik Klean or as we call it Triple K and I had her come in yesterday and clean."

"So normally it's not this neat?"

"Hello no, but it pays to have a good friend who cleans for a living."

"I guess it does."

"Your office seems to be equipped with everything."

"Just the typical stuff, PC, laptop, printer, copier, and a scanner."

"We couldn't survive without these things, could we?"

"In this day and age, not at all."

"It's a well-equipped office."

"Let me show you my room."

"Your love nest?"

"I wouldn't call it that. You've got to be getting some love to call it that."

"We can resolve that."

"Is that right?"

"Your wish is my command."

"We'll see about that later."

"Straight."

"You are silly. Anyway, this is my room."

"Nice and very tasteful."

"Thank you."

194

The master bedroom was taupe colored with blond hardwood floors. The bedroom set was bleached wood, and the bed was a canopy with taupe sheer netting. There was a bay window with a tan leather chaise. On the wall that faces my bed, there was a fifty-five-inch flat screen. The master bathroom was taupe also, but it was also mixed with gray and off white, with the separate marble shower and tub. There was a separate room for the toilet. On the other side of the bathroom there was a door which led to a huge walk-in closet.

"Uh Nia, do you think you have enough closet space?"

"So far so good but that's only because I have all the closets in the house, once I have a family we can't live here."

"This is really nice. Once you have a family, you can have a house built with a closet the size of two bedrooms, that should be enough."

"I don't know, but we'll see."

"Have you ever considered interior decorating?"

"You're too kind, but I'd be too bored with that."

"Where is my room for the next week? Hell, half your place is your bedroom, is the guest room a pill box?"

"As a matter of fact, it is. You're only a guest, you don't need much space."

Laughing. "Is that right?"

"C'mon, let's see what your living quarters will be like."

We entered the guest room, and from the look on my face, she knew I was pleased. There was a black lacquer bedroom set with a queen-sized bed with a black leather tufted headboard. The room also had the blonde hardwood floors, but the walls were painted with taupe and black polka dots. There was a private bathroom with a separate shower and tub. There was also a forty-two-inch flat screen.

"This is very nice. You may never get rid of me."

"I hoped you'd be happy with your accommodations."

"I think I'll be all right during my visit."

"Well, that's good to hear. Let's go downstairs."

While we were in the kitchen, she went to the refrigerator to get a glass of Ocean Spray Cran-Cherry.

"Would you like a glass?"

"Yes, thank you."

"I know this is your first day here, but after today you will no longer be company."

"And the reason you're stating this?"

"I ain't a maid."

"I understand."

"I just want to make it clear."

"If it's okay, I'm going to take a short nap. I'm a little tired."

"No problem let me take you back upstairs."

We climbed the short flight of stairs, and she led me back to the guest-bedroom which was adjacent to her bedroom.

195

"I hope you find your accommodations to be sufficient."

"I'm sure they are fine, just as nice as a five-star hotel but without the maid service."

"There's fresh linen on the bed, as well as in the bathroom. There's also a cordless phone, satellite television and an Echo Dot if you want to listen to music."

"Like I said, just as nice as a five-star hotel. I like that."

"Casa De Witherspoon aims to please. My cousin stays in this room during her visits, and she requested, no she demanded all this stuff."

"She must be spoiled."

"Oh yeah, but she's done very well in school and my family is proud of her. Especially me."

"Well, I'm very happy with my amenities. Thank you."

"You're welcome. I'll be downstairs preparing dinner if you need me for anything."

"All right. One question before you leave."

"What's that?"

"Can I make a long-distance call?"

"Sure, as long as you're not calling any ancestors in Africa."

Laughing, "Damn! I wanted to call my cousin Edafe in Zimbabwe, but I guess I'll have to wait."

Also laughing, "I guess you will. Be sure to tell Edafe I said hello when you call him from your house."

"I'll be sure to do that."

"I'll be downstairs."

Damn! I'm finally in St. Louis visiting the one and only Nia Witherspoon. It took me one month to persuade her into allowing this visit, so I'm going to make the best of it. Damn! She's finer than I remember, even in casual clothes without any makeup. I want her but I know I must take my time. Her crazy ass ex has left her reluctant to try a relationship. She's been open to friendship, and I know she likes me, but it's imperative she's comfortable on taking the next step.

Melina's still calling but I don't want her no-ambition-wig-wearing-dependent-ass. A brotha is done with her ass. Nia's the kind of woman I not only want in my life, but I need. I'm at the point in my life where I've done everything I've wanted to do, except really fall in love, marry, and have children. Nia is God fearing, witty, intelligent, independent, and to top it off she's beautiful. Her ass is as flat as a chalkboard, but that's the only flaw I can see. From the looks of this townhouse, along with her 4Runner and her Mercedes, she's been very successful. Success is a big turn on for me, but I guess it would be after dealing with Melina's, spend-my-money-clingy-no-ambition-having ass.

Nia seems to be just as driven as I am. I really think we'd complement one another. I know how important her friends are to her, so I hope tonight is a success. Honestly, like me or not, I'm going to pursue Miss Witherspoon. I guess it would be easier if they accepted me and liked me, so we'll just have to see. That's a bridge I'll cross when I get to it.

Nia

I went downstairs to begin the dinner preparation. Before that, I asked Alexa to shuffle my jazz playlist on my Echo Dot and got another glass of Cran-Cherry. David Sanborn's horn began to fill the interior of my townhouse. First things first, I put two bottles of Pinot Noir and Armand de Brignac on ice. I preheated the oven to three hundred and fifty degrees. I removed the T-bone steaks from the refrigerator, washed them off, and seasoned them with a mixture of salt free seasonings I created. I cleaned the baked potatoes, covered them with cooking oil, Mrs. Dash, pepper, and then placed them in the oven on a cookie sheet.

I removed the broccoli, corn, cauliflower, and carrots from the vegetable bin so I could cut whatever needed to be cut, and wash everything off. I cleaned them with vegetable cleaner and placed them in a bowl.

Malik knew what was on the menu, but he had no idea I had prepared his favorite dessert, lemon cheesecake with a homemade graham cracker crust. He mentioned it was his favorite, and I stored that information in my memory bank. I prepared the cheesecake when I got home from work last night.

Time was passing at a fast pace. It's already five-fifteen, so I placed the meat on the grill outside and began to sauté the shrimp in the garlic butter sauce I'd prepared. Once the shrimp were done, I placed them in a glass dish in the oven to keep warm. I also fried four strips of bacon to make bacon bits for the baked potatoes. I checked on the steaks and removed my wok from the cabinet. I washed it last night. It would be used to steam the vegetables. I retrieved the steaks from the grill and placed them in the oven to keep warm. I went upstairs to shower. I could hear Malik was up and moving around.

Malik

I heard Nia moving around in the next room. I could smell the aroma, so I guess her dinner preparations were complete.

How I wish I could see her prepare herself. If I could I'd position myself in between her bedroom and bathroom, and just observe. Both upstairs bathrooms have glass door showers. I'd watch her lather and rinse. I'd then watch her lotion herself. I'd ask if she needed assistance, if she did, I'd willingly and gladly oblige. There's something about a woman taking care of herself which turns me on. I'm sure my dick would be as hard as Chinese arithmetic, but I'd be willing to deal with a case of blue balls just to observe.

God made a beautiful creature when he designed the black woman. Just the curves of their bodies are an aphrodisiac. I love to watch women lotion themselves from their toes to their buttocks, to their breasts to their shoulder blades.

Enough of the daydreaming about Nia, I need to get dressed. I showered and lathered myself with the shower gel that Nia provided. I also washed my hair. I dried myself and looked to see what I was going to wear. I chose a pair of black linen slacks and put on a short gray sleeve knit shirt. I put on the D&G belt that I'd purchased earlier, and my black leather Ralph Lauren sandals. I decided to let my dreads hang loose. I was about to go downstairs, but something caused me to stop at her door, I just stood there expecting her to feel I was there waiting. I even reached out to touch the door, and I could feel her essence. Reluctantly I proceeded downstairs. When I got downstairs, I saw an Echo Dot and asked Alexa to shuffle Neo Soul. Jill Scott's voice filled her house.

Over Nia's mantel were pictures of her and, I assume, her mother. She had a picture of her, and it looked like her father because she looked just like him, skin color and all. There was also a picture of her and her girls from the cruise. Nia had on a long silk skirt and a halter. She was oozing sex appeal. I remember the outfit and the hard on that accompanied it. I'm supposed to be here for five days. I hope I can make it.

Nia

I entered my room, undressed, began my shower, and searched my walk-in-closet for something to wear. I decided on a red, Calvin Klein halter linen dress I found on sale at the Beverly Center in Los Angeles. The dress had a deep V in the front, so I decided I was going to work the cleavage tonight; it fit perfectly and ended about two inches above my knees. I was hoping to WOW him with this dress. I paired the dress with my red three-inch heeled Ralph Lauren sandals. I'd overlook my no shoes in the house rule for the evening.

After wrapping my hair, I stepped into the shower. I lathered myself with Unforgivable shower gel and I used an apricot scrub on my face to exfoliate.

After I rinsed off, I dried off and then used my Unforgivable lotion. I sprayed my cologne between my breasts, behind my ears, on my neck, in the bend of my arms as well as the bend of my legs. There wasn't a spot on my body where he wouldn't be able to smell me.

Knowing my girls like I do, they'd be on time. Well, Lexy and Licia would be anyway. I wanted to be the one to greet them, as well as make the re-introductions.

As I was dressing, I could hear Vivian Green's voice crooning about being on an 'Emotional Roller Coaster'. I guess Malik was downstairs making himself at home.

I massaged peppermint foot lotion into my feet and put on my toe rings. I put on my dress and began to apply a light layer of makeup. I applied a brown eye shadow over my entire lid, brushed mascara onto my already long eyelashes, applied eyeliner, lined my lips, and applied my lip gloss. I stepped into my sandals, checked myself in the mirror, realizing I forgot to unwrap my hair. I went into the bathroom, unwrapped my hair and used my Sebastian Shaper hair spray to ensure the unruly strands would remain in place. Since my primping was complete, I proceeded downstairs.

Malik

I was chillin' in the family room reading the latest issue of *Essence* magazine when she appeared. I saw her legs on the cruise, or so I thought. Her legs were beautiful, and her sandals were at least three inches tall. How I love a sistah in high heels, and a short skirt. Her dress fit in all the right places, and her skin was flawless.

"Nia, baby you look beautiful."

Blushing, "Thank you, Mr. Black, you look mighty fine yourself."

"Thank you for the compliment."

"You're welcome."

"You're awfully tall today."

"I know, it's my sandals and fortunately, you're tall enough and I can wear my high heels."

"What, you've dated some short brothas?"

"I don't discriminate, but I will admit my preference is a brotha at least six feet two inches."

"Well, that includes me."

"I guess it does since you're six four. I've actually come to the realization, there are more average to short men than tall men."

"I think I agree with that observation. You've got pretty feet."

"I do, don't I?"

"We're awfully modest about our feet, aren't we?"

"Yes, I am. There are some sistahs out here with monkey toes, but I've been blessed with pretty feet."

"How often do you get a pedicure?"

"Every three weeks faithfully. Have you ever indulged?"

"Actually, I go about once a month in the summer."

"What! A man who gets pedicures on a regular, that's impressive."

"My boys drove me for a while, but I explained women don't want rough feet rubbing against them."

"That's true."

"Now all of those niggas get pedicures."

Laughing, "You've started something."

"Yeah, I know."

"Does a sistah do your pedicures?"

199

"Naw, we go to;' the Asian people. Why, you go to a black woman?"

"Without a doubt, and you haven't had a pedicure until you've been rubbed on by Lisa."

"Is that right?"

"Yes. I'm going to see if she can get you in while you're in town."

"That's cool, and if I like her, I'll-."

"Not only will you like her, but you'll love her."

"Since you're so sure I'll like her, it will give me one more reason to visit St. Louis frequently."

"One more reason. What would the other reason be?"

"You of course, Miss Witherspoon."

"We'll see, you may never want to see me again after this visit."

"That's not likely. If anything, I'm going to want to see more of you."

"Do you mean that literally?"

"Yes and no."

"Yes, and no? It's one or the other. It can't be both."

"Actually, it is both. Let me explain."

"Please do."

"I won't lie and say I don't want to see more of you. I'd love to see you naked as well as make love to you, but I know we're working on a friendship first although we are attracted to each other. I respect your wishes. So, right now I'll have to settle for spending time with you fully clothed."

"You can always see me naked in your dreams."

Grinning, "I already do."

"Is that right?"

"Oh yeah."

"May I ask you a question?"

"Of course."

"Are black and gray your favorite colors?"

Chuckling, Malik looked at me and shook head. "Is that supposed to be a transitional question to change the subject?"

"Is it that obvious?"

"Yes, it is, but I understand."

"Are you going to answer the question?"

"Sure." Still smiling, he added, "Yes, those are my favorite colors."

"The first time I met you in Dallas you had on a black suit with a gray shirt and tie. On the cruise, your attire was the same."

"For some reason, there's very little color in my wardrobe. I may go to the mall and see something with color, but I always find something in black or gray I like better. I did bring some color with me for this trip."

"Well, it looks good on you so if it ain't broke don't fix it."

"Again, thank you. You look good in red."

"Other than black it's my favorite color. I think it brightens my complexion, if that's even possible."

200

"You're working that dress and I don't remember your legs being that pretty."

"I guess you weren't really looking on the cruise."

"Oh, so you know you have pretty legs?"

"Yes, I do."

"Some would say you're arrogant."

"Well, if they saw my legs in high school they would understand."

"Why is that?"

"As a student at University City High School I was skinny, with big breasts and chicken legs."

"Is that right? I'd love to see that."

"I may be able to dig up some pictures if you promise to not laugh."

"I'll try my best."

"I'd appreciate it. I've dealt with enough teasing to last two lifetimes."

"Back to your legs on the cruise, believe me when I say I was looking, but I was more focused on your face."

"Mr. Black, you always know what to say. You're one smooth operator."

"Not an operator, just truthful."

"Anyway, can I offer you something to drink while I'm steaming the vegetables?"

"Nia, there's no need to put yourself out, you told me I could make myself at home, and I plan to do just that."

"Well, I meant it, and I appreciate it."

"No problem, you go ahead and steam your vegetables."

"I'll do that."

"Is there anything I can help you with?"

"There is something. Can you set the dining room table."

"Okay, where is everything?"

"Everything is already on the dining room table."

"Cool, I'll hook it up. Is there anything else?"

"There is. Could you please put Sheba in the laundry room? There's a pillow she sleeps on."

"Sure, but may I ask why? Don't all your friends know her?"

"Yeah, they do, but when she smells food, she will get in your face. She is a Rottweiler, and she has a huge appetite."

"I understand. After I set the table, I'll put her in the laundry room."

"Thank you."

"You're welcome."

As I left the kitchen to enter the dining room, I thought about Nia. So far, I like everything about her. She carries herself with such class. She is truly a lady. The fact that she's oozing sex appeal like Neosporin doesn't hurt, but it's all of her I want.

I continued to listen to the music I chose as I set the table, and then became thirsty. That would be my excuse to reenter the kitchen and sneak another peek. I led Sheba into the laundry room first. She went straight to her pillow to lie down and then she closed her eyes.

I headed in the direction of the kitchen. I stood in the doorway and just stared at her. The woman was truly amazing. The entire time I was with Melina I never felt this way about her. It wasn't love, or at least I don't think it was, but there was a need to protect and cherish her. When I'm home in Dallas, the need to hear her voice and see her is overwhelming. It was a relief to me when she agreed to this visit.

"Malik! Malik!"

"Oh, I'm sorry, did you say something?" Damn! I'm trippin', I stood there and spaced out just staring at her.

"Are you all right?"

"I was in a daze."

"Are you sure you're all right?"

"Yeah, I'm cool. I came in to get a glass of water."

Pointing, she said, "Oh, okay, the glasses are in that cabinet."

"Thank you."

"You're welcome."

Nia continued to cook the vegetables in the wok, and I leaned up against the counter.

"You look very comfortable doing that."

"What? Cooking?"

"Yeah."

"Well, it's what I do. Cooking is my thing."

"I can't wait to taste the food."

"I think you'll be pleased." Wiping her hands on a towel, she said, "I'm finished with the vegetables, I just need to put the rolls in the oven and set the timer."

"You made rolls?"

"Yeah"

"Homemade rolls?"

"Yes, crazy man!"

"How old are you?"

"You know how old I am."

"Well please tell me again because if you made homemade rolls, I must've transposed the numbers."

"Aw, so I'm 93 instead of 39?""

"All I know is, most women your age don't cook, and they damn sure don't make homemade rolls."

"You know black folks like bread with every meal."

"True dat."

"And remember Mr. Black, I'm not most women."

"That you aren't Miss Witherspoon. That you aren't."

Just then the doorbell rang. The clock indicated it was six thirty. It was time to greet the guests.

202

"I know this is Alicia, she's the prompt one."

"Is that right?"

I answered Malik by answering the door, "Hey Licia, hey Kevin."

Hugging me Alicia said, "Hey sweetie, how are you?"

Kissing her cheek I said, "I'm good. You remember Malik?"

"Of course, how are you?"

"I'm fine, thank you for asking."

Licia made the introduction, "Malik, this is Kevin."

"Hey Kevin, what's up?"

Giving each other the black men dap, Kevin replied, "Nothing much, it's nice to meet you and welcome to our city."

"It's good to be here."

"Licia, you and Kevin can go into the family room and make yourselves at home. Malik, you can join them if you like."

"If it's all right with you, I'd like to greet everyone along with you."

"Okay, that's fine. We'll be in shortly."

"Oh okay."

"Would you also ask Alexa to turn the volume down?"

"Sure, did you need help with anything else?"

"Naw, I got everything else together."

Right after I gave Licia those directions, the doorbell rang again.

Malik said, "Who is this since you knew when Alicia arrived?"

"This should be Lexy and Jake."

Laughing he asked, "How do you know Miss Cleo?"

I joined in the on laughter before stating, "I know my girls. Licia's the prompt one, down to the minute. Lexy gets to her destination five to ten minutes after the allotted time but Kenya. Kenya is always late. She's just extremely slow, and a true procrastinator. Why was she polishing her toe nails the morning we were leaving for the cruise?"

"She's definitely a procrastinator."

"Without a doubt."

Opening the door I said, "Good evening."

Lexy hugged me first, "Hey baby! You look beautiful."

"Thanks, so do you."

"Thank you, Ma'am."

Jake was right behind Lexy. He kissed me on the lips because that's how we do, "My baby always looks beautiful."

"You, Mr. McFarlin are biased."

"I'm supposed to be, I'm your brother."

"If I had a biological brother, I doubt I'd be this close to him, but you are my boy, and I love you."

"Love you too, baby girl."

203

"Jake, I'd like you to meet a very special friend of mine. Malik, this is Jake, my brother and best male friend, and you already know Alexis."

With his hand extended toward Jake, Malik said, "What's up man. It's nice to finally meet you. Nia has told me a lot about you." Looking in Alexis' direction, he said, "Alexis, it's good to see you again."

Jake shook Malik's hand, but he also looked him up and down, I guess to size him up. When he saw that Malik didn't flinch, he began grinning, "What's up, man? Nia's told me a lot about you too."

"I hope it was all good."

"It was."

"I'm glad to hear that."

"Did she happen to mention how overprotective I am?"

I interjected, "Jake don't start."

Malik didn't seem fazed at all, "Baby, it's cool. Actually, she did, and I'm glad she has someone to look out for her when I'm not here."

Sarcastically, Jake asked, "Is that right?"

"Yes, it is."

At that point, Lexy interjected, "All right fellas, drop your weapons. It's time to join everyone else. You can argue about Nia later. Please and thank you!"

"Thanks a lot Alexis, with your non-refereeing ass! I was just about to comment about you and Jake being together. It's about time."

"Girl, Jake called and told me he was picking me up. I didn't have a choice in the matter."

"What? Jake was demanding?"

"Yes, ma'am."

Laughing Jake said, "If you believe that Nia, then you don't know your boy at all."

"Oh, I know better than believing the story you had to twist Lexy's arm. Anyway, Alicia and Kevin are in the family room, go make yourselves comfortable."

Whispering, "Nia, I thought Licia was dating J.R."

Through clenched teeth I said, "Lexy, I don't get in grown folk's business.

"Cool. My lips are zipped."

"Malik and I are going to wait on Kenya's slow ass. She's coming with Craig."

"Well, I'm going to fix me a drink."

"Nia, do you have any Corona's in the fridge?" Jake's beer drinking ass wanted to know.

"Now Jake, have you ever been to my house and there wasn't cold beer?"

"A'ight, I get the point, I'm going to the kitchen."

"You do that."

After they retreated into the kitchen, Malik spoke. "Damn! Your boy is a trip. You told me the two of you never dated, but does he know that?"

204

"Yeah, he knows, but sometimes he takes his brother act a little too serious."

"I'll say. Is he always this overprotective?"

"Yes, he is, and it's worse now because of what I had to go through with Ben."

"I'm not Ben."

"I know that, and Jake will soon realize it."

"He'll have to because I'm going to be with you."

"Is that right?"

"Ya' damn skippy!"

The doorbell was doing its thing again. Malik did the honors this time and opened the door.

Bowing I said, "Hello your lateness."

"Nia, I'm really not in the mood."

"Girl whatever! Your ass is always late. Hey Craig, how are you?"

"I'm fine Nia. Thank you for having me."

"Don't mention it. Craig, this is Malik, a special friend."

"What's up bruh?"

"What's up man?"

"Where are you from?"

"Originally Florida, but for the last thirty-two years I've lived in Dallas, why do you ask?"

"I can hear a slight accent."

"I'm sorry bruh but I don't have an accent."

"Bruh don't take it the wrong way. You just don't talk like an average African American in St. Louis."

I jumped in, "That's not saying much."

Malik's curiosity got the best of him, and he asked, "What do you mean Nia?"

"Some of the African Americans in St. Louis butcher the English language daily."

Kenya commented, "Nia has a valid point."

I said, "You all go in the family room. I need to go into the kitchen. I have to take the rolls out of the oven and put everything on the dining room table."

Malik said, "Baby, do you need assistance?"

Kenya started elbowing me and she had goo-goo eyes when she said, "Baby, damn, it's like that?" Of course, I ignored her crazy ass.

"No Malik, I'm fine, but thank you."

Malik

Once everyone was in the family room, Craig and I began talking again.

"How does the average African American in St. Louis talk?"

"Just listen to Nelly or the St. Lunatics."

205

Alicia said, "What Craig means is, Nelly and the St. Lunatics exaggerate, but they've got the gist of it, and in my opinion, it's laziness."

"Give me an example."

"Instead of saying hair, you'll probably hear haar. Instead of there, you'll hear therrre."

I understood. "You mean like Nelly's hit "Hot in Herre."

"Exactly. The same as Chingy's hit, 'Right Thurr', it exaggerates our dialect also." Kenya said.

Lexy said, "I went to school in D.C., and my friends would laugh at me, but I never thought I was saying anything different. I quickly made a conscious effort to correct it."

Kevin said, "What people fail to realize is that each part of the country has its own dialect. People in the northeast speak fast. Those in the south, of course speak slow with their southern drawl and people on the west coast speak very proper."

I asked him, "How would you describe the Midwest?"

Craig responded with, "I think it's a mixture of it all."

Kenya interjected and said, "I agree with Craig."

Nia reentered, "That's enough about dialect, I cooked and it's time to eat."

Nia

The eight of us entered the dining room. Malik and I sat at the ends of the table. Kevin, Jake, and Craig sat on one side of the table, while Lexy, Kenya and Licia sat on the other side, across from their dates.

Alexis said, "Nia, the table settings are beautiful."

"Girl, Malik set the table."

With a stunned look Kenya said, "What, a man who sets the table? I'm very impressed. You may have to keep him girl."

Laughing, "I'll consider it."

Malik was grinning ear to ear, and Jake just glared at him before asking, "Did he arrange the flowers too?"

"Ha-Ha funny Jake! I got the flowers from a florist this morning."

Malik just stared at Jake like he was crazy. He understood our closeness, but it was almost as if Jake was jealous. That couldn't be the case. I'd deal with Jake later.

Licia said, "Well the arrangement is beautiful."

"Thank you, Alicia. Malik, would you please say grace?"

"Sure, if everyone will bow their heads, and hold hands." Everyone did as requested. "Heavenly Father, we come together tonight as friends, some old, some new, but friends, nonetheless. We exalt you. We thank You for bringing us together and we ask You to bless each of us with a safe return to our homes. We thank You for the opportunity to fellowship, and we thank the person who lovingly prepared the meal we're about to partake in. We also ask

206

she receive a special blessing for her generosity, for she is truly a blessing to all of us. (Alexis grabbed my hand and squeezed it when Malik said that) Father, we give You glory, honor and praise in the name of Your Son, our Savior Jesus Christ, Amen." All followed suit by saying, "Amen."

Kenya said, "Malik, that was really nice."

Lexy said, "I concur, because if Jake had done the prayer, it would've gone like this, she placed her hands in front of her and bowed her head again, "Heavenly Father, You know you're good, You know you're great, please make sure Nia prepares my plate, cause if she don't, it won't be nice, I'll be the one who causes strife."

Everyone erupted in laughter, everyone except Jake. He expressed his disdain over her mockery. "Aw, so Lexy's got jokes?"

"I guess I do. Is that a problem, Mr. McFarlin?"

"I'll let it pass right now, you and I will deal with this later."

"Hmmm......Now that sounds interesting."

"Well, we'll see how interesting you find it."

Grinning Lexy said, "Can't wait."

Grinning and shaking my head I said, "You all really are made for each other, I knew it."

"I don't know Nia, your girl is crazy."

"That she may be, but so are you."

"Yeah whatever."

"Anywho, let's eat," I stated.

I chose the dish with vegetables and spooned some onto my plate and passed the dish. Lexy then passed the platter with the baked potatoes; I chose the one I wanted and passed it to Jake. Lexy then handed me the platter with steaks, I cut it in one in half and passed the platter on.

Jake said, "Girl, you know you're going to eat more than half."

"Actually I'm not, I don't eat much."

"Well, when we were in high school-"

"But we ain't in high school now." Totally ignoring Jake's crazy ass. "Malik, would you please pass the condiments for the baked potatoes?'

"Sure."

"Thanks babe."

Grinning from ear to ear from my term of endearment he replied, "No problem."

I placed butter, bacon, and cheese on my potato, and began to eat.

"Something's missing, oops! I forgot, the shrimp scampi. Excuse me."

Licia and Lexy looked at each other and grinned. Lexy spoke, "Damn! We get Nia's famous shrimp scampi?" Malik looked confused, but Alicia was going to explain to clear up his confusion.

Licia said, "Malik, it's like this. Nia cooks for Event Solutions, but she never cooks for us and if she does it's simple stuff like wings and fries. We never get the good Nia gourmet food, but you come to town, and we get steaks, potatoes, steamed mixed vegetables, her famous shrimp scampi and homemade rolls."

"I heard that shit!" Sitting the dish with the shrimp scampi on the table. "How you gone talk about me like I'm not here?"

Lexy said, "Well, it's true, you don't cook for us."

"You all know how to cook, I don't see any of you cooking and inviting me over."

Malik interjected, "Ya'll leave my baby alone. She cooks for a living, and sometimes she needs her rest."

"Malik, you don't have to explain anything to these food fiends."

Jake said, "Baby girl, I invited you over for dinner last week."

"Jake, I appreciated the invite, but it was for burgers and fries man! That don't count."

"Well, you know a brotha is not a gourmet chef."

"I know, and just because I am doesn't mean I want to be constantly harassed about cooking. Shit harass Alicia, she is my partner, and she cooks as well."

Alicia said, "Don't any of you crack-heads call me to cook a meal."

"Oh, so I can cook, but you can't?"

"Girl, stop fronting, you know I'm the brains behind Event Solutions, whereas you're the brains and the cook."

"Yeah, okay but I will not be your personal chef."

Kenya grinned at Malik, and then looked at me, "Well, we could always call Malik in Dallas and see if he'd be willing to fly in."

Malik looked at me and then back at Kenya and she said, "Knowing Nia's sometimes ornery ass, he'd come to town, and she still wouldn't cook."

"You got that right you greedy heifers. After tonight, I will not be cooking until the next holiday."

You could look at Alexis, Kenya and Alicia and see them thinking. I knew they were trying to figure out what the next holiday would be. I decided to help them out. "The next holiday will be Independence Day, but I haven't decided if I'm going to invite you all over or not. I may tell each and every one of you to go to your mammy's houses or Red's BBQ." I stated, with a sly grin on my face.

"Red's is good." Kenya said.

"Agreed so your 4th of July meal may come from there."

That evidently hit a nerve with Jake because he had an opinion, he immediately shared with us.

"Nia Elizabeth Witherspoon-" Before he could get anything else out, I looked at him like he'd lost his mind. Lexy, Alicia, and Kenya first gave each other the oh-no-he-didn't look, and then they gave me the same look. There was an unwritten rule, my middle name was to never be mentioned. I loved my grandmother and I'm honored my parents had decided to name me after her, but honestly, I don't share my middle; it's super personal to me.

"Jake Theophilus McFarlin-

In unison, Kenya, Alicia, and Alexis, shouted, "Theophilus?" The three of them began to laugh. Malik obviously found this amusing because he leaned back in his chair and began laughing too. Jake didn't think it was funny Malik was laughing at his expense. He voiced it. Directing his anxiety toward Malik, he said, "Nigga, what's funny?"

Malik looked around to see who it was Jake was talking to. Jake turned all the way around so Malik would know without a doubt he was talking to him. He also articulated it, "I'm talking to you, Malik."

"First off, don't single me out when everyone laughed. Secondly, I'm laughing at the name Theophilus."

"Well, who gave you the okay to laugh at my expense?"

When Malik heard that, he laughed louder, "Who gave me the right-

I interrupted by saying, "Jake, that's- Malik raised his hand to silence me and although I would never go for that, in this case I understood, and I was silent. He looked in my direction with an apologetic look on his face. Malik had a very serious look on his face when he said, "Jake let me explain something to you. First and foremost, Nia means a lot to me and for that reason, and that reason alone, I will never disrespect her or anyone that means something to her. I apologize if I offended you for laughing at your name. I'm sure if I shared my middle name you'd laugh as well, but please don't think because I'm visiting and won't be here after next week you can punk me. I respect Nia, but I'll leave before I allow that." A pin could've dropped in the room, and everyone would've heard it. Malik had stood up to Jake in a very dignified manner. I was impressed although I know that was not his intention. Jake just sat there stunned. Very seldom did anyone stand up to him seeing that he stood at six feet and six inches and weighed two hundred pounds. He also had a mouth on him.

Jake began to smile, and with that Alicia, Kenya, Alexis, and I knew Malik had gained Jake's respect. He expressed as much. "All right bruh, my bad." Extending his hand for a handshake he asked, "We cool?"

Shaking his head Malik extended his hand, "Yeah man we cool." Malik then gave me an I-don't-believe-this-nigga look. I gave him an I'm-so-sorry look. What else could I do?

Alexis quickly jumped in to say, "Are we done with testosterone time? I'd like to finish eating."

Alicia, Kenya, and I looked at one other and then Alexis and in unison, we said, "Shut up Lexy." Everyone began to laugh. The ice was broken.

We finished eating our meal while sharing conversations about safe subjects. I went into the kitchen to retrieve saucers, Cool Whip, and the lemon cheesecake I'd prepared for dessert.

"Dessert is served." I said when I arrived back in the dining room.

Kevin who'd been quiet most of the evening, but always had a sweet tooth asked, "What are we having?"

As if cued, Alicia, Kenya and Alexis snickered and said, "Coochie pie."

Looking directly into Malik's eyes I responded with, "Excuse the queens of comedy. They have no home training. I made a lemon cheesecake," then I looked at Alicia, Kenya and Alexis and shook my head.

Innocently Alicia asked, "What? Why did you shake your head at us?"

"Alicia Fox I am not going there with you."

Malik didn't respond but he knew I'd made it just for him because it was his favorite and I'd evidently taken great notes. I'd just scored some points with Mr. Black. That I was certain of.

Good food. Good wine. Good music. Good friends. I couldn't ask for a better evening. I was just glad the tension was over. I had a surprise for everyone. One of my business associates from the Pageant was able to get me eight tickets to the jazz explosion they were having tonight. The artists performing Will Downing, George Duke, Rachelle Farrell, Chante Moore and Najee. It was guaranteed to be a great show.

"So did everyone enjoy the meal?" I was bombarded with "Hell Yeahs", "Of course" and "As if you didn't know". I was very grateful everyone enjoyed the food I'd graciously prepared. Those who love to cook also like to hear praise from those partaking in the meal.

"Nia, you know we always enjoy your meals. You just don't invite us over enough." This was Kenya's never-cook-a-meal ass.

Agreeing Jake said, "Real talk."

I looked at Alexis and Alicia and asked them both, "Do you all have anything you want to say?"

Alexis said, "I ain't saying nothing because I'll be back over to eat as soon as Malik leaves town and I won't say anything to jeopardize that."

Alicia added, "I second that because I live less than one minute away and if my girl is cooking, I'll definitely be eating."

"When will that be?" Jake inquired, but no one knew what he was talking about. Everyone looked at him with that what-are-you-talking-about look.

"Babe, what are you talking about?" Alexis asked. We stopped whatever we were doing and looked at Alexis first and then Jake. Did she just call him babe? I wanted to know and I'm sure everyone else was curious. So, I directed this comment to Jake, "Yeah, BABE answer her because I have a question for you and Miss Knight."

With a grin on his face Jake said, "I was just wondering when Malik would be leaving."

"Why Jake? He's staying with me as my guest, so why should you be concerned?"

He tried to clean it up, but I knew he was trying to be this overprotective big brother, and although I appreciated his concern, I am a big girl and Malik is my concern.

"Nia, I was just wondering because," directing this question toward Malik he asked, "Bruh, you play ball?" Malik answered, "Yeah man, when I have time." Redirecting his conversation back to me, "Like I was saying, I was

210

wondering when Malik was leaving because I was thinking we could get together one day and shoot some hoops."

Shaking my head I said, "Yeah okay Jake, whateva."
"I'm for real." Jake declared.

"Well now you've answered that question for me, I have one for you."
"What would that be, Nia?"
"When did you and Alexis start calling each other babe?"
"That's none- Alexis cut him off and said, "Nia, that's really between Jake and I, but if you must know, we've decided to give the relationship a try. We've been friends for a long time and now that he's single, feelings have developed between us." Her news was noticeably a shock to everyone because we sat there stupefied. I knew there was something between them, but I didn't expect them to pursue a relationship so suddenly. Jake had just broken up with Kayla, but they're grown, and you know you can't tell grown folks anything. I let it go. It was none of my business.

"Anyway, I'm glad you all enjoyed your meal, but now-"
Malik interrupted by saying, "Nia excuse me for interrupting you but I wanted to tell you I sincerely appreciate the dinner. You prepared all my favorites and I immensely enjoyed everything. The cheesecake was delicious."

"You are very welcome and I'm glad you enjoyed everything. I was hoping you would." After I said that he got up, walked over to me and gave me a kiss on the cheek. Of course, I blushed like a twelve-year-old and everyone was amused because they were all grinning.

"Before I was so eloquently interrupted, I was about to tell all of you about my surprise. I think-"
Kenya's anxious ass blurted out, "What surprise, Nia?"
"Damn Kenya, if you let her talk, she'll tell us. Your ass has been anxious since the eighth grade, just slow down and listen, and she'll let us in on the surprise." Alicia explained. Kenya rolled her eyes at Alicia, but she shut up so that I could finish.

"Okay this is the surprise. You know Alicia and I have done some functions at the Pageant and on Wednesday one of the owners called me to inform me he had some tickets to the jazz explosion they're having tonight. I explained Malik would be in town and I'd be entertaining other guests as well and if possible, I'd need eight tickets. So, he called on Thursday and today, prior to picking Malik up from the airport I went by the Pageant, and I was blessed with eight tickets." After making my announcement, I sat there grinning because I knew I'd done well. It took a while before what I said sunk in because no one was reacting. They were sitting there as if I'd just hypnotized them to prepare them for nap time. I began to repeat myself. "Did you-" Jake spoke up because he got it... finally. "Hold up, did you just say you have tickets to the jazz show tonight? The show including George Duke, Rachelle Farrell, Najee, Chante Moore, and Will Downing?" Grinning because one of these knuckleheads finally got it, I answered, "Yes, that's the show. So, if you all are interested, we can get ready to go within the next twenty to thirty

211

minutes." I got up to go into the kitchen so I could load everything into the dishwasher. I guess everyone else figured they'd help so they began an assembly line into the kitchen. We were able to load the dishwasher within ten minutes. I wiped the dining room table, the counter tops in the kitchen and began the dishwasher.

Looking directly at Jake because he has a Ford Excursion, "So do you want to ride together? I'm sorry Jake, I didn't mean to just volunteer your truck, but your vehicle is the only one we can all fit in."

"It's cool, but I'd prefer we ride in separate cars because I need to hurry home after the show. I have an early ball game in the morning, and you know I live in West County now which is a twenty-minute drive."

"Oh yeah, you got a brand-new house in Town & Country. When are you going to invite us out?" Kenya inquired.

"Nia and Alexis have seen the house."

"What? How is that?"

"They got into their cars and drove over."

"So, I can come see whenever I want?

"As long as I'm home."

"Cool."

Directing this question to everyone, Jake asked, "Do you all have a problem driving your own vehicles since I no longer live in the area?"

"Naw, that's cool." All the fellas except Malik stated.

"Since that's settled, I'm going to the bathroom to freshen up. You ladies should do the same," Kenya stated.

"Well, thank you, mama. Last time I checked Doris Knight resided on Lindell and she's not in our presence tonight," Alexis stated. Kenya just rolled her eyes. We were accustomed to the eye rolling, just like she was accustomed to one of us calling her out on something. We proceeded to the bathrooms to freshen up because we'd be leaving shortly. Fortunately, everyone had dressed nicely for dinner so there was no need for anyone to change. I checked on Sheba in the laundry room before re-joining everyone.

Once we were done freshening up, we proceeded to our vehicles. The Pageant was only eight minutes from my townhouse. The Pageant is a venue in the STL for concerts. It's a small and intimate two-level venue and lots of entertainers have been performing there. The lower level holds a bar running along the back wall. The floor can be set up with or without chairs. It depends on the event. Some events were strictly standing room only. The upper level had seats and was normally the VIP section.

Malik and I jumped in my car, and we proceeded down Delmar. We wanted to find parking spaces near each other so we could enter the venue together and not get lost in the crowd. During the drive, Malik wanted to talk about the evening.

"Nia, I'm really enjoying myself."

"I'm glad to hear it, I was hoping you would."

"I know I've thanked you once already, but again, thank you for dinner. It was delicious."

"Thank you again for the compliment, but I couldn't invite you here and fast-food you to death. The fellas wouldn't let me live that down."

"And what makes you think I'd tell the fellas?"

"Who do you think you're fooling? As close as you, Curly, Mo, Larry and Laurel are, I know what you'd tell them the moment you arrived back in Dallas. I can hear you now; 'Man, I went to visit that woman in St. Louis and all she fed me was White Castles, McDonald's and Outback."

Laughing Malik said, "That's not true."

"Then why are you laughing?"

"I don't know. I guess some of it is true."

"Yeah, I'm sure. You probably believe women in our age group can't cook. I hope I've proved that's a myth."

"Well....there may be some truth to that. The last three women I dated couldn't make a decent bologna sandwich, but you? You got me believing anything is possible." Now I had to laugh at that, a damn bologna sandwich. "You're being a little hard on the sistahs don't ya think?"

"Unfortunately, I'm not. You're the first sistah in a long time who I've met who can really cook, and the food tastes good."

"I appreciate the compliment and I'm glad to know you won't have to tell the fellas I force fed you fast food."

"That won't be the case. I won't have anything but good things to say about you. A great dinner and now you're treating me to what I'm sure will be a great concert."

"Yeah it should be, I love all of the artists, especially Najee and Chante."

"I like them as well. There are so many great African American jazz artists."

"I agree."

"Now this is an interesting area."
We were driving down Delmar. This area reminds me of Georgetown in DC. There are a lot of eclectic shops as well as diverse and eclectic people. Pointing at Squad One Sports I said, "That's where Nelly taped his Air Force Ones video."
"Really?"

"Yeah. This is the University City, Delmar Loop area. This is a fun area to people watch."

"Really? Why is that?"

"Well, if you-"

"Wait a minute, was that a brotha with black and gold hair?"

"See, that's why it's fun for people watching. The diversity down here is amazing. You're likely to see anything."

"I see. I see even the Rasta brothas hang out down here."

213

"Well see, that's where the diversity comes in. Most of those brothas are down here because of 'Blueberry Hill'.

"Have you ever been?"

"Yah Mon, I've been dere. They occasionally have reggae performances."

Laughing at my pseudo Jamaican accent he asked, "Did you like it?"

"The music was really good. Well, we're here."

The line to get into the Pageant was around the corner. Fortunately, we wouldn't have to stand in line, but we did have to find parking spaces. Right then my cell phone rang, I checked the caller ID, it was Lexy, so I answered. "Yeah Lex?" She was obviously distraught over the crowd. "Girl, do you see all of these people?" Now I hate when people ask dumb questions. Hadn't I just driven by the venue, just like her? "Now what do you think?" I responded with all the sarcasm I could muster.

"Damn Nia, do you always have to get smart?", Lexy asked.

"No, I don't but you know I don't like being asked dumb ass questions." I responded.

With an exasperated sigh, Lexy replied, "All right girl, whateva, let's just find a parking space."

I know I'd upset her, but dumb questions are a pet peeve of mine. "Cool, just follow me."

I drove behind the Pageant to the Metro-Link station parking lot, where we lucked up on four spaces, next to each other. We parked underneath the provided lighting and emerged from our perspective vehicles.

I asked, "So ya'll ready?"

Jake was the most eager in the group and made it known. "Baby girl, I'm always ready for some good jazz. I'm so appreciative of you and these tickets."

"It's no problem, I'm just glad I was blessed with enough tickets for everyone to enjoy the show." With that said, Malik grabbed my hand, and we led the way to the entrance of the Halo Bar. We were on the VIP list and because we were going to the bar first, we wouldn't have to stand in the extremely long line. We arrived at the Halo Bar entrance, I gave my name and we entered. The bar was packed, so we decided to make our way through the bar to enter the venue. Because we had VIP seating, our seats were in the balcony, so we proceeded in the direction of the steps. In order to get to the steps, we had to walk in the direction of the bar.

Kenya noticed Michelle. "Ladies, there's Michelle."

"I forgot how much she loves jazz; I should've extended an invitation to her and Brett."

"Well, no need to cry over spilt milk, she's here so let's say hi," Lexy instructed.

As we approached the bar area where she and Brett were sitting, Brett turned around first. When he saw us walking toward them like we were the police, he began grinning. Brett was a cool ass white boy, he treated Michelle like

214

royalty, and he loved him some Kenya, Alicia, Alexis, and Nia. It didn't hurt that he was fine. Yes, he is a fine ass white boy. He's six foot two inches, medium build with muscles, dark olive colored skin, dark green eyes with beautiful eye lashes and naturally wavy jet-black hair. He is also well groomed. He and Michelle make a beautiful couple. Before Michelle could turn around to see what he was grinning at, Brett began calling our names. "Hey Lexy! What's up kwik klean Kenya? Alicia and Nia, it's good to see you all and congratulations." We all acknowledged Brett with a hug and that's when Michelle got up to greet us with hugs also, "Hey girls, what's up? What are you doing here?"

"Michelle, you know-" I was about to explain.

Waving her hand in a never mind fashion Michelle continued, "Never mind, your father was only the biggest jazz lover in all of Missouri, probably the U.S."

"You know that's right."

"Yeah, that's right. Remember when your father gave us a history lesson on jazz? He made us sit on the couch while he lectured us," Michelle conveyed to everyone.

Trying to imitate his voice Kenya said, "You girls are always listening to new music, but you've got to appreciate the old to appreciate the new. There's Bird, John Coltrane, Miles Davis and a slew of others. Michelle you're white, but you should get something out of this as well."

Laughing Michelle said, "Yeah, Mr. Witherspoon wasn't one to bite his tongue, he always said what was on his mind and strangely, I never felt out of place. I miss him."

"Girl, we just had a miss-daddy-Witherspoon-session at Nia's and now we're out to enjoy ourselves, and I say let's do it," Kenya proclaimed.

"I agree and that's what he would want," I proudly announced.

Looking toward the fellas Michelle said, "My girlfriends are so rude, I'm-"

"Chelle, I'm sorry you know these knuckle heads, and this is-"

Extending her hand toward Malik, "Malik, it's so nice to finally meet you. Are you enjoying your visit in St. Louis?"

Shaking Michelle's hand and grinning he replied with, "So far, my visit is going very well. It's nice to finally meet you as well." Looking in Brett's direction and offering his hand he said, "What's up, man?"

Brett responded with an outstretched hand, "It's nice to meet you, Malik."

"Okay enough with the pleasantries, let's go."

We made our way through the extremely crowded venue. It was inevitable we'd see some people we knew. I just didn't think we'd run into Kayla and Ben. We were approximately fifteen feet from the steps when we ran into Ben. Malik was holding my hand and both of us felt the tug my arm received. Malik and I looked back simultaneously. When I saw it was Ben, I frowned. I hope he didn't think he was going to start anything. I ain't up for no bullshit, especially from him. Malik saw the look on my face, so he gave Ben a look that said, 'don't fuck with her.' Unfortunately, He ignored us and the looks we gave. He looked at our joined hands, frowned and asked, "What's up baby?" I looked around because I knew he wasn't calling me baby. He said it again. Still holding Malik's hand, I said, "Hello Ben. For the record my name is not baby, it's Nia." He totally ignored Malik, but I wasn't going to allow that, "Ben, this is a special friend of mine, Malik. Malik, Ben." Malik just nodded his head. That was cool because as ignorant as Ben is if Malik offered his hand, Ben would've only ignored him. Ben was about to say something but before the words were uttered Jake stepped in, "What's up, Ben?" Jake has always intimidated Ben's bitch ass. He knows Jake would protect me at all costs. Apparently, Jake's presence worked because Ben's bitch ass walked away after looking all of us up and down.

"Nia, what did you ever see in that buster? That nigga-"

"Jake let's not go there."

"Okay baby girl. Fuck him. Let's enjoy ourselves." We descended the stairs and made it halfway up when we saw Kayla. Damn! Instead of attending a jazz fest, we apparently stepped into the Ex Fest.

With as much nastiness as she could summon Lisa spoke. "Hello Miss Witherspoon." I was obviously singled out because Lexy was my friend and Jake was now with her. Following her nasty greeting I looked at her and then my posse. On cue, Michelle, Alicia, Alexis, Kenya, and I all responded with a hello. We didn't allow the cattiness we felt to be displayed. We weren't going to stoop to her level. 'Hello Kayla.' Still holding Lexy's hand Jake spoke. "Hello Kayla."

"Yeah whateva nigga! I still can't believe you left me for Lexy's formaldehyde slinging ass."

Lexy said`, "At least I got a job. I ain't waiting on a nigga to take care of me, unlike you."

Jake began to explain himself to Lisa, "I left you becau- nope, I'm not getting into this. We talked about it and this is the best decision for me. You are no longer my priority, Jake is. I chose Alexis because I want to be with her. It has nothing to do with you or Nia for that matter. Please don't start nothing because believe me when I say I will definitely finish it."

We stood there with stunned looks on our faces and I was praying she would just drop it. I knew how Jake could be when he was mad, and it was nothing nice. She needed to just accept his decision and move on. She must've read my mind because after rolling her eyes at all of us she just walked away in a huff. Jake kept the convoy going as if the Kayla incident never occurred. We finally arrived upstairs and found our seats. The fellas took drink orders while we sat and observed our surroundings. Looking into the crowd on the lower level I saw the one and only Amber. It's weird because I was looking through the crowd just observing, not looking for her but when I came across her face, I saw her staring at me. I quickly diverted my glance. Again, I was not in the mood for any bullshit. The fellas returned with our drinks, we settled into our seats because the show was about to begin.

I asked Malik, "Are you okay?"

"Yeah baby. I'm cool. When we were standing in line to get the drinks, I felt someone staring at me. I turned around and it was him."

"Did he say anything?"

"Naw, he didn't say anything. I wouldn't care if he did, I'm here with you and he's not."

"This is true."

First on stage was George Duke, followed by Chante Moore, Najee, Rachelle Ferrell and then Will Downing. They performed by themselves and then they had a set together. While sitting there and enjoying the groove, my cell phone began to vibrate. Someone had sent me a text message. That someone was Amber. She'd sent an apology message. Looking into the crowd below I felt someone staring. That someone was also Amber. She gave me what I guess was her apologetic look, and I gave her what I'm sure was my fuck-you-look. I'll be cordial if, and when I see her, but our 'friendship' is totally a thing of the past. I could never trust her again and without trust, there's nothing. No relationship. No friendship. Nothing. I continued to enjoy the concert.

The artists performed for about three hours and forty minutes, so around eleven-thirty we were preparing to leave.

"So, did you all want to do something else?", I asked.

Lexy suggested a club catering to the thirty plus crowd. "We can go to 'The Signature Room' if you want."

"I'm down for whatever. Malik, are you down for it?" I asked.

"I'm cool. I'm on vacation and down for whatever."

Michelle decided to turn in. "Ladies, Brett and I have to pass. His niece is having a birthday party early tomorrow and we volunteered to help."

Sarcastically Alicia asked about their intentions, "What are you all trying to prepare yourselves for, your first born?"

Brett began to answer Alicia. "I guess we-" Michelle cut their question-and-answer session short. She was going to share her take on this subject. With hands placed on her hips. "Brett please don't go there with Alicia because what she doesn't realize is when we have our first born because we have friends who throw parties for a living, we're taken care of."

"Okay Miss Smarty Pants, I got you," Alicia responded.

"I know you do but I had to go there since you did." Right then there was a glare that blinded us. Up until this moment we hadn't noticed that Michelle had some bling-bling on. Kenya couldn't contain her excitement. "Girl, you and Brett are engaged?" The excitement was infectious.

Simultaneously Lexy, Alicia and I asked, "Engaged, and you didn't tell us?"

"Would you all please calm down? We just got engaged tonight. Before coming to the show, we had dinner at Fleming's and Brett proposed." We exchanged hugs and everyone congratulated them. Of course, us being women, we had to check out the ring. It was gorgeous. It was platinum and gold with a three-carat crystal clear round brilliant cut diamond surrounded by emerald colored (Michelle's birthstone) baguettes.

"So, you'll be the first to be hitched, huh Michelle?", I inquired.

"Looks that way."

"That it does."

Looking at Malik first then me she replied, "Unless there's something you want to tell me."

Malik held his hands up in the surrender position. I guess he didn't want to get into that conversation. I tackled the question. "What would we want to tell you? We just began dating, remember?"

"I'll leave it alone for right now."

With that everyone said their good-byes. Although Jake had an early morning hoop session, he agreed to hang. I was the designated lead and I opted for the street route since I couldn't immediately jump on an interstate or bypass. I headed westbound on Delmar to I-170, which I proceeded on north bound. I exited onto westbound Page Ave. and made a left into Overland Plaza. *The Signature Room* sat on the corner of the strip mall. I'd stopped going out on a regular basis when I turned twenty-eight. At that point I was just burned out, but it's evident people grow at different levels because the same people who were hanging then, are still hanging. I'd been going to clubs since I was eighteen and eleven years was enough for me. We parked and entered the club.

The dance floor is toward the back of the club. Chairs surround the dance floor and there are also tables. Upon entering the club, we were greeted by heat and a very large crowd. Those were the main reasons for my disappearance from the club scene. We paid our ten-dollar cover charge.

Jake located a table, and we planted our asses in the provided chairs. A waitress approached us.

"Would you all like something to drink?" We gave our drink orders. Alicia went first and everyone else followed suit. "I'd like a glass of Zinfandel."

"Give me some Apple Ciroc," Kevin requested.

"I'd like a chocolate martini," Kenya's martini lovin' ass said.

"I'm sorry ma'am, all we have are regular martinis, apple and watermelon," the waitress informed her.

"Okay then, I'll take watermelon."

"I'd like a Heineken," Craig said.

"I'll take Remy on the rocks." Looking at Lexy, he asked, "Baby what would you like?" She responded by saying, "Belvedere on the rocks."

Malik ordered for us, "I'd like Corona with a lime. The lady will have a frozen Midori sour."

"Thank you, I'll be back shortly with your drinks." She left and we began to enjoy the music as well as the sights.

St. Louis was just like other urban areas. The same people who were club fixtures ten years ago are still fixtures. Sistahs who wore hoochie dresses in their twenties are still wearing the same attire now. Although they're in their

218

thirties and forties and have gained twenty, thirty, forty plus pounds, their attire hasn't changed. Old ass men still hanging at the thirty and older spots preying on women when they should be at the fifty and older clubs sipping' on Geritol. The sights were hilarious.

The waitress arrived with our drinks, the fellas paid, and we began to get our sip on.

The dance floor was packed, and they were doing one of the shuffles. I thought white folks were the originators of line dancing, but we've perfected it. The electric slide, the Cha-Cha slide and the shuffle, yeah, we've definitely perfected it.

After shuffling it up, the DJ played St. Louis' own Chingy and everyone went into a Nina Pop frenzy. Malik leaned in my direction and over the extremely loud music asked about the dance everyone was doing.

"Baby, what dance is that? That's a new one." Before I could answer, Alexis jumped in. "That's the Nina Pop."

"The what? Why haven't I heard of it?"

"It's strictly began in St. Louis-East St. Louis."

"Oh really?"

"Yeah. If you watch Nelly's 'Air Force Ones' video as well as Chingy's video for 'Right Thurr."

Alexis chimed in, "They're also doing it in the 'Shake ya tail feather' video with Nelly, P. Diddy and Murphy Lee and Murphy Lee's 'What the Hook Gon Be?"

"Especially Chingy's video. All the dancers are doing it," Alicia stated.

"Well, they're getting their party on. The dance floor is packed. "We continued sipping on our drinks and after playing Chingy, the DJ played 'Like a Pimp', David Banner and Lil' Flip's party anthem. That was Lexy's shit and because she played and sang it so much, it had become a favorite of mine. I asked Malik to dance. Lexy and Jake joined us. While discussing the Nina Pop, Jake said nothing, but I knew he could dance his ass off. He's always been an excellent dancer. We got on the floor and proceeded to shake what our mamas gave us.

For me it brought back memories of Dallas and the first time Malik, and I met. This time it felt natural to be with him. The first time there was a level of naturalness, but I was still nervous.

The DJ was not leaving us room to rest. He played jam after jam after jam. He was doing the damn thing on the 1's and 2's. He followed up 'Like a Pimp' with Ludacris' joint from the '2 Fast 2 Furious' soundtrack, 'Act a Fool'. He played another jam by Ludacris', 'Stand Up'. He followed that with Lil' Jon and the Eastside Boyz, the Ying Yang Twins and the Youngbloodz talking about, 'If you don't give a damn gon' throw it up'. The DJ was on a serious mission. He followed all of that up with the St. Louis Nina pop anthem, 'The Nina Pop Remix' by St. Louis' own, Da Whol 9. Bumping from the speakers we heard, 'Ladies take it to the Floor this yo Song', and with those few words the already packed dance floor became more crowded. The song always sent the club into a Nina pop frenzy. Then he slowed it down with the Isley Brothers/R. Kelly collabo, '*What would you do?*'

Malik asked, "Nia, you wanna keep dancing?"

"This is my jam, but can we sit this one out? I need something cool to drink."

"That's cool, I could use a drink myself. We'll continue on the next song."

As we headed off the dance floor we literally bumped into Ben and Amber. They looked surprised. I very seldom go out and I'm sure they were shocked to see me. I laughed at them and kept walking.

I am convinced she's stupid with a capital S. Less than three hours ago she acted as if she didn't want to be bothered by him. Sending me text messages and shit. Now she's with him. Dumb, and Dumber together. I'm sure he gave her some bullshit excuse as to why they couldn't be together at the concert. How dumb? If they're a couple, there shouldn't be any reason why they should've been apart at the concert. The only reason is her stupidity. He ended up with the right one.

Evidently Alexis saw the interaction I had with them. She is always ready to fight.

"Did that trick say anything to you?"

"Naw girl, I'm cool. I actually think they're funny."

Lexy's love to fight ass said, "You sure, cause I'll snatch both of them off of the dance floor and-"

"Lexy, don't trip. I'm cool. Neither of them is worth it."

"You know I got your back."

"That goes without saying, but there will be no fights today."

Jake felt the need to make an announcement. "Don't worry Nia, Miss Knight won't be fighting anyone but me. We don't have to worry about Ben's bitch ass. I wish either one of them would try and clown."

I shook my head at Lexy and Jake. They were really made for each other, "Yeah okay, Bonnie and Clyde," I commented.

While we were resting Craig, Kenya, Alicia and Kevin were grooving to the slow jams. After the Isley Brothers/R. Kelly collabo, the DJ played '*Officially Missing You*" by Tamia. During that song my eyes locked on Ben. I felt the emotion in the song, and I understood the title of the song, but I could honestly say I no longer missed him.

The DJ followed up with '*Step in the name of Love*' by R. Kelly. That was our cue. Malik looked at me. I looked at him and like magnets we were drawn to the dance floor. We began to get our swerve on Windy City style. Our bodies were in sync. We received a lot of attention, which prompted us to really put our all into our dancing. In other words, we were showing off. I can't remember the last time I'd had this much fun. We stepped ourselves back to the table.

Jake, Kenya, Alicia and I saw a few familiar faces from high school. Surprisingly, we didn't run into Kayla. When she was with Jake, her ass stayed in the clubs like a single woman with no children. I guess it's good she's not here because there would be drama. She's pissed about the breakup because her welfare has run out. That's what Jake was. Welfare. A crutch. If she was with him, she didn't have to work. Her aspirations? Gone. Like yesterday's news. Her goals never matched Jake's, but good pussy sometimes makes men delirious. That's what I've been told anyway. I've been known to have great sex but the men I pick don't flip out over it. Maybe it's not as good as I've been told. Nah…that couldn't be it. Anyway, thank God, he came to his senses. She was about getting what she could get.

We stayed at the club until it closed. Yawning, I asked Malik to drive home.

He asked, "Are you sure?"

"Yeah, why wouldn't I be?"

"Well, it is a Benz, a new one at that."

"I have insurance, but if I didn't, I wouldn't trip. There are more important things than material things. Sure, I like nice things, but they don't make or break me. I don't trip off material things."

Giving me the look he's famous for he said, "Yeah, you're definitely one of a kind." He agreed to drive. It was becoming obvious he was getting to the point where he couldn't deny me anything. We said our good-byes and I asked all the ladies to call me upon arriving at their homes, so I'd know they made it safely. Lexy smooched with Jake before arriving at the car. I'd forgotten she was riding with us. She got into the back seat, and we were on our way. I directed Malik down Page Ave to North & South. We headed south to Delmar. We took Delmar to Pendleton which turns into Boyle. Lexy's condo is on the corner of Boyle and Lindell. She had fallen asleep about fifteen minutes ago.

"Lexy we're here, wake up. Malik you can pull over here, I'll walk her to the door." Turning around in my seat, I continued my attempt to rouse her from her sleep. "C'mon Lexy, wake up." She began to stir in her sleep. I continued to nudge her. "C'mon Lexy, wake up or I'll take you to my house and you can sleep with Sheba." That got her attention. "Nia Witherspoon no, you didn't say I could sleep with your dog."

Laughing, "Yes, I did, but it woke you up."

"Yeah, it woke me up. Let me out of this back seat."

I stepped from the car and pushed the seat release button. The front seat slid forward to accommodate Lexy getting out of the back seat. She wearily got out of the car.

"Malik, I'll be right back."

"Okay. Alexis, I'll see you later."

"Okay Malik, I'll see you again before you leave."

Lexy retrieved her keys from her handbag. We arrived at the outer gate to the condo community, she unlocked the gate and we proceeded to her unit.

"Nia, I really like Malik and I like the two of you together."

221

"Girl, I know I feel so giddy. I really like him, but I want to take things slow."

"You're not going to give him any?"

"Girl, I want to, and anything is possible in my dick-deprived state. I'm horny as hell and he's sexy as hell, but again, I want to take things slow. I don't want to rush things."

"I hope he's the one. You deserve to be blessed."

"So do you."

Hugging me she replied with, "I think Jake is my blessing." Stepping out of our embrace but still holding onto her arms, I asked, "For real?" Before she could answer I said, "I knew it!"

"Yes, girl. He has been wonderful, everything I've prayed for and wanted in my life."

"Like I said, I knew it. I knew you all would be good together."

"You did, didn't you? I just hate we wasted all these years. Hell, my daddy already likes him and that's a definite plus."

"You're right, but you all hooked up when you were supposed to. It wouldn't have been right at any other time."

"I guess you're right. Let me go inside. I had a ball but now I'm tired."

"Okay girl, get some rest, but don't forget the concert tomorrow."

"I won't. Jake and I wouldn't miss it. You know he loves Whodini."

"Yes, he does. I'm going to surprise Malik tomorrow when we arrive at the Ambassador. I guess we can eat there. Their food is good."

"Yeah, their food is off the chain. You're not going to tell him before ya'll arrive?"

"Nope. He won't even know we're hanging out with everyone again."

"He's in for a surprise."

"Yep, that's the point."

"Okay, tomorrow it is. Holla back."

"Okay sweetie." I turned to walk back to the car and Lexy went into her condo.

I got into the car, put on my seat belt, and explained why it took me so long, "I'm sorry about that, we had to discuss something."

"Girl talk?"

"Something like that."

"Okay. I need directions to your house."

"Make a U-turn and then make a left onto Lindell."

We rode in silence. I guess we were both tired. At Lindell and Euclid, I explained that the next light would be Kingshighway and we'd be making a right. The third light would be Delmar and there we'd be making a left. I laid back to relax but stayed awake because I didn't want him to get lost.

Malik

I'm pretty good with directions so once Nia and I arrived at Delmar, I felt confident I could find my way back to her home.

"Nia, if you'd like to go to sleep, I can get to your house."

"You sure?"

"I am and I know you're tired."

"Actually I am. Thank you for being so thoughtful."

"No problem. I'll wake you when we arrive."

"Or if you get lost."

Laughing, "Yeah that too."

She took that as her cue. She adjusted her seat so she could lean back. Closing her eyes and crossing her legs, she began to relax. I continued driving. Thinking. I'm really enjoying myself and surprisingly her friends are cool. That includes the white couple I met at the concert. Granted, I only deal with white people on a professional level, but they are cool. I can see why they're friends of hers.

I knew we'd run into her ex. The world is small after all, no matter what city you're in. I didn't know he'd be so ignorant. When he tugged on her arm, I almost floored his ass. I wasn't going to stoop to his level though. I allowed Jake to handle it only because the STL is his territory. I don't need a grown ass man to handle anything for me. Trust.

Jake ended up being hella cool. Initially, I thought he had some serious feelings for Nia but now that I've seen the interaction between him and Alexis, I know the truth. That's his girl and he does not want to see her hurt. Again. I totally understand. She doesn't have any biological brothers, so he takes his brother role to heart.

I glanced at Nia as she began to snore lightly. While looking at her I noticed because of the way that she was sitting, some thigh was exposed. This woman was fine. I could think of a lot of adjectives to describe her, but fine fits best.

As we pulled in front of Nia's house, I called her name to wake her while pushing the button on the garage door opener that was attached to the visor. I noticed a black Chevy Tahoe parked in front of Nia's, but I thought nothing of it. I figured someone on the block had company.

"Nia, baby wake up."

Rubbing her eyes she asked, "We're here?"

"Yes, sleepyhead."

"I'm sorry I fell asleep. Was I snoring?" I ignored her question. We got out of the car, closed the garage, and went into the house. She deactivated the alarm system.

"I'm going to let Sheba out. You still haven't answered my question."

"What question would that be?"

223

"Was I snoring?" Opening the door to the laundry room, Sheba stood up. She wagged her stump. It couldn't be called a tail. Her wagging let us know she was happy to see us. "Hey girl! How are you?" Nia began to talk to her dog as if she was a friend. "Malik isn't answering my question. What do you think I should do about that?" I began to rub her head and when I left the room, she and her master followed. When we arrived at the back door, I announced to Nia that I'd hang out with Sheba while she handled her business outside. "Nia, I'll go outside with her."

"Okay, if you want. I'm going to wash this make up off of my face."

"I'll let Sheba back in when she's done. Oh, and for the record, yes, you were snoring."

She gasped, "Was I loud?"

"As hell." By this time, I was laughing.

She gasped again, "Aw shit! For real?"

My laughter continued, at her expense of course, "I'm just joking."

"Whew. That's a relief."

"Oh, don't get it confused. You were snoring but it was only lightly."

"Still a relief. I've been known to snore like an old ass man with Emphysema."

"So, I finally know one of your flaws."

"I have many."

"If you say so." Sheba and I went into the yard.

Nia

Damn if this nigga doesn't know the right shit to say. All the time. I undressed and showered so I could wash away the club smell. I would drop my dress at the cleaners tomorrow. I really enjoyed myself tonight.

On Saturday, we did the ghetto tourist thing. Most people who visit St. Louis want to go to the obvious tourist spots, The Arch, The Zoo, the Aquarium, City Museum and the Science Center. Well, I wanted Malik to experience St. Louis through my eyes. The tourist stuff is cool, and I'd be sure to drive him by those spots, but I wanted to show him what black folk do. We jumped in the 4Runner, and we began our day by having breakfast at 'Goody Goody' on Natural Bridge and Goodfellow. It was a very small diner, and they'd been around since the forties. Goody Goody was to breakfast what The Best Steak House was to lunch and or dinner. Malik followed my lead and duplicated my order. I always get the same thing. The sampler platter includes ham, bacon, sausage, two eggs, grits or rice and toast or biscuits. A good southern breakfast. There's nothing like it and Goody Goody always delivers. Today would not be an exception.

After the waitress delivered our food to our table, Malik understood why I, as most St. Louisans raved about their food. Everything looked delicious.

224

"Nia?"

I didn't hear him because I was too entranced looking at my plate and licking my lips. I placed butter on my rice followed by sugar. He repeated my actions.

"Nia?"

I finally snapped out of it so I could answer him. "Malik, I'm sorry but this food has me in a trance."

"I see why, this spread looks like something my mother used to cook on Sunday mornings."

"I know. I can cook like this, but who has the time?"

"You can cook like this?"

"That should be obvious after last night's meal."

"True dat. You got me." We began to partake in the very scrumptious meal which had been prepared for us by the staff. While eating, we were interrupted several times because of people I knew stopping to talk. We ran into Alexis, Johnny, and Amber. Alexis was there with one of her employees.

"Hey Malik. Nia."

"Hey girl, what brings you-never mind, I know why you're here, the same reason I'm here."

"Exactly. Hey, this is one of my new employees, Nicole Brown. Nicole this is one of my best friends, Nia Witherspoon and her friend Malik Black."

Malik gave Nicole the black man nod that says, "What's up?" and I spoke, "Nicole, it's nice to meet you."

"You as well."

"So, you're one of those people that likes dead people too?"

Laughing Nicole responded with, "Yeah, I'm one of those people. Unlike those who are alive, they don't talk back or give unwanted opinions and or conversations."

"No, they don't."

"Nia, we're heading back to the funeral home. We just came here for some fuel. We have a lot of work to do."

"Okay girl, I'll talk to you later. When Malik and I leave here, we're going sightseeing."

"Well, enjoy. I'll call you on your cell if I need anything."

"Okay," I replied.

Malik said, "Good-bye ladies."

They departed and we continued to eat. Of course, it would be impossible to finish eating without being interrupted. We were trying to complete our meal when Johnny appeared. Johnny is an ex-high school classmate who turned crackhead.

"Nia. Nia Witherspoon is that you?" This question caused Malik and I to look up.

"J? Johnny Reed?"

"Yeah baby girl, it's me. I know I'm looking bad but it's me."

225

"It's okay, J." Looking at Malik, I introduced them, "Johnny Reed, this is a very special friend of mine, Malik Black. Malik, this is an old friend of mine Johnny Reed, but I call him J."

They gave each other dap and said, "What's up man?"
I could tell he wasn't doing well. He was thin, he hadn't had a haircut, his clothes were dirty, and he was missing teeth. He also looked as if he hadn't eaten. "J, have you eaten?"

"Naw, baby girl but I'm good."
I was about to offer him food and a seat but prior to the words leaving my mouth, Malik spoke up, "Naw man, that ain't cool. You gotta keep your strength up." He got up from his seat and said, "Here, take my seat. Nia baby, get the waitress and order him what we just ate." I did what Malik asked me to do. Johnny's pride was getting the best of him, "Bruh, you don't have to do this. I just came over to speak."

"Man, it's cool. Don't let your pride stop you from getting a good, hot meal. Nia and I have both been blessed and as she would say, 'You can't be blessed unless you bless someone.' I began smiling because he not only listened, but he understood. "I'm beginning to believe that."
Johnny looked at him and then at me, "Baby girl where'd you find this one?"

"He's not from here, can't you tell?"

"Hell yeah, so you keep him. I always believed you were to be treated like a queen." Directing his comment to Malik, "Man, she always had a good heart."

"Bruh, I ain't going nowhere unless she wants me to."
At that moment, the waitress brought J's food to the table, Malik grabbed a spare chair from another table and as he ate, we talked and caught up.

"So J, how are your parents?"

"They're good, praying for me and loving retired life."

"Yeah, my mother enjoys being retired as well. I know she misses my father, but she's strong."

"Yeah, she is. Hey, how's Nandi? She still married?"

"Yeah, but how did you know? I haven't seen you since my father's funeral."
J looked off in space before he said, "I'm still so sorry about your father. He was an amazing man."

"Yeah, he was, but it's okay."

"Are you really okay?"

"I'm good."

"I'm glad to hear that. Anyway, I talked to Jake awhile back and he told me Nandi had gotten married and moved somewhere down south."

"I wonder why Jake didn't tell me you all talked?"

"I asked him to not because I knew you'd come looking for me, and at that time I didn't want to be seen."

"Uh, okay. Anyway, Nandi lives in Montgomery, Alabama with her husband Kevin and their twins, Keenan and Kai."

226

"Twins? Nandi has twins?"

"Yep, a boy and a girl."

"What? Next time you talk to her tell her hi. Your mom too."

"Oh, you can tell mom hi tomorrow when you see her."

"How am I going to see her tomorrow?"

"I guess I should ask first."

"Ask what?"

"Would you like to join us for church?"

"Actually, yes I would. I haven't been in a while."

"Cool. Where do you want us to pick you up from?"

"I'll be at my parents in U.City- In unison we said, "On Watts across from Heman Park." We began laughing. "J it is so good to see you."

"You too, baby girl. Thanks for accepting me and not avoiding me."

"Why would I do that?"

"Because of how I look?"

"J, I am no better than you or anyone else for that matter. You and I have been friends too long for me to act like that plus you know that ain't me."

"Baby girl, you haven't changed at all."

"You know me, I don't know how to be anyone except Nia."

"I miss you."

"Well, you won't have to miss me anymore because we won't be losing touch."

"That's cool. I'd love to go to church with you and Malik."

"Cool. We'll be in front of your parent's house at seven-thirty."

"AM?"

"Yeah."

Sighing J replied with, "Okay, I'll be ready. Hey baby girl, isn't that Amber, Dante's little sister?"

Malik and I both looked in the direction he was looking in. We just couldn't escape her. "Yeah, I think that is her." I didn't want J to know she and I were no longer close, so I attempted to get around the subject. "We saw her last night at the Pageant."

"What was going on there?"

"There was a jazz set and Jake, Alexis, Alicia, Kevin, Kenya and Craig, Malik and I were there. We also ran into Michelle and her fiancee'."

"White girl Michelle we went to school with? Ya'll still stay in touch?"

"Yeah, that's my girl. She's our attorney?"

"Damn! She's a lawyer now?"

"Yeah, she's with her dad's law firm downtown."

"Straight! That's cool."

Malik had been sitting there allowing us to reminisce, but I knew it was time to go, we had a lots to do.

"J, I don't mean to cut this short, but we have a lot of stuff to do, but we'll be at your parents in the morning."

"Cool. I appreciate this. I really do."

227

"No need to thank me, we go waaaaay back." J looked at Malik and he was about to say something, but Malik beat him to the punch.

"Bruh, you don't have to say anything. A friend of Nia's is a friend of mine."

"Thanks man."

"No problem." Malik grabbed the bill and proceeded to get up.

"Baby, I'll pay the bill."

"Now Nia, what kind of brotha would I be if I let you pay? I let you pay yesterday. I won't go out like a busta and allow you to continue to pay. I am a man."

"All right."

J was obviously impressed and said, "Nia, I think you should let the brotha handle his business."

"I guess I should." I stood up to hug him, and he and Mailk exchanged dap. To keep J from asking too many questions I spoke to Amber, but that was it. Malik paid the bill, and we exited the restaurant. I drove through the city so I could show him the regular tourist spots as well as what's important to black people in the STL.

I showed him Beaumont high school, Lexy's alma mater. I also drove him by my mother's alma mater, Sumner High School. I proudly showed him the new Vashon High School and Cardinal Ritter. Both were predominantly black high schools in the heart of the city. I took him down Washington Ave. to display what a black owned company had done. How they'd transformed the entire area. We drove by Union Station, the new federal building, the old courthouse where slaves were once sold and the Arch. I asked him if he wanted to go up in the arch, but he declined that idea altogether. After the scenic tour, I asked if he was interested in some shopping? He indicated he was, so I decided to take him to the *West county Mall*. I jumped on I-40 westbound, but I decided to get off at Kingshighway to show him the *St. Louis Science Center* and *Forest Park*, which is home to our Zoo. After showing him both of those attractions, I hopped back on the interstate. I remained on I-40 to interstate I-270 south bound and about one and a half miles in that direction brought us to the Manchester Rd. exit. I exited the interstate and within ten minutes, we were in Nordstrom's. I found a pair of boots, and Malik purchased a pair of slacks.

After leaving the mall, we went back to the house to take a much-needed nap. Two hours is all we needed because we both woke up around the same time. I was still lying in bed when I heard a knock at the door.

"Come on in."

"Hey sleepy head."

"Hey you."

"What's up for tonight?"

"Actually, I have a surprise for you."

"Oh really. What is it?"

"Now, it wouldn't be a surprise if I told you."

"I guess not. Well, are we staying in or going out?"

"Going out so dress casual."

"Cool. What time?"

I looked at my watch before I answered. It was four o'clock. "We'll probably leave here around six."

"I'll be ready."

"Well, I think I'm going back to sleep. Would you please wake me if I'm not up?"

"Sure, enjoy your rest."

"Oh, I will." I turned over and went back to sleep within seconds. I woke up on my own at four forty-five. I went to check on Sheba and came back into my room to shower and dress. While I was outside with Sheba, I'd decided on my outfit. I was going to wear a pair of black linen cropped pants with a red sleeveless wrap blouse. With the outfit, I was going to wear my black and red Gucci wedge sandals and carry the handbag to match. I left my hair wrapped and jumped in the shower. I chose my Blue cologne by Ralph Lauren as the fragrance for the evening. After dressing and applying a light coat of make up, I went in search of Malik. While I was in the shower, I thought I heard a knock at the door but of course I couldn't answer it.

Malik

I was at Nia's door promptly at five, but I guess she'd gotten up on her own. I knocked, but after listening closely, I could hear that she was in the shower. She said we're leaving in an hour, so I better return to my quarters to get ready. I'd decided on a pair of gray wide legged cuffed slacks, a short sleeve black and gray silk sweater and my black sandals. During our shopping at the *West County Mall*, I'd purchased a new men's fragrance. It's called *Hanee Mourii* and it smells really good. I think she'll like it. I showered, dressed, and pulled my dreads into a black leather band. Now, I'm ready to find Miss Witherspoon.

We ran into each other in the kitchen. Nia had just come from the backyard with Sheba. "Hey, don't you look nice."

"Well, thank you sir. You look pretty good yourself. I love that sweater."

"Thank you, ma'am. The sweater was a gift from my mother."

"She has good taste."

"Yeah, she does all right, she's been dressing my father for the last forty-four years."

"Well, there you have it. Are you ready to go?"

"Ready when you are." I noticed Nia was taller than normal, so I looked down to see the cause and I saw a pair of Gucci wedges. "Nice wedges."

"Thank you. I had to have them when I saw them."

Laughing, I responded with, "I'm sure you did."

229

"Let me go upstairs to get my handbag and then we can leave."

"Okay, I'll meet you in the garage."

"All right."

I ran upstairs to grab my handbag, made sure I had the tickets for the concert and met Malik in the garage.

Nia

We jumped in the ride, pulled out of the driveway and as I was pulling onto North and South, I saw a black Tahoe. It looked just like Ben's, but it couldn't be. I drove away and didn't think anything else about it.

Malik

"So, are you going to tell me where we're going now?"

"Nope." To prove her point, she changed the radio station to 100.3 The Beat and began to bop her head to Mariah' Carey's "Always Be My Baby." I laughed and decided to just enjoy the music. She headed west on Delmar to I-170 North. Two and a half to three miles up the interstate she jumped on I-70 east bound to Lucas and Hunt Boulevard going north. After driving down Lucas and Hunt Boulevard, we came across West Florissant, which is where the Ambassador is. She pulled onto the lot, and we were greeted with a long line of people waiting to get inside.

"Okay, do you want to tell me what's going on?"

"Yeah, I guess so."

"Okay, what's up?"

"We're going to a concert."

"A concert? What-Who's concert?"

"Cat got your tongue?"

Laughing I said, "I guess so. So, who's in concert?"

"Um, there's UTFO, Chubb Rock, Kurtis Blow and Whodini."

My eyes bugged out. "Are you serious?"

"Hell yeah, we're about to get our party on."

"Nia, thanks so much. I'm having a helluva time."

"You're welcome. Let's go, everyone's waiting for us."

"Who's everyone?"

"You know...everyone...my peeps."

We parked and got out of the car to get in line. As we walked toward the line, I heard Nia's name being called. It was one of her boys, Scott Simpson and his fiancée Sandra. He went to Normandy High School, Nia's high school's biggest rival. I learned from her that's the thing in St. Louis. When someone asks you what school you attended, they never mean college, they mean high school. She couldn't explain why, but it's what matters in the STL. Anyway, she and Scott met after high school while she was dating one of his boys and they remained good friends. She spoke.

"Hey Scott, Sandra. How ya doing?"

Sandra responded, "We're good girl. I had to threaten Scott's ass to get him to come, he'd rather shake his tail feather at Two Brothers."

"Nia don't believe the hype."

"I'm sorry, I'm being rude. This is Malik, he's visiting from Dallas."

"What up bruh?" Scott and I exchanged dap, and then Scott introduced Sandra.

"This is Sandra, wifey-to-be."

I held out my hand to Sandra, "It's my pleasure."

Scott asked Nia, "Where's Lexy?"

"She should be here." Just as she said that we heard Lexy's voice. "Nia."

She and Jake had obviously arrived early because they were at the head of the line. We headed in their direction after saying our good-byes to Sandra and Scott. Nia reached out to hug Alexis and Jake. I hugged Alexis and Jake, and I shared dap. I'm excited about the concert and about being here with Nia.

Nia

The line was extremely long, and I couldn't help but express my feelings about that, "Damn this line is long."

"Yeah, the thirty and over crowd are about to get their party on. I saw some people from school, people I haven't seen in a long time. It was wild running into them", Lexy announced.

Excited I asked Lexy, "Girl, guess who I saw today?"

"Who?"

"J."

"J as in Johnny Reed? That went to school with you?"

"Yes, girl."

"How's he doing?"

"He's not his normal self, but he seems to be on the road to recovery."

"That's good. I'd love to see him."

"You may get the chance."

"Cool. This concert should be off the chain."

"Yeah, it should. All I want to hear is 'I'm a Ho,'" Jake said.

I said, "Yeah, that was the shit back in the day. We used to party like crazy at the Kappa Skating parties at Saints."

With an I-remember-yesterday look on her face Lexy said, "I used to love Kappa Skating parties."

"They were cool. Those cane twirling niggas could throw a party," Jake agreed.

While we were reminiscing, the doors to the Ambassador were opened. I explained to Malik the one negative aspect about the Ambassador was all the

231

shows were mostly general admission, which meant to get a decent seat you had to arrive early or get VIP. For this concert I'm glad Lexy and Jake took it upon themselves to arrive early. Once we were inside the venue, we found a long table in the VIP section. A majority of the crowd was there but we were still waiting on Kenya, Craig, Alicia, and Kevin. The show was set to begin at eight, but I'm sure the venue was on CP time. The rest of the gang arrived around eight-thirty. Kenya couldn't believe the crowd, "Damn! It's packed up in here."

"Yeah it is," I replied.

Jake asked, "Is anyone hungry?"

"And thirsty. I could use some food and a drank," Kenya said.

Laughing, Craig asked, "A drank?"

"Yeah, that means I'm extra thirsty and a drink won't do."

"Girl, stop frontin', we all know your ass is a lush."

"Call me what you want. I just like an occasional drink."

Alicia sarcastically asked, "Occasional. When did every other day become occasional?"

"Fuck you, Alicia."

"Love you, too."

I interjected, "Ladies. Ladies. We're here to have a good time, cover your horns."

Standing up and ignoring what was said, Jake announced he and the fellas were going to get food. The ladies stayed at the table enjoying the sights and the music the DJ was playing, it was all ol' school. I was bopping my head to Stetsasonic's 'Sally' when I felt a tap on my shoulder. It was evident none of my girls had noticed because none of them alerted me. When I turned around to see who it was, I looked into Ben's eyes. His bald-headed ass is getting bolder and bolder.

"What do you want Ben?"

"I just came to speak."

"Well hi, and bye."

"Damn Nia after everything we shared it's like that?"

"And that's the way it is."

"You know I ain't giving up, right?"

"Whateva!"

"I'm for real."

"You know what?" Before he could answer, I continued. "Our joke of a relationship is over, and you are a lost cause."

"Baby, why are you trippin'?" As the word baby escaped his mouth, the fellas arrived back at our table. Malik had an angry look on his face, but he held his composure. Malik placed the food on the table. He looked Ben up and down and then he looked at me with concern etched on his face. "Baby, are you okay?"

"Aw yeah, I'm cool." Ben sulked away when he realized I was Malik's main concern.

"I was waiting for his bitch ass to say something crazy," Jake commented.

"Man, he ain't crazy. Tonight, will not be a repeat of last night."

"I hear you bruh," Jake commented. Unknowingly, Malik had just gained more points with Jake. Since Jake takes his brotherly role to heart, he's always looking out for me but since Malik has joined the watch-over-Nia crusade I know Jake has a little more respect for Malik.

Craig was obviously hungry because he said, "C'mon ya'll, let's get our eat on before the show starts." They'd purchased a little of everything: fried wings, hot n' spicy wings, catfish, shrimp, green beans, corn, spaghetti, fries, and onion rings. We began eating as if our lives depended on this meal.

You know black folks. We can never start an event on time or be there on time. It went from being eight-thirty to nine-thirty it seemed, within a matter of minutes. The show still hadn't started. The DJ was doing his thing on the 1's and 2's, but we were getting antsy. Thankfully, our wait wouldn't be much longer. One of the DJs from 96.3 was now on stage about to announce the first act. The crowd was hype. First on stage was Chubb Rock, who was followed by UTFO. Of course, their biggest hit was 'Roxanne, Roxanne' and we began doing the dances which were popular during that era. One of the kings of rap entered the stage. The one. The only. Kurtis Blow. He, of course, did all his hits and even graced us with some of his break-dancing moves. Last but definitely not least, Whodini hit the stage. I think they had the most hits as well as the biggest fan base. The crowd went completely crazy. They did everything from, *'Five Minutes of Funk'* to *'I'm a Ho'* and everything in between. We were partying so hard all of us were sweating. You know black folks create heat like sticks make fire. When the concert was over there was a discussion of what was next.

Kevin asked, "So, are we hanging tonight?"

"You know I'm down for whatever," Kenya's always ready to party ass stated.

"Well, unfortunately Malik and I won't be hanging." Looking at my watch I said, "It's one-thirty which means that it's Sunday, and unlike you heathens, we're going to church."

"All right girl, I'll call you tomorrow," Lexy said before she reached over and hugged me. We then said our good-byes and headed to the car to begin our journey home.

"Nia baby, I really enjoyed myself and I sincerely appreciate you taking me."

"Oh, it's not a problem. I enjoyed it as well."

"I really liked Whodini's performance."

"Yeah, me too. It's amazing none of them have aged. They all look the same."

"Especially the brothers in UTFO. They look young as hell, like it's still nineteen eighty-six."

233

"I know, it's amazing but like they say, good black, don't crack."

Laughing he said, "It's so true. We have to thank God for the excessive melanin in our skin."

"Yes, we do."

"Again, thank you. This will definitely be a memorable trip for me."

"I'm glad."

We continued the drive home in silence. Once we arrived home, I let Sheba out and then we both went to our perspective bedrooms. We'd be getting up in a matter of hours. We both said, "Good night."

Although we were out late, we dragged our tired bodies out of bed to attend the early service at my church. I was impressed Malik was up before I was. Last night I mentioned to him I normally attend the eight o'clock service, but I guess he assumed it because I told J we'd pick him up around seven-thirty. I got up around six forty-five and I heard Mr. Sexy man moving around. Without grabbing my robe, I went and knocked on his door. Ten seconds elapsed, then the door swung open. Smiling, I said "Good morning, Mr. Black". I was thinking to myself, 'with your sexy ass'. He stood there in his pajama pants and no shirt. Staring. He looked at me from my wrapped head to my French manicured toes, but he never said anything. I caught him staring at my breasts, but he quickly diverted his gaze. I immediately realized not getting my robe was a mistake. It was evident from the moistness between my thighs and the heaviness in my breasts. Still, he said nothing and continued to stare. I couldn't continue to stare at his fine ass with that sexy ass hairy chest. If I did, I couldn't be held accountable for my actions. I began to look behind me to see if I could see what he was staring at, although I already knew.

"Malik, what are you looking at?"

"You."

"Me? Why?"

"You're beautiful."

"Yea right. I have no makeup on, my hair isn't combed, my legs are ashy, and my breath is funky. As well as I slept last night, I probably have dried up slob around my mouth."

"All of that may be true but you're still beautiful."

"Well, I guess I should just accept the compliment, so thank you."

"You are welcome."

"Since you're up, would you like to attend church with me?"

"Of course. Are you trying to be funny?"

"No, not at all."

"That's why I'm up, I've already showered."

"A man who likes to attend church, I'm impressed."

"I'm not trying to impress you, but church is an important part of my life."

"I heard that, Mr. Black. I think I should hop in the shower so we can be on our way. I hate being late."

234

"That's cool. I'll meet you downstairs."

"That'll be fine, would you like breakfast?"

"Actually, I'd like to take you to brunch. Jake told me about this place downtown. I think it's the Hyatt Hotel. He told me they have a really good brunch."

"Malik, you're visiting me, I can pay for brunch."

"Nia, I want to treat you, would you please allow me that?"

"Yes, Mr. Black and thank you in advance."

"Trust me, it's my pleasure."

"Okay enough with the pleasantries, I need to get ready. My mother should be calling. Would you please answer the phone if it rings?"

"Sure."

"Would you also let Sheba out?"

"No problem."

"I'll give her some water before we leave."

"Don't worry about it, I'll take care of her."

I went back into my room, made my bed and I happened to glance at the mirror over my dresser. My nipples looked like marbles and I instantly knew why he was staring at my breasts like he's never seen a pair before. I'll question him about that later.

I stepped into my bathroom and turned the shower on. I went to my sink to use my Plax. While swishing that around in my mouth, I put toothpaste on my toothbrush and did my morning ritual which ended in me using Listerine. A sistah had to have fresh breath. I reentered my bedroom to step into my spacious walk-in closet to choose a dress for today's service. I stood there a second or two but couldn't decide. I decided to turn on the news to check the weather. Our local NBC station informed me we were in for another hot day. With this knowledge, my search for an outfit would be easy. It would be hot outside, but my car and the church's air were in great working condition. I chose an outfit comfortable in all environments. I also knew if we were going to brunch, the hotel would be running their air as if Satan was a patron and they were trying to freeze him out. I chose a Dana Buchman dress. It was a trapeze pleated dress with ivory, peach, and pale pink polka dots. I chose my ivory 9 West wedges, and my ivory Coach bag. I also grabbed a cardigan in case the air conditioner was making the church feel like Antarctica.

I stepped back into my bathroom and wrapped my hair. I checked the temperature of the water, disrobed, and stepped into the shower. I washed and then I used my "Glamorous" shower gel to ensure my fragrance would linger throughout the day.

When I emerged from the shower, I checked the time and I had about twenty minutes to get ready. I applied my lotion and put on some deodorant. I put on a light coat of mascara and eye liner. I covered my lips in a sheer peach gloss. I unwrapped my hair. combed through it and began to dress.

235

Malik

No, Nia didn't just walk in here with nipples as hard as jawbreakers. I hate she caught me staring, but shit, they were staring at me. She couldn't expect to come in here with those shorts, that tight shirt and those breasts looking like a sex goddess and not expect a reaction from me. And that's what happened. My other head reacted because he doesn't know any better and it's been a while.

I was relieved when Nia left my room to go get dressed. I'd already showered and trimmed my beard. To rectify my situation, I needed a cold shower. I obliged myself, again.

Nia thought I didn't have any color in my wardrobe, but I'd brought along my brown Sean John suit, with my peach silk shirt, handkerchief, and tie. I saw Michael Warren in the Soul Food movie with these same colors on and he looked good. So, I figured I'd try the colors myself. I completed the ensemble with my brown Kenneth Cole shoes and D&G cologne. As I began to dress, the phone rang. I reached over to answer it but the only thing to respond to my "Hello" was silence. So, I repeated my greeting and again the response was silence, so I hung up. I resumed dressing and the phone began to ring again. After two rings I answered. Again, silence followed my greetings. I looked at the phone, hunched my shoulders and hung up the receiver. Again, I finished dressing. Just as I was tightening the knot in my tie, the phone rang. Again, I reached over to answer the phone but this time I didn't give my greeting immediately. I think I was waiting for the caller to say something although they'd said nothing during the previous two calls. Well, this time a female voice came across the line.

"Hello, Nia."
I could hear the nervousness in her voice and from the sound of her voice I knew it was Nia's mother.

"No ma'am' this is Malik, Nia's friend from Dallas."
"Yes, young man. I've heard a lot about you."
"Likewise, Mrs. Lawson."
"Are you enjoying your visit so far?"
"Yes ma'am, I am. Nia has been a great hostess."
"Well, you know what they say?"
"No ma'am, what's that?"
"She get it from her mama." Silence went through the phone line like gossiping women. "Malik?"

What does Nia's mother know about Juvenile? Her comment just threw me off. What's up with that? "With a slight chuckle I answered, "Yes ma'am', I'm here."

"Well, where is that daughter of mine?"
"She's getting ready for church."
"Will you be attending with her?"
"Yes ma'am', I wouldn't miss it."

236

"Good, we will be meeting you this morning."

"Great, I'm looking forward to it."

"Did Nia prepare breakfast for you?"

"No ma'am' but I plan on taking her to brunch after service. Jake told me about the Hyatt Hotel. I'd love it if you'd join us. Both you and Mr. Lawson, my treat of course." Just then I received the beep on the line that tells us there's another call trying to get through. "Excuse me Mrs. Lawson, I need to answer the other line."

"Okay baby, you go right ahead." "Thank you, just a moment." I hit the flash button. "Hello?" Silence followed my greeting....again, I repeated my greeting again. "Hello?" Again, silence encompassed the phone line. Just as I was about to return to Mrs. Lawson a man's voice bellowed across the line.

"Uh...may I speak to Nia?"

"She's not available right now. May I take a message?"

"Who is this?"

"Excuse me."

"Never mind, just tell her Ben called." Click.

It was such an abrupt click I took the phone from my ear and looked at it. It was quite evident he was ignorant. I've seen his ignorance all weekend; Friday's concert, last night's concert and now this phone call. Some niggas could be so rude, but I'll let Nia deal with that.

Ben

No, she is not allowing that nappy-dread-fake-wanna-be-Eric-Benet nigga to answer her telephone. If he answered the phone that means more than likely he spent the night. That's the same nigga on the cruise all up in her face. He was hangin' with her and her peeps Friday night at the jazz set and at the ol' school set last night at the Ambassador. She's flaunting this nigga like he's, her man. I ain't having it. Benjamin Eric Jones is not having it! Nia and nappy head better recognize.

Malik

I returned to her mother. "Mrs. Lawson, sorry about that."

"That's okay. Thank you for inviting Eddie and I to brunch, but I have some things to do at the house after church. I would like to spend some time with you this week though. When are you leaving?"

"I leave Wednesday afternoon and I'd love to spend some time with you this week."

"Great. As much as I'd like to join you and Nia, I must go home if I plan on preparing a hearty meal for dinner."

"Nia did mention you were cooking. May I ask what you're cooking?"

"No, you may not young man. You'll have to wait."

Laughing, "Okay Mrs. Lawson, I'll wait."

She had joined in on the laughter by now, "Just remember who taught Nia how to cook."

"Yes ma'am, I'll remember that."

"Good. Think about what day would be good for you and tell me at dinner tonight."

"Yes ma'am', I will and thank you."

"No problem, see you in church."

"I can't wait to meet you."

"Please don't forget to tell Nia I called."

"I won't. We'll see you in about a half hour." We both hung up, I put on my suit jacket and headed to the mirror to inspect myself. If I had to say so myself a brotha was dapper. I looked good like a black man should. I decided to let my locks hang loose, but I did moisturize them with jojoba oil.

I went to knock on Nia's door. After knocking I quietly heard, "Come in." Nia was bent over strapping her shoes. When she looked up, she was smiling, dimples and all. The only thing I could think of was how fine she was, but I didn't say anything. I'd been commenting on her looks since I arrived in St. Louis, and although she is fine, there's so much more to her. She's intelligent, independent, and ambitious and her having a vast knowledge of our history is a big turn on for me. I was very impressed by her knowledge. It was an aphrodisiac. She obviously loves our people and cares about our future. Most often these women don't care at all. I know there's no comparison between Nia and Melina. That would be like trying to compare the Cadillac Escalade to the Kia Sportage, but like the SUV's, there's no comparison. None at all.

One of the things I admire about Nia is her need to give back to our community. No matter what city you come from, black America belongs to each and every one of us. On several occasions I suggested to Melina she should give back. Unfortunately, she could never grasp the concept. Her world revolved around one thing. HER. She was very selfish and thinking about it now, I don't know how I dealt with it.

Nia's in a different class. Hell, she's got class where Melina Brooks had none although she thought she did. Nia's almost too good to be true. She stood up and she wore this beautiful dress. What a coincidence, the colors in her dress matched my shirt, tie, and handkerchief. I know she noticed, but I guess she decided to say nothing. I wouldn't either.

Nia

Malik knocked on the door as I was slipping my feet into my wedges. "Come on in." When he walked in, I was sitting on the edge of my bed strapping my wedges, so my head was down. When I looked up, the vision I was presented with was beautiful. And of course, those dimples were dancing for me. I spoke first, "Well, well, well......Silence

"What does well, well, well mean?"

238

Standing up and adjusting my dress, I replied, "It means you Mr. Black, clean up very well."

With a slight chuckle, he said, "Is that right?"

"Yes, sir. You clean up damned well."

"Well Miss Witherspoon, you look pretty good yourself."

"Thank you. Service begins in forty minutes, and we need to leave. Remember, I told J we'd pick him up at seven-thirty. I'll meet you downstairs. Let me get my Bible out of my office. I can't remember If I have an extra one or not. "

"Nia, don't worry about it. I packed mine, let me get it out of my suitcase."

I was mentally checking things off my things-I-want-in-a-man-won't-settle-for-less list. So far there was only one item left on the list and that was sexual compatibility. I was sure we'd eventually make love, but I wasn't ready. Not yet anyway. I was tired of giving it up fast because I always end up hurt. This time I wanted it to be different. Malik wasn't pressuring me but a brotha has needs. This I know. As fine as he is I'm sure women throw coochie at him constantly; he was probably known as the coochie catcher. Shit, I want to jump his bones now, but church waited for no one including Nia and Malik.

"All right sir, I'll meet you downstairs." I went to the office to retrieve my Bible and headed to the kitchen. There it was again. That sight. There is nothing finer than a black man. In a suit. In sweats. In jeans and Timberlands. In boxer briefs. In the nude. Nothing finer. Absolutely nothing. Okay, I better quit before the luscious begins to tingle. His fine ass got me thinking about sexual thangs before entering the Lord's house!

"I'm ready if you are." Slipping on his Dolce & Gabbana shades, he held the door separating the kitchen from the garage open and said, "Ladies first."

"Thank you, sir."

"You're welcome. Oh, before I forget, while you were getting ready, Ben and your mother called."

"Oh, okay. We'll see my mother at church."

We were very prompt arriving at J's parents' home, and he was outside waiting for us. Malik got out of the passenger's seat to allow him to get into the backseat.

"Good morning."

Malik mumbled, "Good morning. "

I announced, "Praise the Lord J, it is a good morning."

We arrived at seven-fifty a.m. I located a parking space and the three of us headed to the church doors and into my mother's open arms.

"Good morning, Mama. You look beautiful." I kissed her cheek. Mrs. Lawson was exquisite in an ivory suit, with a sequined lapel, ivory hose, ivory sling back low-heeled pumps, a sequined clutch, and a matching hat. You know black women cannot go to church without their hats.

"Good morning, baby. You look beautiful also. Is that a new dress?"

239

"No mama, it's not new, you just haven't seen it."

"Well, it's beautiful."

"Thank you, ma'am. Mama, this is Malik. Malik, my mother Mrs. Diane Witherspoon-Lawson." She opened her arms, and he walked straight into them. Now that was something that never happened with her and Ben. In the two years with him, he never embraced her. Not even during holidays. My stepfather and I aren't close but even he and I embrace during the holiday season. My mother has great intuition when it comes to people. She never liked Ben, but I can tell her feelings for Malik are totally different.

"Hello, Mrs. Lawson."

Looking him up and down. "Good morning, young man. It's nice to finally meet you."

"The pleasure is all mine." After they exchanged courtesies, J stepped in between us, and my mother recognized him immediately.

"Johnny Reed? Is that you?"

"Yes it is, Mother Witherspoon."

"Praise God. Well, come here and give me a hug." He went into her arms without any hesitation. As she hugged him, she rubbed his back and mouthed the words, 'It'll be all right.' When he stepped away from her, he had tears in his eyes.

"We should go in and take our se-" She paused looking at Malik and I in amazement. "Wait one minute." We both looked at my mother trying to figure out what was up. "Are you two dressed in the same colors?"

Laughter began in the pit of Malik's stomach and emitted from his mouth. It was infectious and my mother and I joined him. "Mrs. Lawson it's a coincidence, we had no idea what the other would be wearing."

Shaking her head, "Well, let's go inside now." Malik and I chuckled, he grabbed my hand and hand in hand, we followed my mother and J to her favorite pew. This was the same pew she and my father shared. I think it's the reason Eddie Lawson won't attend church with his wife. My mother is in love with a dead man. She knows it and unfortunately, so does he. I don't think she should've remarried, but I know my mother. The thought of being alone frightens her. She raised us to be the total opposite of what she is. Dependent. She and my daddy were together for forty years, thirty-five of those years were spent as husband and wife, and my mother was very dependent on her husband. Although my father had been dead five years, he haunted their marriage. A dead man intimidated Eddie Lawson. The love my parents had, Eddie and Diane would never have. For this reason, I understood the intimidation.

For approximately 90 minutes, we listened to the praise and worship team as they lifted their voices. We were also blessed by the pastor's lesson. He taught forgiveness. He talked about how we as Christians say we forgive, but until we forgive in our hearts, our actions don't reflect forgiveness. He also stressed the importance of being nonjudgmental. By being nonjudgmental,

240

forgiveness is an easier concept to grasp. I think this sermon was just for J's ears.

Malik, without trying, impressed me again. Whenever the pastor gave a chapter and verse, he went straight to it without any stumbling blocks. He obviously knew his way around a Bible. A lot of these men will say they attend church to impress but they can't get to Genesis without help. Malik was a man of his word, so far.

The pastor ended his sermon, and it was time for the weekly announcements. I'm sure Malik and J were both dumbfounded when I stood up, walked past them and my mother and went and stood in front of the podium. I began to speak.

"Good morning brothers and sisters. How are you?" The church answered together. "Blessed, and highly favored." I continued. "Glory to God. For those who don't know me, I'm Sister Nia Witherspoon and I'm blessed to be a member of this congregation and the chosen one to read our weekly announcements, when I'm in attendance (that created some chuckles from the congregation). I want to thank Sister Carol Jones for reading the announcements during my absence. For those of you who may not know, Sister Nina James had to be rushed to the hospital." The congregation responded with concerned ahhhs. "Not to worry because we know God is good, not some of the time, but all of the time. She was having chest pains but she's home recovering. Please lift her up in your daily prayers. Also, next Saturday the youth of our church are holding their annual Six Flags outing. Tickets will be on sale after service as well as throughout the week. Please support our youth. If we don't, no one will. Also, next Friday is singles night, so if you are single come out and enjoy the service. If you have time, please meet and greet my visitors; Mr. Malik Black is a good friend from Dallas, Texas. My other friend is Johnny Reed, we attended high school together and I ran into him yesterday. He accepted my invitation to worship this morning. Have a great week and Be Blessed." I returned to my seat and the pastor said the final prayer.

Service concluded at nine forty-five. Malik, J, and I stood around while some of the church members greeted them both. We said our good-byes, informed my mother we'd arrive at her house for dinner at six and headed for the exit.

"Did you enjoy service?"

"Yes, I did. Thank you for including me."

J said, "Yeah Nia, it was really nice. I'd like to go with you next week if possible."

"Of course J, I'll pick you up at the same time next Sunday." Directing the next comment to Malik, I said, "I'm glad you agreed to join me. My ex- I'm sorry I didn't mean to bring him up."

"No, it's okay, you can tell me."

"Well, the truth of the matter is, he never attended service with me. Honestly I can't tell you the last time the heathen attended church."

Laughing as we relaxed in the car, "Don't be too hard on the brotha."

"He's not worth discussing anyway. After I drop J off it shouldn't take us long to get to the hotel."

"Bruh, would you like to join us?"

"Malik, I sincerely appreciate the invite, but I've got some thinking to do and I'm sure you and baby girl want to spend some time alone."

"Well, I'd like to see you before I leave."

"That's cool. Nia has the number, just call me." Right at that second, I pulled up in front of J's parents' home. "All right, I'll talk to you all later."

Malik's stomach growled at that time. "Good because as you can hear, a brotha is hungry."

"Yeah, I'm hungry too."

Our arrival at the Hyatt Hotel was met by a large crowd. St. Louis is a city where you're liable to run into someone you know almost everywhere. I'm a native St. Louisan as well as a minority business owner therefore I know lots of people. That's evident from the people I saw Friday and Saturday. I was certain I'd run into someone here as well. Brunch was set up buffet style so after being seated, we got in line for our food. Malik headed for the omelet line, and I entered the line for the basics, bacon, scrambled eggs, and toast. While in line someone called my name.

"Nia!" I began looking around but couldn't see the culprit. It was a man, but I didn't recognize the voice. Again, I heard my name bellowed across the room and this time the culprit said my whole name. "Nia E. Witherspoon. Girl, you better not act like you don't know me, I know your mammy." At that time Malik was walking toward me and walking next to him was Malcolm E. Hill. He was my boy in elementary, Jr. high and high school. I was as close to him as I was Jake and Johnny. I hadn't seen him since high school graduation. He went into the Air Force the day after, and we lost touch. I tried contacting his parents, but they'd moved, and their number wasn't listed.

Malcolm was some kind of fine too. I say this not because he's my boy but because it's a fact. He reminds me of fine ass Idris Elba except he's the light skin version and we know that he's fine. I prefer chocolate men, but I've got to admit Malcolm is fine. You gotta give props when they're due. He and Kenya dated in high school but that didn't pan out for whatever reason. Damn, it was good to see him.

Malcolm followed Malik and I to our table so I could place my plate on the table to get a hug. Malcolm hugged me, which ended up in him picking me up and swinging me around.

"Boy, put me down."

"Like I did graduation night?"

"Hell no, just put me down on my two feet." He did just that while Malik stood and looked at us crazy. I guess introductions should be given.

"Malcolm, this is a friend of mine from Dallas, Malik Black. Malik, this is a dear friend of mine from grade school, Malcolm Hill a.k.a. the class clown."

Giving each other the pound Malcolm said, "Man, do not listen to her. She was dropped on her head as a child. It took a while for us to figure out what was wrong but that's the conclusion we drew."

"I'm not going to substantiate that comment with a response. Are you here alone?"

"As a matter of fact, I am. I work at the downtown Post Office, I just got off and I figured I'd get me some grub before I go home to watch sports and hold my balls."

I gasped in horror, "Malcolm!"

Placing his hand over his mouth like he'd just been caught doing something wrong, Malcolm said, "We do have company, don't we? I'm sorry, baby girl." He remembered the pet name that he, J and Jake called me.

"Yeah, sure you are. Come join us since you're alone."

"You sure?"

I looked at Malik and he smiled. I took that as okay. "Of course, c'mon."

"I'm not the one to argue with you."

"Smart man, good memory too."

Malik obviously thought this was funny because he was laughing his ass off. "You all are too funny. I've got to ask, what did he do graduation night?"

"Should I tell the story, or do you want to?"

"I'll tell the story. I don't trust you to tell the whole truth and nothing but the truth."

"Whatever Miss, it is still Miss, isn't it?"

"Yes, Mr. Hill."

"If you don't get the story right, I'll jump in."

"You can jump all you want. Anywaaay....After graduation, me, Malcolm, Jake, Johnny, Alicia and Kenya went to a party. And man did we party. Afterwards we were hungry, so we went to IHOP. On the way out of the restaurant Malcolm was giving me a piggyback ride and Jake did the same for Alicia. I was laughing and begging Malcolm to put me down. This fool put me down all right. He dropped me."

Malik gave Malcolm a no-you-didn't-look, "Bruh, no you didn't."

Malcolm tried to explain himself, "Man, don't let Nia fool you. I didn't intentionally drop her, she was moving around, she got heavy, and she fell."

"What! Heavy! Nigga, I weighed one hundred and fifteen pounds when we graduated. You're six foot three inches tall and probably weighed two hundred and twenty pounds then. You dropped me but of course you won't fess up. That's why you took your butt into the Air Force. You knew once I healed up, I was coming to look for you to beat your ass."

"Baby girl don't be that way. I'll fess up. I dropped you but I swear it wasn't intentional. You know I love you like a sister and I'm sorry."

"Yeah okay, I love you too, but I owe ya." We began to eat, and the conversation was free flowing. The dreadful subject of marriage reared its ugly head.

243

Malcolm had the nerve the bring the subject up, "So, no one has made an honest woman out of you?"

"I'm an honest woman now."

"You know what I mean. I've heard about Event Solutions but, I just-"

"You knew about me and Alicia's company, but you haven't called or come by to see us."

"I was going to call but I've been hella busy."

"Busy. Too busy for your girls? What kind of BS is that?"

"Look Nia, I'm sorry, but I have a wife and son now and-

"Wait a minute. Did you say you have a family?"

Malcolm couldn't contain his smile. "Yeah, Autumn and I have been married for two years and little Malcolm is one."

"Autumn. What a pretty name. Did she go to school with us?"

"Naw I met her while I was stationed in San Diego." Malik and I continued eating again while Malcolm sipped on a cup of coffee.

"So, tell me everything since I missed the wedding."

"There wasn't a wedding."

"Why not?"

"I was about to be shipped off when I found out she was pregnant."

"So, you did the right thing?"

"Well, I loved her before Malcolm was conceived so it was only natural, we marry."

"A bruh who takes care of his responsibility. That's admirable," Malik commented.

"Admirable? Bruh, I didn't have a choice. My father raised a man not a boy and to do anything other than taking care of my seed was never an option."

"Yeah, your father, Mr. Hill definitely raised a man."

"It's amazing to me black men who take care of their children are commended. I don't understand, taking care of our children is our responsibility. It's nothing to be commended for. It shouldn't be out of the ordinary," Malcolm explained.

I commented, "Well, there are so many men not handling their responsibility it has become out of the ordinary."

Shaking his head, Malik said, "It's really sad. I don't have any children, but I couldn't imagine them growing up without me. I will take care of mine. If I make em', I'll provide for em'."

I asked, "So tell me about your wife? Is she-"

"Before you say anything, yes she's younger than me. You know I like them young."

"You sure do R. Kelly."

"Nia, don't go there. The women I date are legal. The only time I dated a girl under the age of eighteen was when I was also underage."

Directing the conversation to Malik, "I remember when we were seniors in high school, Malcolm was dating this girl in the eighth grade. Granted she looked twenty, but she was only thirteen or fourteen."

"I didn't know she was that young."

"Okay, I'll give you that. She lied but even after she told the truth, you kept dating her."

By this time all of us were laughing. "You got me baby-girl. I don't know why but I got a thang for younger women."

"Now, tell me about your wife. How young is she?"

"Autumn is thirty." He looked at me because he knew I was figuring out the difference. "I know that look baby girl, she's nine years younger than me."

"What does she want with your old ass?"

"That's my secret."

"I won't even ask you to divulge the 'secret'. I'm sure it's something I don't want to hear about."

"You asked."

"I did. You did always look young, so I guess it's why these women want your old ass."

Shrugging his shoulders and lifting his eyebrows in a playful manner, Malcolm responded. "Yeah, that could be one of the reasons."

Laughing, "Ewwww! Anyway, finish telling me about her."

"Okay. I met her in San Diego. She's five foot two, light with freckles, shoulder-length hair and so far, she's been a good mother and a good wife."

"Well, I'd love to meet her."

"I guess I can arrange a meeting, but no funny shit Nia."

"What do you mean?"

"I know you. No Chester-the-molester comments."

"All right Malcolm." I wrote my phone number on the back of a business card, "Here's my number, give me a call and I'll cook dinner."

"You? Cook dinner?"

"I think you'll be pleasantly surprised."

"Is that right?"

Before I could answer him, Malik spoke up, "Man she ain't no joke in the kitchen. When you come make sure you bring your appetite."

"Damn Nia, it's like that?"

Smiling from ear to ear I proudly said, "Yes sir, and that's the way it is."

"Hey, I gotta get out of here. I promised MJ we'd go to the Zoo today before I get too relaxed."

"Aww, isn't that sweet?"

"Family life is great. I am truly blessed."

With what I'm sure was a dreamy-I-wish-I-had-a-family look on my face I said, "Yes you are."

Shaking Malik's hand he said, "Bruh it was nice meeting you. You've got a good one."

"I don't have her yet, but I'm working on it."

245

Kissing my cheek he said, "Good luck."

"Hold up, Malcolm we can walk out together."

Malcolm and Malik paid the bills and we left. "Nia where did you all park?"

"On Chestnut."

"Yeah, me too."

We headed to our perspective vehicles. We arrived at my car first.

Looking impressed, Malcolm asked, "Baby girl, this you?"

"Yeah."

"It looks like you. Business is obviously good?"

"We're blessed."

"Well, my car is parked up the street from yours. I promise to keep in touch."

"All right. You better keep in touch Malcolm. I can't wait to tell Kenya and Alicia."

"I can't wait to see them either. It'll be like a class reunion."

"Yeah, it will, especially since you missed our ten and twenty year."

"All right, I'll be in touch." Directing the comment to Malik, he said, "Malik I have a feeling I'll be seeing you again."

Grinning he responded, "I hope so."

Malcolm went to his car and Malik, and I began our journey home. I was ready to take a nap. Our drive home was about twenty minutes, and within thirty minutes after changing into a pair of sweats and a tee shirt, I was asleep. I don't know if Malik took a nap, but I was out. The phone rang and I looked at the clock, the red illuminated numbers read four forty-seven. I couldn't believe I'd been asleep as long as I had. "Hello."

"Hey baby." Damn! When is he going to give up? I didn't feel like being bothered so I just hung up the phone. I guess that's what I get for answering the phone without checking the caller ID first. The phone rang again but this time I checked the caller ID, it was my mother. I answered the phone, "Hey Ma."

"Hey baby. Are you and Malik still coming?"

"Yeah we'll be there. Isn't dinner still at six?"

"Yes, and it's almost that now. I hadn't heard from you, so I didn't know if you all were still coming."

"Ma you know me better than that. Let me get up now and we'll see you at six."

I dragged myself from my bed and went in search of Malik. I found him in the family room, watching what else? ESPN.

"Hey."

"Hey Sleepy Head?"

"Did you go to sleep at all?"

"Yeah I napped for about an hour and a half."

"I guess I was more tired than I thought."

"It's understandable considering all the partying we've been doing."

246

"True. I haven't kicked it like this in a long time." As if cued, Malik's stomach growled. "Hungry?"

"Yeah, just a little."

"From that growl, I'd say you're real hungry. That was my mother the second time the phone rang, and dinner should be ready by six, so we've got an hour to get ready."

"I'll be ready. What should I wear?"

"Something casual. Knowing my mother, you should probably wear something with an elastic waist. She probably cooked a Thanksgiving Day type meal."

"Straight? A brotha is hungry. Is it cool if I wear sweats?"

"Yeah, that's what I'm wearing."

"Okay, I'll be ready."

"I'm going to get in the shower."

"Okay."

Malik

Nia had been gone less than five minutes and the phone began to ring. At first, I wasn't going to answer it because I thought she'd answer, but after two rings she hadn't answered. I decided to answer.

"Hello." No one responded so I repeated the greeting.

Ignorant ass opened his mouth to utter ignorance, "Man put Nia on the phone."

"Excuse me."

"You heard me."

"Who is this- never mind, I know who it is, but you can't talk to Nia."

"Why not?"

"One she's unavailable and two she doesn't want to talk to you."

He began screaming like a child, "Nigga I said put Nia on the-"

This nigga is a fatal attraction but if he keeps fucking with Nia, he'll be the last attraction. I hung up because I was not going there with him. The phone began to ring again. I ignored it. He called at least three more times. He has some serious issues, but he needs to get over them. She's going to be my woman and nothing he can say or do will change that. Hell, he messed up, I didn't. I got up to go shower.

Nia

My shower refreshed and woke me up. I was extremely tired. I threw on some sweats, my Air Shox and a Howard University sweatshirt that Jake gave me. I threw my hair into a ponytail and went to meet Malik in the family room.

"You ready?"

"Yes I am. Oh, before I forget, your boy called."

247

"Who Jake? What did he want?"

"No, not Jake, your ex."

"Oh him, who cares?"

"Well, he wanted to talk to you, and he tried to get belligerent, but I just hung up on him."

"What he needs to do is get over himself. I don't want him, and I've told him that."

"Well, he wants you back but I ain't having that."

"Is that right."

"As your boys from the STL would say, Fa Sho Derrty!"

Laughing I told him, "You've been in St. Louis too long."

"Let's go eat. I already put Sheba outside."

"Thank you, let's go."

The drive to my mother's house was a short one. We parked and entered through the side door. The door went straight to the kitchen. I knocked and we walked in.

"Hey Ma."

"Good evening Mrs. Lawson."

"Hey, c'mon in. The food is already on the dining room table and Eddie's waiting. I wouldn't let him snack today."

We washed our hands prior to joining Eddie in the dining room and I was right. My mother prepared a huge meal. We had roast beef, fried chicken, collard greens, sweet potatoes, corn-on-the-cob, seven-layer salad and homemade rolls. I remembered Malik and Eddie had yet to be introduced so I made the introductions before we began to partake in the meal.

"Eddie this is Malik, a very special friend of mine. Malik this is Mr. Eddie Lawson, my stepfather." They shook hands and we sat down to eat. Other than the jazz my mother was playing the only sound heard was chewing and silverware hitting china. After about ten minutes of silence Malik said, "Mrs. Lawson, this food is delicious."

"Thank you baby, I'm glad you're enjoying it."

I commented, "Yeah mama loves people who love to eat."

We continued to eat and then my mother asked all of us, "So who wants dessert?" Malik and I rubbed our stomachs and gave her a sheepish grin.

Malik commented first, "Mrs. Lawson, I don't think I have room."

"Are you sure? It's peach cobbler."

"Peach cobbler with fresh peaches?"

"How else would I make it?"

"In that case, I can make room."

My mother jumped up with a smile on her face. She asked, "Would you like vanilla ice cream with yours?"

"Yes ma'am."

"Nia baby would you like some?"

"No ma'am, but I would like to take some home."

"I'll wrap you some to go."

248

"Thanks Ma."

She returned with a bowl for both Malik and Eddie. Both jumped right in. My mother and I held a conversation.

"So, what's up for this week?"

"Well, I still have to go into the office, but I cut my hours. Alicia's going to take up my slack."

"That's good baby." She then directed the conversation to Malik, "Malik how about we catch a movie tomorrow and do lunch."

"I'd like that Mrs. Lawson, what would you like to see at the show?"

"I don't know, we can decide when we get there."

"Sounds good."

"Good, that's settled. I'll call tomorrow morning to let you know what time I'm picking you up."

"Yes ma'am, I'll be ready." He didn't know he'd just scored major points with my mother. She could never get Ben to spend time alone with her. My father always told Nandi and I, if a man was serious and had good intentions, he wouldn't have a problem spending time with our parents, or our friends. There were so many signs with Ben, yet I chose to ignore them. The things we do in the name of so-called love. Malik finished his cobbler and we prepared to leave. We were going to the show. "Ma, we hate to eat and run but we're going to see The Hitman's Bodyguard."

Shaking her head, "That should be good, Samuel Jackson is good. Well, you all enjoy."

"We will," I kissed and hugged my mother and headed for the door.

Rubbing his stomach, "Mrs. Lawson, thank you for the great meal. I'm looking forward to tomorrow." He kissed her cheek, and we told Eddie good-bye and we left.

We went to AMC Creve Coeur Twelve on Olive St. From my mother's I hopped on I-170 north bound to west bound Olive St. The theater was about 3 miles down so our trip was quick. Malik paid for our tickets and after we found our seats, he announced he was going to the concession stand.

"Uhh…Mr. Black didn't you just eat?"

"Yeah, but…"

"And didn't you eat dessert?"

"Yeah, but…"

"And you're still hungry?"

"I'm a growing boy."

Laughing at him I said, "If you say so."

While he was at the concession stand, I called Colett.

"Hey girl."

"What's up?"

"Nothing much."

"Busy?"

"At the show with Malik."

"I'm just getting ready for school tomorrow."

249

"You?"

"Just chillin'."

"Are you enjoying your company?"

"As a matter of fact, I am. We've had a really good weekend."

"I wish I…" Just as she was going to express her desire to be in the STL kicking it with us, I saw Malik on his way back. I cut her off. "I'm sorry to cut you off girl but he's on his way back. I'll call you from the office tomorrow."

"Okay. Don't forget."

"I won't." I hung up the phone right as Malik sat down with popcorn, candy, and a soda. He certainly has an appetite but if he can eat like that and look as good as he does, I say go for it. I just looked at him and shook my head.

"What?"

"Nothing."

"You want some?"

"Some what?"

"Don't get fresh Miss Witherspoon unless you can hang."

"In that case I'll take some soda. Is it Pepsi?"

"Yeah."

They dimmed the lights and began to show the previews. The movie began and we became engrossed. Samuel Jackson has played an array of characters; I really enjoyed him in this and the collaboration with Ryan Reynolds and Salma Hayek was awesome. We left the theater headed in the direction of University City. Smooth jazz was our backdrop during the drive.

"Did you enjoy the movie?"

"I did. I'm a huge Samuel L. Jackson fan."

"It was cool. The theater is nice."

"That was my first time there and it is nice."

"In Dallas they have mega theaters with like thirty screens."

"That one is not the largest in this area but in south county there's a theater with twenty screens."

"How far is that?"

"About 25-30 minutes away."

"We'll go during my next visit."

"Okay. Well, I'm about to retire." I leaned down to kiss him on the cheek. I didn't notice he turned his head and when I thought I was kissing his cheek my lips landed on his lips. It was our first official kiss. I thought it was going to be a peck, but it turned into a full fledge kiss and neither of us tried to end it. Somehow, I ended up in his lap feeling the evidence of his arousal. While my tongue was mixing with his I began to think if I didn't stop this we were going to the next level. I wasn't ready for that. I pulled back.

"Malik, I'm so sorry. As much as I want you, I'm not ready for this."

"It's cool Nia. I just couldn't resist."

"Me either, but I just can't."

"Seriously, it's cool. You better get some rest for tomorrow."

250

He was trying to get me out of there probably because he was somewhat embarrassed. I got the message, so I got up to leave. Again, I bent down to kiss him on his cheek and this time he didn't turn his head.

"Good-night Malik."

"Good night baby sleep tight."

In my bed, I tossed and turned for a short time until I finally fell into a deep slumber. I was only hoping his night was as fitful as mine.

The following morning, I got up and prepared for work. I was quiet because I didn't want to wake Malik. I left him a note on the refrigerator before I departed. Around eleven, he called me at the office to inform me my mother had called, and she was on her way to pick him up. I wished them well and got off the phone. He didn't mention the note I left him on the refrigerator, so I assumed he hadn't seen it yet. About two minutes after we hung up my assistant informed me that Mr. Black was on line two for me again. I guess he found my note. I answered the line, "Event Solutions, Nia Witherspoon speaking." All I heard was him reciting the note I'd left. Yep, he'd found it. "Malik, I want to thank you for the wonderful time I'm having. You've become a major part of my life and you're slowly but surely restoring my faith in black men. I hope you enjoy your day with my mother. Always, Nia." After he finished reading, there was silence on the line. He broke the silence, "Nia that was so sweet of you. It means a lot to me." I know everyone in the office was looking at me because of the smile plastered on my face. "It was nothing really. I just wanted you to know you're on my mind and I'm glad you're here." Again, silence flooded the phone line. "Nia, you expressing your feelings means so much to me and believe it or not, I know how difficult that was for you. I'll see you when I get back to the house from hanging out with your mother."

"Okay, enjoy yourself and just in case I'm not home yet, there's an extra key in the kitchen under the door mat."

"Enjoy the rest of your day. I think I hear your mother blowing."

"Have a good time."

I worked through the rest of my day without any problems. I decided to order pizza for dinner if that was okay with Malik. When I arrived home, he was there watching Bad Boys II so I kicked my shoes off and joined him on the couch. Between Will and Gabrielle, acting like they weren't a couple to keep Martin in the dark, he and I began to have small talk.

"So, how was it hanging with Mrs. Lawson?"

"It was cool. It was like hanging out with you. You all really act alike."

"That's what everyone says."

"How was your day?"

"It was cool. Busier than I expected."

"That's good for business."

"Yeah, it is. I'm not going to complain about my blessings. I'm just going to be thankful."

251

"You hungry?"

"You know me. I'm always hungry but I don't feel like cooking. I was thinking about ordering pizza."

"From where? Pizza Hut?"

"Actually I want you to try Imo's."

"What kind of pizza do they have?"

"It's thin dough and really good. They also have a good salad with amazing house dressing. and tasty wings."

"I'll take your word for it. Let's order. Pause the movie."

"All right." I went into the kitchen to retrieve their phone number, but before ordering I figured it was best to see what he likes on his pizza. I yelled into the kitchen, "Malik, what do you want on the pizza." He yelled back, "Everything." I picked up the phone to place the order and rejoined him in the family room.

"So what did you order?"

"An extra-large deluxe, an order of wings, garlic cheese bread, and a salad." As the last syllable left my mouth, I heard his stomach grumble, "Hungry?"

"I guess my stomach can answer that."

We continued watching Bad Boys II until the delivery person rang the doorbell. I went to grab my handbag out of the kitchen but by the time I reached the door, Malik had already paid for the food and took it into the family room. I stopped in the kitchen to grab two waters, and a couple of paper plates, and re-joined him. We began to eat while we finished watching the movie. After the movie we turned on VH-1 to catch my ratchet Monday night line-up, which included 'Love & Hip-Hop Atlanta and Basketball Wives.' Following the lineup, we decided to retire.

The next morning, I awoke, showered, dressed, and prepared to leave. As I entered the kitchen, Malik greeted me. What a surprise! He had prepared a light breakfast for me. There was fresh pineapple, sliced bananas and strawberries, yogurt, and orange juice. He'd evidently taken great notes or had a great memory. I'd mentioned during one of our phone conversations when I ate breakfast, it was a light one. He'd retained what I said.

"Malik, you didn't have to do this."

"I know but I wanted to."

"You tryin' to spoil a sistah?"

Laughing, "Yeah, something like that."

"Well, I appreciate it."

"It's not a problem."

We ate in silence until it was time for me to leave for work.

"So, what are your plans for today?"

"I'm hanging with Jake and David. They said they'd be here around ten. We're going to find somewhere to shoot hoops. They mentioned something about the Wohl Center on Kingshighway and MLK or the rec center on Twelfth and Park."

"I'm sure you all will have luck at either of those locations."

"Well, have a good day at work."

"I will. You have a good time hangin' with the fellas and again, thank you for the breakfast."

"You're welcome."

I went on my merry way. I had a short workday. I arrived home around two in the afternoon and Malik was still gone. I decided to take a nap. When I awoke from my nap Malik hadn't returned so I decided to call Lexy and hang out with her for a minute. I called her at home but got no answer, so I tried her cell phone. She answered.

"What's up girl?"

"Nothing much."

"Tired of playing house?"

"Girl, what are you talking about? We're just hanging out and having a good time. I called because I want us to hang out for a minute. It's four o'clock. You down?"

"What do you have in mind?"

"Let's meet at the Cheesecake Factory in the Galleria for a drink."

"That sounds like a plan. What time?"

"I can be there in thirty minutes."

"Thirty minutes it is."

I hopped in the shower, threw on a pair of jeans with a tank and my flip-flops. I left a note on the refrigerator for Malik, put Sheba in the backyard and exited through the garage. We stayed at Cheesecake for about one and a half hours and then I headed home. Surprisingly, when I arrived home not only was Malik there, but he'd cooked dinner for me. My nose caught the aroma as soon as my left foot landed on the garage floor, and I burst through the door. "Hey Chef-brotha-dee!"

"That must be the ghetto version of Chef-boy-ardee."

"Yeah, something like. What's for dinner?"

"Jambalaya and dinner rolls."

"Jamba-" I began looking around trying to see where he was hiding the cook.

"What are you looking for?"

"The person who cooked this food."

"I cooked."

"Yea right. Is your mother here? Or did you hire someone from New Orleans to come and cook for us?"

"You got jokes?"

"Well, most men can't cook. They can fry a burger but that's about it."

"Well, I'm not most men."

"I'm beginning to see that more and more each day."

"Are you ready to eat?"

253

"Yes, I am. Let's eat in the family room. I want to see 'Queen Sugar on OWN."

"Go on in there. I'll bring the food to you."

"Thank you."

"You're welcome."

I entered the family room, turned the television on and relaxed on the sectional. He set up TV tables and we ate and enjoyed the program. I caught Malik making an appreciative grunt toward the sisters on the show, but I ignored him. We watched the show and then turned to HBO to catch a rerun of 'The Wire' with sexy ass Idris Elba. Stringer Bell was the best reason to watch that show.

This would be our last night together. His flight leaves tomorrow evening but I'm tired.

"Hey, I know it's your last night but I'm tired."

"I understand."

"No, you don't. I was with Lexy's-drink-you-under-the-table ass and alcohol makes me either horny or sleepy. I'm not ready for us to go to the next level so sleepy is what you get."

With an understanding look on his face he said, "We can just chill down here and watch a movie and you can fall asleep on my shoulder."

"That's cool. What are we going to watch?"

"Let's flick through the channels to see what we can find." Flicking through the channels we came across 'American Gangster' on Black Starz. It wasn't a new movie, but it was pretty good, and Malik had no qualms about watching it again. An hour into the movie I was asleep on his shoulder. I'm assuming later that night he also fell asleep because we both woke up on the couch the next morning. I didn't wrap my hair, so I looked a hot ass mess, but he never let on about my appearance. He still looked at me like I was one of the most beautiful women he'd ever seen. He makes me feel things, I've never felt with a man before.

"Good morning."

"Good morning, Miss Witherspoon."

Stretching I asked him, "How did you sleep?"

"I was actually quite comfortable."

"To my amazement, so was I."

"Would you like breakfast?"

"I'm cool. I need to get out of here because I plan on leaving work early so that we can have an early dinner before your flight leaves."

"Baby, that's sweet of you, but you don't have to do that."

"I want to do it."

"You sure?"

"Yeah."

"Just call me from the office and tell me what time to be ready."

"I will."

I showered and went downstairs. He was fast asleep on the couch. I kissed his forehead; he stirred a little and I was out. I called him at two o'clock and asked him to be ready at four o'clock. When I arrived, he was there waiting in the garage with his luggage. I blew the horn, and he came out, placed his luggage in the trunk and jumped in the passenger seat. Our ride over was quiet, we listened to the DJ on 96.3. His afternoon show was always hilarious. I'd made reservations at Morton's Steakhouse in Clayton, which was not even five minutes from the house. Upon our arrival, we valet parked and entered the restaurant. I hadn't eaten lunch, so I was famished. I enjoyed a twelve-ounce NY strip, and he had a twenty-two-ounce Porterhouse. Both medium well. Both delicious. Our time spent together. Almost perfect.

Looking at my watch I said, "Are you ready? Your flight leaves in an hour and thirty minutes."

"Yeah, I guess we should go. I really don't want to leave."

"I don't want you to leave either but you gotta get home."

"I know. We better head to the airport."

We arrived at the airport in about twenty minutes with the traffic. I parked in short-term parking for the main terminal, and we entered to locate which gate he'd be departing from. After finding out that information we headed to concourse C to enter TSA where I'd say goodbye and he'd leave to find his gate. The entire time neither of us said anything. We held hands the entire time. He finally broke the silence.

"Nia, I want you to know I had a great time. I enjoyed both concerts, the time spent with your family and friends and most importantly, the time spent with you."

"I enjoyed your company as well."

"I can't wait to see you again." Just then they began boarding, so he grabbed his luggage and got up. I followed him and we hugged each other. In his ear, I whispered, "I can't wait to see you either." Stepping out of the embrace, he planted a peck on my lips and turned to walk away. I stood there feeling as if I'd just lost someone very special to me. In this short time, he'd become a part of my being. What was I going to do until our next visit?

Big State, Big City, Big Visit.....

Toward the end of Malik's visit, he and I agreed I'd visit him in Dallas. Approximately four weeks later, I prepared for the trip. We'd become very close by talking on the phone daily. Sometimes we'd talk three to four times in one day. I felt like he was a good friend. I could be myself and that was rare. Most of the time when I'm dating someone, I can't be myself right away. I should say I don't feel comfortable being myself right away. The truth of the matter is, I'm thirty-nine, I'm single and I don't have any children. I want a husband and children so I feel the need to be the perfect date so the man I'm dating will think I'm the perfect mate. I know it sounds crazy but I'm scaling the

255

wall of desperation like a secret agent. I just want out. Out of the single life. I'm not so desperate as to accept whomever, but I know I'm ready. Is Malik that special someone? I don't know and I don't want to speculate so I'll have to wait and see. I'd hate to say because I've made those assumptions in the past and I've been DEAD WRONG! Anyway, he purchased me a round trip ticket and told me it would be at the gate when I checked in. Alexis agreed to drop me off and pick me up.

Nia

I arrived at DFW right on time. Surprisingly, the chauffeur at the arrival gate greeted me. He was holding a sign with my name on it. Upon close inspection, I saw it was Mike. Why was he holding a sign with my name? He knows who I am and how I look. I guess he was really in his acting mode.

"Hey Mike."

In a professional tone he said, "Welcome to Dallas Miss Witherspoon. How was your flight?"

Again, I guess he was in his acting mode. "The flight was fine. It's not often I fly first class."

"Mr. Black wanted to make sure you were comfortable."

"I was. You don't have to be so formal with me. Where's Malik?"

"He's awaiting your arrival ma'am."

By this time, I began laughing. "So, he sent you as acting chauffeur?"

"Yes ma'am, I'm to take you to the Black residence."

"Okay, I know ya'll got something up your sleeves, but I'll play along."

"All right Miss Witherspoon. Do we need to go to baggage claim?"

"No sir we don't." Lifting my garment and tote bag I said, "This is all I have."

Taking the bags out of my hands, he said, "I'll take these, and if you'd please follow me."

Saluting him armed forces style I said, "Yes, sir."

I followed Mike through the airport to the parking garage. Waiting for us was a black Cadillac Sedan De Ville limousine. He pushed a button on a remote which activated the engine. The Dallas heat smothered me like an insecure lover. Since he was able to start the engine remotely, I was able to enjoy the cool interior of the limo. After he opened the door to let me in, he placed the luggage in the trunk, and I sank into the plush leather seating. Mike got in behind the wheel of the car. Prior to driving off he said, "Miss Witherspoon, help yourself to anything in the bar. Make yourself comfortable. We should be there within thirty minutes."

"Thank you sir."

"You're welcome."

I'd gotten so comfortable that I fell asleep. One minute we were at the airport, the next Mike was waking me up. I got up, popped two pieces of Dentyne Ice into my mouth so my breath wouldn't be tart. Stepping out of the car, I was welcomed by God's gift of light and a modest yet beautifully landscaped home. It was evident he not only had good taste, but business was good.

Mike retrieved my luggage from the trunk and with his own key he unlocked and opened the door. I was greeted by Anita Baker's sultry voice. She hadn't made a CD in years, didn't matter, her voice was still awesome. The song playing was 'You're the Best Thing Yet' off her Songstress CD. Was he trying to tell me something? I entered the foyer in awe. It was beautiful. There were bleached hardwood floors. On the wall to the left was a huge mirror trimmed in pewter colored wrought iron. His taste was exquisite. As I walked into the foyer, I noticed his living room was on the right. I expected the typical bachelor furniture, the dreaded black leather. Surprisingly, his color scheme was burgundy, navy, and brown. The colors contrasted together perfectly. In the room there was a fireplace which was surrounded by brown marble. There were floor-to-ceiling bookshelves on both sides of the fireplaces. On those bookshelves were books and artifacts. Mike instructed me to sit down, "Miss Witherspoon, feel free to sit down and make yourself comfortable." I did as he suggested and as soon as I sat down, Malik entered the room, wearing an apron. He and Mike shared a few words and then Mike prepared to leave.

"Nia, it was good seeing you. I hope you enjoy your visit."

"I'm sure I will Mike. Thank you for picking me up from the airport."

"Not a problem Miss Witherspoon. You know I'll do anything for my boy."

"I know. Have a good one."

"You too. Peace." Mike was out the door and gone.

"Hey beautiful."

"Hey yourself Mr. Black." He walked toward me, I stood up and we hugged. Any nervousness I felt immediately left once I smelled his essence.

I liked his chef get up and decided to voice it, "I like your attire."

"You diggin' the apron?"

"Yes, I am. I get a soft spot for men in uniform." His laughter filled his living room.

"Are you hungry?"

"Actually I am. What did you cook?"

"Let's go in the dining room and I'll show you what I've prepared." His dining room furniture was beautiful. It was an exquisite cherry wood with an African design. He pulled a chair out for me to sit in and then he proceeded to uncover the covered dishes. There was lobster, shrimp, crab legs, twice-baked potatoes, dinner rolls and a salad.

"So, who cooked because I know you only wore the apron to place the food on the table?"

Shaking his head, "Nia, Nia, Nia, you always got jokes, but it's cool. I'm sure you've never had a man with my culinary talents."

"That's an understatement."

257

"Well, this brotha can cook, I prepared all of this just for you so let's eat."

Eat is what we did. We fed one another and filled our bellies with the delicious food he'd prepared.

"Malik, I can't believe you cooked all of this. This food is delectable. Who taught you to cook?"

"That would be Mrs. Black. She can throw down in the kitchen and you should've known from that meal I prepared in the STL."

"I see, and now I need a nap. Before I forget, tell your mother she's no joke in the kitchen."

"I'll be sure to give her the message. Well, your bedroom awaits you. Once we wake up from our naps, what do you think about us going to Dave & Buster's?"

"That should be fun. I haven't been in a minute."

"Cool, that's what we'll do. Let me show where you'll be sleeping."

His home was ranch style so there were no stairs to climb. He led me down the small hallway and into the fourth room on the right.

"This is the room you'll stay in. It has its own bathroom."

"Really? I thought you Texans used out houses."

"Ha Ha funny."

"It was kinda funny and you know I was just playing."

"Yeah, I know."

"Malik, this is nice." There was a beautiful black lacquered bedroom set and a queen-sized bed that looked very comfy. Mike delivered my luggage to the room soon after our arrival.

"Is this okay?"

"This is great. I can't wait to crawl into bed."

"Well, you go ahead. I'm going to clean the kitchen and then take a nap myself."

"You want help cleaning the kitchen?"

"No, it's cool. I'm just going to load everything into the dishwasher."

Yawning, I said, "Okay, I'll see you in a few hours."

"Get some rest."

"I will, oh Malik?"

He turned around, "Yeah?"

"Thanks for the meal, it was really good."

"You're welcome. It was my pleasure."

As soon as Malik left the room, I turned the light out and crawled into the bed.

Malik

I can't believe this woman is in my house. I've been waiting for this ever since Tom Joyner's cruise. I want her to enjoy herself, so she'll want to come back. I cleaned the kitchen and went to my bedroom to take a nap. I'd gotten up early to clean and cook and I was tired.

258

Approximately two hours later, I awoke, got up, showered, and threw on some casual clothes. It was kind of cool outside, so I chose a navy-blue Nike jogging suit and my matching Jordans. I let my locks hang loose and I went in search of Nia. When I got to her door I knocked.

Nia

I'd gotten up about twenty minutes ago, wrapped my hair and jumped in the shower. When I got out of the shower, I checked my cell to find out what was going on with the weather. It was going to be cool, in the low fifties. I brought my red and white Nike leggings and jacket, so I put those on with my all-white Air Max Plus. I unwrapped my hair, combed through it so it just hung loose. Just then, there was a knock at the door. "Just a minute." I finished applying my lip gloss and then opened the door. In walked His Fineness, looking good as usual.

"I see you're ready."

"Yes, I am, I was applying my lip gloss when you knocked."

Staring at me he said, "I see. Well, let's go."

"Before we go, can I get a tour?"

"Sure you can. There's not much to see but I'll show you."

Walking down the hall to his bedroom I asked, "How many bedrooms are there?"

"Three, mine, the guest room which is where you slept and another room I use as an office." We walked into his bedroom, and I was very impressed with the furniture. Again, I expected the typical bachelor pad stuff. You know, a waterbed with mirrors, some shit like that. I got the exact opposite. He had a whitewashed wooden canopy bedroom set. It was complete with the dresser, nightstand, armoire, and chest. All the furniture had marble tops. The furniture was elegant. Over his bed was a beautiful WAK painting of a black man locked in chains with a frame that matched the bedroom furniture. The hardwood floors were beautiful.

"Who does your floors?"

"I do."

"Really? You do a beautiful job."

"Thank you. Another talent from my mother, she made sure I could cook, clean, wash, and my father made sure I could do all the manly stuff."

"Manly stuff like what?"

"Cut grass, change the oil in a car, put shelves up, clean gutters, etc. Manly stuff, that's what my father called it anyway."

"Aw, so you're a jack of all trades."

"Naw, but I can fend for himself."

We then walked into his bathroom, and it was beautiful. Everything was black. The tile on the floor. The sink, the toilet, the bathtub, and the shower. The

259

shower had a glass door with his initials on the door. He decorated it with gray and white accessories. For a man, he really had style.

"All right, who decorated the bathroom?"

"Uh, that would be me."

Giving him my I-don't-believe-you-look, I began to tell him I didn't believe him but before I could get it out, he asked, "What, you don't believe me? A man can't decorate his own crib?"

"Yeah, but-"

"No buts. I did the decorating without any feminine assistance."

Sheepishly I looked away and said, "Okay I believe you. You did a great job on the entire house."

"Thank you very much. You ready?"

"When you are."

He grabbed my hand and said, "Let's go."

During the drive to Dave & Buster's we tuned into one of Dallas' local stations, they played old school hip hop. While riding we did all the old school dances, like the snake, the cabbage patch, and the prep. We were having such a good time we broke a sweat. It was weird because I'd never felt this comfortable with a man, not this soon anyway. The comfort level I have with him normally doesn't come until at least six months to one year of dating.

We arrived. Malik pulled into the parking lot.

"That was fun."

"Yes it was, but we always have a good time."

"Yes we do."

Rubbing his hands and grinning like a child in a candy store he said, "All right, let's go relive our childhood."

"I'm always ready."

"Is that right?"

"Without a doubt."

He got out of the car, laughing. When he got to my side of the car, he was still laughing. He opened the door for me. Always the perfect gentleman. Chivalry ain't dead. No sireee, it's not dead at all. I got out of the car, and we entered the very crowded establishment. It's a grown child's paradise. On several occasions I tried getting Ben's tired trifling ass to go, but he'd stopped hanging with me like that. We used to hang and have a good time; comedy shows at the Funny Bone or the Fox, plays at the Black Rep or the Fox, musical concerts at the Kiel Center, the Fox, the Pageant or Riverport. You name it! We did it! All of that ceased and I should've accepted it as my sign from God. Why we choose to ignore the signs, I'll never know, but the issues continue until we open our eyes.

Upon entering the spot, we smelled the aroma of food and simultaneously Malik and I grabbed our stomachs.

I asked, "Aw, so you're hungry too?"

"I wasn't until I smelled the aroma."

"You wanna order something?"

"Hell yeah."

Laughing he said, "C'mon greedy!"

"You plan on eating too?"

"Well....yeah."

"Then I guess you can be labeled as greedy right along with me."

"Girl, let's take a seat at the bar because if we wait for a table, it could take all night."

"Cool. I already know what I want."

We proceeded to the bar and grabbed the last two available bar stools. Malik ordered a glass of Hennessy and a Corona, and I decided to chill with a glass of Pino Grigio.

"Okay, what do you want to order?"

"Do you want to start with dessert?"

"Do you?"

"Naw, I was just checking to see if you really wanted to relive your childhood."

"Hell, in my childhood I never ate dessert before dinner. The Blacks weren't having it."

"I hear ya. Neither were the Witherspoons."

"So, order whatever you want."

"You sure. I gotta big appetite."

"Go for it."

"Okay." When the bartender came over, I ordered wings, waffle fries, chicken quesadillas and a slice of caramel cheesecake for dessert. While waiting for the food, we finished our drinks, ordered another round, and continued to talk. Our food arrived and we began eating. When we completed our food, the cheesecake arrived, and we shared the delectable slice. We really enjoyed ourselves. After completing everything we got up to go to the recreation area. We played basketball and golf. We played a couple of the shooting video games. Malik did well, but I always ended up dead.

"I thought I'd do better because I'm the bomb at Tomb Raider."

"Is that right?"

"Yeah. The next time you come to the STL, I'll show my skills."

"I'm looking forward to it. What do you want to play next?"

"I've always wanted to go jet skiing, but I've never tried it."

"Never?"

"Nope. Kenya and I went to Aruba in ninety-eight for Sinbad's Seventies Music Festival and we considered it, but I chickened out."

"Well, we'll have to take a trip together so we can jet ski."

"You've done it."

"My parents live in Orlando, so yeah, I've gone jet skiing. I've even swam with the Dolphins at Sea World."

"So, you got skills? Let's see how you do on the assimilated jet ski game."

"I'm down for whatever. Let's go."

We arrived at the game, but we had a short wait. A couple was playing, and they were just about done. Since they were on together, we decided to try it together.

"I'll get in the front first so you can get a feel for it."

Raising my eyebrows and giving him a mischievous grin, I asked, "A feel for what?"

"I could go there with you, but I won't. You know what I'm talking about, so c'mon." He offered me his hand and I climbed on the jet ski behind him and put my arms around his waist. He inserted the tokens, and the machine began to do its thing.

"Hey, this is fun."

"Just the fact your arms are around my waist excites me."

I had to laugh at him because being this close to him was exciting to me as well, but I didn't want to admit that. His ride lasted about ten minutes and I then I took over with him holding me by my waist. While we rode the jet ski, I felt the evidence of his excitement. I wasn't ready for that yet, so I began to yawn. I was tired because I'd had a long twenty-four hours.

"Are you tired?"

"I guess I am. It's been a long day and alcohol normally makes me sleepy."

Looking at his watch, "Well, we have been here for three hours."

"Really? Time flies- we both said, "When you're having fun."

Grabbing my hand he said, "We've had a good time so let's go home."

Swinging his arm I said, "Let's."

We arrived at his house in thirty minutes. He hinted around to wanting to sit and talk.

"I'm sorry Malik but I am so tired. I'd really like to go to sleep."

"Okay, that's cool. What would you like to do tomorrow?"

"If it's okay with you I'd like to stay in all day so we can chill, talk and get better acquainted."

"That sounds good to me, but would you like to go to Sambuca's tomorrow night?"

"Yeah, that sounds like a plan."

"Cool. Sleep tight and I guess I'll see you in the morning."

I walked over to him and gave him a long hug. "Thank you for tonight, I really enjoyed myself." I stood up on my tip toes and gave him a soft kiss on the lips. I was tempted to deepen the kiss, but I chose not to. "Good night, Malik."

"Good night beautiful."

I went to my room, and I guess he went to his. I showered, brushed my teeth and put on my pajamas. I turned the TV on to catch ESPN's Sportscenter. As I listened to the program, I decided to call Lexy. I hadn't called anyone at home since my arrival. I grabbed my cell phone out of my handbag, turned the power on and waited for AT&T to inform me my phone had entered their service area. I dialed Lexy's number and waited for her to answer. After three rings, someone answered but it wasn't Lexy, it was Jake. Damn, things are really going well. Alexis Marie Knight has never allowed a man to answer her phone. Never. Things do change, I guess.

"Hello."

"Uh, hel-Jake?"

"Yeah baby girl, it's me. What's up?"

"Is Lexy there?"

"What? You don't wanna talk to your boy?"

"I'm extremely tired and I just need to talk to Lexy for a minute."

"Okay. You ain't got no conversation for your boy, but it's cool."

"I'll talk to you but not right now."

"Aight baby girl, let me get Lexy." Jake took the phone away from his ear and called for Lexy, "Baby, Nia's on the phone."

She responded to Jake with, 'Got it' and picked up an extension, "Hey girl, what's up?"

"Nothing girl. Why is Jake answering the phone?"

"He's been over here all day. We played hooky all day."

"Did you all do it?"

She began whispering so I knew the answer before she told me. "Yeah, girl and it was beautiful. I think I loved-ed him."

I started laughing after the loved-ed comment. That fool knows she doesn't talk like that, "Lexy, I'm happy for you and Jake. You all deserve each other, and I mean it in a loving manner."

"Thanks girl. Enough about me, you obviously got to Dallas safely."

"Yeah."

"Are you enjoying yourself?"

"You know I am. Girl, this nigga cooked for me."

"What did he cook?"

"Lobster, shrimp, crab legs, twice baked potatoes, dinner rolls and salad."

"Damn!"

"Right, and it was good."

"You would know Miss Caterer."

"I guess I would."

"Are you going to give him some?"

"I'm not ready."

"Well, take your time because you know once ya'll get busy it's going to take it to another level."

"Don't I know it? I'm not going to keep you, but I wanted you to know I got here safely, and I wanted to give you his phone number."

"Cool. Let me grab a pen." Lexy laid the phone down to retrieve a pen and then picked the phone back up. "Okay, what is it?"

"It's 9-7-2-5-5-5-7-6-4-9."

"Got it."

"All right, I'm going to sleep."

263

"Okay, enjoy your visit and I'll talk to you soon."

"Okay, sleep well."

"You as well." I turned the phone and TV off prior to turning over and drifting into dreamland.

It was evident from the time I woke up; Malik had allowed me to sleep late. When I looked at the clock the time was eleven o'clock and although I didn't mean to sleep that late, I felt well rested and refreshed. I reluctantly climbed out of bed and went to shower. Since Malik and I were staying in until later tonight, I threw on a pair of shorts, a tee shirt and a pair of flip-flops. Then I headed to the kitchen to find something to eat. There I found Malik in a pair of gray basketball shorts, a tee shirt, and house shoes. We obviously had the same idea.

"I don't know if I should say 'good morning' or 'good afternoon'."

He turned around with smiling dimples and walked toward me before saying, "Just say hello," and kissed me.

I kissed him back and said, "Okay. Hello."

"Hello." Just then my stomach began to growl. Loudly. He began laughing. "I guess you're hungry."

"If I ain't, my stomach's tellin' me I better be."

"Don't trip, I'll fix something to eat."

"I'll cook."

"You sure?"

"Yeah I'm sure but it didn't take you long to go along with me cooking."

"I'm sorry, would you like me to cook?"

"No, I'll cook."

"You sure?"

"Yeah, go relax."

"Cool, I'll be in my bedroom watching TV."

"Is that where we're hanging today?"

"If it's not a problem for you."

"I don't have a problem with it."

"Cool, just yell when the food is ready."

"Okay."

I found bread, potatoes, onions, eggs, sausage and bacon to begin cooking. I made fried potatoes with onions, fried eggs, bacon, sausage, and toast. I poured two glasses of orange juice and placed our plates on a tray I found in Malik's pantry. When I arrived at Malik's doorway he was engrossed in, what else, Sportscenter. What did men do B.S.? Before Sportscenter? I cleared my throat, and he looked up.

"Hey, let me help you with that." He jumped up and took the tray from my hands. "I thought you were going to yell for me to come into the kitchen."

"I decided to give you brunch in bed."

"Well, thank you. I really appreciate it."

"It's no problem." I climbed into his huge king-sized bed, and we began eating. We ate our food and watched First Take on ESPN. I took the dirty dishes to the kitchen and loaded them into the dishwasher. When I got back to his room, he was no longer watching TV, TV was watching him. He'd gone to sleep quickly. Just like black folk. Eat. Go to sleep. He caught a case of the ITIS. I climbed in bed, grabbed the remote and found Lifetime. I watched TV and I watched him. He was beautiful and he looked so peaceful as he slept. Eventually, sleep claimed me as well.

Malik

I must have dozed off because when I woke up Nia was asleep. I didn't remember either of us going to sleep. Looking at the TV, I definitely did not remember switching the TV to the Lifetime channel. I grabbed the remote and turned on what else, ESPN. I watched the baseball highlights and looked at Nia while she slept in the fetal position. She hadn't gotten under the cover so I could see her beautiful chocolate legs and the lower part of my body responded from a mere glance. She began to stir so I adjusted my response. She sat up and stretched and with that very innocent gesture, my body began to respond again. I'm sure it had everything to do with the fact when stretching, I saw a peek of her flat stomach and noticed her nipples were hard like the lower part of my body. Again, I adjusted my response. Thank God I was lying down.

"Hey sleepy head."

"Hey yourself. When I came back from loading the dishwasher, you were knocked out, so I figured I'd nap also."

"You know black folks-" Together we said, "Eat and go to sleep." We broke out in laughter, and I reached over and began tickling Nia. She became a different person. She was laughing and trying to kick me off her, but a brotha can be relentless. I continued to tickle her, and she kept the fight up. Somehow, she was able to get her arm around my neck and began to tickle me under my neck. She'd found my spot. She kept tickling me and in doing so I let my defenses down. She managed to get my arm behind my back trying to get me to surrender.

She shouted, "Say Uncle!"

"Nope, I won't do it." She twisted my arm again. For her to be so small, she was strong.

"Malik, say Uncle and I'll stop."

"Nope, I'm not punking out."

She said, "Okay," and twisted a little harder. We continued and I managed to flip her over, so I was in control. I sat on top of her, and she tried to sweet talk me.

"Baby, let me up."

"Aw, so now you wanna sweet-talk me?"

She continued, "Baby let me up."

"No can do, not until you say auntie."

"Okay, auntie."

265

I tickled her, "You promise to behave."

She batted those damn eyelashes at me and sweetly said, "Yes," so I let her go. I should've known better because within five seconds, she had me in a head lock screaming, "Say uncle!"

"Okay Nia, I give up."

In a teasing voice she said, "You can't just give up you gotta say uncle." I mimicked her, "You can't just give up. You gotta say uncle."

"Aw, so you wanna mimic me? Just say uncle."

"Aight girl, uncle." She released me and we both laughed.

"I'm thirsty, you?"

"Yeah I am."

"Good. When you get yourself something to drink would you grab something for me?"

"Girl, you are a trip." I went in search of something to drink. I got me a 7UP, and Nia a glass of Cran Cherry.

Nia

Malik evidently has a great sense of humor. While he was in the kitchen, I straightened the bed because it looked a hot mess when we finished wrestling. I was surfing channels when he walked in.

"Hey what you go there?"

"7UP for me, Cran Cherry for you."

"That's sweet of you."

"What?"

"I know you didn't just have Cran Cherry."

"True. I went to the store yesterday and got some."

"Well, I appreciate it."

"Okay, what do you want to do now?"

"We can drink up and go into phase II of NWL?"

"NWL? What the hell?"

"Duh!! Nia's Wrestling League."

"Girl, you are crazy," We began to laugh together.

"You wanna watch a movie?"

"What do you want to watch?"

"I don't know. You pick."

"Do you have 'A Man Apart'?

"The oldie but goodie with Larenz Tate?"

With a dreamy look in my eyes, I responded with, "Yeah. He's some kinda sexy and I don't like short men, but Larenz? Now that's a different story."

"What, no mention of that brotha Vin Diesel?"

"Nope, he doesn't do it for me. I like my men brown or better."

"No light skinned brothas for you?"

266

"Never for me, I've always dated darker hued men."

"Really?"

"Yeah, light skin went out before the DeBarge brothers in my opinion."

"A lot of brothas would argue the point."

"And I'd argue back with the likes of, Morris Chestnut, Method Man, Chris Weber, Idris and Denzel Washington to name a few."

"I'm a dark brotha but in defense of light skinned brothas like LL Cool J and Boris Kodjoe; they're still black men they just have less Melanin in their skin."

"Yeah, they're still black men but my preferred choice-of-chocolate is dark chocolate."

"You'll leave the white chocolate to those who prefer it?"

"Exactly. I just find dark chocolate to be more appealing, and sexy as hell."

"I don't think I like you referring to other men as sexy, but I can live with it.

"Cool. Let's watch the movie." For the next two hours we watched the movie and then I decided to take a nap.

"That movie was pretty good. I think I'm going to take a nap now."

"I think I'll join you."

We napped until about five. I woke up first. I woke Malik up and the phone began to ring. He leaned over to answer it. I could hear his side of the conversation.

"Hello."

"What's up Mike?"

"We just woke up from a nap."

"We've been chilling all day."

"Yeah, we're going to Sambuca's for dinner, drinks, and jazz."

"You and Monica may be there?"

"That's cool."

"Just hit me on my cell if you decide to join us."

"Yeah, I'll tell her."

"Peace." He disconnected the line.

"Mike said for you to have a good time while you're here."

"That was nice of him."

"Are you hungry?"

I grabbed my stomach, "Damn, did you hear my stomach?"

"No, but I know how mine feels. Let's get dressed so we can get a move on?"

"Do you know what the weather is supposed to be like tonight?"

"No, but I'll check."

"Thank you."

"You're welcome." After changing the channel, he said, "Okay, here we go. It says the temperature should be in the low seventies."

"That's not bad, now I just have figure out what I'm going to wear."

"I'm going to wear my gray suit."

"Damn! You're doing it like that?"

"I feel like looking a little dapper this evening."

267

"Well, I wouldn't want you to look bad hanging with me, so I guess I can find something appropriate."

"Yeah okay."

I retreated to my room to get ready. It took me about forty-five minutes. When I walked into the kitchen, he was already there leaning on the counter and drinking a Corona. He was so fine in his suit.

"Well don't you look nice?" He chose a gray, it looked like gabardine, single button blazer with matching slacks. He had on a black shirt with no tie and his black Gucci loafers. As always, he looked good as hell.

"Thank you, ma'am. You look beautiful as always."

I spun around, "Thank you sir." I chose a blue and gray Adrienne Vittadini wrap dress with sheer gray hose and my gray Anne Klein sling-back pumps. He turned up his Corona like it was a forty, activated the alarm and we were off in the Jaguar.

Upon our arrival we valet parked and entered the venue. We arrived early so fortunately there wasn't a wait, and we were seated immediately. I ordered a glass of Pinot Noir and he ordered another Corona. There was a jazz quartet beginning their set. The atmosphere was very laid back.

"Are you enjoying yourself so far?"

"So far so good, but can a sistah get something to eat? A piece of bread? Some nuts? Some chips?" He started laughing like we were at a comedy club instead of a jazz club. "I'm sorry baby, we can order."

"Thank you."

He ordered the jumbo scallops, and I decided to try the shrimp and crab linguini. While waiting for our food, we continued to enjoy the music, the conversation, and each other's company. Our food arrived and we indulged. We ate our food and decided to dance. Just as we were about to get up, Malik's cell phone rang.

"Hello."

"What up bruh? You and Monica on your way?"

"So you all are going to stay in?"

"Well all right then I'll holla at you tomorrow." He hung up. We got up to dance.

At two in the morning, we decided to call it a night. We arrived at Malik's home and were in the kitchen talking when the phone rang.

The Showdown

One of his boys better be in trouble. Or......it better be a family member. Someone had to be in need, calling at this time of the morning. Or. It was the usual. A woman. She thought she was still his woman. The dreaded Ex. The one who wouldn't let go. She just wouldn't go away. She couldn't, wouldn't and didn't move on. I'd been there before. Loved so deep, he was a part of my essence. I could smell him when he was nowhere to be found. I'd seen him

268

with other women, and of course, I clowned like women sometimes do when they hurt. I don't blame brothas for their doggish ways. If anything, I blame us. Us as in black women. We choose to ignore their infidelity because we love them so. We think the pain of infidelity isn't as bad as the pain of being alone. Once we wise up, we realize pain is pain and the sooner we deal with the pain, we can heal and move on. No need to prolong the inevitable.

One thing I know for sure, guys would not do the shit they do if women would stop acting as if sleeping with as many men as they can, is a good thing. I don't believe in double standards, but women need to realize that in society's eyes, a man sleeping around is all right, but when women do it, they'll be labeled as hoes. Also, women need to respect other women's relationships. A lot of men lie about being in a relationship, as well as being married, but there are lots of truthful men. It doesn't seem to matter; some of these women are so desperate for dick, they'll fuck your man, her man, and his man. It's as if the men with women are the only ones with dicks. It's like single men are dickless. I'm thirty-nine, single and childless so I'm very aware of the single woman statistics, but I refuse to believe there isn't a single man out there for me. Singlehood. It's really a sad situation. It's downright scary.

After the second ring, I looked at him. He looked at me. We simultaneously looked at the phone. I do like a man who doesn't hide anything. He had already told me about Melina, the dreaded ex, although I was surprised she was still calling. Women's intuition was a muthfucka, and it kicked in. I knew it was her. He answered, and of course I could only hear his side of the conversation. "Hello."

    "Melina, what do you want? It's over between the two of us."

    "Yes, I have company. I already told you about Nia."

    "No, I do not want to talk to you. We have nothing to talk about."

    "Yes, I care about you, but I've moved on. You need to do the same."

    "I'm sorry you feel that way."

    "Yes, my choice is made, and it's Nia."

Sighing. "Again, I'm sorry you feel that way."

    "Melina, it's been over for more than a year."

    "I know we had sex six months ago, but it was just a quickie. You seduced me..... remember?"

    "We've grown apart."

    "Again, I do have company, and talking to you is being rude to her. I'm about to hang up. Take Care."

Click! Immediately after hanging up, he began to explain.

    "Nia, I am so sorry about that. For some reason she can't move on."

    "It's okay."

    "Is it? I don't want to jeopardize anything we could have together. You know how long it took a brotha to convince you to try a relationship with me?"

"Well, the good thing is you've been honest from day one. Honesty is very important to me."

"I know it is. You know how I feel about you, but I'm glad you made me slow down. This is my first friends-first relationship."

"It was time to try a different approach, considering all of my relationships fail for one reason or another. This is also my first long distance relationship."

"I think we've done all right considering."

"Yes we have. Malik, you know I've been through a lot, and I've admitted I am somewhat insecure. So, I've got to ask. Is the M&M Show over?"

"The M&M show. What are you talking about?" His face had this puzzled look.

"You know, Malik and Melina, sweet, like a bag of M&M's." Laughing. "You are crazy! Seriously though, it's undeniably over. I'll always care about her, but I fell out of love two years ago. I only stayed because of all the years we'd been together and the comfort level."

"I just want to be sure because I've begun to care for you deeply and I don't want any BS!"

"I can't say I'll never hurt you, but I can promise it will never be intentional. I've done some doggish shit in my days, but I've turned in my dog collar and buried the bone. I am sincere when I say I am tired too, and ready to settle down."

"Are you sure you won't miss Melina? I know you all share a history."

"History is the operative word, her ass is history. She is in the past. Where she'll stay! I am thirty-five years old, and in the four years I was with Melina, I never wanted to marry her."

"Really? Why? Men are quick to say what they think we want to hear. I want the whole truth. Nothing but."

"Believe it! She's a beautiful person when she's not acting like Sheniqua, the wicked witch of Texas. She lacks ambition, which is a quality I like in my woman. She also doesn't have many friends and therefore she wants to be in my mix at all times."

"Oh, she's a SWF?"

Looking puzzled. "A SWF? What a single white female?"

Laughing. "Hell no! She's definitely not white, is she?"

"Nia don't play with me, you know I don't do white girls."

"I know. I was just playing. It stands for, sistahs without Friends. My ex is a NWF. Like NWF's, SWF'S are big trouble too!!"

"Unfortunately, Melina and I just grew apart. My mother told me she wasn't the one, and surprisingly, my father agreed. I guess they were right."

"Well Thank God, she never got pregnant."

"She tried to say she was at one time, when we were having problems. I would've handled my responsibility, and loved my child but she was trying to trap a brotha?"

270

"You think?"

"Without a doubt. In the beginning, she had goals but as our relationship progressed, her goals died along with her ambitions."

"Were you supportive?"

"As much as I could be considering my business was taking off, and it kept me very busy."

"Do you think she was jealous of your success?"

"I don't know, but I feel like she was using me. I was her excuse to not excel. I guess because I made decent money, she was satisfied. She didn't need any extra money; I gave her everything she needed. She wanted us to live together, but I wasn't having it. Our relationship was changing, and I didn't like her anymore nor was I happy in the relationship."

"When did you finally realize she wasn't the one, the two, or the three?"

Laughing. "You know what?" Before I could answer, he answered. "You are a clown. Actually, I realized she wasn't the one when I met you in Dallas in March."

"Malik we only met one another, danced, shared a drink, and shared light conversation."

"I know, but I knew."

"You knew what? Please don't give me the love at first sight shit!" Men know when they talk that talk. We fall for it. Most sistahs are vulnerable, especially after getting out of a mentally or physically draining relationship. We want to believe in and hear the love at first sight shit, but deep down we know it's bullshit. I think most women want the fairy tale although we know it's not reality.

"All I knew, after talking to you at Sambuca's, I knew I'd been wasting my time with her. You were full of life, confident and ambitious. All qualities I want in my woman."

"Well Mr. Black, thank you for the compliments."

"You're welcome, Miss Witherspoon. You know you're the first woman I've really opened up to. Most sistahs are so concerned about themselves, and their drama, they never listen. Sistahs will talk you to death, but they don't give five fucks about a brotha's dreams and aspirations. It's hard being a black man and a lot of the gold diggin' sistahs have no compassion."

"I disagree. There are a lot of women who are into their man and are supportive. I can't comment on the gold diggin' because my girls and I are self-sufficient."

"What? I pick the wrong ones?"

"That appears to be your dilemma," yawning.

"I know you're sleepy, it's two-thirty and we have a big day ahead of us."

Right then the contraption that Alexander Graham Bell invented began ringing. Again.

Shaking his head in a frustrated manner, "Now we both know who's calling again, I say we let voice mail answer it."

"You won't get any argument from me."

"Nia, I know we haven't been intimate yet, but I'd like to hold you."

"I think I'd like that, just one thing."

"What's up?"

"Turn the damn ringers off, please."

"Your wish is my command."

"Is that right?"

"Oh yeah, I promise."

"That I'll have to see."

While Malik was going through his house turning off ringers, I used the bathroom to brush my teeth. I also took a quick shower. I put on the top that goes to Malik's pajamas, and he'd put on the bottoms after showering. I was a little nervous. During our previous visits we always slept separately. Him in my guest room. Me in his guest room. Never together. Always separately. Not tonight. Tonight, will be the start of something new. The possibilities are endless. The fear is inescapable. My nervousness. Unavoidable. I guess I'm nervous because I've wanted his sexy ass for the last three months, but I've held out. I wasn't holding out to play a game, but I wanted to try a new approach. You see, brothas will leave. One week. Six months. It doesn't matter. If all a brotha wants is the LUSCIOUS! Time is never an issue. Brothas can look at sistahs and immediately they know. If they want to just hit it and quit it. Or if they want a relationship. They know. Sistahs know also, but sometimes we're tricked. Tricked like its April Fool's Day. I was tired of playing the fool. Again, I was holding out to try a different approach. I wanted us to become acquainted on a non-sexual level. Malik said he would be down with it if he could be with me. I know the sex will be the bomb because of the passion we ignite in one another. I want more with Malik. Hell, sex has never been an issue. Keeping a man. Now that's the issue. It took a while before he convinced me we should try it to see where it takes us. I was finally willing to see where we could ultimately land. I'm not a pessimist, but I am a realist. Malik's a different kind of man, but Ben's fatal attraction ass left me reluctant to start something new. I know Malik is not Ben, nor is he Will, Ron, Tommy, or Damon but it's hard to forget. Like Erykah Badu sings, 'Bag Lady you gon hurt yourself, draggin' all them bags like that'. You all know how the rest of the song goes. Sistahs have a lot of baggage, me included. To have a successful relationship I had to let go. Malik could be Mr. Right-For-Me but I want to utilize my brain instead of my heart to decide.

I actually dated a guy who was true to me, but I messed it up. My insecurities drove him away after three years. I didn't trust him. I accused him of sharing the dick with every Tomika, Deja, and Helen, but not once did he accuse me of sleeping with every Tyrone, David and Harold. This man was faithful the entire time and believed in me as well as our love. Total monogamy. That's what he gave me. Now he's happily married to a beautiful woman who adores and more importantly trusts him. He deserves that. He was my biggest regret. I did the coulda, woulda, shoulda dance for a year, if not longer. I finally realized it was my loss and I let go.

Surprisingly, we're good friends now. He even met Malik. Celia is okay with the friendship Ron and I share, although she's familiar with our background.

Malik and I haven't been intimate, but the panties have been moist for the last three months. Let me keep it real, wet would be a better description. I was afraid to open my heart because it's followed by vulnerability. At this point, I want it, but I want it to happen naturally. Natural like the sun rising. Natural like the moonlight. Natural like Aretha Franklin singing, 'Natural Woman.'

He completed his task of turning the ringers off and stepped in the bathroom to shower. As he began the task of cleansing himself, I began playing a sexy and soulful playlist with ballads by talented soul singers; there was Javier, Jill Scott, Maxwell, Bilal, Erykah Badu, Alicia Keys, Ledisi, Ella Mai, and Kem to name a few. I laid in his gigantic king-sized bed.Thinking. About me. Him. Us. About ten minutes later, Malik walked out of the bathroom with just a towel wrapped around his waist. Mmmm...Mmmm...Mmmm....Is there anything finer than a black man?

He said, "Excuse my attire, or lack thereof, but the pajama bottoms weren't in the bathroom." Smiling like a woman in heat I said, "I understand." I kept smiling and staring. He was beautiful, as most black men are. He began looking around for the bottoms, but he couldn't find them, and I was in such a daze I forgot I had them under the sheet with me.

"Nia, have you seen my pajama bottoms, the ones matching the top you have on?" I kept staring at him in awe. This man was beautiful inside and out, but he wasn't arrogant at all. He was truly a jewel within the sea of black men within the USA. "Nia."

"I'm sorry, did you say something?"

"Uh, are you all right?"

"I'm fine, why do you ask?"

"I called your name twice, but you didn't answer."

"I'm sorry, I must be trippin. What did you say?"

Malik was laughing by this time, "I asked if you knew where the pajama bottoms are?"

"Why are you laughing at me?"

"You're really giving me that look."

I started turning my head, as if I could really see myself, "What look?"

Shaking his head, he said, "Never mind."

"Never mind, bump that, tell me what kind of look I'm giving you."

"There's no need to get your thong in a bunch, it was nothing. Have you seen the bottoms?"   Pulling them out from under the sheet, "Oh, here they are." Swinging them around my finger like a hula-hoop. I decided to give him the come-gimme-some-look. He was too sexy in that towel. I was ready to take our relationship to the next level. "Thank you Miss Witherspoon." Damn! Damn! Diggity Damn! He must've missed my look because he grabbed those bottoms and went to change without another word. Oh well, celibacy lives on.

Malik

I entered the bathroom to change but I didn't miss the look Nia gave me. A brotha is trying to keep his composure, but DAMN! It's hard. She's giving me the look. Is she really ready for what I've got? She looks so sexy. In my bed. In my pajama top.

Nia

As Malik emerged from the bathroom, I was enjoying the music. He climbed into bed. We laid there staring at the ceiling, I guess we were both nervous.
"Nia?"
"Yes."
"Can a brotha get a kiss?"
"I don't know. Does your breath stink?"
"No. Why, does yours?"
"Hell no, but I have to be sure yours doesn't."
Laughing he said, "Yeah okay."
He turned on his side to face me and took my face in his hands. He began to tenderly kiss each part of my face. My forehead, eyelids, chin, cheeks and lastly, my lips. When he reached my lips, the Luscious was like a waterfall. Wet and overflowing.
At that exact moment, I knew we were going to the next level.
I anxiously accepted his mint flavored tongue. Our tongues danced together like the Alvin Ailey dance group. His tongue traced my lips in a slow and sensual way. I reciprocated the action.
I began to explore his body. His arousal didn't surprise me. It enticed me. I pushed his pajama bottoms off, and at the same time he unbuttoned his pajama top off me. We stared at each other's nakedness. He was so beautiful! So African! So male! We spoke at the same time. "You are so beautiful!" We shared a laugh, and it eased our nervousness.
He reached out and caressed my already aroused and extended nipples. His tongue replaced his hands and my center erupted like a volcano. His touch was so calming. It eased the nervousness I was feeling, but it also excited me. I moaned and then eagerly took him into my hands, caressing his long and thick shaft. I thought to myself, 'Brotha is hooked up!' I had lived up to my reputation of being a BDM (big dick magnet). I planned on riding him like a Buffalo Soldier. I don't know who was moaning the most or the loudest. There were three months of sexual frustration built up between us. He laid me on my stomach. "Nia, are you sure about this? I can wait."

Without any hesitation I said, "Yes, I'm sure."
He then proceeded to love me down. He licked, kissed and sucked me from my head to my toes. From my hair shaft to the heels of my feet. Then he began to kiss my back. For his size his touch was so gentle. He had found my spot. I don't know what it is, but a brotha kissing my back always sends me over the edge. My back began to form an arch the more he licked. I had three orgasms just from him licking and sucking my back. After my first orgasm he saw my reaction and he kept going. I could feel his dick moving over my legs, ass and back. I tried to touch him, but he wouldn't let me.
This was his show. I was merely a patron.
"Baby, why can't I touch you?
"I want you to feel good. Just lay here and enjoy."
He continued to love me in all the right places. After lavishing my back, he turned me over. He took my left breast into his mouth and licked the aureole until my nipple was as hard as a pebble. He then pushed both of my breasts together to give them both attention. He continued south to my belly button and ran his tongue over it. My body was on fire. He then reached the Luscious. She was a faucet. Turned on. Full force. He began to trace the lips of my vagina with his tongue. I was literally trying to climb the posts on the bed. Malik held me tight and continued to lavish me with his tongue. My moans got louder if that was even possible. My body was like a candle with a wick waiting to be put out. I was so hot I knew smoke had to be emitting from the luscious. DAMN! I found a brotha who believed in foreplay, not child's play. He then pulled me up so I was on all four, and I was eagerly waiting on the dick. I just knew he was also ready to give it to me.
Instead of feeding me the dick, he began to partake in the luscious as if it were an all-you-can-eat lunch special. He licked my clit in a circular motion, and then sucked on my nub as if it were a jolly rancher. He took me from behind where he had better access. I'd never had it this good. Brotha was devouring me, and it was all good. Again, I tried to touch him, but he moved so I couldn't.
"Nia, I want you to be satisfied so just relax." I obliged him by holding onto the headboard. I trembled and savored each orgasm as he bestowed them upon me. After the fifth one, I wanted to be on the giving end instead of the receiving end. I'd like to consider myself an equal opportunity lover. The licker deserved to be the lickee.
"Baby, stop."
"For what, you taste scrumptious."
"There's something I want to do to you, and for you."
He ignored me and continued to enjoy my smorgasbord. After another fifteen minutes of pure ecstasy, he stopped. I turned over and dazed into his beautiful, golden brown, sexy eyes. He stared back, and I took one of his hands and began to suck his fingers to taste my own juices. As I sucked his fingers, he closed his eyes and moaned. He feasted on his fingertips also. I began to aggressively rub his dick. I laid him on his back and began a tongue

275

exploration of my own, from his thighs up to his head. I licked until I got a response and then I moved on. On my way north, I stopped at his dick, and gave the tip a quick lick before I headed up north to those luscious lips of his. His breathing increased. I ran my fingers through his locks and gave him a wet and passionate kiss, taking his tongue and suckling on it like a breast-fed baby! I then began my descent south. I landed in the central region. I kissed the inside of his thighs before licking his smaller head. He moaned which prompted me to take all of him into the warm confines of my mouth. I fervently sucked his dick, taking all of it in like a hot pickle with a peppermint stick. I fondled and licked his balls. I didn't want them to feel neglected. While I played with his balls, I licked his shaft up and down. His penis began to emit pre cum which I accepted like a baby accepts his mother's milk. I wanted to please him, so I resumed. Fifteen minutes passed before he was ready to climax. His legs locked, and his upper body began to jerk. Oral sex was one of my favorite pastimes. I believe in pleasing my man. I took in all his love juice, so much so it was dripping from my lips. After swallowing because that's what pros do, I continued to suck him, so he'd stay hard. I know men sometimes have a problem with keeping an erection after having an orgasm, but I had to see what I was working with. Was he up for the challenge? From the looks of it, he was.

"Nia, baby, what are you doing to me?"

"The same thing you're doing to me."

He then reached in his nightstand drawer for a Magnum condom. Any other condom wouldn't do. I took the condom out of his hand, ripped the package open, and placed it on his dick with my mouth. I decided I wanted to be in control, so I straddled him. I sat on his dick like it was a Lazy Boy chair. I sat still while adjusting to his blessed size.

"Ooh Malik, baby you feel so good inside of me." I began to slowly rise and fall on his thickness! In the rise position, I would rotate my vaginal walls around his thick shaft. Malik was enjoying our first time together and so was I. We were about to reach our orgasm together.

"Maaaalik!"

"Yes baby!"

"I'm cumming!"

That was my seventh orgasm for the day. My Boo wasn't finished. He picked me up and leaned me over the bed. I did as he requested, and he inserted the DICK from behind and began massaging my clit. This was by far my favorite position. I was so wet my love juice was running down my thighs. The sound of his dick sliding in and out of my vagina pushed me over the edge. We reached our climax together again. We both trembled until goose bumps appeared on our arms like a rash. He retreated into the bathroom to retrieve wash cloths for us to use while my breathing regained some normalcy.

We climbed into bed, and I laid my head on his chest, and he embraced me while placing a kiss on my forehead. Had I known it would be this good, I would've given him some two months ago. He pulled the covers up on us, and we drifted off to sleep. Smiles were on our faces. This felt so right.

Malik

I can't believe the sexual chemistry I have with this woman. This is something new to me. I have never experienced lovemaking this powerful before. Sistahs got skills, but it's more than that, our lovemaking was more emotional than anything and I'd never experienced this. Not even with Melina. I think she may be the one. They say men know when they've met the one.

Nia

I woke up still in his arms. When I peeked at the clock, the blue light illuminated five a.m. The Luscious was still tingling. I'd gone without far too long. I had to have some more. Was he up for it? Ain't nothing to it but to do it! He was lightly snoring. I began to massage his hairy chest, and my hand traveled south. Yep! He was up (literally) for it. I rubbed his smaller head back and forth before I began licking him. I licked him up and down before accepting him into my mouth totally.

Suffice it to say, he woke up. "Boo, whatcha doing?"

"Would you like me to stop?" Questioning him while looking up from the southern region of his body.

"Not no, but Hell No!"

"Well then, lay back and enjoy."

I placed him between my breasts and continued to lick him. This was an obvious turn on for him. He came almost immediately. It was like Maxwell House! Good to the last drop.

I got up in the bed next to him. We were laying side by side, my back to his front. He began to fondle one breast with one hand and rubbed my clit with the other. Brotha was doing a sistah right! This time he slipped on a condom and took me from behind. I put my left leg over both of his so that he could gain better access. His rhythm started slowly and matched my bumpin' and grindin'. It was so good. He then very gently began to stroke that spot again. Damn! He throws the dick and strokes my spot too! Fuck the chicken dinner! I've found me a winner!

"Baby, that's it...keep it like that...."

"Niaaaaaa........"

After our trembling subsided, we fell asleep again holding one another in the wet spot. The next time we woke up, it was nine o'clock. We made love in the shower.

The lips to the luscious were swollen, but the dick, like crack. Addictive. I couldn't get my fill.

I left the shower first so I could start breakfast. I prepared sausage, eggs & biscuits. We completed our meal, and then somehow, I landed coochie up on the kitchen counter with him doing the damn thing! We got our freak on! Again!

"Boo, I could love you all day, but we won't get anything done and I want to go to the Galleria."

"Are you sure you don't want anymore?"

"No, I'm not sure, but I know Lexy's birthday is Tuesday and I have to get her a gift."

"All right girl, I'll leave your sexy ass alone until later."

"Well, thank you Mr. Black, I'll load the dishwasher, and you jump in the shower."

"Sounds like a plan to me. Can a brotha get a kiss?"

"Sure Boo,'" I kissed him on the forehead.

"Damn, it's like that?"

"With you Mr. Black it has to be. If it were up to you, I'd be coochie up all the time."

"You weren't complaining a while ago."

"Not complaining, just stating a fact."

"Really?"

"I like what you do. How you do. When you do. But I have to get to the mall."

"All right, all right, I'll be ready in twenty minutes. I'll tell you when I'm out of the shower."

"Actually, I'll shower in the guest-bathroom."

"What? You don't trust me?"

"Nope. I sure don't!"

He laughed and left to go shower. I loaded the dishwasher, as well as cleaned off the counter and stove top. I wanted to hear some music, so I put on Jaheim and shuffled his music. I've been a fan of his since his first album, Ghetto Love. As I was about to climb the stairs to shower, the doorbell rang. I called out for Malik but didn't get a reply. So, I opened the door. A woman. That woman. I knew it was her. Half of the M&M duo had arrived. Melina. She looked disheveled, but I could tell she was pretty. She looked at me up and down, noticing I had on the top to his pajamas.

"Hello Melina, may I help you?"

"Bitch, why are you in my man's house?"

"Bitch?" I looked behind me to see who she was talking to. I was the only person there, so I guess I was the bitch. She really had no clue and why would she? She doesn't know me. I guess she wants to become acquainted with my fist. "You need to skip your ass down the yellow brick road, visit the Wiz and ask for some sense, because you don't have a clue."

Totally ignoring me she asked, "Where is he?"

She then began sniffing, I guess she smelled the sex aroma on me.

"Girl, you better leave. That's what you better do."

"Whateva! Where is my man?" No, she didn't try and dismiss me like I'm nothing. Like I don't figure into the equation at all.

"Malik, my man, is in the shower. If you like you can leave a message."

"Yeah, all right bitch, here's the message; Tell Malik I'm sorry I beat your ass."

Laughing, "I'm not fighting over Malik. He chose me. Oh, and just an FYI. I'm from the STL and we don't play."

Swinging, "Well, I'm un-choosing yo ass for Malik! You being from St. Louis don't mean shit to me."

If not now, when? If not me, who?

I know Jill Scott said "Queens shouldn't swing", and I know what she means, but when she got in my face, I bypassed the Vaseline. I ducked. She missed. I jabbed her twice, once in the eye, and the other in the mouth. I then Taebo kicked her ass out the door, and down the porch. That's when Malik appeared with only a towel wrapped around his waist. "What the fuck?"

Just then she grabbed my hair, so like they say, "What's good for the goose, is damned sure good for the gander." I grabbed her braids, and they came off. I mean just like that, they came off. This was some Maury Povich shit. Underneath the braided wig, was a tiny spotted Afro. It looked as if she'd had some chemical damage to her natural hair. As I took her wig off, her natural reaction was to release my hair, and touch hers. My natural reaction was to laugh .

Malik said, "Melina what the hell are you doing here?"

"I'll tell you what she's doing here. The other half of the M&M duo is here trying to clown. I don't fight over niggas, but I don't get my ass beat either."

Right then Melina regained her composure and stared at both of us. She had blood on her face.

Melina said, "Malik aren't you going to do something? That bitch hit me, ripped my wig off, and laughed at me!"

I said, "Your stupid ass swung first, and you were dealt with."

Talking to Melina, Malik said, "Melina, first of all my woman is not a bitch, and you will not refer to her as such, and secondly I am no longer your man. Did you hear our conversation last night, or the ones we've had for the last six months? I stopped being your man eight-nine months ago, but our shit was flat more than a year ago. I'll always care about you, but I no longer love you and it's over."

Melina crying, "You fucked her while we were together?"

"Not that it's any of your business, but I just met Nia four months ago, and we began dating two months ago. She is my choice."

Melina said, "What, you love her?"

"Again, that's none of your business, but yes, I do love her, very much."

279

When I heard his confession, my head snapped around, and we just stared at one another with a he's/she's-the-one-grin on our faces. I got the warm feeling I get when I fall into the abyss of love.

We were in such a daze neither of us noticed Melina leaving. Finally, after what seemed like an eternity, Malik spoke. "I know we've only known each other for 4 months, but it's how I feel. I'm not going to pressure you, but I want you to know, I love you, and I'm not interested in feeling this way about anyone else."

"Malik, I'm crazy about you, and I heard what you said to Melina, last night and today, but I will not fight every time I visit Dallas. That's high school shit!

"I know baby, but you handled yourself like a young Holyfield. It won't happen again."

"How do you know? Hell, she doesn't seem too balanced. I can just see myself, thirty-nine-years old fighting her outside, of all places. I have business down here, and I can't risk it happening again. What if one of Mr. Wells' associates would've seen me, or better yet, Mr. Wells himself?"

"I know, and all I can say is, I'm sorry. I'm going to have a heart-to-heart talk with her after you leave."

"After I leave? Fuck that! That doesn't sound right. Why not talk to her while I'm here? Is there something you're trying to hide? I do live in St. Louis, which is approximately seven hundred miles away, and she's here. It would be easy to play both of us."

"What? I told you I'm through with Melina. I'm also through playing games. What we shared is over. Yeah, she calls but I have caller ID so we don't talk. I called her three months ago after she left several messages at my office, and at home. She didn't want anything, just the same ol', "Can we get back what we had?" and each time I gave her a resounding NO! If you weren't in the picture, I still wouldn't be with her."

"How did she know I'd be here this weekend, and why did you answer the phone?"

"I didn't tell her you'd be here, but one of her girls may have seen us at Sambuca's. I answered the phone because I'm not hiding anything. I didn't want to be one of those brothas turning the ringer off when he has company. I DO NOT want Melina! I love you, but it has nothing to do with you. I knew before I met you, I no longer wanted a relationship with her, and yes, meeting you confirmed it."

"I just want you to know I'm in no mood for any bullshit, and if you need time to figure things out, I'll give you plenty of it."

"Now what does that mean? It sounds like you're ready to throw in the towel. Melina is part of my past. She has nothing to do with my present or future. I don't need time to figure anything out. I know what I want and who I want. Tuesday I'm going to see about getting a restraining order."

"We'll have to see what happens."

"Please don't let this morning's episode ruin our day, or what we shared this weekend."

"I'd never allow her to steal our joy!"

"Cool, that's what I wanted to hear. Give me a kiss and I'll go put my clothes on."

Malik

I went into the bedroom to get dressed, thinking to myself. 'I can't believe this bitch clowned with Nia, but my boo held her own. Melina's stupid ass obviously forgot I've got a nasty little secret of hers. I guess she conveniently forgot I walked in on her coochie up with Keisha. She begged me to stay with her. She claims she was just curious. She asked me to keep it a secret. I may have to use the secret as leverage. I won't allow anything to come between Nia and I.'

Twenty minutes later both of us emerged from our perspective rooms. I was dressed in jeans, a polo shirt and a pair of Air Max Plus. What a coincidence? She had on a pair of jeans, a tee shirt and her Air Shox. Weren't we a cute couple? I asked if she was ready.

She replied, "Yeah, just let me grab my handbag."

"I got it for you."

I handed her the Coach backpack, and we headed to the garage hand in hand. The weather was fairly warm, so I considered driving my convertible. "Nia, are you going to get Alexis' gift only, or are you doing more shopping?"

"I don't know, why?"

"The trunk in the Jag isn't that big, so if you're going to do some serious shopping, I'll need to drive the truck."

"Naw, the convertible should be fine."

"All right let's go. Do you mind if we let the top down?"

"No, not at all."

I let the top down, and we were on our way. Garland, Texas is a suburb of Dallas, and about thirty minutes from the Galleria. We rode in silence still holding hands and listening to Earl Klugh and George Benson's 'Collaboration'. I'm sure we were both thinking about what happened last night and this morning. At the same time, she was probably thinking, 'Why do I always pick men with drama? I want a drama free man. The only drama I want is the shit on TV. Although she hasn't told me this, I think she loves me but she's afraid of letting go. She can't take any more nonsense. Lord knows we've both been through enough. I'll just hold on and see what happens." After twenty-five minutes in the car, we arrived at the Galleria. Prior to getting out of the car, I faced her.

I asked, "Boo, are you all right?"

"I'm just in deep thought, but I'm okay."

"Is everything cool?"

"Yeah, we're cool, as long as we keep the lines of communication open, and we continue to be honest with each other."

"I plan to do my part. May I have a kiss?"

"Sure, and for future reference, after what we shared last night and this morning, you don't have to ask for a kiss. They're yours for the taking."

Nia

He smiled, caressed the side of my face while staring into my eyes, mouthed the words I-L-O-V-E-Y-O-U, and then gave me the gentlest kiss I've ever experienced. He got out of the car, came to my side of the car, opened my door, and we entered the Galleria, again, hand in hand. A man who doesn't fear or shy away from public displays of affection. I could get used to this.

I didn't know what I wanted to get Alexis for her birthday, but I wanted to get her something she could use. Our first stop was in the Hallmark store. I found an appropriate Mahogany card for her. I then decided to browse in the Coach store for a briefcase. She just mentioned she needed a new one.

On our way to the Coach store guess who we ran into. You got it, the M&M half. Melina was with a beautiful woman. I guess it was one of her girlfriends. Melina had on a large pair of sunglasses, to hide the scars inflicted by me. Malik spoke first, "Hello Melina and Keisha. Keisha this is my lady, Nia. Melina's already met her."

Keisha spoke, "Hello Nia, it's nice to meet you."

I spoke, "Likewise."

Malik spoke again, "Ladies take care, we have shopping to do."

Neither of them replied but the entire time, Keisha shot daggers at Malik with her eyes. I could still feel the daggers as we walked away.

I spoke first, "What's up with Keisha? Is that one of her girls or what? She's real pretty."

"Yeah, really pretty and really freaky too."

"How would you know that?"

"I walked in on the two of them fucking?"

"You what! You are lying!"

"That's another reason we broke up. I caught them, and Melina had the nerve to ask if I wanted to do a menage a trois?"

"Well, did you?"

"Hell no, unlike most niggas, I ain't trying to share, not even with another woman."

"Damn with your skills, strictly dickly sistahs should be satisfied."

"Melina claimed she was curious, and Keisha coerced her into doing it, but I ain't buying that. Not at all. I think she's bi-sexual but didn't want to tell me because she knows I'd never get with it."

"What's up with Keisha shooting daggers your way?"

"I think she's always wanted Melina and hates the fact Melina feels for me like she does. She's never been a big supporter of the relationship I had with Melina."

"I guess not, not when she was trying to confiscate your coochie."

"What? You got jokes? Laughing...... "There's the Coach store, let's go in." I found Lexy a really nice Coach briefcase in black. They gift wrapped it for me. I'm sure she'll like it, but if she doesn't, she can return it to one of the Coach stores in St. Louis. After we left there, Malik wanted to go to the Bally store because he was looking for some loafers. He purchased two pairs of loafers, and a belt. He also purchased me a pair of loafers.

"Baby, thank you for the loafers."

"It's no problem, I wanted to do it."

Now we were hungry, so we grabbed three steak sandwiches (two were for him) from Steak Escape, along with some bottled water; we headed to the house to eat. After eating I took a nap, and Malik played with his Playstation. Men and their toys.

I'd been sleeping for about an hour when I felt Malik's arms go around me. I guess he decided it was naptime also. We napped together for another hour. Upon waking up, we shared another lovemaking session. Early evening breath and all. It was so intense. It was like he was trying to love away what happened earlier with Melina. We then showered together and decided to dress for dinner. We were going to Pappadeaux's. A definite favorite of mine. Our attire was casual. Malik had on a pair of black wool crepe slacks, a gray silk shirt, and the black Bally loafers he purchased earlier. I had on a long navy silk skirt with an ivory silk wrap blouse, and my navy Michael Kors wedges. I changed handbags and grabbed my navy Gucci.

Malik's parents. They would be proud. Milk had done his body good! Damned good, I might add. He was simply fine! There is nothing like the beauty of a black man. So, I complimented my man.

"Damn you look good!"

"Thank you, Miss Witherspoon. You don't look so bad yourself."

"You're biased, Mr. Black."

"True dat."

We hopped in his Yukon and arrived at the restaurant in about thirty minutes. As usual, they had a crowd. The wait was forty-five minutes, so we sat outside and talked. He asked me to meet him in Orlando in two weeks, to meet his parents. That weekend was supposed to be his St. Louis visit. We try to see each other twice a month. I visit him, and then he visits me. The next visit would be different. It was time to meet the parents. I didn't want to wig out because he'd met my mother and all my friends without any reluctance, but I'm nervous. I love him and therefore, I want his family to like, or better than that, love me. It was time.

"Are you sure you're ready for me to meet them?"

"Why wouldn't I be sure?"

"Well, I don't know, it hasn't been too long since you broke up with Melina and our relationship is new."

Rolling his eyes and shaking his head he said, "Nia, please don't start. I don't want Melina, and my parents don't like her. I've been talking about you to them for the last two months, and they know I love you. I agree our relationship is new, but our feelings are real."

"Well, if you're sure, then I'll meet you in Orlando because what we have is definitely real."

"Well, I'm definitely sure about that, my parents are looking forward to meeting you."

"I want to meet them as well, but I will admit I am nervous."

"Nervous.....about what?"

"About meeting your parents. I know how much you love them, and I really want them to like me."

"Like you...they're going to love you."

"You love me but you don't know if they will."

"I say it because you're good people, and my parents will sense that. My ex always had a plan, and they saw it, but I couldn't."

"Well, you know they say love is blind."

"I guess."

"Seriously. That's a disadvantage of loving someone."

"What do you mean?"

"A lot of the time, we fall in love before we really know the person, and in the end, it just doesn't work out. Wouldn't it be easier if we could know the person, I mean really know the person before the three words are spoken."

"I guess, but that's idealistic, not realistic."

"I know. I know. No, let me finish. Loving someone is a good thing, and although the relationship may have ended it was all a part of God's plan."

"Is that right?"

"Yes. What we should do is treat every failed relationship as a learning experience, a stepping-stone. Like the saying goes, "You've got to kiss plenty of frogs before you get your prince.""

"Oh, I got it. Melina was the frog with the big warts?"

"Yeah, if that's how you want to look at it. I mean if I refused to love again after every heartbreak, my last love would've been Dante who was my high school sweetheart."

"I see your point, I guess I never considered that perspective."

"Women bounce back from hurt a little better than men."

"Yes, ya'll do."

"I'm getting off of the subject, but while we're in Orlando, can we go to Universal Studios?"

"Sure. If you want."

"I love roller coasters and they have the Hulk which is the bomb."

"My parents love Universal so I'm sure they'll want to join us."

"Your parents like amusement parks?"

"Yeah, I think that's one of the reasons they moved back to Orlando." Just then we heard, 'Black party of two'. "That's us and I'm starving."

Grabbing his hand I said, "Me too. Let's go."

We were seated. I ordered a "Swamp Thing", Pappadeaux's frozen specialty drink and Malik ordered a Corona. He also ordered fried crab fingers and fries as an appetizer. As the waitress walked away, I looked into his eyes and in doing so a peace came over me. I really love this man and I want to express those feelings and put myself out on a limb like that. Unfortunately, I'm scared. I must play the nonchalant game because if I let on that I'm really diggin' him, he'll act up. I know, maybe he won't, but maybe he will. I just don't know. I'll contemplate my next move.

"Baby, I'm going to the rest room."

"I'll be right here."

He came back and took a seat. I sat there quietly, thinking.

"Hey, why are you so quiet?"

"No reason in particular. I'm just thinking."

"A dollar for your thoughts."

"I thought it was a penny?"

"The economy is kinda jacked up, so I figured a dollar would be a better offer than a penny."

"In that case, I'll accept your dollar and share my thoughts."

"Okay, what's up?"

Here goes. I'm going out on this limb, and I hope it doesn't break.

"I've been thinking." I became silent. Malik was also silent. I guess he wanted to allow me time to gather my thoughts. I also think I was taking too much time because he cleared his throat to prompt me on. "Oh I'm sorry. This is just kind of hard for me."

"Well, take your time. I'm not going anywhere."

"Okay here goes." I took a deep breath and began walking out on the limb. "I was reluctant to start a relationship with you because of what I'd just gone through with Ben. I agreed to become your friend, but you always made it known you wanted more. Over the last few months, we've become very close, and I respect you as a man and a friend. Last night, I shared my body with you and that's special to me. I-"

"It's spec-"

"Please. Allow me to finish."

"I'm sorry."

"It's okay. As I was saying I don't sleep with just anybody, but in my heart you're special. I'm going out on a limb, but I want you to know I love you." His eyes popped out of his head, and I resumed. "I know we can't see the future and therefore we don't know what will happen between us, but I want you to know I expect honesty. If you feel you can't be honest, please tell me so I can decide what I want to do. I promise to keep an open mind and check any baggage I may have from previous relationships. All I ask is that you, again, remain honest with me." The silence hung between us. When he spoke, he stumbled over his words.

"You. I can't believe. Did you say, love?" I began laughing and he joined me. He reached across the table to grab my hands, looked me in my eyes and began to speak after the laughter subsided. "I know how hard it was for you to put yourself out there, but it means a great deal to me. I love you and want to be with you. When I told you I was through playing games, I meant it, so I promise to be honest with you."

"Then we should be fine."

"Yes, we should." He still held onto my hands. I tilted my head to the left, like Sheba sometimes does when she's trying to figure what's going on with me. "Did you want to say something else?"

"Yeah, could you say it again?"

"Say what again?"

"You love me." His request caused my lips to turn into an inviting smile and I knew I'd oblige him. "Malik Black, I Nia Witherspoon, love you."

"Thank you."

"For what?"

"For letting go of the fear and the demons and allowing your heart to open up to opportunities."

"Granted, it was a hard decision, but your actions made it easy." Right then the waiter arrived with our appetizers and drinks, and we indulged. We fed each other and ourselves. We enjoyed conversation, laughter, and love. We ordered another round of drinks and ate our entrees when they arrived. After our bellies were full, Malik paid the bill and hand-in-hand we left to return to his place.

We arrived at his place and went straight to his room. I think my admission of love mixed with the alcohol got both of us aroused. I was leaving tomorrow which also had something to do with it. When we entered his room, candles and Najee greeted us.

"Who did this?"

"My fairy God fathers."

"What are their names?"

"Mike, Rick and Ray."

"So, you didn't go to the rest room at Pappadeaux's? You went to use the phone?"

He held up his hands and said, "Guilty as charged."

"Well, tell the fellas I said thank you."

"I'll tell them tomorrow. We're meeting for drinks after I drop you at the airport."

"Well, I think I'm going to hop in the shower." I didn't want to talk about the fact I'd be leaving tomorrow. I'd just admitted I loved him and missing him was unavoidable, but I wanted to prolong the reality of the situation.

"Aw....o...kay."

"Would you like to join me?"

"I think I'd like that."

"I began disrobing and sensually walking into the bathroom." His arousal was evident by the tent in his pants. He followed me like a lost puppy. While in the shower, we shampooed each other's hair. The gesture was so sexy. That night we made passionate love. We clung to each other like it would be our last time seeing each other. The experience was so tender, and I think both of us hoped it would hold us until we saw each other again.

When I meet a man and we're vibin' I always get the 'he-must-be-the-one' feeling, but so far, it's been wrong. I pray this time my feelings are correct. The following morning, I awoke to the aroma of bacon, eggs, and toast. After our night of lovemaking, I was hungry. I climbed out of bed so I could brush my teeth and wash my face. I slipped on one of his shirts and went downstairs. I tiptoed down the steps because I wanted to surprise him. My subtlety worked out well. He had no idea I was now standing in the kitchen doorway observing him. What I saw brought a smile to my face. My man was lovingly preparing a meal for me. I tiptoed to where he was standing and hugged him from behind.

"Hey you."

"Hey right back at you. Thank you for preparing breakfast for me. I'm starving."

"My pleasure. I don't want you flying with an empty stomach." He turned around, hugged me, and kissed me on the forehead. "Go sit down so I can serve you."

"Oooh....I feel so special."

"You are special."

"We'll see if you still feel that way in six months."

"I'll do you even better. I think I'll feel this way in one year."

"Yeah okay. We'll see. You know men change when they get comfortable."

"And so do women, but you and I are better than that."

"I hope so baby. I really do."

"Don't worry, it's all good."

We ate breakfast and cleaned the kitchen. I decided to take my shower because my flight was scheduled to leave at noon. I started the shower and then I brushed my teeth. By the time I stepped into the shower the entire bathroom was full of steam. I stood under the showerhead and allowed the water to cascade down my body. It felt so good. I stood there for a while and enjoyed the warmth of the water. While indulging myself in the warmth, the door to the shower opened and in stepped my man. Neither of us said anything, we just stared at each other. He pulled me into an embrace and just held me while the water continued to cascade over our bodies. We were officially beginning to miss each other although I hadn't left yet. We remained in the shower until the water began to chill us.

"I guess we should get out."

287

"Yeah, it's time to get ready. My flight leaves in three hours."

"Please don't remind me."

"Baby, it'll be okay. We'll see each other in two weeks."

Drying my body off he said, "Yeah, two weeks. That'll be here before we know it." As he wrapped the towel around my body, his phone began ringing. He grabbed his towel and went into the bedroom to answer the phone. I followed him into the bedroom to get some lotion. From his conversation I could tell that he was talking to one of his boys. "Yeah man, I'll meet y'all at Houston's. Nia's flight leaves at noon and I should be there by twelve-thirty." He then hung the phone up. "That was Rick confirming we're meeting after I drop you off."

"Be sure to tell them hello."

"Them niggas just wanna be nosey." Mimicking their voices, "What ya'll do man?" "Did you all make love?" I began laughing, so he asked, "What are you laughing at?"

Still laughing, I responded with, "I'm laughing because you and I both know they are not going to ask if we made love, instead they're going to ask if you hit it?"

"You got me there, but I didn't want to come across rude."

"I appreciate that, but I know how ya'll talk, remember Jake is my best friend."

"True dat."

"Well, let's get dressed. I don't want to be rushed at the airport."

"Okay. No need in me trying to prolong the inevitable."

We dressed in silence. Malik loaded my luggage in the back of his SUV and I met him in the garage. We pulled out and began our journey to the airport. We rode in silence, holding hands and listening to jazz on one of their local jazz stations. The flow of traffic allowed us to have a smooth arrival at the airport.

"Baby, you go on in and check in, I'll grab your luggage."

"Thank you baby. I really appreciate it."

I checked in, got my boarding pass and while looking at the arrival/departure monitors, Malik walked up with my luggage.

"You don't have to wait with me."

"Sure, I do and anyway, I told the fellas I'd meet them at twelve-thirty, that's an hour and twenty minutes from now."

"Are you sure? I have a book I can read."

"I am."

"All right. I can't wait to get home. I miss Sheba."

"I'm sure she misses you too."

"A lot of people don't understand the love pet owners have for their pets."

"I understand, they're like family members."

"Enough about Sheba. I'm going to miss you."

"Shit, I miss you already."

288

Running my thumb over one of his eyebrows, I said, "I know baby, but we'll talk every day and like I said, two weeks will be here before we know it."

"I guess it'll have to do."

Time went fast. Over the PA system a voice announced my flight. "Delta Airlines, flight twelve seventy-three from Dallas to St. Louis will begin boarding in ten minutes."

"Well, that's my flight." We stood and began to walk toward security. I placed my tote on my shoulder and placed my arms around his waist. He reciprocated my actions. We hugged for what seemed like an eternity, then he kissed my forehead and my lips.

"I better let you go."

Reluctantly I said, "Yeah, I better be going."

Trying to prolong my departure he said, "Yeah I guess you should be going."

I began laughing and he of course questioned that, "Why are you laughing now?"

He joined in on the laughter. "I know what you're trying to do but I really must go. Two weeks will be here faster if I leave."

"Okay I'll let you go just give me a kiss."

So, we kissed, and I walked toward the TSA agent to give her my ticket and boarding pass. As I was about to remove my shoes for TSA, he called my name.

"Nia!" I turned around and he said, "I love you."

I responded with, "I love you too. I'll see you in two weeks and I'll call you tonight." I proceeded to my gate. I was asleep before we were in the air.

Malik

After dropping her off at the airport, I headed to Houston's. All the fellas were there to greet me. They'd already been seated.

Rick was apparently amused because he was laughing when he asked, "What's up nigga?"

I replied with, "What's up?"

We ordered our drinks and our entrees. Mike got to the point because he's a to-the-point brotha, "So, how was the weekend? Did you hit it?"

I thought about the conversation Nia and I had prior to her leaving and I laughed. Mike used the same terminology Nia said he'd use. Mike wanted to know what was funny. "Man, what's up? What's funny?"

"Nothing man, nothing at all."

"Well, are you going to answer my question?"

"Yeah, I'll answer it." I looked at each of them and they looked at me like they were dogs waiting to be fed. "No, I did not hit it, but yes, we did make love."

Ray asked, "Straight, how was it?"

289

Rick bumped shoulders with Ray and said, "What kinda question is that? It's new pussy which means it was good."

"You know I love you all, but this is different so please don't refer to Nia as new pussy."

They all leaned back in their seats and together said, "DAMN!"

Mike was the first to say anything, "You really dig her huh?"

"It's deeper than that, I love her."

Again, they leaned back in their seats and gave me another, "DAMN!"

Stuttering, Rick asked, "F...f....for real?"

"Yeah, but the good thing is, she loves me back."

They all looked at me, and then each other before they asked, as if rehearsed, "Straight?" I guess they were all at a loss for words because silence encompassed our table. Our waiter arrived with our entrees, and we began to eat. Ray broke the silence, "Malik, man I'm happy for you. You've been diggin' on ol' girl for a minute, so I'm glad things went in your favor."

"I appreciate it Ray. She's special and she's different."

"Yeah I'm happy for you too. After that fiasco with Melina, you deserve some happiness," Mike said.

"Thanks Mike."

Rick was the last to say something, but I knew he was sincere, "Bruh, if you're happy, I'm happy. From the looks of it, she makes you happy."

"I appreciate it because ya'll my boys and it's important you all like her."

Mike's logical ass said, "Man, you don't have to worry about that, Nia is hella cool and we'd love to have her as a sister-in-law." Ray and Rick shook their heads in agreement. This was a big load off my mind. Now, I just hope my parents love her.

"She's meeting me in Orlando in two weeks. We're going to hang out with the parents."

"Bruh, after Melina, your parents will welcome Nia with open arms," Ray stated.

"Shit, just the fact she has a job will make your parents happy," Rick said.

"Yeahhhh man, Melina was a no-job-havin'-no-ambition-havin'-gold-diggin-trick. I'm thankful you finally woke up because she was not the one," Ray said.

"Yeah man, you woke up. Good pussy can't keep a relationship going, not unless it's a relationship where you're only fucking. If you want mental stimulation and a woman who's got your back, good pussy won't keep you there," Mike stated.

"I know and agree with everything you all are saying that's why I finally left her trick ass alone. I'm just glad I met Nia. I think she's the one."

Ray's dumb ass asked, "The one for what?"

Rick nudged his shoulder, "The one man! The future Mrs. Black."

290

Ray's eyes popped out of his head, "Straight! That's cool man. Nia and her crew are cool."

With that we continued to eat, drink, and talk shit. We must've stayed at Houston's for at least two and a half hours. Nia was heavy on my mind. It was going to be a long two weeks.

Nia

My flight took two hours. I embarked upon the city I call home and my girl Lexy was there waiting for me. I put my luggage into her trunk and climbed into the front seat.

"Hey girl."

"Hey Lex!"

"How was your trip?"

"My trip was good and before you ask, the dick was the bomb."

"For real?"

"Girrrrrl, the dick talked to me. It's like it was made just for me."

"Tell me more. Tell me more."

"Girl, I finally have a man who believes in foreplay. He's got the equipment and knows what to do with it. They say brothas have their sexual peak around the age of twenty, well Malik has defied that myth."

Fanning her face, she said, "Whew girl! I know what you mean. Good dick is hard to find, and you know I'm like Sommore."

"What does Sommore have to do with this?"

"Nobody knows good dick like I know good dick. Sommore claims she knows good dick, but she ain't met me."

Laughing, "Girl, you are crazy, but I know what you mean. Hard dick is easy to find, a man's dick will get hard when the wind blows, but good dick, that's another thing. Good dick is hard to find and I'm glad I've found the complete package."

"And what is the complete package?"

"A brotha, cause you know he's got to be a brotha, that's-"

"Yeah cause your daddy would probably haunt your ass if you dated a white boy."

"And you know it, he was not havin' it. Hell, I remember he treated Kevin like he had the plague because he was light skinned. Too close to white is what he'd say."

"Yeah, black folks and their hangups."

"Ain't that the truth."

"Anyway, finish telling me about the complete package."

"The complete package is an intelligent and ambitious black man who loves God and puts him first. He cherishes black women and would never think of insulting the matriarchs in his family by dating a white woman. He is affectionate, loving, witty, hardworking, and strong. He has a strong sense of

291

self, and he loves his people. It doesn't hurt if he's handsome, most black men are and, has a big dick."

"Girl, you just said a mouth full. Don't forget, brothas do have their issues."

"Yes, they do, but so do we."

"True dat. Well, I'm glad you're home and I'm glad your trip was good."

"Oh snap! I almost forgot."

"What?"

"I had a fight while-"

"You had a what?"

"A fight with-

By this time Lexy was fuming and yelling. Nobody messes with her girl, "A fight with who?"

"Girl, if you allow me to finish, I'll tell you."

"Okay, I'm sorry. Finish telling me."

"As I was saying, I had a fight with Malik's ex." Just then my cell phone rang. "Hold up Lexy, let me get this." I answered without looking at the caller id, "Hello."

"Hey baby." It was Malik.

"Hey!" I'm sure my grin told Lexy who was on the other end of the phone.

"Are you home yet?"

"Yeah, I'm with Lexy now."

"Aw okay, I won't keep you, I'm still at Houston's with the fellas." As soon as he said the fellas, I heard all of them say, "What's up Nia!"

"Tell them I said hello."

"I will baby, you go ahead and enjoy your time with Lexy. Tell her hello for me."

"I will and I'll call you when I get settled at home. I have to get Sheba from my mother's, and I need to go by the office to check on things. We have a gala we're hosting Friday and I need to make sure things are going as scheduled."

"Okay I'll talk to you later. Have a good day."

"You too boo."

"I love you." There. He'd said it. In front of his friends. He really did love me because brothas certainly don't make that claim in front of their friends unless they mean it. They'll tell you when they're fucking you because they think it's what the woman wants to hear, or they'll say it when it's just the two of you. Yeah, Mr. Malik Black had just shown more than he realized. My feelings were also sincere, so I voiced them in front of my girl. "I love you." Lexy's eyes popped out of her head, but I ignored her. "I'll call you later." We said bye and hung up. Alexis couldn't wait to begin questioning me. "Miss Thang, you got some explaining to do."

"I know girl but let me finish telling you about the fight."

"Yeah, c'mon with it because I will go to Dallas if I need to."

292

"Girl, ain't no need, I handled my business."

"That's my girl. Now, give up the details."

"Melina, that's her name, called Saturday night and he told her it was over, that it's been over for eight months. After the fiasco he turned the ringers off in case she called again. We chilled, made love, and got a good night of rest. Sunday morning, we had breakfast and then we were preparing to go to the mall. While Malik was in the shower someone rang the doorbell, so I answered." I continued telling her what happened.

"No, that trick ass bitch didn't come over there and clown?"

"Yes, she did."

"Well, I'm glad you handled her ass."

"You know how I am about fighting, I don't like to, but I will if I have to."

"Yeah, I know but sometimes you do what you gotta do."

"A to the men on that."

"So let me tell you about the lovemaking and the confession of love."

"Let's grab something to eat at Pasta House."

"The one in University City?"

"Yep?"

"Ok, let's do it."

"Oh, okay." On our way to the restaurant, I told Lexy all about the lovemaking and the admission of love. We arrived at the restaurant and continued our conversation while ordering. She also filled me in on her relationship with Jake and its progress between bites.

"Before I forget. You know Malik and I have been seeing each other every two weeks."

"Yeah?"

"Well, time to meet the parents. He wants me to meet him in Orlando."

While sucking on a chicken wing she said, "Well he's met your mom it's time you met his people."

"I guess you're right, it doesn't stop me from being nervous though."

"About what?"

"About meeting them."

"Girl, they will love you."

"I hope so."

We completed our meals and she drove me to my mother's. By that time, I was tired, so I picked up Sheba and I told my mother I'd call her tomorrow. I stopped by the office to see how things were going. Alicia was on the phone, but quickly hung up when she saw me.

"Hey jet setter."

"Hey!"

"What's up girl?"

"Nothing much, just real tired but I wanted to stop by here to see if everything's okay."

"Everything's fine. We're just preparing for Friday night's gala."

"Cool. Is it okay if I go home to rest?"

"Yeah, it is. Go ahead and I'll see you in the morning."

Walking out the door I said, "Thanks, eight am sharp."

I got in my truck and Sheba, and I headed in the direction of home. When we arrived, I put Sheba in the backyard and began checking my messages. My voice mail was overloaded. There were eighteen messages. Eight were hang-ups. Two were from my credit card companies making customer service calls. Two were from my mother's forgetful self, calling while I was in Dallas. Four were from Ben making his weekly I'm-so-lonely-gimme-another-chance calls. The last two calls were from Michelle. She said she had something urgent to discuss with me. I didn't plan on returning any phone calls because I was on my way to relaxing. Grabbing the mail, I let Sheba in the house, grabbed a Pepsi from the refrigerator and went to my bedroom. Sheba followed me and when we got there, she laid at the foot of the bed. I turned the TV on and began to browse through my mail. I received my new Essence with Mary J. Blige on the cover. She was gracing everyone's cover promoting her new CD, her love, and her happiness. I couldn't be mad at her. Just as I was finishing up the monthly 'In The Spirit' article in the Essence, the telephone began to ring. Only a few knew I was home, so I answered without looking at the caller id.

"Hello."

"Hey baby."

"Who is this?" I knew it was Ben's dumb ass, but I didn't want him to think I still knew his voice.

"Aw, so because it's been a couple of months, you don't know my voice?"

With agitation in my voice, "Who is this?"

"It's me, Ben and please don't hang up."

"What do you want Ben?"

He sighed before he said, "I want to say I'm sorry. For everything."

"Is that it?"

"I'd like to see you."

"Not possible."

"Why not?"

His question amused me, "Bye Ben."

"Wait a minute Nia, don't -" Before he could get his plea out, I hung up. I was not in the mood for his nonsense. I continued reading through my magazine and the phone began to ring again. I ignored it and eventually it stopped. I immediately drifted off to sleep. The phone rang again, and my eyes glazed over. I was obviously tired, but I found enough energy to lean up and peek at the clock. The time showed eight-thirty, so I'd been asleep for about three hours. I grabbed the handset to the phone and greeted the party on the other line, "Hello."

"You sleep baby?"

"Just waking up. What's up?"

"Nothing, I was just calling to see how your day was?"

294

"Same ol' same ol', what about-"

"I miss you." Silence shot through the phone line like lightning shot through the sky.

"I miss you too."

"I can't wait to see you."

"Two weeks. We'll just have to keep busy until then."

"I guess you're right. So, what's up in the STL?"

"Ben called tod-"

"What did his busta ass want?"

"I don't know. I hung up on him."

"He's persistent."

"Yes he is, but all the persistence in the world won't help."

"He'll get it sooner or later and for his sake I pray that it's sooner. I'm about to lay it down baby. You wore a brotha out this weekend and I must rest so I can go to work in the morning."

"All right Boo. I'm still tired so I think I'm going to order carry-out Chinese, take a shower and go back to sleep."

"I'll call you from work tomorrow."

"Until then, sleep well."

"I will." After hanging up the phone, I got up and did what I said I was going to do. Soon thereafter, I acquiesced to the fatigue invading my body.

For the next two weeks, I went through my normal routine. Work, home, and phone calls to Malik. The gala we catered for was a huge success for Event Solutions. Hopefully, the success of the gala will bring us even more business. We received a very positive review on STLToday.com and in the St. Louis American (St. Louis' premiere black weekly newspaper).

I was scheduled to leave for sunny Orlando, Florida in two days. The nervousness was kicking in like Jet Li, but Malik really wanted this. It was my duty to make sure I came through for him.

That First Visit

When I arrived in Orlando, Malik met me at baggage claim.

"Hey baby!", he pulled me into an embrace.

Kissing his lips, I said, "Hey yourself."

"How do you feel?"

"I'm good, just a little nervous."

"About meeting my parents?"

"Yeah."

"Don't worry, plus I have a surprise for you."

"What?" I began looking around expecting his parents to be there as part of a welcome committee. "Please don't tell me that your parents are here, at the airport?"

"C'mon, let's walk while I tell you about the surprise." He took off walking, looking at his watch and leaving me behind. I didn't budge. What the hell is he rushing for? After taking ten steps he realized I wasn't walking beside him, so he stopped.

"Baby, why aren't you walking?" He looked at his watch again. Giving him a quizzical look, I asked, "Why do you keep looking at your watch and why are you rushing?"

"That's part of the surprise, so please trust me and come on."

"Okay Mr. Black, this better be good." We began walking but not in the direction of the parking lot. I didn't say anything. I was supposed to trust him, right? He finally began to speak, "Remember during your visit when we discussed jet skiing?" I began to get excited. He was taking me jet skiing. "Aw baby, that's sweet but isn't it kinda cold to be in the water?"

"That's the surprise, we're going to Cancun." He waited for my reaction.

"Can-what? For real?" Before he could answer to confirm, I grabbed him and began kissing and hugging him. I'd made a spectacle with my display of affection. During my temporary state of euphoria, a light bulb went off and I realized I couldn't go to Cancun. I didn't have my birth certificate or my passport. I couldn't go to Cancun or any other destination outside of the USA. Malik must've noticed my change in demeanor because he asked, "What's wrong?"

I whispered, "I can't go."

"What do you mean you can't go?"

"All I have is my driver's license. I don't have the appropriate ID to leave the states." He went to pull something out of his back pocket and handed it to me. "What's this?" I opened it and saw that it was my passport. "How did you get this?"

"Mrs. Lawson was kind enough to mail it last week."

"So, you got my mama involved?"

"A brotha's gotta do what a brotha's gotta do. She even sent me some of your summer clothes, so you'd have something to wear in the heat."

I kissed him and said, "Thank you and my mama for doing what you had to do. When does our flight leave?"

He looked at his watch, "In about thirty minutes."

I grabbed him around the waist and said, "Let's go."

He placed his arm around my waist, and we began our trek to the gate. We had a few minutes, so we sat down and waited.

"This is so nice of you. No one has ever surprised me like this."

"You're very welcome. I'm glad I'm the first to give you this type of surprise. I promise it won't be the last."

"Somehow I believe that."

"You should."

"I do. You've allowed me to trust, I mean really trust men again."

"That's good baby. I'm just glad your heart allowed you to love me."

296

"Me too."

"For the record, I'll be the last man you'll be trusting cause I'm not letting you go."

"Is that right?"

"If you only knew." The airline was ready to begin boarding. It was a chartered flight, so we were in the second group to board. Malik got up to retrieve his luggage the attendant was holding behind the desk.

"Okay baby, let's go."

"Let's."

Our boarding passes were checked, and we boarded the plane. We got into our seats, and I was excited because this was our first official trip together.

"Hey baby."

"Yeah?"

"I just thought of something."

Buckling his seat belt he asked, "What's that?"

"This is our first trip together."

"I guess we can't count the Tom Joyner Cruise because we didn't go together."

"No, we didn't."

"Don't worry baby, this is the first of many trips to come." He closed his eyes to nap. I grabbed his hand, which caused him to open his eyes and look at me questioningly. "We need to pray."

"You're right, I'm tripping. I'm sorry." He lowered his head, and I did the same. I lead the prayer. "Heavenly Father, we come to you with thanks, praise, glory, and honor. I want to thank you for this very special man beside me. I know he is truly a gift from you." He squeezed my hand and I continued. "As you know we've boarded this aircraft and we're asking you to bless us with safe travels. We ask this in the name of your son, our savior, Jesus Christ." We both said, "Amen." He leaned over and kissed me.

"Baby, I'm going to sleep."

"Not before me you aren't."

We both drifted into dreamland prior to the plane taking off. We arrived in beautiful Cancun, Mexico within one hour. We caught a taxi to our hotel, the JW Marriott Cancun Resort and Spa. The grounds and the hotel were stunning. The entire view was breathtaking.

"Baby, this is beautiful. I've stayed at the Casa Magna Cancun Marriott and it's nice, but this hotel is newer and nicer."

"I'm glad you like it. Gerald and his ex-came here and he said the experience was a good one."

We checked in and after browsing around the lobby, we went in search of our room. My mouth dropped in awe. Our room was beautiful, and the view had us in a trance. It was so vivid that it looked like an artist had painted the scenic view from our patio door. The bed was huge. Malik and I looked at the bed and from the look on our faces we had to be thinking the same thing, and that is, 'We're going to tear that bed up.' We began to laugh.

"What do you want to do first?"

I looked at my watch, "Well it's too late to jet ski but," I rubbed my stomach and gave him my I'm-hungry look, "I could always eat."

"I'm sure you can. Kenya was right."

"I doubt it because she's very seldom right, but what is she supposedly right about?"

"She said you have a big appetite. You can and will get your eat on, but that's cool cause I can't stand those salad and fruit eating heifers."

"Well, I like food too much for that."

"Well then we should get dressed."

"Yes, let me take a look in this duffle bag to see the conservative outfits my mother chose."

"I think you'll like what's in the bag. Your mother didn't mention it, but I think she had Alexis pick some stuff out of your closet."

I sat on the bed and began to look through the bag. He was right. Lexy had a hand in choosing my outfits. In the bag there were shorts, halters, three swimming suits and underwear. The main outfits she chose were my strapless black Capri jumper and my brown linen halter dress. For shoes, she included my all-white Air Shox, my flip-flops, my black and red Gucci wedges with the matching handbag and my tan BCBG strappy sandals and a matching clutch. "You're right, I'm happy with what Lexy chose. I'll thank her when I get home."

"Cool. I'm going to jump in the shower so we can get out of here."

"Where are we going?"

"Where would you like to go?"

"I don't know, let me think-"

"I'm in the mood for steak and lobster, and there's this restaurant here called.... Damn, I can't think of it."

"Well, I really like Captain's Cove, they have good food, and it sits right on the beach."

Snapping his fingers, "That's it, that's what I was trying to remember. Gerald said they had delicious food."

"Yeah, they do so let's hurry up because a sistah is starving."

We both showered and dressed. He looked extremely handsome in a pair of brown linen slacks, a short sleeve tan silk tee shirt and brown leather sandals. He was acting nervous and fidgety, but I couldn't figure out why. I guess he's nervous about this being our first trip.

"You have on a color other than black and gray?"

"Yeah I peeked in the duffle bag and decided to get some items to match your colors."

"Well you look nice."

"Thank you and so do you."

We caught a taxi to the restaurant. There was a crowd so there was a slight wait. It was a beautiful night but that is the norm for Cancun. He was still acting nervous, but again, I didn't know why.

"Malik, are you okay?"

298

"I'm cool. Why do you ask?"

"I don't know. You're acting nervous."

"No, I'm cool. Other than being hungry, I'm cool."

The host informed us we could be seated, and she sat us by an open window. It was nice because there was a slight breeze.

"What do you say we get a bottle of Moet?"

"And what may I ask are we celebrating?"

"Us. Our love. Our first trip."

"I'm in Cancun Papi` so I'm down for whatever."

The waiter came by and introduced himself. His name was Eduardo and although his accent was strong, I could understand his English without any problem. Malik ordered the bottle of Moet and we continued to chill. He was still acting nervous, but again, I didn't know why.

"Baby, are you sure you're okay?"

Looking back like he was expecting someone, he said, "I'm cool, why do you ask?"

"Because you're acting nervous, and you act like you're expecting someone."

Still looking nervous, "I'm not expecting anyone." He then leaned back in his chair and began trying to relax. It appeared to be working. In the restaurant, there was a pianist, who played a mixture of Latin, pop, jazz, and easy listening music. The restaurant was dimly lit and therefore very romantic. I was immensely enjoying the ambience as well as the company. Eduardo arrived with our champagne, and we indulged. Later when he returned to take our order, Malik surprised me by ordering in fluent Spanish.

"Eduardo, te gusta carne des res y langosta, carne de res o camarones y dos vaso de agua."

Eduardo responded with, "Si` senor."

"Muchos gracias."

"I didn't know you spoke Spanish."

"Yeah, it comes in handy living in Texas."

"I'm sure it does."

While waiting for our food to arrive we discussed current events and we both talked about work. Luckily our wait wasn't long. Eduardo arrived with our meals, and we began to eat.

"Hey, can I taste your lobster?"

"Sure." He dipped a piece of lobster in butter and fed it to me." Since he felt bold enough to feed me lobster in public, I surprised him by sucking on his finger. In public.

Jerking his finger away, "Baby, what are you trying to do?" I just grinned and continued eating my food.

"Is your food okay?"

With food in my mouth I just shook my head. The food was just like I remembered. It was delicious. Ben and I had traveled together but I can honestly say in the short time Malik and I have been here, I was certain our

299

time would be better than my wildest dreams. We finished our food and continued to enjoy the ambience and the music. Malik ordered a dessert in Spanish, but I didn't know what it was. I was trusting him and waiting on the surprise. While we were enjoying the ambiance, we shared several moments of silence. They were comfortable moments of silence not the-I've-run-out-of-things-to say silence. I could hear the waves rolling in, but I also saw a shimmer of light. It was almost as if someone was having a bonfire, but that couldn't be it. He broke the silence. "Are you having a good time?"

"Yes I am. Thank you so much."

"You are welcome." Just then I saw another flicker of light on the beach, but we didn't know what caused it. There was no lightning, so I couldn't figure it out. It got everyone's attention because everyone in the restaurant looked out the windows. From our seats we couldn't make anything out, so we stood up. My mouth dropped in awe, and I blinked my eyes to make sure they weren't deceiving me. The pianist began to play a beautiful ballad but for the life of me, I couldn't think of what it was. On the beach there were individual lights, they appeared to be candles and they were illuminating a message. As I read the message, tears began to well up in my eyes. I read it a second time, it said, 'Nia, will you marry me?' By the time I turned around all the patrons were standing and looking. At me. Eduardo had arrived with two covered dishes and Malik was lowering himself to the floor. I sat back down. He took one of the dishes and uncovered it to display a ring box. It hit me. Like a ton of bricks. Malik was proposing. Now I realized what song the pianist was playing. It was 'Here and Now' by Luther Vandross. He was going to ask me to marry him. That's why he was nervous. With this acknowledgment tears began to fall from my eyes. He took my left hand and began to speak with tears in his eyes.

"Nia, I know this proposal is soon, but I know what I feel. I've thought about making you my wife since the first time I held you in my arms. As a matter of fact, I don't have to date you for years to know I want you as my wife. I can't promise I'll always be perfect, but I promise I'll always love and honor you. You have become my everything by filling the void in my life and I want to spend the rest our lives loving you." He opened the ring box to display a two-carat princess cut solitaire diamond set in white gold with an eternity band. It was exquisite. "Would you please accept my proposal to become my wife?"

Without any hesitation I replied with, "Yes." He slipped the ring on my finger, and we kissed. I heard clapping and I realized everyone in the restaurant had become our audience. I heard male voices yelling Malik's name. When I turned around, there they were. Mike, Ray, and Rick. I waved them over and hugged each of them. "So, he put you all up to this?"

Ray's smart-ass said, "Naw, we were just in Cancun making bonfires on the beach."

I punched him in the shoulder, "All right, smart ass."

Mike said, "Congratulations are in order."

"Let's order champagne," Rick suggested.

300

"There's a bottle already chilling," Malik informed them.
We all sat down and began to talk.

"On a serious note, Nia I know I speak for all of us when I say Malik couldn't have picked a better woman to be his wife. He's our boy and we love him like a brother. I say all that because we expect you to treat him like the king he is and I guarantee he will treat you like a queen," Mike expressed.

"Mike, don't worry." Looking at Malik I said, "I love him and as corny as this may sound, I've been waiting for him all my life. I won't be letting him go for the next forty to fifty years. We're going to grow ancient together."

"That's good to hear cause we don't hit women, but we'd have to beat you down," claimed Ray. That got a laugh out of all of us. We stayed at the restaurant for another hour before we got ready to depart.

"We hate to cut this time short but we're going to Daddy-O's and I'm sure the two of you want to do some private celebrating," Mike stated.

"Yep, my fiancée and I have a date on the beach." The fellas looked at us and just shook their heads.
We thanked the restaurant management and Eduardo. They left for the club, and we went back to our hotel.

"We were in the lobby when he said, "Baby, have a seat, I'm going to run to our room and then we'll head for the beach."

"Okay babe but don't take too long."

"I won't."
I waited in the lobby. He retreated to our room, and I sat in one of the wing back chairs and waited. While waiting I stared at the band of love on my finger. I'd wanted this my entire life. A man just like Malik to love me. A man like my father. For me. Completely. Unconditionally. Well, I got what I asked for. God does answer prayers. I'd just received a huge blessing. After kissing toads for the last seventeen years, I could now throw the mistletoe away and relax. I'd been attracting the wrong men for-fuckin-ever. Losers were attracted to me like gold and platinum teeth to rappers. In this case, I'd finally attracted and got a winner. He knew what he wanted and what to do to get it.
He reappeared with a blanket and his cell. "Baby, I'm ready."
"What's that for?" Pointing at the stuff in his arms, "What are you doing now?"
Holding out his hand to me, "Another surprise, c'mon." I placed my hand in his. He led me to the back of the hotel, out a rear exit and onto the beach. We found a spot on the beach. From this moment on, it would be known as our spot. He spread the blanket out and we sat down. He played music from a playlist on his cell and Jagged Edge's music filled our spot. 'I gotta be the one you love, I gotta be the one you need.' That particular song was my favorite of theirs. Malik offered me his hand, I got up, accepted his hand and we began to dance. He held me close, and our bodies swayed to not only the beat of the music but the breeze. Jagged Edge's voices faded as Ginuwine began to tell his woman how she'd made a difference in his life. 'My whole life has changed, since you came in', his voice continued to float through the breeze.

301

After enjoying his melodious voice, Mya began to sing about "Fallen". Her song was appropriate because we had definitely fallen. In friendship. In love. In lust. We'd fallen into everything.

While we were swaying to the beat Malik looked at me through honest eyes. This man loved him some Nia. I was certain my eyes, like his, told the undeniable truth. Nia loved her some Malik. He lowered his head, and I parted my lips anticipating the arrival of his tongue. Our tongues began the dance they'd become quite familiar with. As we continued our kiss, the music of various artists continued to float through the air. During our kiss Malik not only lowered me to the ground but my halter-top was lowered to my waist. I removed his shirt and our bare chests touched. I must've gone into a daze because the next thing I knew we were both butt-ass-naked sitting on the edge of the beach with waves rolling under our asses. Making love on the beach has always been a fantasy of mine and it was about to happen. I guess when he went to our room, he grabbed some condoms. He slipped one on Zulu and I rode him as if this would be our last time making love. The experience was so intense, and the funny thing is neither of us seemed to care who saw us. We were butt-ass-naked in a public place. I guess that's what love, and lust do to you. We loved one another but, on this beach, our only concern was doing the damn thing. Our moans floated through the breeze like birds fly south for the winter. It was the norm. We held each other and cherished this moment which would be forever etched into our memory. I had tears in my eyes. Although I had been blessed in so many ways I always wondered and second-guessed God as to why I had to go through what I've gone through in relationships. Why hadn't I been blessed with a man to love me enough to marry me? Why this? Why that? I know everything is done in His time, but it's hard to not second guess when others around you, are in your opinion living foul but still being blessed. This is obviously my time and I thank God for this moment and this man. Malik, his love, and his proposal all came when I least expected it. I fought the urge to be with him. It was too soon after the Ben fiasco. Wasn't it? I guess not. We're blessed when He sees fit. Well, I'm a definite believer in things happening in God's time. What I've been through with men and just life in general, have molded me into being the best wife I can possibly be. I will try my best to emulate my mother.

As our lovemaking subsided, we just held each other. He whispered something but I didn't hear him.

"I'm sorry baby. I didn't hear you.

"I said I love you."

"I know baby. I love you too."

"I don't think you understand Nia. Loving you feels my heart with....I can't explain it but when I look at you and when those three words are spoken I can actually feel it in my heart. It's almost as if I can feel my heart expanding." He was holding his head down. With my left hand and my ring finger, the finger that he'd glided a band of love on, I tilted his chin up so I

302

could gaze into his eyes as I spoke. "Malik I do understand. Loving you completes me, and I honestly never believed I'd be this blessed. You are such a blessing I've pinched myself on more than one occasion. So, believe me when I say I understand."

"I'm glad you do."

"Me too. Baby, can we go to our room? I'm getting cold."

"Yeah, let's get dressed." We grabbed our belongings and started toward the hotel in silence. When we arrived in our room, I was the first to shower and climb into the bed. I was tired. He followed my lead. He climbed into bed, and we fell fast asleep in the well-known spoon position. We told the fellas we'd meet them on the beach at noon to begin our water excursions.

The following morning neither of us was in a hurry to get up. We stayed in bed until eleven. As the time neared, we climbed out the bed to shower together. We changed into our swim attire and hand-in-hand we went to the beach. The fellas were on time and waiting. Mike was the first to greet us, "What's up hubby and wifey to be?"

Malik answered for us, "What's up? Ya'll ready?"

"Yeah man, we were born ready."

"I just don't want you clowns drowning."

Rick looked at Ray and Mike before he said, "Man, I'm a Pisces. I ain't got no problem with the water. Now those two, you may have to keep an eye on."

"Nigga whateva! I'll swim laps around your fishy ass. Pisces, Taurus, or Scorpio, I don't care what your zodiac is."

"Ya'll need to bring your silly asses on," I demanded. If it were up to them, they'd stay here and argue over nothing. We headed to the water sports area and for the next four hours we indulged. For two of those hours, we jet skied. Me behind Malik holding on for dear life. Me leading and him holding on. Me on my own jet ski. All five of us having a great time. Me fulfilling a desire I've had for years. When we tired of jet skiing, we decided to go parasailing. This was the one area I had a little experience in where they had none. From there they decided they wanted to scuba-dive. In my head I decided I wanted a nap. We'd decided on eating at *Ruth Chris' Steakhouse* and I knew I'd need some sleep before that. I pulled Malik aside to ask if he was tired, "Baby, are you tired?"

"No babe, are you?"

"Yeah I am. Would you mind if I went back to the room to lie down?"

"Of course not. Do you mind if I continue to hang with the fellas?"

"Not at all." I kissed his cheek, waved bye to the boys and went to nap. As I was walking away, I heard Ray ask Malik, "Man, where's Nia going?"

"She's going to take a nap so let's go scuba-diving."

That's what they did. When I woke up and looked at the clock, I realized I'd been sleeping for two hours. Malik was in the other room with a towel around his waist asleep on the couch. I chose not to wake him. Instead, I decided to prepare myself for the evening. Just as I was stepping out of the shower, Malik appeared in the bathroom. "Hey baby. How was your nap?"

"It was good. I really needed that. You and the fellas wore my ass out today."

"Well, they plan on wearing you out tonight also."

"At Ruth Chris'?"

"After dinner they want us to hang with them at *Daddy-O's.*"

"Daddy-O's two nights in a row?"

"Yeah, they really enjoyed themselves."

"Obviously. Well, I guess we should get ready. Our flight leaves tomorrow afternoon, right?"

"Yeah. It leaves at one and we should be in Orlando no later than three. We need to cut our stay with my parents short because I want to be with you when you tell your family and friends the news."

"Really? You mean that?"

"Yeah baby. I wouldn't leave you to do it alone."

"I appreciate you."

"We're a team and I wouldn't have it any other way."

Placing my arms around his waist I said, "That's why I love you so much." He patted my ass and responded with, "Let's get ready. The fellas will be ready."

We put our clothes on and left to meet the fellas. They were of course on time and just like Malik said, waiting on us at a table. We joined them at the table and geared up to partake in the good food Ruth Chris' always prepares. We completed our meals and shared a round of drinks before we headed to Daddy-O's. At the club I was the luckiest girl in the club, I had four men to dance with and we kicked it. We partied until three in the morning. Malik and I said our good-byes because our flight was scheduled to leave before theirs. Upon our exit, the fellas were still getting their party on with three Mexican beauties.We walked along the beach together and in silence. There were a lot of couples with the same idea. We packed our bags when we arrived in our room and fell fast asleep. The following morning, we woke up, made love, ordered room service, showered, ate, and caught a taxi to the airport.

Time to Meet the Parents

We arrived in Orlando at three and as soon as the aircraft touched the ground the nervousness in my stomach began. Malik had rented a car. We put the bags in the trunk and headed in the direction of Mr. And Mrs. Black's home. We rode in total silence and the entire time I thought to myself, 'What if they don't like me?' That question cut me like a knife because I really love their son and it's important to me, they like me. I know a lot of women don't care if the family and friends care for them, but for me it matters. I realize you not only marry this man or woman, but the entire family. For this reason, it's important they like me.

Malik grabbed my hand and the sweat covering it easily gave away my nervousness. "Baby, what's wrong?"

"I…I'm nervous."

"About meeting my parents?"

Okay here we go with dumb questions. "Well what other reason would I have to be nervous about?"

Laughing, "Don't get snappy with me young lady."

"I'm sorry baby. I'm just really nervous."

"There's no reason to be. My parents are cool people, and they'll love you."

"What if they don't?"

"I've known them my entire life. They'll love you."

"If you say so but if they don't it's your ass."

"Is that a threat?"

"It sure is."

We continued the ride in silence. Ten minutes later we were in a gated residential area. We passed several streets before we turned onto a tree-lined cul-de-sac. Their home sat in the middle of the cul-de-sac. Their home was a brick ranch style home.

"It's a nice home."

"They just down sized. Their previous home was a two-story and since they're getting up in age, they chose this home."

"It's nice."

"It's cool. It's not too large and not too small, it's just right for them." He put the car in the park, cut the engine off and turned in his seat to face me. "Baby, are you still nervous?"

"Yeah, but I know I must go through with this."

"Yeah since we're going to be married."

Sighing, I said, "Let's do this."

He grabbed my hand and gave it a squeeze before he opened his door. I said a quick prayer before Malik arrived on my side of the car. As he led me to the front door, we saw that we had company. His parents must've heard the car when we arrived. They were waiting in the doorway. Mr. Black looked like an older version of his son. As the saying goes, 'he spit him out'. The only difference was the fact that Malik had locs and his father had a low cut. If I did older men, I'd do him. Mrs. Black was Halle Berry's complexion with a salt and pepper short hair style. She was a petite woman and very shapely. She has a mole above her lip just like Malik's. That's probably the only thing he took after her because he was truly the spitting image of his father. As we were walking up the steps, his father walked onto the porch. They were smiling and to me that was a good sign. His father opened his arms, "Come here young lady." I walked straight into his embrace, and it felt natural. It was like hugging my father. "Hello Mr. Black, Mrs. Black. It's so nice

305

to meet both of you." Mrs. Black didn't hug me, and I found it a little strange, but this was our first meeting. We went inside and sat down in the living room. Malik and I sat on the love seat and his parents sat on the couch. I grabbed Malik's hand and he smiled at me. That gesture helped my nervousness a little. There was an awkward silence, but his father talked which eased a lot of the awkwardness.

"So, Nia, we finally meet. Our son has told us so much about you." "He's told me a lot about both of you as well." Mrs. Black finally said something, "So how was your trip?"

Gazing into my man's eyes I said, "It was great. We really had a good time."

"Good. Good. Did you all get the opportunity to jet ski? Malik told us you'd never been."

"No ma'am I hadn't but Malik taught me and now I think I'm a pro." That got a laugh out of everyone.

Mrs. Black was obviously proud of her son's accomplishments. With a lot of pride, she asked, "Did he happen to mention he's swam with the dolphins?"

"Yea ma'am he did. I can swim but I don't know if I'm brave enough to swim with the dolphins."

"He always did swim like a fish. He told me you don't like airplane food, so I prepared a meal. Are you hungry?"

"As a matter of fact, I am."

"Good. You all go wash up and meet us in the dining room."

Like a hungry panting dog Malik began to salivate. "Ma, what did you cook?"

"Don't worry baby, I made all your favorites. Nia, I hope you like Cajun food."

"Yes, ma'am I do. During Malik's last visit in St. Louis, he prepared jambalaya, and it was delicious. I thought he was hiding you in the house somewhere."

"A young lady with a sense of humor, I like that," Mr. Black said. I followed Malik to the bathroom to wash up while his parents went to the dining room.

While we washed our hands I whispered, "I don't think your mother likes me."

"Baby, just give her time. She's somewhat leery after Melina."

"I hope that's all there is. I really want her to like me."

"Baby, don't trip. She'll love you."

"When are we going to share our news?"

"As soon as we're done eating."

"Okay, I'll just follow your lead."

We re-entered the dining room and found the feast his mother prepared. She had outdone herself. She'd prepared shrimp etouffe`, jambalaya, dirty rice, catfish fillets, greens, hot watered cornbread and miniature shrimp and catfish

306

po' boys. It was like I was standing in the middle of the French Quarters. "Mrs. Black, I know we just met but I love you and all this food you've prepared." I figured I'd compliment her to death. If the compliments and her seeing the way I treat her son don't work, oh well. "How did you learn to cook this well?"

"Malik didn't tell you?"

Stuffing my cheeks with dirty rice, "Tell me what?"

"I was born and raised in New Orleans."

"No, he didn't tell me. This food is delicious. I would love it if you shared some of your recipes with me for my business."

"That's right, he told Brad and I you and one of your girlfriends have an event planning business."

"Yes ma'am, we've been very blessed."

"So, you're a good cook?"

"I don't know if I can burn like this, but I do all right."

Malik spoke up to sing my praises, "Ma, don't listen to that noise. She can burn in the kitchen. During my visit she cooked for her friends and I and prepared a delicious feast. Her mother also cooked for me, so I know she got her cooking skills honestly."

"Mrs. Black don't listen to Malik; he's biased when it comes to me."

"Well young lady he always sings your praises and I'm glad we've finally met you."

"I feel the same way. Your son has become very special to me in a short time, and I assure both of you I love him very much."

It appears his mother was softening up, "Well, it seems as though he feels the same way. I apologize for being standoffish but after we-won't-mention-her-name, I must be leery."

"That's understandable Mrs. Black. I had the pleasure of meeting we-won't-mention-her-name, so I know what you're talking about."

"Ma, I'm glad you and pop like Nia but I knew you would. I want to tell both of you something."

His father acknowledged him, "Go ahead son, your mother and I are listening."

"Okay, well, you know what I've been through in my relationships, and you also know how I feel about Nia. She's very special to me and in a very short time she's proven her love and loyalty. I love her because she reminds me a lot of," looking at his mother, "you and I've always wanted a relationship like the one you all have had over the years."

"A relationship like ours is hard work," his mother admitted.

"We know Ma, but Nia and I want to work at it. So, I just wanted you all to know while in Cancun, I asked for Nia's hand in marriage, and she has accepted." His father was the first to respond. He was evidently pleased with our announcement and expressed those sentiments, "Son that is wonderful news." I patiently waited for his mother to express her feelings. I honestly didn't know if she was happy or not. She didn't intend on me waiting long. "Baby, I agree with your father. This is great news and you've made an excellent choice in choosing a wife. I'm normally really good at feeling people

out. If you'll remember, I knew from day one your ex wasn't the one but the feeling I get after being around Nia in this short time is very positive."
I felt the need to say something, "Mrs. Black thank you so much for accepting me. I felt the distance you initially placed between us, and I understand. Malik has filled me in on his previous relationship and I am so glad you were able to open your heart to accepting me." She got up from the table and walked to where I was sitting. She pulled me up by the arm and we embraced each other. She even surprised me by kissing me on the cheek. "Welcome to our family. As long as you treat my son right, I will never have a problem with you."

"You won't have to worry about that."

"Miss Witherspoon, I believe that."
Mr. Black had something else on his mind, "All right with all of that. What Barbara and I want to know is when she should we expect grand babies?" Malik and I looked at each other and went into a fit of laughter. We had discussed this, and we knew our parents would ask the same thing. I think parents are born just to be grandparents. We decided Malik would be the one to answer this question when it arose so that's what he did. "We've agreed on two children, and we've decided to start trying after our first-year anniversary." With a concerned look on her face, Mrs. Black asked, "Why may I ask are you waiting so long?"
I decided I'd tackle this question. "We'd like to enjoy each other and married life for one year and that's why we decided to wait but don't worry, you'll get your grandbabies."
Looking at her husband she said, "Brad it looks like they've made up their mind."
"I guess so sweetheart, so we'll have to be patient."
"I guess so."
Malik had something else to say, "There's something else I have to tell you."
"What is it son?"
"Nia and I can't stay until the end of the week. We're going to leave tomorrow because I want to be with her when she shares the news with her family and friends."
"I understand but I was really looking forward to your visit and me getting better acquainted with my daughter-in-law to be," Mrs. Black expressed.

"I was looking forward to it as well, but I promise to visit within the next month. We can hang out and get to know each other. I really want us to have a close relationship."

"Ditto. Now let me look at the ring my son chose." I held my left hand out and she examined my ring. "Brad, our son did pretty good for himself. This ring is exquisite." Malik listened intently while his parents talked about him. He sat there with an arrogant look on his face. From everyone's reaction, he knew he'd chosen well.

"So when are you all leaving?" his dad asked.

"Unfortunately, tomorrow."

"Well, we better make the most of the time we have together."

For the rest of the evening, we sat around the house talking. We discussed the wedding, our careers, the trip we'd taken and current events. Truth be told I was tired and wanted a nap. I couldn't stop yawning so I asked if I could retire. Mr. Black reacted by telling Malik they should get our bags out of the car. Mrs. Black led me to the room I'd be using.

"I hope this is all right."

"Yes ma'am, it's fine."

Soon thereafter Malik and his dad arrived with our bags. Mrs. Black asked, "What time does your flight leave?"

Malik answered her, "Not until three and it's a two-hour flight so we should be in St. Louis around four with the different time zones. We're going straight to her mother's when we get there."

"Well, you all should get some rest. Nia, do you think you'll sleep for the entire night?"

"I seriously doubt it. I'll nap for about two hours and then I'll probably wake up hungry."

"After all you just ate?" Mrs. Black inquired.

Malik began to laugh jovially. His parents looked at him trying to figure out why he was laughing. He and I knew he was laughing at my appetite. I joined in on his laughter. His parents began to look at both of us strangely. Malik began to explain our fit of laughter to them, "Ma, Pops, it's like this. Nia's the first woman I've met who eats, I mean really eats. Her appetite is almost as hearty as mine." Mrs. Black gave him her I-don't-think-so look. He caught the look, "I said almost. Anyway, she has a pretty good appetite to be as small as she is, but I like it."

Smiling at me, she commented, "Baby, don't pay him no mind. I'm sure you don't eat like him. I don't think there's anyone who eats like him. Well, no one besides his father and Shemar."

"Speaking of Shemar, where is he?" Malik asked about his brother.

"You know he's playing with a jazz quartet and right now they're in Paris."

"I can't wait to share my news."

"Son, he'll be excited," Mr. Black stated.

"Let's get out of here so the girl can get some rest," Mrs. Black remarked. His parents left but Malik stayed. "So, is everything okay?"

I leaned over to land a peck on his lips, "Everything is great and I'm glad I finally met them so I could get over this nervousness."

"I told you there was nothing to worry about. My peeps are cool."

"Yes, they are. Your mother was leery but she's cool."

"Yeah, she's a little overprotective but she'll be all right."

"You know mothers, no matter how old we get we'll always be their babies."

"Yeah. Well, I'm going to hang out with Pops while you sleep."

"Okay, I'll see you when I get up."

I slept for two and a half hours. When I woke up, I found Malik and his father in the kitchen talking.

"I'm up."

"How was your nap young lady?"

"It was good Mr. Black but just like I thought, I'm hungry."

"Well – you did say you'd be ready to eat."

"Where's Mrs. Black?

"She went to bed early. She apologized but she got up early today to cook. She left you a po' boy sandwich."

"Thank you, Mr. Black. If it's okay with you, I'm going to take the sandwich along with a glass of water upstairs and watch TV."

"That'll be fine."

"Nia, do you need help?" Malik questioned.

"Naw baby, I'm cool. You go ahead and enjoy your time with your father."

"Okay but if you need me, just call me."

The following morning Mr. and Mrs. Black treated us to breakfast at *IHOP*. I hadn't been to Orlando in years, so we did a little sightseeing. I couldn't believe how much the city had grown. All the amusement parks were huge. Within the Disney compound was the *St. Louis Cardinals'* training camp. We drove there and I was able to see the growth of the city. Years ago, Orlando was *Disney* country but now there's Universal *Studios, Warner Brothers, and Sea World* wasn't far away. It was amazing to see so many amusement parks in one place. After driving around, we went back to the house and just lounged around. At one o'clock we prepared to leave for the airport. Malik placed our bags in the car earlier. His parents walked us to the car.

I expressed my gratitude, "Mr. and Mrs. Black thank you so much for your hospitality. I really enjoyed my visit and I'm glad we were finally able to meet."

Mr. Black said, "We're glad also and, you keep your promise and come and visit us next month."

"I'll do that. If it's okay with you all I'd like to get your number from Malik, and we can keep in touch."

Smiling, Mrs. Black said, "I'd really like that. I think you're going to be a good daughter-in-law."

"I hope so."

Everyone hugged and we were on our way. When we arrived at the airport we found our gate, boarded the plane, prayed, and fell asleep.

The Moment of Truth

When we arrived in St. Louis, we left the airport and went straight to my mother's house. I'd left my SUV in long-term parking. She knew I'd be home today, but she had no idea Malik would be with me.

310

We arrived at my mothers in University City. We decided we would tell her as soon as she opened the door by waving my left hand at her.

We parked and prior to emerging from the car Malik grabbed my hand and asked, "Are you ok?"

"Yeah baby, I'm cool. I'm just a little nervous."

"Don't worry, everything will be fine." With that said, we got out of the car and, hand in hand, we proceeded to my mother's door. Malik rang the doorbell and after about forty-five seconds Eddie appeared.

"Hey Eddie. You remember Malik?" Before I allowed him to answer, I continued talking. "Is my mom home?"

"Yeah, she's in the kitchen. Come on in." We entered the foyer, and we could hear my mother yelling from the kitchen. "Eddie! Who is it?" Before he could answer, I placed my index finger to my lips to shhh... him. His eyes became as large as ghetto gold medallions when he saw the ring on my finger. Since he didn't answer, my mother repeated herself, "Eddie!" By then, I was entering the kitchen. She was at the sink washing her hands. She turned around and was surprised to see her oldest daughter. "Nia, hi baby!" As I was about to respond, I noticed my mother was looking over my shoulder. She must see Malik. "Malik! What are you doing here?" She bypassed me and went straight into Malik's arms. I like the fact she really likes him. She never had this kind of closeness with Ben.

"Hey Mrs. Lawson. You're looking as beautiful as always."

Blushing she said, "Talking like that will get you anything you want?"

He decided to milk it for what it's worth, "What about a peach cobbler?"

"It'll be ready tomorrow."

Kissing her on the cheek he replied with, "Thank you Mrs. Lawson." After the interaction with Ben, she gave me some attention. Kissing my cheek, she greeted me with, "Hey baby girl, what brings you by?" Like a pop-up jack-in-the-box, Malik grabbed my left hand and in one swift motion he displayed the ring. My mother is obviously getting older and doesn't catch on fast. That was evident when she said, "Nice ring baby. How was your trip?" Malik and I gave each other a look, and I answered her question. "The trip was good. Malik's parents are really nice." Busying herself with what smelled like homemade chicken n' dumplings, she replied with, "That's good baby." I don't know if she's trying to be funny or what, but I didn't know what to do. Malik, being the man he is, made the decision for me, or should I say for us. He grabbed my hand, looked me in my eyes, mouthed the words I-Love-You and proceeded to speak, "Mrs. Lawson, I'm sure you're aware of my feelings for Nia. I love her very much." Her attention was now piqued because she turned around and began looking at us. He continued. "I apologize for not getting your blessing first. My parents have always told me I have a one-track mind when it comes to getting something I want. Anyway, I surprised Nia with a trip to Cancun, and during our visit I asked for her hand in marriage. She accepted and I hope you approve of me becoming your son-in-law." By that time, tears had welled up in her eyes, and with women, crying is normally contagious,

311

tears began to moisten my cheeks also. My mother looked at Malik first and then wiping my tears she asked, "Are you happy?" I was so overwhelmed with emotion for a few seconds, I couldn't find my voice. When I found it, I answered, "Yes ma'am. I'm very happy. I just wish Daddy were here." She then pulled me into an embrace and said, "Your father is always with you and don't you forget it." After about two minutes of embracing, she released me and went to Malik and began embracing him. As their embrace ended, she held his hands and began to speak, "Malik as parents we try to not label one child as our favorite, but Nia is our firstborn, and she was her daddy's baby. Her father loved Nandi, but he adored Nia. He was so proud of her and all her accomplishments. College. Grad school. Everything. He knew one day she'd become a successful entrepreneur. I'm saying all of this to say I'm sure if he were here, he'd be happy with Nia's choice of a husband. I think you'll make her a great husband, and I couldn't be happier."

"Thank you, Mrs. Lawson. I love Nia very much and I promise to do everything in my power to be the best husband I can be."

"I know you will baby. I know you will. Do your parents know?"

"Yes ma'am. We told them while we were in Orlando. They love Nia, but I knew they would."

Mama began yelling into the other room, "Eddie! Come here so I can tell you the news. Would you all like something to eat?"

"No mama, we came straight from the airport, and we need to go home."

Just then Eddie walked into the kitchen. "Di, what are you fussing about?"

My mama was grinning when she said, "Eddie, my baby is getting married."

Grinning he said, "What you say? Congratulations!" He shook Malik's hand and hugged me. "When is the wedding?"

Malik and I looked at one another, shrugged our shoulders and he spoke, "We haven't set a date yet, but we'll both check our schedules to see what's doable." I added my opinion, "It won't be a long engagement." My mother was glad to hear that, "That's good to hear baby. What do you think about Windows on Washington for the reception?

"That's perfect, but I want Malik to see the place first. This is his wedding also."

"Good idea, but I'll call tomorrow for prices."

"Okay Ma, thanks."

"Does Nandi know? The twins can be ring bearer and flower girl at the wedding."

"No, Nandi doesn't know yet. I haven't called her yet."

"Let's call her now."

"Ma, I'm tired."

"I know baby, just a five-minute phone call."

I acquiesced, "Okay Ma."

She dialed Nandi's number, pushed the speaker phone button and Kevin answered. "Hello?"

"What's up brother-in-law?"

"Hey Nia, what's up?"

"You baby." After we exchanged pleasantries, my mother chimed in. "Hello Kevin."

"Hey Ma, how you doing?"

"I'm fine baby. How are Keenan and Kai?"

"Who, two times the trouble?"

"Don't you talk about my grandbabies."

Laughing he replied with, "All right Ma."

"Yeah, how are my favorite niece and nephew?"

"Favorite? They're your only niece and nephew."

"That doesn't mean they can't be my favorite. I could hate their spoiled behinds."

"You're half the reason they're spoiled."

"That's what aunts are for."

"If you say so."

"Hey brother-in-law, where's my sister? Is she at the hospital?"

"No, she's here, just a minute." We could hear him calling her name. "Nandi baby, your mother and retarded sister are on the phone."

"Hey big-head, I heard that."

"Sorry sis, I couldn't resist." Right then, we heard Nandi enter the room. "Kevin, stop talking about my sister."

"That's right Nandi, you take up for your big sister."

"You know I got yo back sis! Hey Ma."

"Hey sweetie how are you?"

"Well, between being a mommy, wife and doctor, I'm hanging in there by God's grace. How are you?"

"Baby, I'm fine. Eddie and I are thinking about taking a cruise."

"That will be nice Ma. Keep me posted about the dates."

"I will."

"So, what's going on? You and Nia never call together unless you have something to tell me. Is it gossip about the family? Please don't tell me Aunt Patti left Uncle Mark again."

That got laughter from my mother and I because we knew all about the family antics. "No, it's nothing like that, but Nia has some news."

"Oh okay, what's up sis?"

"Well, your big sister is getting married."

"Yeah right."

"I'm for real. What, you don't think a brotha would want me as his wife?"

"It's not that, you just keep attracting bums like Ben, and Daddy would've never approved of him."

"I know Nandi. I just had a lapse in judgment."

313

"Are you really getting married? Ma, is she serious?"

"Yeah baby, she's serious and your father would approve of this one."

"Who's the lucky man? And I mean that."

"That's so sweet Nandi."

"I mean it, I know how good you are and how big your heart is. I know it was only a matter of time before God blessed you with a man worthy of being your husband."

"Girl, you've got me in tears. You know I love you right?"

"Never doubted it a day in my life, now tell me who he is."

"Malik Bla-" Before I could get his last name out of my mouth she blurted, "That fine man you told me about from Dallas?" Malik began grinning from ear to ear.

"Well, you just made his day."

"He's there? I'm sorry if I embarrassed you."

"Girl, please. He's the man I love so it's cool."

He spoke up, "Hello Nandi."

"Hey brother-in-law-to-be. I can't wait to meet you."

"Me either, Nia's told me all about you."

"Well, from my outburst, Nia's told me a lot about you as well."

"Yeah, I guess she has. I can't wait to meet Kai and Keenan either. Nia loves them like crazy."

"Yeah, they love their auntie too."

Out of the blue, Nandi asked, "So where will you all live?"

Our mother quickly chimed in and gave her opinion, "I didn't think of that. My other child won't be living in St. Louis either."

Malik stepped in to answer. "Actually Mrs. Lawson, I'll be relocating to St. Louis. I can open an office here."

"That's wonderful. You really do love my daughter to leave everything behind."

"Well, I'd be a fool to leave her in St. Louis. My business will thrive in any city because I offer services all companies can utilize. Not only that, but I'll also delegate more responsibility to my Vice-President so the Dallas office will remain up and running. My parents and brother already live in a different state and my boys, my Dallas family, they'll come and visit. I'll also visit them in Dallas."

"Ma, while Malik's in town we're going out to Town & Country to look at homes."

Nandi then asked, "Isn't that where Jake just purchased a home?'

"Yeah, he lives in the Pinetree subdivision, which I believe is in Town & Country."

"Well, it sounds like you got it all figured out," my mother commented.

"I agree Ma. It sounds like my big sis is in good hands."

"Thank both of you ladies."

In unison they responded with, "You're welcome."

"All right Dr. Bradshaw, we have to go, Malik and I came straight from the hospital, and we're tired."

"All right girl, I'll let you go. Ma, Kevin and I will be there in three weeks."

"Good, cause I miss my babies."

"They miss you too, all they talk about is Nana and Auntie Nia."

"I can't wait either. I saw the cutest Burberry dress for Kai," I stated.

"You cannot continue to spoil my children."

"And why not? They are my niece and nephew, and God has blessed me financially."

"It's not worth arguing over."

"No, it's not. I'll talk to you later."

Nandi chimed in, "Oh, before I forget, Malik can you make it that weekend? Kevin, Keenan, Kai and I would love to meet you."

Looking in my direction, Malik asked, "Baby is that all right?"

"Of course, I want you to meet Nandi and her tribe."

"Hey! Watch those tribe comments or I'll start praying that you are blessed with a tribe."

Laughing, I told her, "Sis, slow your roll, I've got plenty of time."

"Is your biological clock telling you time is your friend?"

"Let's leave my clock out of this."

"Anyway, I'll see you all in three weeks."

"Kiss my babies for me."

"Will do. Ma, I'll call you later in the week. Malik, you take care of my sister."

"Don't worry, I got her...always."

"Okay then. Love you."

My mother and I both responded with, "Love you too."

The conversation was over. As always, it was good talking to my baby sister.

"Ma, I didn't mean to cut things sh-"

"Baby don't worry about it, I'll just call you tomorrow. I know you all are tired."

Kissing her cheek, I said, "Thanks Ma." Malik followed suit by also kissing her cheek. He shook Eddie's hand, and we were on our way. When we got into the truck, I asked him if it would be okay to invite all my friends over to share the news. "Baby, I know you're tired, but I'd like to invite Michelle, Brett, Lexy, Kenya, Jake and Alicia over to make our announcement."

"That's cool baby but don't tell them I'm with you. I want to surprise everyone."

"That's cool. It will definitely be a surprise." My memory kicked in and I remembered the main reason I went to my mom's was to pick Sheba up. "Damn!"

"What's wrong?"

"I forgot to get Sheba."

"Damn! How did we forget her?"

I climbed out of the SUV and went back to the front door. This time I could hear her barking inside. Before I rang the doorbell, my mother opened the door. "She started barking as soon as you walked out the door."

"Thanks for keeping her Ma."

"It's no problem, she's a good dog."

"Yes, she is."

She opened the door, and Sheba came out wagging her stump. "Hey girl. How are you? I missed you." I started toward the SUV, and she followed. I opened the back door, and she jumped right in. We then proceeded to the house, which was only three minutes away. Using my cell phone, I called Lexy first. I love my girls, but I feel especially close to Lexy and Colett. Lexy answered after the second ring. "Girl, it's about time you got back. I missed you."

"I know girl, I missed you too."

"So, what's up?"

"I just got Sheba from my mother's."

"What are you going to do now?"

"I'm going home to chill and find something to eat."

"Are you going to cook?"

"Not if I don't have to."

"Well, I'm hungry too. I'm going to Chong Wah to get some food and then I'll be over."

"That's cool."

"What do you want?"

"I haven't eaten since early this morning. You know how I am before I board a plane."

"I know, you're a punk and you have a weak stomach."

Laughing. "Whateva! All I know is I'm starving. Let's do a pig out."

"Damn! We ain't did that in a while. So, what does your greedy ass want?"

"I don't know. Why don't you get a variety of shit?"

"Like what?"

"Mmmm...Let me think. Get two orders of hot braised boneless chicken and-"

"Damn greedy ass!"

"Whatever! I love hot braised chicken. Also, get a full order of duck & noodles, a full order of special fried rice without the bean sprouts, a whole order of beef n' broccoli, and an order of crab rangoon."

"Damn girl! Did you get knocked up in Orlando?"

"Hell no, just hungry. I haven't eaten in hours. Don't trip, I'll give you the money when you get here."

"I ain't trippin' off the money, I'm trippin' off your greedy ass! You sure Malik didn't knock you up?"

Laughing I asked, "Did Malik knock me up? What? Upside my head? Girl, hell to the naw. He did not knock me up. I told you I'm hungry."

"Whateva! You want egg rolls?"

"Yeah, but I-"

"Nia I know, you want everything but the egg rolls from Chong Wah. The egg rolls you want from Jack In The Box."

"Damn you're good."

"I'm not good, I've just been friends with your greedy ass too long."

"Yeah whateva, love you too."

"I'm about to hop in the shower, I'll be there within the hour."

Right then I pulled in front of my townhouse and opened the garage.

"Okay, girl I'm home, I'll see you when you get here. Someone is ringing my other line."

I hung up and prepared to get out of the SUV while answering my line. It was Jake.

"Hey baby girl."

"What's up Jakey?"

"Nothing much. What are you doing?" Malik busied himself by getting Sheba and retrieving our luggage.

"I'm on my way over to your girl's."

"Who Lexy? How's that going?"

"It's going pretty good. She doesn't smother a brotha."

"That's because she has her own life, and Kayla didn't. You were her life. She put more into you than she did her own child."

"Yeah, she was a trip and I just thank God, He delivered me from her."

"Yeah, me too."

"My bank account couldn't take it."

"Amen to that."

"I think Lexy's the one."

"I already knew that."

"You did, didn't you?"

"Yeah, but it's a good thing. Hey, you may as well come over here."

"Baby girl, I told you I'm on my way to Lexy's."

"I know, but she's on her way over here."

"Straight? I was trying to surprise her. I got her twelve assorted roses."

"Awww, ain't that sweet?'

"Nothing but the best for her."

"Well, you're going to have to surprise her over here. Don't worry, it'll still be a surprise, she doesn't expect you here."

"True dat. I'm on my way."

"Okay, I'll see you in a minute."

Malik had gotten settled in the house by the time I entered the kitchen. Sheba was in the back yard handling her business. I checked the mail. Lexy had been kind enough to collect it daily. There was a large pile on the island in the kitchen. While I was going through the mail, I picked up the phone to call Kenya.

"Welcome home Miss Witherspoon."

"Thank you, Miss Martin. What's up?"

"Nothing much."

"Are you busy?"

"With what? I ain't got no man."

"Well, I ain't a man and even if I was, I don't think I'd want to be bothered with your crazy ass. Why don't you come over?"

"I think I will, and you can tell me all about your trip."

"That sounds like a plan. Would you bring some food?"

"You are always hungry. What do you want?"

"I want some Chinese food."

"That's cool. I haven't had any in a while."

"I'll see you when you get here."

After Malik let Sheba back in the house, he informed me he'd just had a conversation with my dog.

"What did you all talk about?"

"I informed Sheba we're getting married."

"Is that right? What did she have to say about it?"

"She's cool with it."

"Well, that's good to know considering her opinion doesn't matter." Malik grabbed me from behind and kissed me on my neck. I really love him, and he's been a real blessing to me. I turned around while still in his arms and kissed him. Laying my head on his chest I whispered the words; I love you so much. Evidently, my whisper wasn't much of a whisper because he replied with, "I love you too baby." The way he said it was so gentle, it brought tears to my eyes. For the first time in my adult life, I feel really loved by a man. A man other than my father. Malik loves me with every fiber of his being. The way he looks at me, holds me, kisses me. and takes care of me. They say actions speak louder than words, well his actions are screaming. The best thing about being in love with him is he doesn't care who knows and more importantly, I know. If he never told me, I would still know because of his actions. We continued to embrace until I remembered people were on their way.

"Baby, I hate to spoil the moment, but I still have to call Michelle and Alicia."

"That's cool. We'll just finish up after everyone is gone."

Reaching for the phone, I said, "It's a date." I began dialing Michelle's number, after two rings Brett answered.

"Hey Brett!"

"What's up Nia?"

"Nothing much as usual."

"How was your trip?"

"It was good."

"Hold on, let me get Michelle."

"Thanks Brett."

Michelle got on the phone. "Hey girl."

"Hey, what's going on?"

"Nothing much, Brett and I are just chillin' we were just about to decide what we're going to eat tonight." I'm thinking to myself it must be my lucky night; all my friends are hungry. But what's new?

"Perfect timing."

"Perfect timing. For what?"

"Lexy's on the way over here with Chinese food and before you ask, there will be enough."

"We'll come over, but we'll stop at Lam's Garden to get some extra."

"If you insist."

"I do, so we'll see in thirty minutes."

"Until then."

Next, I called Alicia.

"Hey Nia. Welcome back."

"Thanks girl, I'm glad to be home."

"Whatcha doing?"

"I'm about to take a shower and chill."

"You up for some company?"

"Sure, why not."

"Cool, I'm gonna jump in the shower, I just completed my daily run."

"That's good, I don't want you over here smelling like fried rice."

"I ain't trippin' off of you Nia. I'll see you in a few."

As I hung up the phone, I noticed Malik raising his eyebrows, "What's the look for Mr. Black?"

"Well, you mentioned a shower and I think we shoul-"

"Hold up baby! What does we, have to do with shower?"

"I think we should take a shower."

"Together?"

"Of course."

"Is that right?"

"Yeah, it will relax both of us."

"You Mr. Black are incorrigible. If we shower toge-" I placed the index finger from my right hand in my mouth and my thoughts drifted to the shower Malik was suggesting.

"I got you thinking, huh?"

"Yeah I'm thinking, but I know you and we won't just shower, and I am not going there with you."

"Have it your way Mrs. Black-to-be but let me give you fair warning."

"And what warning is that?"

"As soon as your last friend leaves, it's on."

"Promise?"

"No doubt."

"You have a date sir."

"Well, while you're waiting on the posse, I'll be in the bedroom hiding out."

"Very well, after the doorbell rings five times, c'mon down so we can face the noise together."

"Okay, but are you going to take your ring off?"

"Yes, you can hold it."

Kissing me on the lips he said, "See you in about thirty minutes."

As he went upstairs, I opened the refrigerator to make sure there were cold beverages for everyone. Ice cold Pepsi's and bottled waters for the girls and ice-cold beer for the fellas. Everything was in place. I decided to play some music. I was in the mood for Frankie Beverly & Maze; their music always relaxes me. It's very laid back. I grabbed a glass of Cran-Cherry and went into the family room to wait on my peeps.

While sitting there Colett popped into my mind. She'd kill me if I told everyone about my up-and-coming nuptials and not include her. I decided to call her now to share the news. I got up, turned the music down, and yelled upstairs. "Malik!"

He responded, "Yeah!"

"Could you please come here?"

"Give me a minute."

"Okay." Two minutes later he appeared.

"What's up?"

"Since Colett won't be here, her being in the ATL and all, I'd like us to call her now to share the news."

"That's fine."

"Allrighty, follow me in the kitchen."

Patting me on the ass he said, "I'll follow you anywhere."

"You are so silly." We entered the kitchen; I hit the speaker phone button and began dialing her number. After three rings, she answered, "Hello."

"Hey girl."

"Hey Nia, how was your trip?"

"The trip was good. I really enjoyed meeting his parents."

"Other than meeting Mom and Pop Black, how was the trip?"

"Real good."

"How good?"

"If only you knew

"Huh? What –"

Before she could continue, I continued. "Actually, it was better than good. It was so good I am now the future Mrs. Black. And we're-"

"Wait one damn minute! Did you just tell me you're getting married?"

Malik spoke up, "Hey Colett!"

"Hey Malik! Is this real?"

"Most definitely. Your girl has agreed to become my wife."

Malik and I could hear Colett sniffing. She was crying. My eyes began to tear up, but I refused to succumb to the moment. Malik sat there with his mouth open. He was at a total loss for words. I wasn't really concerned because I knew although there were tears, they were tears of joy.

320

"Colett, sweetie stop crying before I start."

"Girl, I'm sorry, but you know how I am."

"I know and I understand. If you were you getting married, I'd be the same way."

"I am so happy for both of you."

"Thank you."

"Malik?"

"Yeah?"

"You take care of my girl. You're getting a good one."

"You don't have to worry, I know it. I love this woman."

"I know you do."

"She's in good hands."

"I know she is, and I want to thank you."

"Thank me? For what?"

"For really loving her. She is so deserving of a man like you."

"Thanks for the compliment, but I'm the lucky one."

"Damn why can't we clone you? Seriously, just take care of my girl."

"No problem."

"Well, I have company coming over, so I have to go and Nia before you say anything, I'll call you tomorrow to fill you in."

"That's cool girl, have a good evening."

"All right, love you."

"Love you too."

"Have a good one Malik."

"You too Colett."

I hung the phone up. "Well, baby, one down and six to go."

"Six more, huh?"

"Yeah but my friends are an easy crowd."

"I'm going back upstairs."

"Okay, I'll see you in a few."

After Malik departed to return upstairs, I decided to sit in the family room and continue to listen to my music. In one instant I got butterflies. Nervous butterflies. I know my friends like him but I'm nervous and scared. Scared because everything I've prayed for is now mine for the taking. I've always wanted a family because my family, in my opinion, was the epitome of black family life. No, it wasn't perfect, but it was close. It was the closest to perfection a lot of black families ever had. Nandi and I were blessed to not only have two parents, but we had two parents who sincerely loved one another, and they loved us. I want the same life and now I can have it. I know the God I serve is an awesome God, but fear has crept into my inner being causing me to feel unworthy. I know I'm worthy and I also know the devil is a liar, but I can't help the feelings that have overcome me. I know the only thing taking these feelings away is praying. I muted the music filling the interior of the family room, humbled myself by dropping to my knees and began to pray.

321

"Heavenly Father, I come to you humbled giving you praise, glory and honor. I know I am not perfect but through your grace, I am saved and therefore blessed." At this time tears began to fall from my eyes. I was about to continue when I felt Malik kneeling beside me. When I muted the music, he must've wondered what was going on and came to investigate. This is the first time a man other than my father has prayed with me. It really touched my heart because it was an oddity for black men who I've dated to pray. Openly. I continued, "Malik has asked for my hand in marriage and I've accepted. He has been good to me, and I know he'll be good for me, but I'm scared. I'm asking you to remove this demon of fear from me. I place my faith and trust in you." As I was completing the prayer Malik began to speak, "Heavenly Father, now that Nia is done, I'd like to share some thoughts with you and her. First and foremost, God you are at the head of my life and though I may sometimes fall short or back slide please know my intentions are always to serve you. You've blessed me beyond measure, and I give you honor in my life, and I thank You. Your greatest gift to me, other than my parents, is this beautiful lady kneeling next to me. Nia mentioned she's scared, and I must admit I am as well. I prayed for your guidance, so I know I'm not making a mistake. Our prayers have been answered God and I ask for your guidance through our courtship into our marriage. I'm sure Nia agrees with me when I say we will keep you first in our lives." He grabbed my hand, kissed it and continued, "Father, Nia and I both realize our love is a blessing, and we will treat it as such. We thank You for your grace, our love and the journey we're about to begin. As always we give you glory and honor in the name of your son, our Savior Jesus Christ." We squeezed each other's hand before saying, "Amen." We both opened our eyes and we stared at one another through tear-drenched eyelashes. Simultaneously, we stroked one another's cheek with our thumbs to wipe away the tears.

"I'm sorry I'm so emotional."

"It's cool. This is a big step for both of us."

"Yeah it is, but I feel in my heart we're doing the right thing."

Without any hesitation, he said, "Oh, no doubt. You're the best thing to happen to me."

"Ditto." My smile lit up the room like a Christmas tree. He stood up, helped me up, we hugged, he kissed me on the forehead, and he said he was going back upstairs. I went into the bathroom to splash cold water on my face and returned to the family room. I resumed my music listening and continued to wait on everyone. Thankfully, I didn't have to wait long. My doorbell rang. I felt the finger on my left hand next to my pinkie finger so I could take my ring off but then I remembered Malik had the ring. I answered the door. It was Michelle and Brett with food in hand.

"Hey you two."

Hugging me Michelle said, "Hey yourself." Brett also hugged me.

"Go on in and get comfortable." As soon as the last syllable left my lips, the doorbell rang again. This time it was Jake. He stood in my doorway with an assortment of roses in a beautiful, frosted vase.

"Jake, the flowers are beautiful. Lexy's going to love them."

Stepping into the house and pulling me into a hug he said, "I hope so. She's special to me."

"You're special to her as well."

"Hey, I smell food. Did Lexy arrive already? I didn't see her car. I parked up the street so she wouldn't notice my truck."

"Naw, she's not here but Brett and Michelle just stopped by with some food."

"I hope there's enough."

"You know there's enough."

"Cool. A brotha could eat a lil' sumthin' sumthin'." Jake and I walked into the kitchen, and he spoke.

"Hey Chelle. Brett."

Brett replied, "What's up Jake?" Michelle walked over to him to hug him, "Hey Jake!" What's up?"

"Nothing's up favorite white girl."

"All right with the white girl jokes because you know I can't call you a nig-"

In unison Jake and I said, "Whoa! Watch out now!"

We all began laughing. "Michelle, you know you can't go there."

"I know, but no white girl jokes."

With my hands up I said, "I surrender." Right then the doorbell rang, and I went to answer. I checked the peephole prior to answering the door. It was Alexis so I ran into the kitchen to get Jake. Since I was running, Jake looked at me like I was crazy. "Uh Nia, what's up? Why is your crazy ass running in your own house?"

"It's Lexy at the door and I figured you could answer and give her the flowers."

"Good thinking baby girl." He went in pursuit of his woman. Since I 'hooked' them up, I felt the need to eavesdrop, so I peeked around the corner. Jake opened the door with the vase behind his back, but Lexy had her head down and therefore didn't notice Jake was the one who opened the door.

She slowly began to lift her head as she began to speak, "Damn Nia! What took you s- She began to smile from ear to ear when she saw Jake. "Wh- what are you doing here?"

"What, you're not happy to see me?"

"Of course I am, but how did you know I'd be here?"

"A little birdie told me of course."

"A big head birdie with a flat ass."

"Hey, watch the ass comments," I yelled from the other room.

Leaning in to kiss him she said, "I'm happy to see you."

323

Kissing her back he said, "I'm always happy to see you. How was your day?"

"It was okay. Yours?"

"Mine? Mine was good." She ran her thumb over his eyebrow.

"Why was yours just okay?"

"It's the same ol', same ol'. Dead bodies and silence."

"That's your chosen career."

"True and I love it, it's just-" She became silent.

"It's just what?"

"I watched the news last night and one of the lead stories was of a nineteen-year-old mother beating her three-month-old daughter to death. Since hearing the story, I've been praying we don't get her body."

"Damn! That's real messed up, but that's the world we live in."

"Yeah, I know, but now you know why my day was just okay."

"Well, I hope this helps to brighten it. 'Voila'. He pulled the flowers from behind his back. She began to bat those damn eyelashes of hers and then she innocently asked, "For me?"

He asked, "Who else?" They kissed again. "Thank you, baby. This is so thoughtful of you."

"You deserve it."

"I do, don't I?" She began laughing and it filtered to Jake. I decided it was time to break up all this happy Huxtable family shit.   "Aw, ain't that sweet?"

They both looked at me and stuck their tongues out while still laughing.

"I can't stand either of you."

In unison they said, "We love you too."

"Enough! Let's eat. I'm hungry."

"You're always hungry," Lexy's smart mouth ass commented. I took the food out of Lexy's hand and went into the kitchen. Frick and Frack followed behind me hand-in-hand. As soon as I walked into the kitchen, the doorbell rang again. My home was Grand Central Station. I looked out the window, but I didn't see Kenya's truck, so it had to be Alicia. I opened the door.

"Welcome back to reality Ms. Witherspoon." She began to look me up and down.

"Thank you, Ms. Fox. There's no need to check me out. Nothing has changed. Get in here so we can eat." She stepped into the foyer and hugged me. We began our descent into the kitchen when the doorbell rang. Again. It had to be Kenya. When I opened the door, she stood there, food in hand and arms out. "Girl, I missed you." We embraced each other.

"I missed you too. C'mon in."

"So, how was your trip?"

"Good. Real good."

We entered the kitchen and there was hustle and bustle everywhere. I guess I wasn't the only hungry one, but there were too many people in the kitchen. Kenya must've read my mind because she said, "Hey! Hey, there are too many people in the kitchen. Too much congestion. Why don't you all go into the family room and Nia and I will bring everything in there."

They obviously thought this was a good idea because they all dropped what they were doing and retreated to the family room. Those bums didn't want to help anyway. Kenya and I proceeded to prepare everything. I grabbed Coronas, Pepsi's, and bottles of water from the refrigerator while Kenya busied herself gathering plates, napkins. and utensils. There was plenty of food for all of us. Malik entered the kitchen just as Kenya and I were about to depart to go into the family room. His appearance apparently startled her because she almost dropped the utensils.

"Damn you scared me Ma-"

"Shhh....We want to surprise everyone."

"Well, you should succeed in that."

"Let's go." I had Kenya walk in the family room first. Malik and I followed her. Initially no one noticed so we stood there until someone recognized I'd entered the room with Malik. Brett was the first to notice.

"Hey! Malik, what's up? When did you get here?" Immediately after Brett asked the question the room became still, and all eyes were on us. Malik grabbed my hand, squeezed it (I think that was our new unspoken gesture indicating everything was going to be all right) and began to speak, "What's up everybody?"

The entire room erupted into questions and comments. They were coming so fast neither of us could answer or comment. My voice has always been boisterous, so I spoke up, "Hey, slow your roll! We can only answer one question at a time, and we have something to say."

"What is it?" Kenya's anxious ass asked.

I began, "Well, we-" Malik cut me off and proceeded. "Baby, let me. I'll get straight to the point. When we met in Orlando, I surprised Nia with a trip to Cancun. While we were in Cancun, I asked her to marry me. I know how much you all mean to her, and I didn't want her to tell you without me being present. I love her and I'm going to be the best husband I can be to her." The room fell silent again. Malik went into his pocket and took this moment to place my ring back on my finger.

Jake had this I-can't-believe-this look on his face when he said, "Damn! Ya'll serious?"

"Yes Jake, it's serious. He asked me to marry him, and I accepted. I know it's soon, but it's right." Looking into Malik's eyes, I said, "So right." Right then it was as if my father had given me his blessing. I received a warm fuzzy feeling, and I knew. I knew deep in my heart and soul Malik was my gift from God and my father would have approved of him. Jake continued to stare at us, but he said nothing. When I looked at my girls, all of them had tears in their eyes. Lexy broke down first. The tears wouldn't stop falling from her eyes. She walked over to me and asked, "You're getting married?"

Before I could answer, she embraced me and wouldn't let go. Tears began to flow from my eyes as well. She continued to cry and talk, "I am so happy for

325

you." She finally let go of me and embraced Malik. "Man, you better treat her like the queen she is." Jake finally came out of his trance to agree with Lexy. "I second that. She's like a sister to me."

Malik felt the need to defend himself, "You all have nothing to worry about. God has blessed me with her, I won't mess up."

"That's good to hear."

"Jake, you've been trying to protect Nia since high school and I know she loves you for it, but it's time to let go," Michelle suggested.

"I think she's in good hands," Kenya stated.

Agreeing, Lexy, and Alicia said, "Yeah, she is."
Jake apparently felt the need to say more, "Ya'll don't understand. Nia has always been in my corner, and she's always had my back. Her father asked me to take care of her years ago since she and Nandi don't have a brother and I take that responsibility literally." The room erupted in laughter because everyone present knew how true his statement was. He didn't get the joke. "What's funny?"

Michelle explained, "We know you take your job literally. We know better than anyone." That lightened the mood up. Everyone hugged and congratulated us. My girls cornered me to inquire, "All right, show us the ring." I held my left hand out. "Damn! He really loves you, huh?" That was Kenya's sometimes-ignorant ass.

Lexy could really be sentimental at times. She looked in my eyes and then at the ring and then she said, "Nia I am so happy for you. You deserve all the happiness. You really do. I can't wait to share the news with my parents."

"Thanks Lexy. I really appreciate it. Your parents will be happy, their daughters are getting married. You and Jake won't be far behind."

Michelle said, "I'm happy for you too. Now we can kinda plan our weddings together."

"Yes, we can although we haven't set a date yet. Have you all set a date?"

"As a matter of fact, we have. Our date is November twenty-seventh." Kenya asked," What year?"

"Duh, I guess giving a date without a year doesn't help much. Two thousand and nineteen, which is next year."

"Isn't that the Saturday after Thanksgiving?"

"Yep. We'll have family in town so I figured we could do it then."

"I don't know if we want to wait as long, but Malik and I will have to discuss, but you all will be in the first group to know."
Alicia went to change the playlist to Sweet Back, Miles Davis, and Cassandra Wilson. The music filtered through the house while we enjoyed good food, friendship, and laughter. The TV was on, tuned in to ESPN's SportsCenter but it was muted. The fellas just watched the NFL pr highlights. I tuned in when they showed the Cardinals highlights.

The girls and I were giddy about my future nuptials. I hadn't really thought about the wedding, but I guess I better start. Alicia on the other hand

326

had thought about it, she asked, "So, who are you going to choose as your attendants?"

"Licia, what kind of question is that?"

"A good one, I think."

"To me it's a stupid question. All of you will be attendants in the wedding. You're my girls."

She was really pushing the issue when she asked, "So who will be your maid-of-honor?" That piqued everyone's interest. I decided to drag it out and make them wait before I answered. As soon as I accepted his proposal, I knew who my maid-of-honor would be, so I asked, "Who do you think it should be?"

She didn't hesitate to answer, "Well, I think-"
This was too much. Of course, she's going to nominate herself, but I was stepping in to voice my opinion, "Alicia, don't go there. I know who maid-of-honor will be. I love all of you like sisters, but all of you can't be my maid-of-honor. Only one of you can. Nandi of course will be my matron-of-honor and I hope this doesn't hurt anyone's feelings, but I want Alexis as my maid-of-honor. She and I are tight and when Malik asked me to marry him her name was the first to pop in my head. Again, I hope no one's upset."

Lexy spoke first with tears in her eyes, "Thank you Nia, and I hope this is okay with everyone."

Kenya's friendly ass said, "Girl yeah, it's cool. If I'm included in the festivities, I'm cool. I'm sure Alicia, Michelle and Colett feel the same."

Since we'd had the maid-of-honor talk, we could relax and continue to enjoy ourselves. I think Alicia was a little upset because she and I had been friends since the fifth grade, and she probably felt she should be my maid of honor. Also, because she and I were business partners she probably felt she was entitled to the role. I love Alicia but the one friend who always has my back is Alexis. Financially and emotionally, she has always been there for me. When I lost my job at AT&T before Alicia and I started Event Solutions, Lexy allowed me to work at her funeral home and she paid me five hundred dollars weekly, cash money. Only a friend would do that. I'm also very close to her parents and for all these reasons, I chose her as my maid-of-honor. So, everyone continued eating and talking while enjoying themselves. Around nine thirty the phone rang, and Alexis answered it.

"Hello....just one moment," She pressed the hold button on the phone to tell me there was a female on the line.

I grabbed the phone, released the hold button, and replied with, "Hello." It was Ben's mother. "Hey Mama Jones, how are you?" That got Lexy, Alicia, Kenya and Michelle's attention. Jake asked Lexy who Mama Jones was, and I faintly heard her say, "Ben's mother." After that, I tuned them out to focus in on Mama Jones.

"I'm fine baby, you?"

"I'm good. I can't complain at all."

"Are you busy right now?"

"Well, I have some friends over and we're just hanging out. I'd planned on calling you because I have something to tell you."

"I'm calling cause I got something to tell you too."

"What is it, Mama Jones?"

"Baby you can tell me your news first."

"Naw, Mama Jones, you go right ahead."

"All right baby if you insist. I was calling because Ben's been in a horrible accident." As soon as I heard that, tears welled up in my eyes. No, I didn't want to be with him, but I care about him and his health.

"Aw, Mama Jones I'm so sorry to hear that. Is he okay?"

"I'm sorry baby, but he's dead."

"He's what?" The teardrops began running down my cheeks.

"I'm sorry to tell you this but he died when he arrived at the hospital."

My emotions were getting the best of me, "He what?" I screamed. Malik ran to my side.

"I'm sorry baby, he passed. It was an extremely bad accident."

"What happened?"

"He was on that no-good motorcycle of his and I'm sure he was driving too fast. He must've lost control and hit a wall on I-70."

"Mama Jones, I am so sorry." I tried to pull myself together. She'd just lost her only son. She needed consoling more than I did.

"I know baby, I am too. I told him too many times to slow down on that bike. He was hardheaded though, just like he was hardheaded about you. I don't know how many times I told him to leave them nappy headed girls alone, but he never listened. Baby, he never listened."

"It's okay Mama Jones. He's in a better place now."

"That he is baby. That he is." The phone line became silent, and she was quietly sniffing on the phone. I asked again, "Mama Jones, are you-" Just then her brother, James got on the phone, "Nia, this Uncle Jimmy, Mary Lou ain't too good right now so I'm gon' hang up but I'll have her call you tomorrow."

"All right Uncle Jimmy, I'll talk to you all tomorrow." We hung the phone up and I just stood there in a daze. Everyone was trying to figure out what was wrong, but I'm sure none of them would guess this. I sat down on the couch. I couldn't believe it. Ben was dead. It just couldn't be true. I kept looking at the phone thinking it would ring and be him. He'd call to tell me it was a joke, and he wasn't dead, he just had his mother and uncle to tell me, so I'd feel bad and take him back. He was that dramatic. After ten minutes with no ringing phone, I concluded it must be true. Ben was dead. The first thing that came to mind was Malik's reaction. I swear if he acts in a juvenile manner or acts jealously, I'll call off this damn engagement. I don't need drama in my life. I swear I don't. I guess it was time to break the news to the seven people who were in my family room. They'd asked me over and over what was wrong, but I tuned them out and sat there in a daze. Malik kneeled beside me, took his thumb

328

and wiped away the tears which moistened my cheeks. He then gently asked, "What's wrong? Baby you know you can tell me." My mouth began to move but there were no words coming out of it and I was still in a daze. Malik called my name over and over, and again nothing from me. He snapped his fingers in front of my face, and I snapped out of it. "Baby, I'm sorry but I just received some shocking news."

"We can tell baby, but what is it?"

"That was Mama Jones, Ben's mother. Obviously, Ben was on his motorcycle and had a fatal accident." After I said that, I just sat there silently. Lexy kneeled and hugged me, "Sweetie, it will be all right." Brett spoke up, "Nia, did you say the accident was fatal?"

Leaning out of Lexy's embrace I replied with, "Yeah it was fatal. Ben passed away as soon as he arrived at the hospital." Everyone in the room knew what he meant to me, so they all began to show their concern. That included concern from Malik.

He was genuinely sincere when he said, "Baby, I know you loved him and I know this hurts, but I want you to know I'm here for you and I'll stay in St. Louis as long as it takes." I looked into his eyes and saw only love and sincerity. This man really loves me. I kissed his cheek and hugged him before I said, "Thank you." When I looked up, all eyes were on me. All except Alicia. When I searched the room with my eyes, I saw her in a corner crying. I thought to myself, 'That's strange, but I guess she's upset because I'm upset.' Everyone continued to check on me, and my well-being. It was at that very moment Alicia jumped up, hysterical and crying. She began screaming, "Why are you all so worried about her? What about me?" We all looked at her as if she'd lost her damn mind. It was evident from her outburst she had, but she continued. "Everybody's so fuckin' concerned about Nia. Nia this! Nia that! Shit, what about me?"

Jake glanced at me and then asked Alicia, "Shit, what about you? Nia just lost a man she loved for two years so why are you trippin'?" Suddenly, it hit me. Alicia was fucking Ben. The truck I saw outside of my house I thought was his on more than one occasion. It was his. Her always dogging him was a ploy to take the attention off her. She wanted him. Her rushing off the phone whenever I walked into a room or our office. She was straight fuckin' my ex. I can't believe this shit. I've been this skank's friend since fifth grade, and she pulls this shit. Now, ain't that a bitch? It was cool. Just like the Amber and Ben incident, neither one of them have shit. Nothing from nothing, leaves nothing. I calmly asked Alicia, "Alicia, why are you trippin'? What was Ben to you?" The room became silent, and all eyes were on Alicia. "Nia, I'm sorry but I love him and I'm pregnant with his child." I jumped up to ring her neck, but Malik held me. I can't believe this shit. At the same time Jake and Alexis (my guardian angels) both said, "What do you mean you love him?" Lexy was obviously fuming because her hands were on her hips and the neck was rolling, "What the fuck is going on Alicia? What part of Ben being Nia's man did you not understand?"

Alicia began to stutter, "I' I' I'm sor...sor...sor...sorry I-"

Alexis decided it was time to end this, "Yes, you are sorry, and I think it's time for you to go." Alicia slowly got up and walked toward the door to leave, she turned and looked all of us in our faces. I'm sure the only thing she saw in all our faces was pity. After she closed the door, I looked at Lexy, she looked at me and in unison we said, "Ain't that a bitch?"

Epilogue

After the Benjamin Jones-Alicia Fox-Amber Waller fiasco, I attended Ben's funeral with my man by my side. The funeral was held at William C. Harris's funeral home instead of Lexy's. Amber and Alicia were both there, but neither of them said anything to me. They knew I was not to be fucked with.

As for Event Solutions, I paid Alicia for her half of the company. There was no way we could remain friends or business partners. She had committed the ultimate betrayal. I expected Ben to be a nigga, but I expected Alicia to keep our friendship at the forefront of her thoughts. It's evident, fucking my man was more important than our friendship.

Malik and I jumped the broom in November of 2018. I was escorted down the aisle by Mr. Knight, Alexis' father. We held our reception at Windows on Washington. It was my mother's first suggestion. We stepped into our new life and reception to Anthony David's '4evermore', and our first and second official dances as husband and wife were, 'We Both Deserve Each Other's Love' by L.T.D. and 'A Couple of Forevers' by Chrisette Michelle. We decided to honeymoon in Turks & Caicos and prior to the wedding, we closed on our new home in West County. I sold my townhouse to a young white couple relocating from Chicago.

As we were about to board our plane for our honeymoon, we saw Alicia. Alicia and Ron. Holding hands. Not only was he an ex of mine, but he's married. He was just at our wedding with his wife. If his wife Celia finds out, she'll beat both of their asses. Alicia may as well sign her own death certificate. This trick had the nerve to approach us. Smiling. I'm convinced her elevator does not go to the top floor.

"Hey Nia. Malik." Malik spoke but I just looked at her crazy ass. I did speak to Ron. "Hey Ron, how are Celia and the baby?"

This skank had the nerve to question me, "Why did you have to bring her name up?"

"Are you talking to me?"

"What do you think bitch?"

I began talking to myself because she couldn't be talking to me. 'This trick doesn't know I will snatch her ass in the airport. I don't give a damn.'

"Why are you talking to yourself?" her dumb ass asked.

Malik began to say something, "Alicia c'mon- "That's all I heard because the next thing I knew my fingers were around her neck. Choking her ignorant ass. Malik grabbed me. "Baby, she is not worth it." When I released her, she began sputtering trying to catch her breath because I choked her ass with a tight grip.

After regaining some composure, she said, "You bitch! How dare you."

"Yes, how dare me," I said while laughing.

She rolled her eyes at me and said, "What goes around."

Laughing and shaking my head, I knowingly replied with, "Already came around."

We walked away from her to begin our journey into paradise and our new life together.

The End

About the author

Leslie Rogers was born in Germany but considers herself a native St. Louisan. Leslie has always had a passion for reading and writing. Some of her inspiration comes from some of the great African American authors, such as Kimberla Lawson-Roby, Michael Baisden, Eric Jerome Dickey, Mary B. Morrison, Terri McMillan and, Travis Hunter, to name a few. In her current novel, "What Goes Around…", she is making it okay for sistahs to do for themselves and not wait on brothas to do it for them. True friendship. True love and even true drama can all be found in this piece of work. Once you get to the end, you will definitely be saying, "What goes around, definitely comes around." Leslie currently resides in her hometown of St. Louis, MO and, is working on her next novel. She can be contacted via email at writer4life1@aol.com.

Made in the USA
Monee, IL
14 December 2023

49228225R00184